A Shocking Proposal . . .

Miss Charing swallowed another mouthful of punch. A gentle glow was spreading through her veins. A certain exhilaration infused her brain. She sat bolt upright in her chair, staring straight ahead, the fingers of one hand tightening around her tumbler.

"Freddy!" said Miss Charing suddenly, turning her expressive eyes towards Mr. Standen.

He gave a slight start. "Sorry! Thinking of something else!" he excused himself.

"Freddy, you are quite *sure* you don't want to marry me, aren't you?"

He looked a little alarmed, for she spoke with a degree of urgency which made him uneasy. "Yes," he said, adding apologetically: "Very fond of you, Kit, always was! Thing is, I'm not a marrying man!"

"Then, Freddy, will you be so *very* obliging as to be betrothed to me?" said Miss Charing breathlessly.

Also by Georgette Heyer

The Reluctant Widow
Friday's Child
A Civil Contract
Bath Tangle
The Toll-Gate
April Lady
Sylvester or the Wicked Uncle
Sprig Muslin
Venetia
The Quiet Gentleman
The Foundling
The Grand Sophy
The Unknown Ajax
Arabella

Published by
HarperPaperbacks

GEORGETTE HEYER

COTILLION

HarperPaperbacks
A Division of HarperCollins*Publishers*

HarperPaperbacks   *A Division of* HarperCollins*Publishers*
10 East 53rd Street, New York, N.Y. 10022

Copyright © 1953 by Georgette Heyer
Copyright © renewed 1981 by Richard George Rougier
All rights reserved. No part of this book may be used or
reproduced in any manner whatsoever without written
permission of the publisher, except in the case of brief
quotations embodied in critical articles and reviews. For
information address HarperCollins*Publishers*,
10 East 53rd Street, New York, N.Y. 10022.

Cover illustration by Debby Chabrian

First HarperPaperbacks printing: June 1991

Printed in the United States of America

HarperPaperbacks and colophon are trademarks of
HarperCollins*Publishers*

10 9 8 7 6 5 4 3 2

to
Gerald

❧ *Chapter I* ❧

*THE SALOON, LIKE EVERY OTHER ROOM IN ARN-*side House, was large and lofty, and had been fur-nished, possibly some twenty years earlier, in what had then been the first style of elegance. This, however, had become outmoded, and although the room bore no such signs of penury as a ragged carpet or patched curtains, the bright brocades had faded, the paint on the paneled walls had cracked, and the gilded picture-frames had long since become tarnished. To a casual visitor it might have seemed that Mr Penicuik, who owned the house, had fallen upon evil days; but two of the three gentlemen assembled in the Saloon at half past six on a wintry evening of late February were in no danger of falling into this error. They knew that Great-uncle Matthew, who had made a fortune in the large enterprise of draining the Fen-country, was one of the warmest men in England, and suffered merely from a rooted dislike of spending money on anything that did not administer directly to his own comfort.

The third gentleman gave no indication of thinking about it at all. He did not, like his cousin, Lord Biddenden, level a disapproving eyeglass at a spotted mirror; he did not, like his younger cousin, the Honorable and Reverend Hugh Rattray, comment acidly on the inadequacy of the small wood-fire burning in the hearth. Throughout dinner, which had been served at the unfashionable hour of five, and had been chosen (as Lord Biddenden pointed out to his brother) more with a regard to the host's digestive difficulties than to the tastes of his guests, he had maintained a silence that might have been unbroken had his cousin Hugh not addressed a series of kind and simple remarks to him, which could be easily understood, and almost as easily answered. Upon entering the Saloon, he had drifted to a chair on one side of the fireplace, where he now sat, chewing a corner of his handkerchief, and staring with an expression of vacuity at his elder cousin. Lord Biddenden knew that this gaze betokened nothing but blankness of mind, but he found it disconcerting, and muttered fretfully: "I wish the silly fellow would not stare so!"

"He is doing you no harm," his brother said gravely. However, he picked up a book of engravings from one of the tables, and gave it to Lord Dolphinton, directing him to look at the pictures, and telling him that he would find them very pretty and interesting. Lord Dolphinton, who was accustomed to being told, far less kindly, by his mother, what he must do, received the book gratefully, and began to turn over the pages.

Lord Biddenden said, still in that complaining undervoice: "I cannot conceive what should have prevailed with Uncle Matthew to have invited him! It is absurd to suppose that *he* can have an interest in this business!" He received no other answer than one of his brother's annoyingly reproving looks, and with an exclamation of impatience walked over to the table, and began to toss over one or two periodicals which had been arranged upon it. "It is excessively provoking that Claud should not be here!" he said, for perhaps the seventh time that day. "I should have been very glad to have seen him comfortably established!" This observation being met with the same unencouraging silence, his lordship said with a good deal of asperity: "*You* may not consider Claud's claims, but *I* am not one to be forgetting my brothers, I am thankful to state! I'll tell you what it is, Hugh: you are a cold-hearted fellow, and if you depend upon your countenance to win you a handsome fortune, you may well be disappointed, and there will all my trouble be spent for nothing!"

"What trouble?" inquired the Rector, in accents which lent some color to his brother's accusation.

"If it had not been for my representations of what you owe to the family, you would not be here this evening!"

The Reverend Hugh shrugged his broad shoulders, and replied repressively: "The whole of the affair seems to me to be most improper. If I make poor Kitty an offer, it will be from compassion, and in the belief that her upbringing and character are such as must make her a suitable wife for a man in orders."

"Humbug!" retorted Lord Biddenden. "If Uncle Matthew makes the girl his heiress, she will inherit, I daresay, as much as twenty thousand pounds a year! He cannot have spent a tithe of his fortune since he built this place, and when one considers how it must have accumulated — My dear Hugh, I do beg of you to use a little address! If I were a single man—! But, there! It does not do to be repining, and I am sure I am not the man to be grudging a fortune to either of my brothers!"

"We have been at Arnside close upon twenty-four hours," said Hugh, "and my great-uncle has not yet made known to us his intentions."

"We know very well what they are," replied Lord Biddenden irritably. "And if you do not guess why he has not yet spoken, you are a bigger fool than I take you for! Of course he hoped that Jack would come to Arnside! And Freddy, too," he added perfunctorily. "Not that Freddy signifies a whit more than Dolphinton here, but I daresay the old man would wish him not to be excluded. No, no, it is Jack's absence which has made him hold his tongue! And I must say, Hugh, I never looked for that, and must hold it to be a piece of astonishing good fortune! Depend upon it, had the opportunity offered, the girl must have chosen him!"

"I do not know why you should say so," replied the Rector stiffly. "Indeed, I am at a loss to understand why you should be so anxious to have me offer for a lady whom you apparently hold in such poor esteem! If I did not believe her to be a well-brought-up young woman to whom such persons as my cousin Jack must be repugnant—"

"Yes, well, that is more of your humbug!" interrupted his lordship. "You may be a handsome fellow, Hugh, but you are not an out-and-outer, like Jack!"

"I have no wish to be an out-and-outer, as you term it," said Hugh, more stiffly still. "Nor do I regard his absence or his presence as being of any particular consequence."

"Oh, don't sham it so!" exclaimed Biddenden,

flinging down a copy of the *Gentleman's Magazine*. "If you fancy, my dear brother, that because he gave you your living my uncle prefers you above his other great-nephews you very much mistake the matter! I wonder you will talk such gammon, I do, indeed! Jack has always been my uncle's favorite, and so you know! He means Kitty to choose him, depend upon it, and that is why he is so devilish out of humor! I marvel at his having invited any of the rest of us, upon my soul I do!"

Lord Dolphinton, who occasionally disconcerted his relations by attending to what they said, here raised his eyes from the book on his knees, and interpolated: "Uncle said he didn't invite you, George. Said he didn't know why you came. Said—"

"Nonsense! You know nothing of the matter!" said Lord Biddenden.

Lord Dolphinton's understanding was not powerful, nor was it one which readily assimilated ideas; but once it had received an impression it was tenacious. "Did say so!" he insisted. "Said it last night, when you arrived. Said it again this morning. Said it—"

"Very well, that will do!" said his cousin testily.

Lord Dolphinton was not to be so easily silenced. "Said it when we sat down to luncheon," he continued, ticking the occasion off on one bony finger. "Said it at dinner. Said if you didn't care for your mutton you needn't have come, because he didn't invite you. I ain't clever, like you fellows, but when people say things to me once or twice I can remember them." He observed that this simple declaration of his powers had bereft his cousin of words, and retired again, mildly pleased, into his book.

Lord Biddenden exchanged a speaking look with his

brother; but Hugh merely remarked that it was very true, and that in such a contemptuous voice that Biddenden was goaded into saying: "Well, at all events, it is as much to the purpose that I have come as that Dolphinton has! Folly!"

"I'm an Earl," said Lord Dolphinton, suddenly reentering the conversation. "*You* ain't an Earl. Hugh ain't an Earl. Freddy ain't—"

"No, you are the only Earl amongst us," interposed Hugh soothingly.

"George is only a Baron," said Dolphinton.

Lord Biddenden cast him a glance of dislike, and said something under his breath about impoverished Irish peers. He had less patience with Dolphinton than any of the cousins, and the remark, moreover, had slightly wounded his sensibilities. He was a man of more pride than genius; liked to think himself the head of a family of great consequence; and was ambitious to improve his condition. However poorly he might think of Irish titles, he could never see Dolphinton without suffering a pang. A juster providence, he felt, must have reversed their positions. Not that he wished to exchange more with Dolphinton than his title: certainly not his snug inheritance for Dolphinton's Irish acres, mortgaged to the hilt, as he had good reason to suppose they were. Dolphinton was an only child, too, and that would not have suited his cousin. Lord Biddenden's instincts were patriarchal. He liked to see his brothers and sisters under his roof, and to feel that they depended upon him for guidance; and he was almost as anxious for their advancement as his own. It had been a source of considerable chagrin to him that circumstances had made it impossible for him to bestow his first living upon Hugh. He, and not Matthew Penicuik, should have been Hugh's benefactor, and he could never quite forgive the valetudinarian who was nursing Hugh's Rectory for having grossly outlived expectation. That Hugh's presence within walking distance of Biddenden Manor might not be conducive either to his happiness or to his self-esteem he did not allow to weigh with him, for he was a man with a strong sense of propriety, and he knew that it was his duty to feel affection for all his brothers and sisters. But the melancholy truth was that he could never be long in company with Hugh without becoming vexed with him. He was a just man, and he did not blame Hugh for being a head taller than himself, and very much slimmer; but he did think that Hugh was to be blamed for supposing that his cloth gave him the right to adopt a censorious attitude towards his elders. Regretfully, Lord Biddenden thought of his second brother, Claud, and wished that he were not, at this particular moment, serving with his regiment in the Army of Occupation in France. He would have been glad to have helped Claud to a fortune, for he liked him, and he foresaw, too, that he would be obliged, at no very distant date, to help him to buy his promotion, if not to do the thing outright. Captain Rattray, though deferential to the head of his house, was expensive.

These reflections were disturbed by Lord Dolphinton, who raised his head again, and gave utterance to the thought which had been slowly germinating in his brain. "I'd as lief not be an Earl," he said heavily. "Or a Viscount. Freddy's going to be a Viscount. I wouldn't wish to be. I wouldn't wish to be a Baron, though that's not much. George—"

"Yes, yes, we all know I am a Baron! You need not

enumerate the degrees of nobility!" said Biddenden, in an exasperated tone. "You had as lief not be a peer of any degree! I am sure I don't know what maggot has got into your head now, but that at least I have understood!"

"There is no occasion for you to speak so roughly," said Hugh. "What *would* you like to be, Foster?"

Lord Dolphinton sighed. "That's just it," he said mournfully. "I wouldn't like to be a military man. Or a parson. Or a doctor. Or—"

The Rector, realizing that the list of the occupations his cousin did not desire to engage in was likely to be a long one, intervened, saying in his grave way: "Why don't you wish to be an Earl, Foster?"

"I just don't," said Dolphinton simply.

Fortunately, since his elder cousin showed signs of becoming apoplectic, any further remarks which he might have felt impelled to make were checked by the arrival on the scene of his great-uncle and host.

Mr Penicuik, who had retired to his bedchamber after dinner for the purpose of having all the bandages which were bound round a gouty foot removed and replaced, made an impressive entrance. His butler preceded him, bearing upon a silver salver a box of pills, and a glass half filled with an evil-looking mixture; Mr Penicuik himself hobbled in supported on one side by a stalwart footman, and upon the other by his valet; and a maidservant brought up the rear, carrying a heavy walking-stick, several cushions, and a shawl. Both Lord Biddenden and his brother started helpfully towards their infirm relative, and were cursed for their pains. The butler informed Lord Dolphinton in a reproachful whisper that he was occupying the Master's chair. Much alarmed, Dolphinton removed himself to an uncomfortable seat at some distance from the fire. Mr Penicuik, uttering sundry groans, adjurations, and objurgations, was lowered into his favorite chair, his gouty foot was laid tenderly upon a cushion, placed on the stool before him, another cushion was set at his back, and his nephew Hugh disposed the shawl about his shoulders, rather unwisely inquiring, as he did so, if he was comfortable.

"No, I'm not comfortable, and if you had my stomach, and my gout, you wouldn't ask me a damned silly question like that!" retorted Mr Penicuik. "Stobhill, where's my cordial? Where are my pills? They don't do me any good, but I've paid for them, and I won't have waste! Where's my stick? Put it where I can reach it, girl, and don't stand there with your mouth at half cock! Pack of fools! Don't keep on hovering round me, Spiddle! I can't abide hoverers! And don't go out of hearing of the bell, for very likely I shall go to bed early, and I don't want to be kept waiting while you're searched for all over. Go away, all of you! No, wait! Where's my snuff-box?"

"I fancy, sir, that you placed it in your pocket upon rising from the dinner-table," said Stobhill apologetically.

"More fool you to have let me sit down before I took it out again!" said Mr Penicuik, making heroic efforts to get a hand to his pocket, and uttering another anguished groan. An offer of Lord Biddenden's Special Sort, put up in an elegant enamel box, was ungratefully rejected. Mr Penicuik said that he had used Nut Brown for years, and wanted nobody's new fangled mixture. He succeeded, with assistance from two of his henchmen, in extricating his box from his pocket, said that the room was as cold as a tomb, and roundly de-

nounced the footman for not having built up a better
fire. The footman, who was new to his service, fool-
ishly reminded Mr Penicuik that he had himself given
orders to make only a small fire in the Saloon. "Man's
an idiot!" said Mr Penicuik. "Small fire be damned!
Not when I'm going to sit here myself, clodpole!" He
waved the servants away, and nodded to his young relatives. "In general, I don't sit here," he informed
them. "Never sit anywhere but in the library, but I
didn't want the pack of you crowding in there." He
then glanced round the room, observed that it needed
refurbishing but that he was not going to squander his
money on a room he might not enter again for a
twelve-month, and swallowed two pills and the cordial. After this, he took a generous pinch of snuff,
which seemed to refresh him, and said: "Well, I told
you all to come here for a purpose, and if some of you
don't choose to do what's to their interest I wash my
hands of them. I've given 'em a day's grace, and
there's an end to it! I won't keep you all here, eating
me out of house and home, to suit the convenience
of a couple of damned jackanapes. Mind, I don't mean
they shan't have their chance! They don't deserve it,
but I said Kitty should have her pick, and I'm a man
of my word."

"I apprehend, sir," said Biddenden, "that we have
some inkling of your intentions. You will recall that
one amongst us is absent through no fault of his own."

"If you're talking about your brother Claud, I'm
glad he isn't here," replied Mr Penicuik. "I've nothing
against the boy, but I can't abide military men. He can
make Kitty an offer if he chooses, but I can tell you
now she'll have nothing to say to him. Why should
she? Hasn't clapped eyes on him for years! Now, you

may all of you keep quiet, and listen to what I have to say. I've been thinking about it for a long time, and I've decided what's the right thing for me to do, so now I'll put it to you in plain terms. Dolphinton, do you understand me?"

Lord Dolphinton, who was sitting with his hands loosely clasped between his knees, and an expression on his face of the utmost dejection, started, and nodded.

"I don't suppose he does," Mr Penicuik told Hugh, in a lowered voice. "His mother may say what she pleases, but *I've* always thought he was touched in his upper works! However, he's as much my great-nevvy as any of you, and I settled it with myself that I'd make no distinctions between you." He paused, and looked at the assembled company with all the satisfaction of one about to address an audience without fear of argument or interruption. "It's about my Will," he said. "I'm an old man now, and I daresay I shan't live for very much longer. Not that I care for that, for I've had my day, and I don't doubt you'll all be glad to see me into my coffin." Here he paused again, and with the shaking hand of advanced senility helped himself to another pinch of snuff. This performance, however, awoke little response in his great-nephews. Both Dolphinton and the Reverend Hugh certainly had their eyes fixed upon him, but Dolphinton's gaze could not be described as anything but lackluster, and Hugh's was frankly skeptical. Biddenden was engaged in polishing his eyeglass. Mr Penicuik was not, in fact, so laden with years as his wizened appearance and his conversation might have led the uninitiated to suppose. He was, indeed, the last representative of his generation, as he was fond of informing his visitors;

but as four sisters had preceded him into the world
and out of it this was not such an impressive circumstance as he would have wished it to appear. "I'm the
last of my name," he said, sadly shaking his head.
"Outlived my generation! Never married; never had
a brother!"

These tragic accents had their effect upon Lord Dolphinton. He turned his apprehensive eyes towards
Hugh. Hugh smiled at him, in a reassuring way, and
said in a colourless voice: "Precisely so, sir!"

Mr Penicuik, finding his audience to be unrespon-
sive, abandoned his pathetic manner, and said with his
customary tartness: "Not that I shed many tears when
my sisters died, for I didn't! I will say this for your
grandmother, you two! – She didn't trouble me much!
But Dolphinton's grandmother – she was my sister
Cornelia, and the stupidest female – well, never mind
that! Rosie was the best of 'em. Damme, I *liked* Rosie,
and I like Jack! Spit and image of her! I don't know
why the rascal ain't here tonight!" This recollection
brought the querulous note back into his voice. He sat
in silence for a moment or two, brooding over his favorite great-nephew's defection. Biddenden directed
a look of long-suffering at his brother, but Hugh sat
with his eyes on Mr Penicuik's face, courteously waiting for him to resume his discourse. "Well, it don't
signify!" Mr Penicuik said snappishly. "What I'm
going to say is this: there's no reason why I shouldn't
leave my money where I choose! You've none of you
got a ha'porth of claim to it, so don't think it! At the
same time, I was never one to forget my own kith and
kin. No one can say I haven't done my duty by the family. Why, when I think of the times I've let you all come
down here – nasty, destructive boys you were, too! –

besides giving Dolphinton's mother, who's no niece of mine, a lot of advice she'd have done well to have listened to, when my nevvy Dolphinton died – well, there it is! I've got a feeling for my own blood there's no explaining. George has it too: it's the only thing I like about you, George. So it seemed to me that my money ought to go to one of you. At the same time, there's Kitty, and I'm not going to deny that I'd like her to have it, and if I hadn't a sense of what's due to the family I'd leave it to her, and make no more ado about it!" He glanced from Biddenden to Hugh, and gave a sudden cackle of mirth. "I daresay you've often asked yourselves if she wasn't my daughter, hey? Well, she ain't! No relation of mine at all. She was poor Tom Charing's child, all right and tight, whatever you may have suspected. She's the last of the Charings, more's the pity. Tom and I were lads together, but his father left him pretty well in the basket, and mine left me plump enough in the pocket. Tom died before Kitty was out of leading-strings, and there weren't any Charings left, beyond a couple of sour old cousins, so I adopted the girl. Nothing havey-cavey about the business at all, and no reason why she shouldn't marry into any family she chooses. So I've settled it that one of you shall have her, and my fortune into the bargain."

"I must say, sir, it is an odd, whimsical notion!" Biddenden remarked. "And one which—"

"Whimsical!" exclaimed Hugh, in tones of disgust. "I had rather have called it outrageous!"

"Very well, my lad, if that's what you think, don't offer for her!" retorted Mr Penicuik.

"Pray be silent, Hugh! May I inquire, sir, whether

the whole of your estate is to be bequeathed to the – er – fortunate suitor?"

"To Kitty, once she is safely married. I don't hold with cutting up property."

"And in the event of no offer's being received?"

Mr Penicuik gave vent to another of his cackles. "I ain't afraid of that!"

Hugh rose to his feet, and stood towering above his great-uncle. "I will not be silenced! The whole of this scheme must be repugnant to any female of delicacy. Pray, which of us do you mean to compel her to marry?"

"Don't stand there, giving me a crick in my neck!" said Mr Penicuik. "I shan't compel her to marry any of you. I don't say I wouldn't rather she had one than another, naming no names, but I'm not an unreasonable man, and I'm willing to let her have her pick amongst you. Plenty of you to choose from!"

"But what if she should refuse, sir?" asked Bidden-den anxiously.

"Then I'll leave my money to the Foundling Hospital, or some such thing!" replied Mr Penicuik. "She won't be such a zany!"

"Am I correct in assuming, sir, that Kitty has no fortune of her own?" demanded Hugh.

"Not a farthing piece," said Mr Penicuik cheerfully.

Hugh's eyes flashed. "And you say you do not compel her! I marvel at you, sir! I may say that I am profoundly shocked! Without fortune, what hope can any female, circumstanced as Kitty is, have of achieving a respectable alliance?"

"She can't have any, of course," said Mr Penicuik becoming momently more affable as his great-nephew's choler rose.

"No, indeed!" exclaimed Lord Biddenden, almost shuddering at the thought of marriage with a portionless female. "Really, Hugh, you go too far! I don't know where you learned your fantastic notions! One would say there had never been a marriage arranged before, yet you must be well aware that in our circle such things are always done! Your own sister—"

"I have yet to learn that my sisters were forced into marriages that were distasteful to them!"

Mr Penicuik opened his snuff-box again. "What makes you think marriage to one of you would be distasteful to the girl?" he asked blandly. "Maybe she don't fancy *you,* but that ain't to say there isn't one amongst you she might not be glad to pick. She don't know any other men, so there's bound to be." Inhaling too large a pinch of Nut Brown, he sneezed violently several times. When he had recovered from this seizure, he said: "Going to be open with you! Everyone knows the Charings: good stock, fit to couple with any family! The thing is, Kitty has French blood in her." This information was well known to the company, but he disclosed it with all the air of one making a damaging admission. "Evron was the name. Never knew much about the family myself. They were emigrés, but not noble – at least, if they were it's more than Tom ever told me. They won't trouble you: *I saw* to that! Fellow who said he was Kitty's uncle came here once – oh, years ago! Brought his sons with him: couple of scrubby schoolboys, *they* were. I soon sent him to the rightabout: a very neat article I thought him! No use his trying to bamboozle me, and so I told him! A sponge, that's what he was, if he wasn't worse. However, to the best of my belief he took himself off to France again. I never heard any more of him, at all events. But Désirée – Kitty's mother—" He broke off, and his gaze, which had been flickering from Bidden-den's face to the Reverend Hugh's, transferred itself to the smouldering logs in the grate. He did not finish his sentence, but said, after a pause: "Pretty little thing, Kitty, but she'll never be the equal of her mother. Favors poor Tom too much. Got something of her mother's look: I see it now and then: but Dés – Mrs Charing—Well, never mind! That ain't to the purpose." He stretched out his hand towards the bell-rope, and pulled it vigorously. "I'll have her in," he said. "But, mind, now! *I* ain't compelling her to choose any of you three – well, she can't choose you, George, because you're married already! I don't know what brings you here: I never invited you!"

Lord Dolphinton, pleased to hear his words thus confirmed, turned his eyes towards his elder cousin, and remarked succinctly: "Told you so!"

❧ Chapter II ❧

A FEW MINUTES LATER, MISS CATHERINE CHAR-
ing entered the room, accompanied by an elderly lady
whose sparse gray locks had been crimped into ringlets which dangled on either side of an amiable if not
comely countenance. The absence of a cap proclaimed
her spinsterhood; she wore a high-gown of an unbecoming shade of puce and carried a reticule in one
bony hand. Mr Penicuik no sooner saw her than he exclaimed with unnecessary violence: "Not you, woman,
not you! Think I haven't had a bellyful of your face
today? Go away! go away!"

The elderly lady made a faint clucking noise, but although she looked frightened she did not seem to be
surprised by this unconventional greeting. She said:
"Oh, Mr Penicuik! At such a time – such a *delicate* occasion—!"

"Kitty!" interrupted Mr Penicuik. "Throw that Fish
out of the room!"

The elderly lady uttered a protesting shriek; Miss

Charing, however, pushed her gently but inexorably over the threshold, saying: "I *told* you how it would be!" She then closed the door, favored the company with a wide-eyed and thoughtful gaze, and advanced into the middle of the room.

"Good girl!" approved Mr Penicuik. "Sit down!"

"Take this chair!" urged Lord Biddenden.

"You will be comfortable here, my dear Kitty," said the Reverend Hugh, indicating the chair from which he had risen at her entrance.

Not to be outdone, Lord Dolphinton gulped, and said: "Take mine! Not comfortable, but very happy to—Pray take it!"

Miss Charing bestowed a small, prim smile upon her suitors, and sat down on a straight chair by the table, and folded her hands in her lap.

Miss Charing was a rather diminutive brunette. She had a neat figure, very pretty hands and feet, and a countenance which owed much to a pair of large, dark eyes. Their expression was one of candor and of innocence, and she had a habit of fixing them earnestly (and sometimes disconcertingly) upon the face of any interlocutor. She had a slightly retroussé nose, a short upper lip, a decided chin, and a profusion of dusky curls, which were dressed in the demure style which found favor in the eyes of her guardian and her governess. She wore a round robe of green cambric, with a high waist and long sleeves, and one narrow flounce. A small gold locket was suspended round her throat by a ribbon. It was her only ornament. If Lord Biddenden, a man of fashionable inclinations, felt that a few trinkets and a more modish gown would have improved her, it was plain that his brother surveyed her modest appearance with approbation.

"Well, Kitty," said Mr Penicuik, "I've told these three what my intentions are, and now they may speak for themselves. Not Biddenden, of course: I don't mean *him*, though I don't doubt he'd speak fast enough if he could. What brought him here *I* don't know!"

"I expect," said Miss Charing, considering his lordship, "he came to bring Hugh up to the mark."

"Really, Kitty! Upon my word!" ejaculated Biddenden, visibly discomposed. "It is time you learned to mend your tongue!"

Miss Charing looked surprised, and directed an inquiring glance at Hugh. He said, with grave kindness: "George means that such expressions as *up to the mark* are improper when uttered by a female, cousin."

"Ho!" said Mr Penicuik. "So that's what he meant, is it? Well, well! Then I'll thank him to keep his nose out of what don't concern him! What's more, I won't have you teaching the girl to be mealy-mouthed! Not while she lives under my roof! I have quite enough of that from that Fish!"

"I must observe, sir, that my cousin would be perhaps well-advised to model her conversation rather upon Miss Fishguard's example than upon that set her by – I conjecture – Jack," returned Hugh, pointedly enunciating each syllable of the governess's name.

"Gammon!" said Mr Penicuik rudely. "It ain't Jack's example she follows! It's mine! I knew how it would be: I shan't get a wink of sleep tonight! Damme, I never knew a fellow turn my bile as you do, Hugh, with that starched face of yours, and your prosy ways! If I hadn't made up my mind to it that—Never mind that! I did make it up, and I won't go back on my word! Never have, never will! However, there's no reason for

Kitty to be in a hurry to decide which of you she'll
have, and if she takes my advice she'll wait and see
whether—Not that either of 'em deserves she should,
and if they think they can keep *me* dangling on their
whims they will very soon discover their mistake!"

With these suddenly venomous words Mr Penicuik
once more tugged at the bell-rope, and with such violence that it was not surprising that not only the butler, but his valet as well, appeared in the Saloon before
the echo of the clapper had died away. Mr Penicuik
announced his determination to retire to the library,
adding that he had had enough of his relations for one
day, but would see them again upon the morrow, unless – as was more than probable – he was then too
ill to see anyone but the doctor. "Not that it'll do me
any good to see *him!*" he said. He uttered a sharp yelp
as he was hoisted out of his chair, cursed his valet, and
cast a malevolent look at Lord Biddenden. "And if I
were to sleep all night, and wake up without a twinge
of this damned gout, I still wouldn't want to see you,
George!" he declared.

Lord Biddenden waited until he had been supported out of the room before observing, with a signif-
icant look: "It is not difficult to understand what has
cast him into this ill-humor, of course!"

"Didn't invite you," said Dolphinton, showing his
understanding.

"Oh, hold your tongue!" exclaimed Biddenden,
quite exasperated. "My uncle must be in his dotage!
A more ill-managed business—"

"Ill-managed indeed," said Hugh. "There has been
a want of delicacy which must be excessively disagreeable, not to *you*, but to our cousin here!"

"She is not our cousin!"

"My dear brother, we have thought of her as our cousin ever since she was in her cradle."

"Yes, I know we have," said Biddenden, "but you heard what my uncle said! She's not!"

Hugh said arctically: "That was not what I meant. I am happy to be able to say that such a suspicion has never crossed my mind."

"Coming it rather too strong, Hugh!" said Biddenden, with a short laugh.

"You forget your company!" said Hugh, allowing annoyance to lend an edge to his voice.

Recollecting it, Lord Biddenden reddened, and cast an apologetic look at Kitty. "I beg your pardon! But this business has so much provoked me—! Done in such a scrambling way—! However, I do not mean to put you to the blush, and I am sure we have all of us been in such habits of easy intercourse that there is no reason why you should feel the least degree of mortification!"

"Oh, no, I don't!" Kitty assured him. "In fact, it is a thing I have wondered about very often, only Hugh told me he was persuaded it could be no such thing. Which, I must own, I was very glad of."

"Well, upon my word!" said Lord Biddenden, torn between diversion and disapproval. "Hugh told you, did he? So much for your fine talking, my dear brother! No suspicion, indeed! I wonder you will be for ever trying to humbug us all! You should not be talking of such things to Hugh, my dear Kitty, but I shall say nothing further on that head! No doubt you have a comfortable understanding with him, and I am sure I am glad to know that this is so!"

"Well, I knew it would be useless to ask poor Fish," said Kitty naïvely, "so I spoke to Hugh, because he is a clergyman. Has Uncle Matthew told you that I am *not* his daughter?"

She turned her eyes towards Hugh as she spoke, and he replied, a little repressively: "You are the daughter of the late Thomas Charing, Kitty, and of his wife, a French lady."

"Oh, I knew my mother was French!" said Kitty. "I remember when my Uncle Armand brought my French cousins to see us. Their names were Camille and André, and Camille mended my doll for me, which no one else was able to do, after Claud said she was an *aristo,* and cut her head off." Miss Charing's eyes darkened with memory; she added in a brooding tone: "For which I shall *never* forgive him!"

This speech did not seem to augur well for the absent Captain Rattray's chances of winning an heiress. Lord Biddenden said fretfully: "My dear Kitty, that must have been years ago!"

"Yes, but I have *not* forgotten, and I shall *always* be grateful to my cousin Camille."

"Ridiculous!"

Hugh interposed, saying: "It is you who are ridiculous, George. However, I must agree with you that my uncle has shown a lack of delicacy in this affair which renders the present situation distasteful to any person of refinement. I am persuaded that it would be more agreeable to our cousin if you and Dolphinton were to withdraw into some other apartment."

"I daresay it would be more agreeable to *you,*" retorted his lordship, "and I should be very glad to oblige you, but if you imagine that I am going to bed at seven o'clock you are the more mistaken!"

"There is not the smallest necessity for you to go to bed. Really, George—!"

"Oh, yes, there is!" said his lordship, with considerable acerbity. "No doubt my uncle has a very comfortable fire built up in the library, but if there is one in any other room in the house I have yet to discover it!"

"Well, there is one in his bedchamber, of course," said Kitty. "And, if you did not object to sitting with Fish, there is a fire in the schoolroom. Only I daresay you would not like it very much."

"No, I should not!"

"And poor Dolph wouldn't like it either. Besides, he wants to say something," pursued Kitty, who had been observing with an indulgent eye the spasmodic opening and shutting of Lord Dolphinton's large mouth.

"Well, Foster, what is it?" said Hugh encouragingly.

"I won't go with George!" announced Dolphinton. "I don't like George. Didn't come to see him. Oughtn't to be here. Wasn't invited!"

"Oh, my God, now we are back at that!" muttered Biddenden. "You might just as well take yourself off to bed, Dolphinton, as remain here!"

"No, I might not," returned Dolphinton, with spirit. "*I* ain't a married man! What's more, I'm an Earl."

"What has that to say to anything, pray? I wish you will—"

"Important," said Dolphinton. "Good thing to marry an Earl. Be a Countess."

"This, I collect, is a declaration!" said Biddenden sardonically. "Pretty well, Foster, I must say!"

"Are you being so obliging as to make me an offer, Dolph?" inquired Miss Charing, in no way discomposed.

Lord Dolphinton nodded several times, grateful to her for her ready understanding. "Very happy to oblige!" he said. "Not at all plump in the pocket – no, not to mention that! Just say – always had a great regard for you! Do me the honor to accept of my hand in marriage!"

"Upon my word!" ejaculated Biddenden. "If one did not know the truth, one would say you were three parts disguised, Foster!"

Lord Dolphinton, uneasily aware of having lost the thread of a prepared speech, looked more miserable than ever, and colored to the roots of his lank brown locks. He cast an imploring glance at Miss Charing, who at once rose, and went to seat herself in a chair beside him, patting his hand in a soothing way, and saying: "Nonsense! You said it very creditably, Dolph, and I perfectly understand how it is! You have offered for me because your Mama ordered you to do so, haven't you?"

"That's it," said his lordship, relieved. "No wish to vex you, Kitty – really very fond of you! – but must make a push!"

"Exactly so! Your estates are shockingly mortgaged, and your pockets are quite to let, so you have offered for me! But you don't really wish to marry me, do you?"

His lordship sighed. "No help for it!" he said simply.

"Yes, there is, because I won't accept your offer, Dolph," said Miss Charing, in a consoling tone. "So now you may be comfortable again!"

The cloud lifted from his brow, only to descend again. "No, I shan't," said his lordship wretchedly. "She'll take a pet. Say I must have made poor work of it."

"What astonishes me," said Biddenden, in an aside

to his brother, "is that my Aunt Augusta permitted him to come here without her!"

"Didn't want to," said Dolphinton, once more startling his relatives by his ability to follow the gist of remarks not addressed to himself. "Uncle Matthew said he wouldn't let her cross his threshold. Said I must come alone. *I* didn't object, only she'll say I didn't do the thing as she told me. Well, I did! Offered for you – said I was an Earl – said I should be honored! Won't believe it, that's all!"

"Oh, don't distress yourself!" said Biddenden. "We three are witnesses to testify to your having expressed yourself with all the ardour and address imaginable!"

"You think I did?" said Dolphinton hopefully.

"Oh, heaven grant me patience!" exclaimed his cousin.

"Indeed, you stand in need of it!" said Hugh sternly. "You may be quite easy, my dear Foster: you have done just as my aunt bade you. I believe I may say that no persuasions of hers could have prevailed upon our cousin to have changed her nay to yea."

"Well, you may," conceded Miss Charing. "Only I am very well able to speak for myself, I thank you, Hugh! Are *you* wishful of making me an offer?"

Lord Dolphinton, his mission honorably discharged, turned an interested gaze upon his clerical cousin; Lord Biddenden exclaimed: "This is intolerable!" and Hugh himself looked a trifle out of countenance. He hesitated, before saying, with a constrained smile: "There is a degree of awkwardness attached to this situation which might, I fancy, be more easily overcome were we to converse alone together."

"Yes, but you cannot expect George and poor Dolph to remove to a room where there is no fire!"

objected Miss Charing reasonably. "It would be useless to apply to Uncle Matthew for leave to kindle any more fires tonight: you must know that! Nothing puts him into such a taking as habits of wasteful extravagance, and he would be bound to think it a great waste of coals to make a fire for George or for Dolph. And as for our situation's being awkward, if I do not regard that I am sure you need not. In fact, I am happy to be able to tell as many of you as I can that I have not the smallest wish to marry *any* of you!"

"Very likely you have not, Kitty, but that you should express yourself with such heat – or, I may say, *at all!* – is very unbecoming in you. I am astonished that Miss Fishguard – an excellent woman, I am sure! – should not have taught you a little more conduct!" It occurred to Lord Biddenden that a quarrel with Kitty would scarcely forward the project he had in view, and he added, in a more cordial tone: "But, indeed, I must own that such a situation as this must be considered in itself to have passed the bounds of propriety! Believe me, Kitty, I feel for you! You have been made the object of what I cannot but deem a distempered freak."

"Yes, but fortunately I am very well acquainted with you all, so that I need have no scruple in speaking the truth to you," Kitty pointed out. "I don't want Uncle Matthew's odious fortune, and as for marrying any gentleman who offered for me only because I have the advantage of a handsome dependence, I would rather wear the willow all my days! And let me tell you, Hugh, that I did not think that *you* would do such a thing!"

The Rector, not unnaturally, was a little confounded by this sudden attack, and made her no immediate reply. Lord Dolphinton, who had listened intently to what she had to say, was pleased to find that he was able to elucidate. "Shouldn't have come," he told his rigid cousin. "Not the thing for a man in orders. George shouldn't have come either. Not in orders, but not invited."

"Not want to inherit a fortune!" exclaimed Biddenden, the enormity of such a declaration making it possible for him to ignore Dolphinton's unwelcome intrusion into the argument. "Pooh! nonsense! You do not know what you are saying!"

"On the contrary," said the Rector, making a recovery, "her sentiments do her honor! My dear Kitty, none is more conscious than myself of what must be your reflections upon this occasion. Indeed, you must believe that I share them! That my great-uncle would make *me* the recipient of his fortune was a thought that has never crossed my head: if I have ever indulged my brain with speculations on the nature of his intentions, I have supposed that he would bequeath to his adopted child a respectable independance, and the residue of his estate to that member of the family whom we know to be his favorite great-nephew. None of us, I fancy, could have called in question the propriety of such a disposition; none of us can have imagined that he would, whatever the event, have left that adopted child destitute upon the world." He saw the startled look in Miss Charing's eyes, and said, with great gentleness: "That, dearest Kitty, is what he has assured us he will do, should we or you refuse to obey his – I do not scruple to say – *monstrous* command!"

"Destitute?" repeated Kitty, as though the word were unknown.

Lord Biddenden pulled a chair forward, and sat down beside her, possessing himself of one of her

hands, and patting it. "Yes, Kitty, that is the matter
in a nutshell," he said. "I do not wonder that you
should look shocked! *Your* repugnance must be shared
by any man of sensibility. The melancholy truth is that
you were not born to an independance; your father –
a man of excellent family, of course! – was improvi-
dent; but for the generosity of my uncle in adopting
you, you must have been reared in such conditions as
we will not dwell upon – a stranger to all the elegancies
of life, a penniless orphan without a protector to lend
you consequence! My dear Kitty, you might even have
counted yourself fortunate today to have found yourself in such a situation as Miss Fishguard's!"

It was plain, from the impressive dropping of his
voice, that he had described to her the lowest depths
in which his fancy was capable of imagining her. His
solemn manner had its effect; she looked instinctively
towards the Rector, upon whose judgment she had
been accustomed, of late years, to depend.

"I cannot say that it is untrue," Hugh responded,
in a low tone. "Indeed, I must acknowledge that whatever may be my uncle's conduct today, however improper in *my* eyes, you are very much beholden to him
for his generosity in the past."

She pulled her hand out of Lord Biddenden's warm,
plump clasp, and jumped up, saying impulsively: "I
hope I am not ungrateful, but when you speak of *generosity* I feel as though my heart must burst!"

"Kitty, Kitty, do not talk in that intemperate style!"
Hugh said.

"No, no, but you do not understand!" she cried.
"You speak of his fortune, and you know it to be large!
Everyone says that, but *I* have no cause to suspect it!
If he yielded to a generous impulse when he adopted

me, at least he has atoned for that during all these years! No, Hugh, I *won't* hush! Ask poor Fish what wage she has received from him for educating me! Ask her what shifts she has often and often been put to to contrive that I should not be dressed in *rags!* Well, perhaps not rags, precisely, but only look at this gown I am wearing now!"

All three gentlemen obeyed her, but perhaps only Lord Biddenden recognized the justice of her complaint. Hugh said: "You look very well, Kitty, I assure you. There is a neatness and a propriety—"

"I do not want neatness and propriety!" interrupted Kitty, her cheeks flushed, and her eyes sparkling. "I want elegant dresses, and I want to have my hair cut in the first style of fashion, and I want to go to assemblies, and rout-parties, and to the theater, and to the Opera, and not – *not!* – to be a poor little squab of a dowdy!"

Again, only Biddenden was able to appreciate her feelings. "Very understandable!" he said. "It is not at all to be wondered at. Why, you have been kept so cooped up here that I daresay you may never have attended so much as a concert!"

"Very true," Hugh concurred. "I have frequently observed to my uncle that the indulgence of some degree of rational amusement should be granted to you, Kitty. Alas, I fear that his habits and prejudices are fixed! I cannot flatter myself that my words have borne weight with him."

"Exactly so!" Biddenden said. "And so it must always be while you remain under this roof, Kitty! However little you may relish the *manner* of my uncle's proposals, you must perceive all the advantages attached to an eligible marriage. You will have a position of the first respectability; you will be mistress of a very pretty establishment, able to order things as you choose; with the habits of economy you have learnt you will find yourself at the outset most comfortably circumstanced; and in the course of time you will be able to command every imaginable extravagance."

From his lengthening upper lip it was to be deduced that this sketch of the future made little appeal to the Rector. He said: "I do Kitty the justice to believe that the tone of her mind is too nice to allow of her hankering after *extravagance.* I am not a Puritan; I sympathize to the full in her desire to escape from the restrictions imposed upon her by my uncle's valetudinarian habits—"

"Oh!" cried Kitty wistfully. "I should like so much to be extravagant!"

"You will allow me to know you better than you know yourself, dear Kitty," responded Hugh, with great firmness. "Most naturally, you desire to become better acquainted with the world. You would like to visit the Metropolis, I daresay, and so you shall! You yearn to taste the pleasures enjoyed by those persons who constitute what is known as the *ton.* It is only proper that you should do so. I venture to prophesy that in a very short space of time you would find many of these pleasures hollow cheats. But do not imagine that if you were to bestow your hand upon me in marriage you would find me opposed to the occasional gratification of your wish for more gaiety than is to be found in a country parish! I am no enemy to the innocent recreation of dancing; I have frequently derived no small enjoyment from a visit to the playhouse; and while I must always hold *gaming* in abhorrence I am not so bigoted that I cannot play a tolerable game of whist, or quadrille, or bear my part in a private loo-party."

"Hugh," interrupted Kitty. "George must have *constrained* you to make me this offer!"

"I assure you, upon my honor, it is not so!"

"You don't wish me to be your wife! You – you don't *love* me!" she said, in a suffocating voice, and with tears starting to her eyes.

He replied stiffly: "My regard for you is most sincere. Since I was inducted into a parish, not so far distant as to make it impossible for me frequently to visit my great-uncle, I have had ample opportunity of observing you, and to my regard has been added respect. I am persuaded that there is nothing in your character which could preclude your becoming a most eligible wife to any man in orders."

She gazed up at him in astonishment. "I?" she exclaimed. "When you have been forever scolding me for levity, and frowning every time I don't mind my tongue to your liking, and telling me I ought not to be discontented with my lot? How can you talk so?"

He possessed himself of her hand, saying, with a smile: "These are the faults of youth, Kitty. I own, I have tried to guide you: it was never my intention to *scold!*"

"If you are not constrained by George, it must be by Uncle Matthew!" she declared, snatching her hand away.

"Yes, in some sort," he replied. "It is hard for you to understand the motives—"

"No, I assure you!"

"Yes," he said steadily. "You must know, Kitty – you must realize, however painful it may be – that George has spoken only the truth. Your whole dependance is upon my uncle; were he to die, leaving you unwed, un-betrothed to one of us, your situation must be desperate indeed. I hesitate to wound you, but I must tell you that, the world being what it is, a respectable marriage is hard to achieve for a dowerless and orphaned female. What could you do to maintain yourself, if left alone upon the world? George has spoken of such a position as that held by Miss Fishguard, but surely without reflection! Miss Fishguard is an excellent woman, but she is lacking in such accomplishments as a governess, seeking employment in the first circles, is today expected to impart to her pupils. Her knowledge is not profound; her performance upon the pianoforte is not superior; she has no skill with Water-Colors; little mastery over the French tongue; none at all over the Italian."

She turned her face away, a blush of mortification spreading over her cheeks. "You mean that *I* am lacking in accomplishments."

"Since my uncle neglected to provide masters to supply the deficiencies of your education, it must necessarily be so," he replied calmly. "You know, my dear Kitty, how often I have recommended you to pursue your studies, even though you have left the schoolroom."

"Yes," acknowledged Kitty, without enthusiasm.

"It would afford me much pleasure to be able to direct your studies, and to read with you," he said. "I believe I may say that I am accounted a good scholar, and I am very sure that to guide the taste and to enlarge the knowledge of so intelligent a pupil as you, dear cousin, must be an agreeable task."

Lord Biddenden, who had been listening to his brother's measured speeches in growing disapprobation, could no longer contain his impatience. "Well, really, Hugh!" he ejaculated. "A fine offer to be making the poor girl, I must say! Enough to set her against marriage with you from the outset!"

"Kitty understands me," Hugh said, rather haughtily.

"Well, yes, I think I do," said Kitty. "And George is perfectly right! I should dislike excessively to be turned into a scholar, and I cannot feel, Hugh, that I am at all the kind of girl you should marry. And now I come to think of it, I daresay there is *one* way in which I could earn my bread! I could seek a post as housekeeper. That is something in which I need no instruction. I have had the management of this house ever since I was sixteen, and able to relieve poor Fish of duties for which she is quite unsuited! I expect anyone would be very happy to employ me, too, because if there is one thing I know all about it is the strictest economy!"

"Now, Kitty, don't talk nonsense!" begged Lord Biddenden testily.

The Rector made a silencing gesture with one shapely hand. "If your youth, Kitty, did not render you ineligible for such a post, your birth and your breeding most assuredly do. I hardly think, moreover, that you would find it congenial."

"No, I shouldn't," she said frankly. "But I shouldn't find it congenial to be married to you either, Hugh."

"There! What did I tell you?" interpolated Biddenden.

"I am sorry," Hugh said, grave but kind. "For my part, I should count myself happy to be able to call you my wife."

"Well, it is very obliging of you to say so," retorted

Kitty, "but if you are speaking the truth I cannot conceive why you should never have given me the least suspicion of it until today!"

It was his turn to redden, but he did not allow his eyes to waver from hers, and he replied with scarcely a moment's hesitation: "The thought, however, has frequently been in my mind. I believe it is not in my nature to *fall in love*, as the common phrase has it, but I have long felt for you the sincerest esteem and affection. You are young: you have not yet reached your twentieth birthday; I believed that the time to declare myself was not yet. I have sometimes suspected, too, that you had a partiality for another member of the family decided enough to make it useless for me to address you. It was in the expectation of finding all three of my cousins gathered here that I came to Arnside. I have found only Dolphinton, and in these circumstances I do not hesitate to beg you, Kitty, to accept of my hand in marriage, and to believe that at Garsfield Rectory you may be sure of a safe and an honorable asylum."

"It is not, then, for the sake of Uncle Matthew's fortune that you have offered for me, but from chivalry towards a penniless creature whom you suppose to have been rejected by – by everyone else?" demanded Kitty breathlessly. "I – I would rather marry *Dolph!*"

At these alarming words, Lord Dolphinton, who had for some time been sucking the hilt of a paper-knife, which he had found conveniently to hand, sat up with a jerk, and dropped the knife from his suddenly nerveless fingers. "Eh?" he uttered. "But—Said you wouldn't! Remember it distinctly! Said I might be comfortable again!"

"And so you may, for I meant it!" said Kitty fiercely.

"There is no one for whom I have the *least* partiality, and I don't wish to marry *anyone* in your odious family! I think Hugh is a humbug, and Claud has a cruel nature, and Dolph and Freddy are just *stupid,* and as for Jack I am truly thankful that he was not coxcomb enough to come here, because I dislike him more than all the rest of you together! Goodnight!"

The door slammed behind her, causing Lord Dolphinton to start nervously. Biddenden said: "A ramshackle business you made of it, Hugh, with your damned, long-winded periods, and your fine talk of educating the girl! Much good will your scholarship do you while you have less than commonsense! What in the devil's name possessed you to bring Jack up? Of course she's fancied herself in love with him for years!"

"It is time she left such childish folly behind her," said Hugh coldly. "There can be little in Jack to recommend him to a female of sense and principles, after all."

"If that's what you think, my dear brother, I would advise you to put your nose outside your Rectory and to go about the world a little!" returned Biddenden, with a short laugh. "And don't talk fustian to me about his gaming, and his libertine ways – ay, I know it's on the tip of your tongue! – Jack may be anything you please but he's a devilish handsome fellow, and an out-and-outer – what they call top-of-the-trees! Of course Kitty has a *tendre* for him!"

"No, she hasn't," interrupted Dolphinton, who had been following this interchange with a puzzled frown on his brow. "Can't have been listening! She said she disliked him more than all the rest of us together. And come to think of it," added his lordship, attacked by a sudden thought, "not sure she ain't right!" He nodded, pleased with his flash of insight, and said with unimpaired affability: "Don't see much of him, which accounts for my thinking it was you I disliked the most, George."

Lord Biddenden, after glaring at him in an impotent way for several seconds, strode to the bell-rope, and jerked it vigorously. "Since that miserly old bag of bones has given no orders for our refreshment *I* shall make so bold as to tell the servant to bring some *brandy* to this room!" he announced bitterly.

❧ *Chapter III* ❧

SHORTLY BEFORE SEVEN O'CLOCK THAT EVE-
ning, at about the moment when Miss Charing entered
the Saloon to receive the proposals of two of her cousins, a hired post-chaise and pair drew up before the
Blue Boar, a small but excellent hostelry situated
rather more than a mile from Arnside House, where
four roads joined. The young gentleman who alighted
from the chaise must have been recognized at sight
by the discerning as a Pink of the *Ton*, for although
his judgment, which, in all matters of Fashion, was extremely nice, had forbidden him to travel into the
country arrayed in the long-tailed coat of blue superfine, the pantaloons of delicate yellow, and the tas-
selled Hessian boots which marked him in the
Metropolis as a veritable Tulip, or Bond Street Beau,
none but a regular Dash, patronizing the most exclu-
sive of tailors, could have presented himself in so ex-
quisitely moulded a riding-coat, such peerless
breeches, or such effulgent top-boots. The white tops

of these, which incontrovertibly proclaimed his dandyism, were hidden by the folds of a very long and volu-
minous driving-coat, lined with silk, embellished with
several shoulder-capes, and secured across his chest
by a double row of very large buttons of mother of
pearl. Upon his brown locks, carefully anointed with
Russian oil, and cropped à la Titus, he wore a high-
crowned beaver-hat, set at an exact angle between the
rakish and the precise; on his hands were gloves of
York tan; under one arm he carried a malacca cane.
When he strolled into the inn, and shed the somewhat
deceptive driving-coat, he was seen to be a slender
young gentleman, of average height and graceful carriage. His countenance was unarresting, but amiable;
and a certain vagueness characterized his demeanour.
When he relinquished his coat, his hat, his cane, and
his gloves into the landlord's hands, a slight look of
anxiety was in his face, but as soon as a penetrating
glance at the mirror had satisfied him that the high
points of his shirt-collar were uncrumpled, and the intricacies of a virgin cravat no more disarranged than
a touch would set to rights, the anxious look disappeared, and he was able to turn his attention to other
matters.

The landlord, who had greeted him with a mixture
of the deference due to a wealthy man of fashion, and
the tolerant affection of one who, having been acquainted with him since the days when he wore nan-
keens and frilled shirts, knew all his failings, said for
the second time: "Well, sir, this is a pleasant surprise,
I'm sure! Quite a period it is since we've seen you in
these parts! You'll be on your way to Arnside, I don't
doubt."

"Yes," acknowledged the traveler. "Dashed nearly

dished myself up, what's more! Devilish early hours my great-uncle keeps, Pluckley. Fortunate thing: remembered it a mile back! Better dine here."

The Blue Boar was not much in the habit of catering for the Polite World, but the landlord, secure in the knowledge that his helpmate, a north-country woman, was a notable housewife, received this announcement with unruffled equanimity. "Well, sir, I won't say you're wrong," he remarked, with the wink of the privileged. "A most respected gentleman, Mr Penicuik, I'm sure, but they do say as he don't keep what I'd call a liberal table, nor, by what I hear from Mr Stobhill, he don't let the bottle go round like it should. Now, if you'll step into the coffee-room, sir, you'll find a good fire, and no one but yourself likely to come in. I'll just make so bold as to fetch you in a glass of as soft a sherry as you'll find this side of London-town, and while you're drinking it my rib shall toss you up some mushroom fritters, by way of a relish – for you know we don't have any call for French kickshawses here, not in the ordinary way, and aside from the fritters there's only a serpent of mutton, and one of our goose-and-turkey pies, which I'll be bound you've not forgot, and a bit of crimped cod, and a curd pudding, if you should fancy it."

This modest repast being approved, Mr Pluckley then withdrew; and within a short space of time the covers were laid in the coffee-room, and the guest sat down to an excellent dinner, the bare skeleton, which had been described by the landlord, being reinforced by oysters in batter, some Flemish soup, and, as side-dishes, some calf's fry, and a boiled tongue with turnips. A bottle of burgundy, which had formed part of a particularly successful run, washed the meal down;

and the whole was rounded off by some cognac, the
young gentleman of fashion waving aside, with a horrified shudder, an offer of port.

It was while he was sipping this revivifying cordial
that the landlord, who had lingered in the coffee-room
to regale him with various items of local gossip, was
drawn from his side by the sound of an opening door.
Informing his guest that he would take care no ungenteel person intruded upon him, Mr Pluckley departed. A murmur of voices penetrated confusedly to
the coffee-room, and in another minute Mr Pluckley
reappeared, looking very much astonished, and saying: "Well, sir, and little did I think who it might be,
at this hour of the evening, and the snow beginning
to fall, and her coming on foot, without a servant nor
nothing! It's Miss Charing, sir!"

"Eh?" said the willowy gentleman, slightly startled.

The landlord held the door wide, and Miss Charing,
a serviceable if not beautiful cloak huddled about her
form, appeared on the threshold, and there halted.
The strings of her hood were tied tightly under her
chin, and the resulting frill of drab woollen-cloth un-
becomingly framed a face whose nose was pink-tipped
with cold. There was nothing romantic about Miss
Charing's appearance, but her entrance would not
have shamed a Siddons. "You!" she uttered, in accents of loathing. "I might have known it!"

The Honorable Frederick Standen was faintly puzzled. It seemed to him that Miss Charing was both surprised and displeased to see him. He expostulated.
"Dash it, Kitty, I was invited!"

"I thought better of you!" said Miss Charing tragically.

"You did?" said Mr Standen, sparring for wind. His

gaze, not wholly unlike that of a startled hare, alighted on the table; he fancied he could perceive a glimmer of light. "Yes, but you know what my uncle is!" he said. "Dines at five, or he did when I was last down here! Nothing for it but to snatch a mouthful on the way."

"That!" said Miss Charing, with withering scorn. "I don't care where you dine, Freddy, but that you should have come to Arnside gives me a very poor notion of you, let me tell you! Not that I ever had anything else, for you're as bad as Dolph—worse!"

Mr Standen, considering the matter, was moved to expostulate again. "No, really, Kitty! Pitching it too strong!" he said. "The poor fellow's queer in his attic!" It occurred to him that Mr Pluckley's interested presence might with advantage be dispensed with. He indicated this briefly and simply, and Mr Pluckley regretfully withdrew.

Miss Charing, who shared with her governess a taste for romantic fiction, toyed with the idea of remaining (a statue of persecuted virtue) by the door, but succumbed to the lure of a fire. Seating herself on the settle beside it, she untied the strings of her cloak, pushed back the hood from her ruffled curls, and stretched benumbed hands to the blaze.

"I'll tell you what it is!" offered Mr Standen. "You're cold! Put you in a miff! Have some brandy!"

Miss Charing declined the invitation contemptuously. She added: "You need not have put yourself to the trouble of traveling all the way from London. You have quite wasted your time, I assure you!"

"Well, that don't surprise me," returned Freddy. "I rather thought it was a hum. Uncle Matthew pretty stout?"

"No, he is not! Dr Fenwick said he could be cured of his stomach trouble by magnetism and warm ale, but it only did him a great deal of harm. At least, he said it did, and also that we were all in a plot to kill him."

Gout bad too?" inquired Mr Standen anxiously.

"*Very* bad!"

"You know, I think I made a mistake to come," confided Mr Standen. "Not at all sure I won't rack up for the night here, and go back to London in the morning. The thing is the old gentleman don't like me above half, and if his gout's plaguing him I'd as lief not meet him. Besides, he won't let me bring my man, and I find it devilish awkward! It ain't my neckcloths, of course: never let Icklesham do more than hand 'em to me! It's my boots. The last time I stayed here the fellow who cleaned 'em left a dashed great thumb-mark on one of them! I'm not bamming, Kitty! Gave me a nasty turn, I can tell you."

"You might as well go back to London *now*," said Kitty. "You made a *great* mistake to come! In fact, when I think of your circumstances I am quite shocked that you should have done so!"

"That's all very well," objected Mr Standen, "but I don't like traveling at night. Besides, this ain't a posting-house, and I need a change. Yes, and now I come to think of it, what have my circumstances to say to anything?"

"You are as rich as – as – I can't remember the name!" said Miss Charing crossly.

"I expect you mean Golden Ball," said Freddy. "And I ain't."

"No, I do not! I mean somebody out of history – at least, I think he was, because when you wish to signify that a person is excessively wealthy you say he is as rich as – as *him!*"

"Well, I don't!" said Freddy. "Never heard of the fellow! Nice cake I should make of myself if I went around talking about people out of history! Anyone would think you'd been in the sun, Kitty!"

"Sun? It is snowing!" cried Miss Charing.

"In that case, I'll be dashed if I go back to London tonight," said Freddy. "Not that that's what I meant, but never mind! What's more, I ain't as wealthy as all that."

"You are wealthy enough not to be obliged to offer for an heiress!" said Miss Charing, darting a glance of scorn at him.

"Well, I ain't going to offer for an heiress," said Freddy patiently. A thought occurred to him; in some concern he added: "Kitty, you haven't got this infectious complaint, have you? Don't know what it is, but it goes very much about, they tell me. M'sister Meg was in bed a sennight with it."

"Freddy!" exclaimed Miss Charing, staring fixedly at him. "Don't you *know* why Uncle Matthew sent for you?"

"Said he had something important to say to me. I thought it was a hum!"

"But if you came at all why did you not come yesterday?" Kitty demanded.

"Been out of town," explained Mr Standen.

"Oh, Freddy, I have wronged you!" uttered Kitty, genuinely remorseful. "But George, and Hugh, and Dolph all knew, and so of course I supposed you must too!"

"Eh?" ejaculated Freddy, startled. "You don't mean to tell me *they* are at Arnside?"

"Yes, yes, they have been there since yesterday, and it is too dreadful, Freddy!"

"Good God, I should rather think so!" he agreed, much struck. "Why, if I hadn't met you, I should have walked smash into them! You know, Kitty, the old gentleman must be in pretty queer stirrups! Unless he's been on the mop, and that don't seem likely. Well what I mean is, he must be dicked in the nob to want to such a set of gudgeons at Arnside! Mind, I don't say Hugh ain't a clever fellow: daresay he is; but you can't deny he's a dead bore!"

"Yes, he is!" agreed Miss Charing, with enthusiasm. "And, which is worse, he's a *saintly* bore, Freddy!"

"Devilish!" agreed Freddy. "Know what he said to me the last time he took a bolt to the village? Why, just because he saw me coming away from the Great-Go, he started to moralize about the evils of gaming! Seemed to think I was a regular leg, which, as I told him, is a dashed silly thing to think, because for one thing it ain't at all the thing, and for another you have to be a curst clever fellow to be a leg! What's brought him to Arnside?"

"Uncle Matthew," replied Kitty. "He is making his Will!"

"He is? You don't mean he's had notice to quit at last?"

"Of course he has not, but he chooses to think so!" said Kitty.

"No need to put yourself in a pucker," said Freddy kindly. "Been saying it any time these past ten years! Who's he leaving his moneybags to?"

"To me – upon conditions!"

"What, nothing to Jack?" exclaimed Freddy. "If that

don't beat the Dutch! Not but what I'm dashed glad to hear it, Kitty! Felicitate you!"

"Yes," said Miss Charing, "but it is on condition that I marry one or other of his great-nephews, and *that*, Freddy, is why you were invited to Arnside! You are to offer for me!"

The effect of this pronouncement was quite as great as she could have desired, and, possibly, rather greater. Mr Standen, who had disposed his slender person gracefully in a chair on the other side of the fireplace, was jerked suddenly upright. An expression of the most profound horror transformed his amiable countenance; his eyes showed an alarming tendency to start from his head; and he said, in a voice approaching a squeak: "*What?*"

Miss Charing was betrayed into an unromantic giggle.

Mr Standen looked suspiciously at her. "Now, listen to me, Kitty!" he said savagely. "If you're trying to roast me—No, my God! So that was it! I might have guessed as much! Well, if I don't serve him trick-and-tie, for this—!"

"Who?" demanded Kitty.

"Jack," said Mr Standen. "Mind, I thought it was a dashed smoky thing! In fact, I settled it with myself I wouldn't come. Well, what I mean is, I ain't such a green 'un as to fall into one of Jack's take-ins! But, you know, Kit, this is a devilish business! Why, if I hadn't chanced to meet you I should have found myself dished-up! You might have warned me, my dear girl!"

Miss Charing paid no heed to this, but fixed her eyes most earnestly upon his face, and asked: "Did Jack tell you to come?"

"That's it. Met him at Limmer's last night. Wearing

a coat I didn't like. Told me he let Scott make it for him. Pity! Made him look like a military man."

"Never mind Jack's coat!" interrupted Kitty. "What did he say to you?"

"Well, that's it. Said he was tired of Weston's cut, which made me think he must be a trifle above par. Well, I put it to you, Kit, that's all you *can* think when a fellow says a thing like that!"

"What did he say about – about me?" demanded Kitty.

"Didn't say anything about you. Asked me if I'd had a summons from the old gentleman. Told him I had, and he said I should on no account stay away. That's why I settled not to come. Kept his mouth as prim as a pie, but you know the way he laughs with his eyes!"

The very thought of the way Mr Westruther laughed with his eyes drew a deep sigh from Miss Charing. "Yes," she said wistfully. For a moment she seemed inclined to sink into a reverie, but the melting mood was not of long duration. Once again Mr Standen became the object of her penetrating gaze. "Did Jack – *know* – why he was sent for?" she asked.

"Carlton House to a Charley's shelter he knew!" said Freddy. "That's why he ain't here, of course."

Miss Charing stiffened. "You think so?" she said coldly.

"Not a doubt of it!" responded Freddy. "I must say, I call it a shabby thing to do! Might have told me what was in the wind. That's Jack all over, though!"

Miss Charing accepted this unflattering speech meekly enough, but said, lifting her chin a little: "For my part, I am very glad he has not come. I should have thought very poorly of him had he obeyed such a command."

"No fear of that," said Freddy. "Very likely to have put up his back."

"Yes, perhaps that was it!" said Kitty, brightening. "He is very proud, isn't he, Freddy?"

"Oh, I wouldn't call him proud, precisely. Gets upon his high ropes now and then, but he ain't one of your high sticklers."

Miss Charing meditated for some moments in silence. "*I* did not wish him to come," she said at last, "but Uncle Matthew is excessively vexed that he has not. It is the most absurd thing, but I am persuaded that Uncle Matthew had not the least notion of my marrying anyone else. He was as mad as fire when only Dolph and the Rattrays came to Arnside."

"Anyone would be," agreed Freddy. "Can't think what possessed the old gentleman to invite 'em!" He added modestly: "Or me either, for that matter."

"He has taken a nonsensical notion into his head that he must not favor any of you above another. And you know what he is, Freddy! Once he has said a thing he will never unsay it! I daresay it may not have occurred to him that Jack would not even come! It would serve him right if I said I would marry Dolph!"

"You aren't going to tell me Dolph offered for you?" said Freddy incredulously.

"Yes, he did. If I hadn't been so angry I must have gone into whoops. Poor Dolph! he looked so miserable, and of course I knew he only did it because that odious woman compelled him!"

"Now I see it all!" announced Freddy, nodding his head several times. "Accounts for it! Told you I'd settled not to come, didn't I? Well, it was Aunt Dolphinton who made me change my mind! If I hadn't met her this morning, I wouldn't have!"

Kitty looked very much surprised. "Lady Dolphinton made you come? No, how should she do that? She
cannot have wished it!"

"Well, that's it. Didn't wish it at all. I was in Bond
Street, just on the toddle, you know, when out she
popped from Hookham's Library, and stood there
staring at me. Made my bow, of course: nothing else
to be done! Nasty moment, I can tell you, because I
was wearing a new waistcoat, and I'm not sure that it
ain't a thought too dashing. But it wasn't that. Not,"
he added, considering the matter, "that I feel quite
easy about it. Liked it when Weston showed it to me,
but as soon as I put it on—"

"Oh, Freddy, do stop talking about coats and waist-
coats!" begged Miss Charing, quite out of patience.
"What did Lady Dolphinton say?"

"Said, *So you haven't gone to Arnside!* Silly thing to say,
really, because there I was, in the middle of Bond
Street. So I said, No, I hadn't gone; and she asked me
whether I meant to go, and I said I rather fancied not.
And that's when I took a notion she was playing some
kind of an undergame, because she gave me a hoaxing
sort of a smile, and said I was wise not to go, for it
was all a hum, or some such thing. Seemed devilish
anxious to discover whether Jack had gone, too.
Looked like a cat at a cream-pot when I told her he
hadn't. Playing the concave-suit, that's what I thought!
Well, dash it, Kit, I may not be one of these clever fellows, talking about a lot of dead people out of history,
but a man can't be on the town and not smell out a
bubble! Stands to reason! So I came to see for myself
what was in the wind. Mistake, of course, but there's
no harm done, as it chances. All the same, Jack served

me a damned backhanded turn, and so I shall tell him! A pretty fix I should have been in if I hadn't met you!"

"No, you wouldn't," said Kitty. "Uncle Matthew cannot compel you to offer for me!"

Mr Standen looked dubious. "You think he can't? Not sure you're right there. Fact is, I'm frightened to death of the old gentleman! Always was! I don't say I wouldn't have made a push to come off clear, but it would have been dashed awkward. No, the more I think of it the more I think it was a fortunate circumstance I met you. Seemed to me rather a queer start when you walked in, but I'm glad you did, very!" This reflection had the effect of causing a problem which had for some time been floating in a rather nebulous way at the back of his mind to assume a more concrete form. He said suddenly: "Come to think of it, it *is* a queer start! What brings you here, Kit? No wish to offend you, but not quite the thing, you know!"

Her lip trembled. She replied with a catch in her voice: "I am running away!"

"Oh, running away!" said Mr Standen, satisfied.

"I could not bear it another instant!" declared Kitty, gripping her hands together in her lap.

"Very understandable," said Freddy sympathetically. "Most uncomfortable house I ever stayed in! Devilish bad cook, too. Not surprised the old gentleman has stomach trouble. Quite right to run away."

"It wasn't that! Only when Uncle Matthew put me in that dreadful position, and Dolph offered for me, and then Hugh – *Hugh!* – I wished I had never been born!"

Mr Standen had no difficulty in appreciating this. He said with considerable feeling: "By Jupiter, yes! Not to be wondered at. I wouldn't have Hugh, if I were you, Kit. You'd find him a dead bore. Handsome fellow, of course, but too mackerel-backed, if you ask me. Never saw anyone make a worse bow. Offered to teach him once, but all he did was to look down his nose, and say it was very obliging of me, but he wouldn't trouble me. As a matter of fact, it wasn't. Only did it because everyone knows he's a cousin of mine."

"Oh, he is the stiffest thing in nature!" declared Kitty. "But I didn't care for that! Only he said he would marry me because if he didn't I should be left d-destitute upon the w-world, and it is all out of chivalry, and not in the least because he loves m-me, or wants to inherit Uncle M-Matthew's fortune!"

Mr Standen, perceiving that her eyes were swimming in tears, made a praiseworthy attempt to avert a scene the mere threat of which was already making him acutely uncomfortable. "Well, no need to cry over *that!*" he said. "Never heard such a tale! Bag of moonshine, that's what it is! Lord, though, to think of Hugh's being such a Captain Sharp!"

"George said it too. And Hugh means to educate me, and he says there is nothing I can do to earn my own bread, and they all of them seemed to think I should be *glad* to marry one of you, and I ran out of the room, and then what must Fish do but say that it was romantic! *Romantic!* It was too much, Freddy! I made up my mind I would just *show* them! So I stole the housekeeping money, and I came here, because I know the Ashford stage stops here, and from Ashford, you know, I can get to London."

"Oh!" said Freddy. "Very good notion, I daresay. At least—No wish to throw a damper, but what are you going to do there?"

"That's just it!" said Kitty, her face much flushed,

and large teardrops trickling down her cheeks. "I was too angry to think of that, but I thought of it when I was walking along the lane, and I don't know what I'm going to do, or where I am to stay, for I haven't a friend in the world, and every word Hugh said was *true!*"

"No, no!" said Freddy feebly.

Miss Charing, after an abortive search for her handkerchief, began to mop her face with a corner of her cloak.

Mr Standen's dismay gave place to shocked disapproval. "Here, Kitty, I say! no!" he protested. "Take mine!"

Miss Charing accepted, with a loud sob, the delicate handkerchief held out to her, and blew her small nose with determination. Mr Standen, reflecting that he had several handkerchiefs in his portmanteau, applied himself to the task of consolation. "No sense in crying," he said. "Think of some shift or other! Bound to!"

This well-meant suggestion caused Kitty's tears to flow faster. "I have been thinking and thinking, and there is nothing I can do! And, oh, I would rather die than go back to Arnside!"

At this moment, an interruption occurred. The landlord, not unnaturally consumed with curiosity, had hit upon an excuse for re-entering the coffee-room. He came in bearing a steaming bowl of rum punch, which he set down on the table, saying: "Your punch, sir. You *did* say nine o'clock, sir, didn't you? Just on nine now, sir!"

Mr Standen could not recall that he had said anything at all, and he was about to repudiate the punch when he realized that it was clearly the moment for him to fortify himself. He was thankful to perceive that Kitty had stopped crying, and had turned her face away. He ventured to offer her a glass of ratafia. She shook her head silently, and the landlord, setting two glasses down beside the bowl, said: "Perhaps Miss would fancy just a sip of punch, to keep the cold out. Snowing quite fast, it is, though not laying, sir. I hope no bad news from Mr Penicuik's, sir?"

Freddy, who had been hurriedly inventing a tale to account for Miss Charing's unconventional presence in the Blue Boar, now rose to the occasion with considerable address. "Lord, no! Nothing of that sort!" he said airily. "Stupid looby of a coachman forgot his orders, that's all! Ought to have fetched Miss Charing an hour ago. She's been visiting: obliged to walk back to Arnside. Started to snow, so she had to seek shelter."

If the landlord thought poorly of a story which featured a host so lost to propriety as to permit an unattached damsel to leave his house at dusk, on foot and unescorted, and which left out of account the modest carpet-bag, at present reposing in the passage outside the coffee-room, Kitty at least had no fault to find with it. No sooner had Mr Pluckley departed, than she turned to look admiringly at Freddy, and to thank him for his kind offices. "I had no notion you could be so clever!" she told him.

Mr Standen blushed, and disclaimed. "Made it all up beforehand," he explained. "Daresay you wouldn't think of it, but the fellow was bound to start nosing out your business. Oughtn't to be out alone, you know. Ought to have brought the Fish with you."

"But, Freddy, you must see that I couldn't run away

to London if I brought Fish! She would never consent!"

"Mustn't run away to London," said Freddy. "Been thinking about that, and it won't do. Pity, but there it is!"

"You don't feel that there might be *something* I could do to support myself?" asked Miss Charing, with a last flicker of hope. "Of course, I don't wish to starve, but do you think I should? *Truthfully* Freddy?"

Keeping his inevitable reflections to himself, Mr Standen lied manfully. "Sure of it!" he said.

"Not if I became a chambermaid!" said Kitty, suddenly inspired. "Hugh says I am too young to be a housekeeper, but I *could* be a chambermaid!"

Mr Standen brought her firmly back to earth. "No sense in that. Might as well stay at Arnside. Better, in fact."

"Yes, I suppose I might," she said despondently. "Only I would like so much to escape! I do try not to be ungrateful, but oh, Freddy, if you *knew* what it is like, keeping house for Uncle Matthew, and reading to him, and pouring out his horrid draughts, and never speaking to anyone but him and Fish! It makes me wish he never had adopted me!"

"Must be devilish," nodded Mr Standen, ladling punch into one of the glasses. "Can't think why he did adopt you. Often puzzled me."

"Yes, it used to puzzle me too, but Fish thinks that he formed a lasting passion for my mama."

"Sort of thing she would think," remarked Freddy. "If you ask me, he never formed a lasting passion for anyone but himself. I mean, look at him!"

"Yes, but I do feel she may be right," Kitty insisted. "He hardly ever speaks of her, except when he says

I am not nearly as pretty as she was, but he has her likeness. He keeps it in his desk, and he showed it to me once, when I was a little girl."

"Well, I wouldn't have believed it!" said Freddy, apparently convinced.

"No, but I fancy it was so. Because George, you know, thought I was Uncle Matthew's daughter. Hugh said that *he* never did so, but I have a strong notion he did!"

"Shouldn't think so at all," said Freddy. "George might, because he'd a gudgeon. Daresay Dolph might, but nobody else would. In fact, Dolph wouldn't either, because he don't think anything. If you was my uncle's daughter, he wouldn't behave so shabbily. Wouldn't want to leave his money to one of us, either."

"N-no. I daresay he might wish me to marry one of his great-nephews, but he wouldn't cut me off without a penny if I refused, would he?"

"He don't mean to do that?" exclaimed Freddy, shocked.

She nodded, and gave a rather watery sniff into his handkerchief. "Yes, he does, and of course I quite see that I can never hope to form an eligible connection if I'm to be a pauper. It makes me feel horridly low!"

"What you need, Kit, is a drop of something to put some heart into you," said Freddy decidedly. "If you won't take some ratafia – mind, I don't say I blame you! – you'd better have a mouthful of this. It ain't the right thing, but who's to know?"

Miss Charing accepted a half-filled glass, and sipped cautiously. The pungency of the spirit was inclined to catch the back of her throat, but the sweetness and the unmistakable tang of lemon-juice reassured her. "I like it," she said.

"Yes, but don't go telling my uncle, or the Fish, that you've been drinking punch with me," he warned her.

She assured him that she would not; and since she was now quite warm, and was finding the settle uncomfortable, joined him at the table, and sat there, sipping her punch, and brooding over her unhappy circumstances. Freddy, who was grappling with thoughts of his own, rather absentmindedly refilled both glasses. A frown began to gather on his brow. He broke the silence by demanding suddenly: "Who'll inherit the ready if you don't marry one of us, Kit?"

"Uncle Matthew says he shall leave it to the Foundling Hospital," replied Kitty. "All of it!"

"He does, does he? Seems to me Dolph ain't the only one who's queer in his attic!" said Mr Standen. He stared fixedly at the play of the candlelight on the golden liquid in his glass. "Wonder if Jack knows that?" he said, in a ruminative tone.

"You may depend upon it that he does, for I am sure Uncle Matthew would not tell George and Hugh more than he has told Jack. And I am excessively happy to think that it has not weighed with him!"

"Wonder if he's playing a deep game?" said Mr Standen, pursuing his own meditations. "No saying what might be in his head: a curst rum touch, Jack! Shouldn't have thought he'd whistle a fortune down the wind, though. Rather fancy he counted the old gentleman's rolls of soft his own. Never knew such a fellow for wasting the ready! Played wily beguiled with his own fortune." He encountered a startled look of inquiry from Miss Charing, and added succinctly: "Gamester. Tulip of the Turf. Seems to have come off all right so far, but m'father says he'll end under the hatches. Very down one, m'father!" He dwelt for a moment on the percipience of Lord Legerwood, while Miss Charing eyed him with hostility. Refreshing himself with some more punch, he said: "May be shamming it. Don't care to have his hand forced. Must know you wouldn't take Dolph or Hugh. Must know I ain't hanging out for a rich wife. Means to steer the old gentleman to Point Non-Plus." He drained his glass, and set it down. Still more profound thoughts deepened the frown on his brow. "Same time – may have come about again. Fresh as ever. Don't need the ready. Don't want to be married. Drop the handkerchief when he chooses."

"Drop—*Drop*—?" stammered Kitty. "Do you mean – he thinks I w-would pick it up w-whenever—*Oh!*"

Much confused, Mr Standen begged pardon. "Thinking to myself!" he explained.

She paid no heed to this, but said fiercely: "*Do* you mean that?"

"No, no! That is – couldn't blame him, Kit! Handsome phiz, you know – devil of a Corinthian – never at a stand! Daresay you don't know it, but the fact is any number of caps set at him! High-fliers, too. Queer creatures, females," mused Mr Standen, shaking his head. "Fellow's only got to be a rake to have 'em all dangling after him. Silly, really, because it stands to reason—Well, never mind that!"

"Good gracious, Freddy, as though I was not well aware that Jack is a shocking flirt!" said Kitty untruthfully, but with spirit. "I have not the least doubt that he flirts with all the prettiest ladies in London! Which makes it so particularly stupid and – diverting of Uncle Matthew to suppose that he wished to offer for me! Indeed, I can't imagine why anyone should think he would do so. I should be astonished to learn that he regards me as anything other than a dowdy school-girl!"

"Yes, I should be too," agreed the Job's comforter on the other side of the table.

Miss Charing swallowed another mouthful of punch. A gentle glow was spreading through her veins, dispelling the melancholy which had possessed her. It would have been too much to have said that she was restored to happiness, but she no longer despaired. A certain exhilaration infused her brain, which seemed all at once to be able quite easily to master difficulties that, a few minutes before, had appeared so insoluble. She sat bolt upright in her chair, staring straight ahead, the fingers of one hand tightening unconsciously round her tumbler. Mr Standen, glad to be left in peace to wrestle with the second of the problems confronting him, meditatively rubbed the rim of his quizzing-glass up and down the bridge of his nose.

"Freddy!" said Miss Charing suddenly, turning her expressive eyes towards him.

He gave a slight start, and let his quizzing-glass fall. "Thinking of something else!" he excused himself.

"Freddy, you are quite *sure* you don't want to marry me, aren't you?"

He looked a little alarmed, for she spoke with a degree of urgency which made him feel uneasy. "Yes," he said. He added apologetically: "Very fond of you, Kit, always was! Thing is, not a marrying man!"

"Then, Freddy, will you be so *very* obliging as to be betrothed to me?" said Miss Charing breathlessly.

❧ *Chapter IV* ❧

FOR A STUNNED moment Mr Standen stared into the dark eyes fixed so beseechingly on his face. His horrified gaze, wavering, fell upon the tumbler, still clasped in Miss Charing's hand. A certain measure of relief entered his face; he removed the half-empty glass, and set it down safely out of Miss Charing's reach. "Ought never to have given it to you!" he said, in self-accusatory tones.

"No, no, Freddy, indeed I'm not *inebriated!*"

"Lord, no, Kit! Nothing of that sort! Just a little bit on the go! Call for some coffee! Soon set you to rights!"

"I don't want it! I am quite sober, I promise you! Oh, Freddy, please listen to me!"

Mr Standen, however undistinguished a scholar, was at home to a peg in all matters of social usage. He knew well that it was useless to expostulate with persons rather up in the world. Miss Charing had stretched out an impulsive hand, and was clutching

58

the sleeve of his coat in a way that could not but render him acutely apprehensive, but he refrained from drawing her attention to this. He said soothingly: "Of course! With the greatest pleasure on earth!"

To his relief, she released him. He smoothed his sleeve carefully, and was inclined to think that no irreparable damage had been done to it.

"I cannot and I will not return to Arnside!" announced Kitty. "At least, I suppose I must for a little while, but I won't remain there, meekly waiting for – for some obliging person to marry me! By hook or by crook I mean to go to London! Ever since I was seventeen I have yearned to go. Uncle Matthew will not let me. He says it would be a great waste of money, and that it is not to be thought of. It is useless to argue with him upon that head: in fact, it is much worse than useless, because the last time I begged him to let me go with Fish, for one week, only to see the sights, he went to bed, and stayed there for a fortnight, and would do nothing but throw things at Spiddle and poor Fish, and groan in the most affecting way whenever I entered his room! He said he had nourished a serpent in his bosom, and that I did not care how soon he was dead and buried, besides being giddy, and selfish, and too young to go to London. Of course, the thing was that he could not let me go without Fish, and that would have meant that there would have been no one left at Arnside to order everything as he likes, for he won't employ a housekeeper, you know."

"Very hard case," said Freddy politely. "But it ain't got anything to do with—"

"It has, Freddy, it has!" insisted Kitty. "Only consider! If you were to offer for me, and I should accept your offer, Lord and Lady Legerwood would wish to see me, would they not?"

"Have seen you," Freddy said, entering a caveat.

"Well, yes, but not at all lately. They – they would wish to present me to their acquaintance! Freddy, don't you think your mama would invite me to stay with her, in Mount Street? Just for one little month?"

Mr Standen, perceiving a straw, clutched at it. "Tell you what, Kit! Ask my mother to invite you. Fond of me: very likely to do it to oblige me. No need to be betrothed!"

For a moment her eyes brightened; then they clouded again, and she sighed, and shook her head. "It wouldn't serve. Ever since the buttered lobsters Uncle Matthew is convinced that he has only a few months to live! He had a dreadful colic, you know, and nothing will persuade him that it was only the lobsters, which he *would* eat for supper! He says his heart is very weak, and that Dr Fenwick is a clodpole. That's why there is all this bustle about his Will. He is determined to provide for me before he dies, so, you see, he could never be prevailed upon to let me go to London if I were still unbetrothed. He would be bound to suspect I should elope with a half-pay officer."

"I don't see that," objected Freddy, painfully following the gist of this tumultuous speech.

"Well, I don't either," admitted Kitty, "but it is what he always says, whenever I have asked him if I might not go to London. He has the greatest dislike of military men, and when the militia were quartered in the neighborhood he would scarcely allow me even to walk to the village. But if I were betrothed to you, Freddy, he could not refuse to let me go on that score. He could not refuse on *any* score, because if Lady

Legerwood would be so obliging as to invite me to Mount Street it would not cost him a penny above my coach fare. And there can be not the least necessity for Fish to go too, so that he may be sure that things will go on at Arnside just as they should."

"Yes, but—"

"And, Freddy, only think! He said that if I became engaged to one of you he would give me a hundred pounds for my bride clothes! A – hundred – pounds, Freddy!"

"You know, Kit," said Mr Standen, momentarily diverted, "dashed if he ain't the kind of fellow who behaves scaly to waiters! A Plum wouldn't buy the half of your bride clothes! Forget how much blunt m'father dropped when Meg was married, but—"

"More than a hundred pounds?" said Kitty, awed. "It seems a very great sum to me. But it was quite different in your sister's case! I mean, she is the eldest of you, and I expect your father wished her to have the very best sort of bride clothes. Truly, I think I could contrive very well with a hundred pounds! I don't want *grand* dresses, or jewels, or costly furs. Just – just one or two pretty ones, so that I need not be a dowd! Freddy, I know I am not beautiful, but don't you think I might be *passable*, if I could be more in the mode?"

This appeal awoke an instant response in one whose exquisite taste was the envy of the *ton*. "I know what you mean," said Freddy sympathetically. "Need a little town-bronze! Give you a new touch!"

"Yes, that is it!" she said eagerly. "I knew you would understand!"

"Well, I do, and, what's more, I'd be very happy to do anything in my power to oblige you. Dashed awkward thing to have to say, but not marriage, dear girl! We shouldn't suit! Assure we should not! Besides, I don't want to be married."

She broke into a gurgle of laughter. "How can you be so absurd? Of course we should not suit! I did not mean we were to be *really* betrothed! Only hoaxing!"

"Oh!" said Freddy, relieved. He considered the matter for a moment, and perceived a flaw. "No, that won't do. Bound to find ourselves in the basket. Can't puff off an engagement, and then not get married."

"Yes, we can! I know people often cry off!"

"Good God, Kitty, you can't ask me to do a thing like that!" exclaimed Freddy indignantly.

"But why should you not? I assure you I shan't take a pet, or care for it!"

"Well, I won't do it, that's all!" said Freddy, with unexpected firmness. "Shocking bad *ton!* Now, don't start disputing about it, Kit, because it ain't a bit of use! Good God, a pretty figure I should cut!"

He was evidently a good deal moved. Kitty said placably: "Oh, very well! *I'll* cry off. There can be no objection to that!"

"Yes, but it would make me look like a flat!" protested Freddy.

"No, no! Everyone would say you were very well rid of me! Besides, I daresay it would not make such a stir after all."

"Well, it would. Dash it, notice in the *Gazette* — friends felicitating one — dress party — wedding gifts!"

"I hadn't thought of that," admitted Kitty. "I don't think we should send a notice to the *Gazette.*"

"I'm dashed sure we shouldn't!" said Freddy, with feeling.

"You may easily hit upon an excuse for our keeping

the engagement private. After all, it will only be for one month!"

He blinked. "But there's no sense in being engaged for a month!"

"Freddy," she said earnestly, "*anything* may happen in a month!"

"Yes, I know it may. The thing is I ain't one of these care-for-nothings, and I don't want anything to happen. No, and another thing! I don't want to be roasted all over town, which I should be. Everyone knows I ain't in the petticoat-line!"

"No one will know we are engaged," she coaxed him. "I mean, no one except the family, because we shan't announce it in a formal way."

"Now, listen, Kit!" said Freddy reasonably. "If no one's to know of it, there ain't a bit of sense in it!"

A faint flush stole into her cheeks. "Yes, there is, because we are obliged to hoax Uncle Matthew. And – and I think we won't tell anyone – anyone at all! – that it is all a hum, because – because – perhaps your father would not like it, and – and Uncle Matthew might get to hear the truth!"

"I don't see that," said the captious Mr Standen. "Never stirs outside the house! Who's to tell him?"

"Jack would, if he knew the truth!" flashed Kitty.

"Well, he wouldn't if we—" He broke off, as a brilliant solution presented itself to him. "That's it!" he said. "Wonder I didn't think of it before. Wonder you didn't. Ask Jack to do it for you! Daresay he would: done a lot of ramshackle things in his time. Likes being the talk of the town, too. Regular cool hand!"

"Ask *Jack?*" she repeated, in a very alarming voice. "I wouldn't ask Jack – I wouldn't ask Jack even to frank a letter for me!"

"Wouldn't be any use if you did," said Freddy, always practical. "He ain't a Member of Parliament!"

"I hate Jack!" declared Kitty, her bosom heaving.

Freddy was surprised. "Thought you liked him. Had a notion—"

"Well, I do not! I think he is a great deal worse even than George! In fact, I forbid you, Freddy, to admit him into your confidence about our engagement!"

Mr Standen had a vague feeling that he was treading upon dangerous ground. Why Miss Charing should have become so suddenly agitated he had no idea; but he suspected uneasily that she had some scheme in mind which she had not yet disclosed to him. Her proposal seemed to him absurd, not to say preposterous; he pointed out to her that there was no fear that he might confide in Mr Westruther. "Nothing to confide," he said. "There ain't an engagement."

Miss Charing argued in vain. Acutely uncomfortable, more than a little alarmed, he clung obdurately to his refusal.

"It is such a *little* thing to do for me!" Kitty said.

"No, it ain't. You can't call making such a cake of myself a little thing!"

"You will not: there is not the least occasion for anyone to suppose that you have made a cake of yourself!"

"Well, it's what they would think. What's more, they'll say I did it to get my fingers on the old gentleman's rolls of soft."

"No, because when nothing comes of the engagement they will perceive that they were mistaken!"

"Won't perceive anything of the sort. Only thing they will perceive is that you've tipped me the double! Dash it, Kit—"

"Freddy, *you* would not condemn me to remain at Arnside, used like a – a – a drudge!"

"No, of course I wouldn't, but—"

"Or to marry Hugh!"

"No, but—"

"But, Freddy, you cannot expect me to accept Dolph's offer!"

"No, but—"

"And Claud has not offered at all, besides being an odious person!"

"No, is he?" said Freddy, interested. "Haven't seen him, myself, since he first joined, but I daresay you're right. To tell you the truth, I never liked any of the Rattrays above half. Now, take George, for instance! Know what he—"

"Well, I can't take George, because he is married already," said Kitty, ruthlessly cutting short this discursion. "Besides being quite as odious as Claud! Freddy, you know I would not hold you to it!"

"Yes, that's all very well, but—"

"If this one opportunity – the only one I can ever be offered! – is denied me," declared Kitty dramatically, "all hope is at an end!"

"Yes, but – I mean—No, dash it, Kitty—!"

"And it will be *you,* whom I have always believed to be the kindest of my cousins – at least, you are not indeed my cousin, for I am quite alone in the world, but I have ever regarded you as my cousin – it will be *you* who have inexorably slammed to the gates upon my aspirations!"

"Done *what?*" demanded Freddy.

"Condemned me to a life of misery and – and of indigent old age!"

"No, that's coming it too strong!" protested Freddy. "I never—"

"I should not have asked you to help me," said Kitty, stricken by remorse. "Only it seemed to me that here, perhaps, was a chance offered me of escaping from my wretched existence! I see that it will not do! I beg your pardon, Freddy: pray do not think of it again!"

With these noble words, Miss Charing rose from the table, and retired to stand before the fire with her back to the room. A stifled sob, a sniff, the flutter of Mr Standen's maltreated handkerchief, bore witness to the courageous attempt she was making to suppress her tears. Mr Standen regarded her bowed shoulders with dismay. "Kit! No, Kit, for God's sake—!" he said.

"Do not give it another thought!" begged Miss Charing, brave but despairing. "I know I am alone in the world – I have always known it! It was stupid of me to suppose that there was *one* person to whom I might turn! There is no one!"

Horrified, Mr Standen uttered: "No, no, I assure you—! Anything in my power—! But you must see, my dear girl – dash it, it's impossible!"

Ten minutes later Miss Charing, restored to smiles, was thanking him warmly for his exceeding kindness. "And perhaps we ought to return to Arnside," she suggested. "I must say, Freddy, I shall like very much to see Hugh's face when he learns that we are betrothed!"

Mr Standen agreed that the prospect of making a pigeon of his cousin went some way towards reconciling him to the pitfalls ahead of him; but Kitty's words recalled to his mind the question which had been for some time troubling him. "How am I to take you back to Arnside without creating the devil of a dust?" he demanded. "If no one's to know it's all a fudge, it won't do to let it be known you've been here with me this evening. George and Hugh would be bound to guess it was a take-in."

"Oh, there will not be the least difficulty!" she declared optimistically. "I will draw my hood well over my face, and if you will stop the chaise at the gates, and set me down, I can slip through the shrubbery to the side door, and up the backstairs to my own bed-chamber. I told Fish I should lock my door, because I would not see anyone, I was so cross; and you may depend upon it that no one has the smallest notion I am not at this moment laid down upon my bed. And if you pay off the postboy, he will not be able to gossip in the stables. There is no cause for any apprehension!"

"Yes, but I don't want to pay off the postboy!" objected Freddy. "Hired the chaise for the whole journey, you see."

"Oh, well, the postboy must take it to the Green Dragon for the night!" said Kitty, dealing summarily with this problem. "You may easily contrive that! And when you enter the house, you must say you have come to see me, because I do think, Freddy, we shall go on more prosperously if you do not meet Uncle Matthew until we can confront him together."

With this, Mr Standen found himself to be in entire agreement; and as everything seemed now to be provided for, and the hands of the clock on the mantel-shelf stood at twenty minutes past nine o'clock, he thought they would be well-advised to set forward upon the short journey to Arnside immediately. The last of the punch was disposed of, the chaise bespoken, and Miss Charing once more wrapped in her thick cloak. The travelers climbed into the chaise, the steps were let up, and the door shut; and during the minutes which it took two sturdy horses to cover little more than a mile, Miss Charing coached her reluctant swain in the part he had to play. She was set down at the gates of Arnside, and disappeared, a good deal to the postilion's surprise, into the night. Miss Charing had her own ways of entering the jealously guarded grounds of Mr Penicuik's house; Mr Standen was obliged to wait until the lodge-keeper came out to open gates which were invariably locked against the outer world at dusk. Since visitors to Arnside were rare, and evening visitors unheard of, it was some time before this individual could be roused. By the time Mr Standen alighted at the front door of the house he judged that Miss Charing should have reached the side door, and might even be already in her bedchamber.

Stobhill, the butler, was quite as much surprised as the lodge-keeper to see Mr Standen, but (also like the lodge-keeper) seemed to take an indulgent view of his eccentric conduct. Indeed, as he presently observed to his colleague, Mr Spiddle, there was never any saying what such a harebrained young gentleman might take it into his head to do next. He was perfectly well aware of the errand which had brought Mr Penicuik's great-nephews to Arnside; but when Mr Standen asked in the most nonchalant way if Miss Charing would receive him, his sense of propriety was offended, and he said with some severity: "It's the Master you should be seeing, sir."

"What, is he still up and about?" asked Freddy anxiously.

"As to that, sir, I'm sure I could not say. We helped him up to his room half an hour ago, but I daresay he's not yet abed. If you care to step into the Saloon, where you will find my Lord Dolphinton, my Lord Bidden-den, and the Reverend, I will step up to inquire if the Master will see you."

"No, you won't," said Freddy. "Bacon-brained thing to do at this hour of the evening! Besides, I want to see Miss Charing."

"Miss went up to her room almost immediately after dinner, Mr Freddy!" said Stobhill, still more disap-proving.

"Yes, I know she did, but—" Freddy paused, en-countering an astonished stare. He was momentarily shaken off his balance, but he made a quick recover. "What I mean is, if my cousins are here, of course she did! Anyone would! You go and tell her I'm here, and I beg the honor of a few words with her."

He then moved towards the Saloon, and Stobhill, saying unencouragingly: "I will have your message conveyed to Miss, sir," opened the door for him.

On one side of the fire, the Rattray brothers were playing cribbage; on the other, Lord Dolphinton was doing nothing. Hugh, who had found the cribbage-board, and had inaugurated the game with the self-sacrificing intention of alleviating his brother's bore-dom, wore an expression of determined cheerfulness; Lord Biddenden, to whom cribbage was only less in-supportable than an evening passed in talking to Hugh, was frankly impatient, made his discards almost at random, and yawned over the totting up of points. His chair faced the door, and it was thus he who first perceived Freddy. "Oh, the devil!" he exclaimed.

Hugh, turned to look over his shoulder, and for an

instant it seemed as though he doubted the evidence of his eyes. A slight flush mounted to his cheeks; he compressed his austere lips, as though to check some hasty utterance, and with deliberation pushed back his chair, and rose. By this time, Lord Dolphinton had assimilated the fact that another of his cousins had come to Arnside. He looked rather pleased, and said helpfully: "Here's Freddy! Hallo, Freddy! You here?"

"Hallo, old fellow!" responded Mr Standen good-naturedly. He drew near the fire, nodding affably to his other cousins, and levelling his quizzing-glass at the card-table. "You above par, George?" he inquired, mildly surprised. "Never seen you play cribbage before in my life! Well, I mean to say – *Cribbage!*"

"No, I am not!" replied Biddenden crossly. "It's Hugh!"

"You don't say so?" said Freddy, bringing his glass to bear on Hugh's handsome countenance. "Hugh full of frisk? Well, I wouldn't have thought it of you, Hugh!"

"Do not pretend to be more of a fool than God made you, Freddy!" said Hugh coldly. "You know very well that George did not wish to signify that I was inebriated – if, as I apprehend, that is the meaning of the cant you choose to employ."

"Something thrown you into gloom?" asked Freddy solicitously. "A trifle out of sorts? Daresay you ate something at dinner that's making you feel queasy. Devilish bad cook, my uncle's: never eat a meal here if I can avoid it."

"Thank you, I was never better in my life," said Hugh. "May we know what has brought you to Arnside?"

Lord Biddenden stirred impatiently. "Oh, play off

no airs for our benefit!" he begged. "It is as plain as a pikestaff why he is here!"

"I hesitate to contradict you, George, but I am far more inclined to suppose that Freddy does not know for what purpose he was invited here."

Mr Standen, who had turned to observe himself in the spotted mirror over the fireplace, discovered that his neck-cloth needed an infinitesimal adjustment. Until this delicate operation had been performed, it was plainly useless to address questions to him. Hugh tapped his foot against the floor, his lip curling disdainfully; and Biddenden, who had himself a great inclination towards dandyism, watched with reluctant appreciation the deft straightening of a cravat which had roused his admiration at the outset. He held the poorest opinion of his cousin Freddy's mental ability, but he always took covert note of any new fashion Freddy adopted, and very often copied it; and he would not for an instant have denied that Freddy's rulings on such matters were worthy of respect. "Schultz make that coat?" he asked.

"Weston, George: never let another snyder cut my coats! Mind, if I wanted sporting toggery—"

"You have not yet answered my question!" interrupted Hugh. "What has brought you here?"

"Hired chaise," said Freddy. "Thought of driving myself down, but too far for the tits. Bad weather, too."

"I shall not gratify you by explaining my meaning," said Hugh contemptuously. "You know quite well what it is."

"I came in my own carriage," offered Lord Dolphinton. We changed horses twice, and I had a hot brick to keep my feet warm, and a shawl round my shoulders. I shall have another hot brick put in the carriage when I go back. I shall tell Stobhill to attend to it. My mother said that was what I should do, and I shall do it. Stobhill will know how to set about it."

"I imagine the task need not strain his powers unduly!" said Biddenden snappishly.

"Some people," said Dolphinton, "don't heat the bricks right through." He thought for a moment, and added: "Some people heat 'em too much."

"Fact of the matter is, old fellow," said Freddy, entering into the spirit of this, "it's a dashed difficult thing to do. You leave it to Stobhill!"

"Well, that's what I shall do," said Dolphinton, much gratified. "I'm glad you've come, Freddy. Sensible fellow. You going to offer for Kitty?"

"That's it," replied Freddy.

"You know what?" said Dolphinton. "I hope she takes you. Wouldn't take Hugh. Wouldn't take me. George didn't offer. Couldn't, because he's married. Can't think why he came. Wasn't invited, you know."

Hugh said, with a certain deepening of his mellifluous voice: "We are to believe that, Freddy? You have indeed come for that purpose? I own, I had not thought it of you!"

"Well, if it comes to that," said Freddy. "I hadn't thought it of you! Never took you for a downy one. Daresay I was misled by those bands of yours: very likely thing to happen!"

"*My* motive in offering the protection of my name to our unfortunate young cousin is not, I assure you, a mercenary one."

"Not our cousin," objected Lord Dolphinton. "George said she wasn't. Said my uncle told us so. I didn't follow it all myself, but that's what George said."

No one paid any heed to this remark. Biddenden said with some asperity: "This is a new come-out for you, Freddy! Pray, since when have you been hanging out for a rich wife?"

"Took a sudden notion to get married," explained Freddy, extemporizing cunningly. "Must have an heir!"

"As your father is in the prime of life," said Biddenden, with heavy sarcasm, "and has two other sons beside yourself—"

"Too young to be married," Freddy pointed out. "Well, look at it! Charlie's up at Oxford, and Edmund ain't even at Eton yet!"

"I can tell you now that you have wasted your time! If the girl means to marry any other than Jack, you may call me a zany!"

"Now, that's where you're wrong!" said Freddy, speaking with authority. "It ain't Jack: doesn't seem to like him above half."

Biddenden gave a snort. "She's piqued, I don't doubt. That she doesn't hanker after him you will find it hard to make me believe! As for her entertaining for an instant the thought of marrying *you*—! Upon my soul, I have not been so much diverted since I came to this damned, cold house!"

"Lay you a monkey she takes me!" offered Freddy.

"You must be out of your senses! If you imagine she will accept you for the sake of a title, you much mistake the matter! She has refused Dolphinton already, and he, as he will be only too ready to inform you, is an Earl!"

He had no sooner uttered these words than he re-

gretted them. Lord Dolphinton, who had shown signs
of relapsing into the state of suspended animation natural to him, responded as to a clarion-call. "Only Earl
in the family," he said. "Thought she'd like it. Good
thing to be a Countess. Don't see it myself, but that's
what my mother says. Must know, because she's a
Countess. Seems to like it pretty well. No good Freddy's offering. Only be a Viscount. That's better than
a Baron, but George don't count in any case. Can't
think why he came."

"If you say once more that I was not invited," ex-
ploded the much-tired Biddenden, "I will not be an-
swerable for the consequences!"

"Well, what did you want to start him off for?" said
Freddy reasonably. "You might have known he'd
catch his own name! That's all right and tight, Dolph:
don't pay any heed to George! He's a gudgeon."

"If we are to talk of gudgeons," countered Biddenden, "there is a bigger one in this room even than Dolphinton!"

"Well, why don't you sport a little blunt on the
chance?" suggested Freddy. "I'll lay you handsome
odds!"

"The style of this conversation is quite improper,"
interposed the Rector. "Unless you are in the expectation of being received by my great-uncle tonight,
Freddy, I suggest that we should all of us retire to bed.
I will add that while I cannot but deprecate the free-
dom George uses in discussin such a matter I believe
that whatever may be our cousin's sentiments upon
the occasion, my uncle is much chagrined at Jack's absence from Arnside, and is very likely to wait upon the
chance of his making a belated appearance tomorrow."

"No use doing that," replied Freddy. "He don't mean to come."

"You are no doubt in his confidence!"

"No, I ain't in his confidence, but I've seen the nice bit of game he's been throwing out lures to this month and more," said Freddy frankly.

Hugh looked disgusted, and Biddenden curious. Before either of them could speak, however, the door opened, and to the surprise of everyone except Freddy, Miss Charing tripped into the room.

She was still attired in the rather drab gown she had worn earlier in the evening, but she had dignified the occasion by tying up her locks with a red ribbon. All trace of chagrin had departed from her face, and it was with a beaming smile that she greeted Mr Standen. "Freddy, how glad I am to see you!" she exclaimed, holding out her hand to him. "I had quite given you up!"

Mr Standen bowed in his inimitable style over her hand, saying: "Beg a thousand pardons! Been out of town! Came as soon as I had read my uncle's letter."

Miss Charing appeared to be much affected. "You came at once! So late, and – and with the snow falling! Oh, Freddy!"

"That's it," agreed Freddy. "No sense in letting these fellows steal a march on me. Came to beg you to do me the honor of accepting my hand."

The hand was once more extended to him; Miss Charing said, with a sigh, and modestly downcast eyes: "Oh, Freddy I do not know how to answer you!"

Mr Standen, unprepared for this improvisation, was put out. "Dash it, Kit!" he began.

"For I had come to believe that I had mistaken your sentiments!" said Kitty hastily. "Now I see that it is not so! You, I am persuaded, would not wish to marry me for the sake of Uncle Matthew's fortune!"

"Thing is," said Freddy, recognizing his cue, "never thought my uncle would permit it. Thought it was useless to approach him. As soon as I read his letter – bespoke a chaise and came at once! Trust you'll allow me to speak to him in the morning."

"Oh, yes, Freddy! It will make me very happy!" said Kitty soulfully.

Under the bemused stare from three pairs of eyes, Mr Standen, with rare grace, kissed Miss Charing's hand, and said that he was very much obliged to her.

❧ *Chapter V* ❧

THE APPROVAL AND THE FELICITATIONS WHICH a young lady might have expected to have greeted the news of her betrothal to a man of rank and fortune were denied to Miss Charing. Only Lord Dolphinton was pleased; and as it soon became apparent that his pleasure had its root in the realization that not the most exacting parent could expect him to marry a lady already betrothed to another man, his congratulations were not felt to be particularly gratifying.

Lord Biddenden's chagrin found expression in ejaculatory half sentences, spoken largely under his breath; and while he was very angry with Freddy, who had snatched at an heiress without the justification of being himself in straitened circumstances, he was also quite as angry with Hugh, for having done so little to make his suit agreeable to Kitty.

Whatever of rage or mortification Huge felt, he concealed, merely saying to Kitty in a grave tone: "I had not thought this of you. I beg you will consider well

before you take a step I am persuaded you must regret. I shall say no more. George, I am going to bed.
I daresay you too, Foster, are ready to retire."

But Lord Dolphinton, scenting an ally in his cousin
Freddy, was recalcitrant. He said that he need not go
to bed at anyone's bidding; and went so far as to add,
in a spirit of great daring, that he was going to drink
the happy couple's healths. As Hugh had dissuaded
him, rather earlier in the evening, from pouring himself out a second glass of brandy and water, this announcement was tantamount to a declaration of
independence, and frightened Lord Dolphinton quite
as much as it surprised all those who knew how much
in awe of his clerical cousin he stood. However, the
Rector refused the challenge, merely favoring the
backslider with a long, reproving look before bidding
the company goodnight.

This triumph so much elated Dolphinton that he became loquacious, living over again his victory with
such pertinacity that Lord Biddenden was soon driven
from the room.

"Didn't like it, because I gave Hugh a set-down,"
said Dolphinton, with satisfaction. "Silly fellow!
Shouldn't have come here."

Since his lordship showed every sign of settling
down to make a night of it, Freddy, who wished for
further guidance from his betrothed, was obliged to
exert all his powers of persuasion to induce him to go
to bed. But no sooner had he accomplished his design
than Miss Fishguard came into the Saloon, agog with
sentiment, curiosity, and a determination to chaperon
her charge.

Miss Fishguard's method of entering any room in
which she had reason to believe that a *tête-à-tête* was

taking place, was first to peep round the door with an arch smile, saying: "Do I intrude?" and then, without awaiting an answer, to trip across the floor on tiptoe, as though she feared to disturb a sick person. The habit arose partly from timidity, and partly from a resolve never to presume upon her position; and it never failed to irritate her employers. However, as Kitty was well aware, from Miss Fishguard's fund of reminiscence, of the slights and snubs which were a governess's portion, she creditably hid her annoyance, summoned up a welcoming smile, and announced her engagement.

Since the news had spread rapidly through the household that the Honorable Freddy had arrived at a dissipated hour of the night, demanding Miss Charing, and that Miss had risen from her bed, dressed herself, and gone down to the Saloon immediately, the announcement was not quite unexpected. Miss Fishguard, however, greeted it with upflung hands, and ecstatic exclamations. Mr Standen's tardy arrival and successful suit seemed to her so romantic that, inspiration failing, she was obliged to quote the words of one of her favorite poets. Twittering with excitement, as she dropped a curtsy to Freddy, she uttered: "Oh, Mr Frederick! It reminds one so! 'He staid not for brake, and he stopp'd not for stone, He swam the Eske river where ford there was none!' "

"Eh?" said Freddy, startled.

"Oh, yes, Mr Frederick, surely you remember? 'For a laggard in love and a dastard in war, Was to wed the fair Ellen of brave Lochinvar!' "

"Was he, though?" said Freddy, faint but pursuing.

Miss Charing, more familiar with the poem than her betrothed, was just about to inquire, in a practical frame of mind, whether her preceptress had the Reverend Hugh Rattray in mind, or Lord Dolphinton, when Miss Fishguard, in a gush of sensibility, said: " 'Love swells like the Solway, but ebbs like its tide!' "

Mr Standen, receiving only a blank look in answer to the anguished glance of inquiry he cast at Miss Charing, said politely: "Just so, ma'am!"

"Oh!" cried Miss Fishguard, clasping her hands over her emaciated bosom, and blushing with emotion, "I declare, it is the same, only in real life! Only think, Mr Frederick! – 'One touch to her hand, and one word in her ear, When they reached the hall door, and the charger was near; So light to the croupe the fair lady he swung. So light to the saddle before her he sprung!' And then, you know, he rode off with the fair Ellen, and 'The lost bride of Netherby ne'er did they see! So daring in love, and so dauntless in war. Have ye e'er heard of gallant like young Lochinvar?' "

"Sounds to me like a dashed loose-screw," said Freddy disapprovingly.

Miss Fishguard looked rather daunted; Kitty interpolated in soothing accents: "It comes in *Marmion*, Freddy!" and Mr Standen said, relieved: "Oh, *Marmion!*" rather spoiling his effect by adding a moment later: "Who was he?"

"My dearest Kitty, permit one who has ever had your welfare at heart to wish you happy!" said Miss Fishguard, fondly embracing her pupil. She was obliged to search in the reticule which dangled from her wrist for her handkerchief, for a gush of sensibility brought the tears to her eyes. Wiping them, and dabbing at the tip of her thin nose, she added in thickened accents: "I do not scruple *now* to disclose to you the anxiety which has troubled my bosom since I first learned of your honored guardian's intentions! Delicacy forbade me to unclose my lips, but one question could not but obtrude upon my brain. In the words of that poet whom we both revere, my love, I have trembled before the thought: 'What shall be the maiden's fate? Who shall be the maiden's mate?' If I express myself with unbecoming warmth, in telling you how thankful I am to learn that your choice has fallen upon dear Mr Frederick – 'Steady of heart, and stout of hand,' I am persuaded! – rather than upon another, I must not be understood to mean the least derogation of one whose Calling, indeed, must be thought to place him far above my criticism! Mr Frederick, most ardently do I felicitate you! You have offered for the hand of one reared 'in still retreats, and flowery solitudes', and never, I dare to assert, will you have cause to regret your choice! You will live to echo the words of the poet: 'Domestic happiness, thou only bliss—!' Dear Kitty, I am quite overcome!"

Miss Charing patted her shoulder, in a sustaining manner. "Yes, yes, dear Fish! But pray dry your tears! There is not the least occasion for you to weep, I do assure you!"

Miss Fishguard, having mopped her withered cheeks, given a final sniff into the handkerchief, recovered sufficiently to bestow a watery smile and a fervent handclasp upon her young charge, and to utter: " 'The tear that is wiped with a little address, May be followed perhaps by a smile!' "

At this point, Mr Standen, who had been listening in growing dismay to the conversational style affected by his affianced's preceptress, excused himself. It was not his custom to seek his couch at such an early hour of the evening, but he had rapidly arrived at the con-

clusion that any further colloquy with Miss Charing
was likely to be punctuated by quotations from a class
of persons known to him as Writing Coves, and he decided that bed before eleven o'clock was a preferable
fate. He kissed Kitty's hand, and then, impelled by the
expectant look in Miss Fishguard's eye, her cheek.
Miss Charing received this embrace with equanimity,
merely seizing the opportunity afforded to whisper:
"After breakfast! On no account go to Uncle Matthew
before we have consulted together!"

There might have been those who doubted Mr Standen's ability to shake the world, but none could have
been found with the hardihood to declare that he
lacked social address. His bow indicated to Kitty that
he had perfectly understood her, to Miss Fishguard
the depth of his reverence. A second bow, directed to
this lady, was so nicely graded as to draw from her,
as soon as he had left the Saloon, an encomium upon
his gentlemanly deportment. "Such courtesy, my
love!" she sighed. "Such exquisite regard for the feelings of one who, perhaps believing herself '*not* scorned
in heaven', is 'little noticed here!'"

Miss Charing agreed to this; and, observing that the
fire was burning low, announced her intention of seeking her own couch. Miss Fishguard accompanied her
upstairs to her bedchamber, so obviously determined
to talk the whole matter over that Kitty thoughtfully
reminded her to provide herself with a shawl, Mr
Penicuik's parsimony leading him to view with violent
disapprobation the lighting of fires in any other bedchamber than his own.

Accordingly, Miss Fishguard first sought her own
apartment; while Kitty, encountering the arctic tem-
perature of her chamber, made haste to shed her rai-

ment and tumble into the old-fashioned four-poster bed. This had just been warmed for her by a maid bearing a large warming-pan when Miss Fishguard rejoined her, now swathed in a large shawl of nondescript color and rather tufty appearance. She was in time to see Kitty get between sheets, her nightgown untied, and her cap in her hand, and clucked a faint protest. Kitty, fitting the cap over her head, and tying its strings under her chin, paid no heed; and, indeed, the remonstrance lacked conviction. She pulled the quilt round her shoulders, and said, sitting up against her banked pillows: "Do you think you should stay, Fish? I am sure you will be perished with the cold! If ever I should be mistress of a house of my own, I shall have huge fires burning in *every* room!"

Miss Fishguard was not unnaturally startled by this remark. *"If?"* she echoed. "But, my love—!"

"Oh, yes, of course, to be sure!" said Kitty, recollecting herself. "The – the thing is, it seems strange to me just at first!"

Miss Fishguard could readily understand this. She pressed Kitty's hand in a speaking manner: "A change in your circumstance, dear, but a *natural* one."

Kitty gave an involuntary gurgle. "Well, I must own it doesn't seem a natural thing to me to be engaged to marry Freddy!" she said frankly.

Miss Fishguard forbore to reprove her for this outburst of candor. She said: "A very eligible connection! He has a thousand amiable qualities – most distinguished manners, I am sure! Most truly the gentleman! But, oh, my love, when Stobhill dropped a hint in my ear – so very improper, but one scarecely liked to give him a set-down, for I daresay he meant it for the best! – I declare I felt ready to drop! Pardon me, my dear Kitty, if I am presumptuous enough to say that I had not the remotest guess – never expected – in short, was amazed almost into a spasm! I do not pretend to any extraordinary quickness in these matters: it has never appeared to me that dear Mr Frederick had grown particular in his attentions!"

"No," agreed Kitty, reflecting that since of all Mr Penicuik's relations Mr Standen had been of late years the most infrequent visitor to Arnside, no one could wonder at Miss Fishguard's surprise.

"In another, I might almost have supposed this event to have been occasioned by pecuniary considerations," confessed Miss Fishguard. "I hasten, however, to assure you, my love, that in connection with Mr Frederick such a suspicion has only to occur to one to be banished! I am persuaded that he has too much delicacy of mind and sensibility of heart ever to be swayed by mercenary impulses! Besides," she added, "I cannot but be aware that he was born to the comfort of a handsome fortune."

"I must say, I do hope that others besides you will think that," remarked Kitty thoughtfully. "I quite see that it would be very disagreeable for poor Freddy to be supposed to have offered for me only to acquire Uncle Matthew's money."

"So ignoble a thought," declared Miss Fishguard, "will not for an instant be permitted to obtrude!"

"I own, I cannot imagine how it should," agreed Kitty, hugging her knees, and looking, with one curl escaping from beneath her cap, and a bow tied at a skittish angle under her chin, absurdly youthful. "But he seemed to think it would. Oh, well! Very likely he quite mistakes the matter, for he is the most foolish creature!" She realized that she had shocked her governess, and added hastily: "I mean – I mean – he takes odd notions into his head!"

"Kitty!" said Miss Fishguard, her voice sinking a tone, and her cheeks suffused with color, "can it be that you have mistaken your heart?"

Kitty made haste to assure her that she had not. Miss Fishguard, her fingers writing together, and her eyes cast upwards, said tremulously: "Let one whose vernal hopes were blighted by the ambition of a parent assure you that 'love will still be lord of all!' Dear Kitty, do not, I implore you, be seduced by thoughts of worldly advancement!"

"No, no, I promise you I will not!" Kitty said. "But – but what *were* your vernal hopes, dear Fish?"

"Alas!" sighed Miss Fishguard. "His situation was inferior, and although I must always hold to the belief that his character was respectable, I could not but acquiesce in my dear father's decision that it might not be." She met Miss Charing's inquiring gaze, and sank her head, saying in a stricken under-voice: "He was the apothecary's assistant. He was a very handsome young man, my dear, and looked quite the gentleman. I can see him now, putting up the pills which poor papa was forced to take to alleviate the pangs of indigestion. But of course it would not do!"

"Of course not," said Kitty, overawed by the mental vision of Miss Fishguard in the throes of love for an apothecary's assistant.

"For my revered papa, as I need scarcely remind you," said Miss Fishguard, "was, like Mr Rattray, in Holy Orders."

This name aroused Kitty from her reverie, and she said with a good deal of feeling: "Do not speak to me of Hugh, I beg of you! Only fancy, Fish! He would have me believe he offered for me out of *pity!*''

Miss Fishguard, who was at once afraid of the Rector and resentful of his efforts to prevail upon Mr Penicuik to replace her with a governess able to instruct Kitty in the Italian tongue, clicked her tongue, and shook her head, saying that she feared Mr Rattray was guilty of dissimulation. "I do not know how it is, my love," she said impressively, "but although he is excessively handsome I can never bring myself to trust him! His manners are reserved, and although I am sure I hope he *may* be a man of rectitude, one cannot but reflect that instances *have* been known when outward piety has served but as a cloak for – well, consider Schedoni, dearest Kitty!''

But the thought of a comparison's being drawn between Hugh Rattray and the villainous monk in Mrs Radclyffe's popular romance set Kitty off into such a fit of giggling that Miss Fishguard became offended, and was with difficulty mollified. Indeed, only her desire to discover what circumstance it had been that had impelled Mr Standen so suddenly to declare himself kept her seated still beside Kitty's bed. Feeling that she could not improve upon the words she had spoken in the Saloon, for the benefit of her other suitors, Kitty repeated them. Miss Fishguard was at once affected by the thought of the pangs endured by Freddy while concealing his hopeless passion for Miss Charing. She was put so much in mind of all her favorite heroes that for several minutes she forgot what she could not but consider to be the superior claims of Mr Westruther. But these presently recurred to her memory, and she ventured to inquire whether tidings had yet been received of this gentleman.

"Dear me, no!" replied Kitty airily. "I assure you, I do not expect to see him at Arnside on this occasion!"

Miss Fishguard sighed. "How often one may be deceived in one's fellow creatures!" she observed. "When Mr Penicuik was so obliging as to make known to me his intentions, I must own it was Mr Jack whom I expect to see at Arnside, ahead of all!"

"*I* had no such expectation!" said Kitty. "Nor had I the smallest wish to see him here."

Miss Fishguard looked timidly at her, for she sounded rather fierce. Encountering a dangerous sparkle in those big eyes, which met hers full, she said doubtfully: "I have sometimes wondered, my love . . ."

"You have wondered what, dear Fish?" prompted Kitty, with deceptive sweetness.

"Only that—Such a *very* handsome man, and of the first style of elegance! Air and address everything that they should be!" faltered Miss Fishguard. "And one cannot but recollect that it is he who has been most often at Arnside, after all!"

"Certainly, for he is quite Uncle Matthew's favorite!" responded Kitty swiftly. "As for the rest, I believe that he is a very dashing blade, as Freddy would say! My dear Fish, has he added you to his many conquests? The most shocking flirt in town, I am persuaded! He does very well for – for one's entertainment, but the female who receives his advances seriously will be destined, I fear, to sad disappointment! But do not let us be talking about such a rattle! The thing is, Fish, that Freddy is very desirous of presenting me to his parents, and means to carry me off to London almost immediately."

"But, Kitty, you are already acquainted with dear

Lady Legerwood!" objected Miss Fishguard. "And with Lord Legerwood too, for now I come to think of it, he accompanied her ladyship to Arnside, on the occasion of—"

"Yes, yes, but that is more than a year ago!" Kitty pointed out. "Lord Legerwood's relations, too – I believe he has many, and you must know that I have never met them! Besides, there will be all my bride clothes to order from the warehouses, and – and—You must perceive, Fish, that it will be proper for me to visit the Legerwoods!"

Miss Fishguard acknowledged it, but ventured to inquire who was to fill Kitty's place at Arnside while she went away on this visit of duty.

"Why, you, to be sure!" declared Kitty, with a brilliant smile.

Miss Fishguard had already faced with a sinking heart the prospect of being obliged, at an advanced time of life, to seek a new position, and it spoke volumes for the real benevolence of her character that she had been able to face it with fortitude, resolutely stifling every selfish wish that her pupil might remain unwed, and thus in need of her continued chaperonage. The tidings that her services would still be needed at Arnside, so far from relieving her mind of its most pressing care, threw her into disorder and no little agitation. "Remain to keep house for Mr Penicuik?" she almost shrieked. "Oh, I could not! Oh, Kitty, how can you think of such a thing? You know how much he dislikes me!"

"Fiddle!" said Kitty bracingly. "It is only that you will let him bully and browbeat you, Fish! Depend upon it, he would be very much vexed if you left Arnside! You must be firm! Remember how much he hates to have strangers about him! If he should throw his stick at you, or fly into one of his absurd rages, you have but to tell him that you mean to leave Arnside immediately, and I assure you he will mend his ways!" She perceived that dismay still dwelled in Miss Fishguard's countenance, and said imploringly: "Pray, Fish, do not fail me, I beg of you! He will never let me go to London if you too desert him! It will only be for one month! Oh, Fish—!"

Much moved, Miss Fishguard shed tears, and declared that no power on earth should prevail upon her to fail her dearest Kitty. But she felt bound to add, as she wiped her reddened eyes, that she was by no means persuaded that the betrothal would find favor with Mr Penicuik! "My love, it is my duty to utter a warning!" she said, hiccuping on a sob. "I believe him to have intended, from the outset, to bestow you upon Mr Jack! You cannot have failed to observe how vexed he is that Mr Jack has not come to Arnside, how he delayed to make known his intentions for a whole day! Spiddle told me tonight – not that I would have you suppose that I have been gossiping with the servants, but you know how they will talk!—Well, he told me that Mr Penicuik is in such a taking as never was, not having imagined that Mr Jack would absent himself upon such an occasion. I have the greatest apprehension that you and dear Mr Frederick may encounter strong opposition, and that there is little likelihood of his consenting to your proposed visit to London."

But when the affianced couple obeyed a summons to Mr Penicuik's dressing-room next morning, he surprised them both by receiving them with almost alarming affability. In what spirit he had greeted the news of the engagement, obligingly conveyed to him over-

night by his valet, Spiddle naturally did not inform the
happy pair. The night had brought counsel; and had
anything further been needed to confirm the old gentleman's resolve to pursue a Machiavellian policy it
was supplied by an early visit from the Reverend Hugh
Rattray, whose discourse so much enraged Mr
Penicuik that he declared himself thankful at least that
his ward had not been so misguided as to become engaged to such an intolerable stick of a parson. He then
indicated his burning desire to see his house rid of his
great-nephews, and charged the Rector with a message for his brother and for Dolphinton, that they
need not put themselves to the trouble of taking formal leave of him.

By the time that Kitty and Mr Standen (no early
riser) presented themselves, Mr Penicuik had consumed a sustaining repast, and was seated in a winged
chair before the fire in his dressing-room, a shawl over
his knees and another round his shoulders. His sag-
ging form and apparently palsied hand informed the
initiated that his rôle this morning was one of senile
decay; but there was nothing very senile in the needle-
sharp glance he cast at his ward, as she approached
his chair.

"Well, my dear!" he said. "They tell me I'm to wish
you happy. Hey?"

"If you please, sir," responded Kitty, dutifully bending to kiss his cheek.

"I *do* wish you happy!" said Mr Penicuik, with strong
resolution. He turned his penetrating eyes towards
Freddy, but instantly shut them, his countenance con-
torted, possibly, by a twinge of gout. "I felicitate you,
Frederick!" he said. He opened his eyes again, took
another look at the successful suitor, and averted them

with a visible shudder. But this was unfair: the Honorable Frederick had done justice to the occasion by arranging his necktie in the style known as the *trône d'amour,* a mode as difficult to achieve as it was beautiful to behold. Any one of a score or more aspirants to fashion would have been glad to have studied its intricacies, and several dashing blades would have had no hesitation in demanding the name of the genius who had designed his waistcoat. It was not so with Mr Penicuik. He reached out a trembling hand for his snuff-box, recruited his forces with a large pinch of Nut Brown, sneezed violently, shut the box with a snap, and said with all the air of one who had made up his mind to perform a painful duty: "Very well! You have my blessing!"

Kitty looked at her swain in an expectant way, but Freddy, quite unnerved by the basilisk glance he had encountered, forgot his carefully conned part, and merely said that he was very much obliged. Kitty, realizing that little could be hoped for from that quarter, made the best of it, and said brightly: "Yes, sir, and Freddy wishes me to go to Mount Street, to be formally presented to his parents, if you should not object to it."

Recalled to a sense of his shortcoming, Freddy made hasty amends. "Very likely to have forgotten her," he explained. "Good thing to remind them!"

"Imbecile!" said Mr Penicuik. His gaze rested thoughtfully on Kitty's face. There was a tense pause. "London, eh?" he said at last. "What do you mean to do there, miss?"

Kitty's heart began to thump. "If – if Lady Legerwood should be so obliging as to invite me, sir, I – I shall do whatever she desires, of course!" she produced.

"Don't tell me!" said Mr Penicuik. "Go raking about town, that's what you want to do!" He turned his eyes upon Freddy. "I suppose Emma – your mother – goes to all the swell places? Almack's – box at the Opera – Carlton House parties? She was dressed as fine as fivepence the last time I saw her: I daresay fifty pounds wouldn't have paid for what she had on her back! Not that it's any concern of mine if your father chooses to let her squander a fortune on trumpery!"

"No," said Freddy.

"What do you mean, *No?*" demanded Mr Penicuik, glaring at him.

"No concern of yours," said Freddy, with unimpaired amiability. "What's more, fifty pounds wouldn't have paid for her dress, let alone her hat, and her gloves, and the rest of it. Dash it, sir, m'mother don't buy made-up clothes in Cranbourne Alley! Never heard of such a thing!"

Mr Penicuik's hand clenched on his ebony stick, and his demeanour was for a moment so alarming that Kitty feared her betrothed might flee from his presence. But as Mr Standen had just then caught sight of a piece of fluff, adhering to the lapel of his riding-coat, and was carefully removing it, he remained entirely unconscious of the danger he stood in. By the time he had leisure to turn his attention again to his great-uncle, Mr Penicuik had regained control over his emotions, and merely said: "Plump in the pocket, your father!"

"Oh, very!" agreed Freddy.

Mr Penicuik regarded him with narrowed eyes.

"Suppose I let Kitty go to London?" he said abruptly. "Think your mother will take her to the *ton* parties?"

"Bound to," said Freddy reflectively. "Only parties my mother goes to."

"H'm!" grunted Mr Penicuik, taking another pinch of snuff. He gave a sudden cackle of laughter. "Ay, you're a sly puss!" he told Miss Charing. "Damme, I'll let you go!" His mirth ceased; a look of anguish entered his face; he said, with a moan: "But you'll be wanting to waste my money on finery!"

"No, no!" faltered Kitty, tightly clasping her hands. "Only — only a *very* little, sir, I promise!"

"I can't afford it!" said Mr Penicuik, relapsing into decrepitude. "You'll ruin me!"

"You *did* say I should have a hundred pounds for my bride clothes!" Kitty reminded him desperately.

He shook his head sadly. "You'd want more. Peacocking about the town! *I* know!"

"No, indeed I should not!" she assured him.

"Yes, you would," interrupted Freddy. "Told you so last night!"

"Oh, Freddy, do pray hold your tongue!"

"Dashed if I will!" said Freddy, feeling himself to be on firm ground. "You can't buy town rig for a hundred pounds: shouldn't think it would purchase more than one gown, myself."

"What?" screamed Mr Penicuik.

"Well, say a couple!" conceded Freddy, willing to stretch a point.

"Oh, Uncle Matthew, pray don't heed him!" begged Kitty.

Perceiving that he had dealt his aged relative a severe blow, Freddy said kindly: "No need to put yourself about, sir: daresay m'mother will buy Kit some toggery. Always ready to sport the blunt!"

This turned out to be a lucky suggestion, for however much he disliked spending money Mr Penicuik disliked still more to be thought impecunious. He instantly raised his drooping head, and withered Freddy with a few well-chosen words. After that, stifling another heavy groan, he desired Kitty to fetch him the box she would find in the cupboard beside his bed. This being done, he produced a key, and unlocked the case. Taking care that neither she nor Freddy should obtain a glimpse into the interesting box, he searched in it, and presently produced a roll of bills, tied up with tape. He regarded it wistfully for a moment, and then thrust it into Kitty's hand, turning away his head, and moaning: "Take it! Put it up safely, girl! Oh dear, oh dear! Don't let me see it again! To think of all that money squandered!"

Kitty stuffed the roll into her pocket, terrified lest his feelings should overcome him and he should change his mind. She tried fittingly to express her gratitude, but he cut her short, saying that no one need accuse him of stinting her. Hardly had he spoken the words than a fresh nightmare presented itself to him, and for some agonizing minutes it seemed as though the whole scheme must fail. The problem of Kitty's transport to London appeared to be insoluble. Her suggestion that she should travel on the stage was rejected, for, as Mr Penicuik pointed out, she had no maid to accompany her. He added that he had no doubt she expected him to engage one for her, but as such an idea had never so much as crossed her mind she was easily able to assuage his indignation. She ventured to suggest next that one of the chambermaids might go to London with her, but the thought of being obliged to pay this damsel's coach fare to London and back again cast him into renewed fury. A further, and most unwise, suggestion that Kitty should hire a post-chaise and pay for it with some of the money he had given her, shocked him so much that he seemed much inclined to take the bills back again. After a painful interlude, during which he reckoned up the extortionate charges of post-boys, the exact number of changes which would be necessary on the journey, and every other expense she might be expected to incur, Freddy, who was getting bored, intervened with a very simple solution. "Take her to town with me," he said.

This offer, which, as he instantly perceived, relieved him of all the expense of his ward's journey, found instant favor with Mr Penicuik; and he regarded Freddy with real if brief approval. It was Kitty who demurred. She could not but feel that Lady Legerwood might wish to receive notice of the impending visit – even of her eldest son's betrothal. Both Freddy and Mr Penicuik thought this frivolous, Mr Penicuik being outraged by the suggestion that his niece might not welcome any ward of his into her family; and Freddy maintaining that the thing was more likely to come off right if his parents were taken by storm than if they were allowed time for reflection.

This speech caused Mr Penicuik to direct one of his penetrating looks at him; but he said nothing, merely inhaling another pinch of snuff, and glancing sideways at Kitty. She still could not like the scheme, but as her fond guardian informed her that if she did not choose to go to London with Freddy she should not go at all, she was obliged to yield.

Mr Penicuik then relapsed into profound thought,

but just as the engaged couple, having exchanged speaking looks, were about to leave him, he emerged from his abstraction, and said: "No need to puff it off in the newspapers yet!"

Freddy, who had no desire to advertise his engagement, accepted this with relief unmarred by any ulterior thought. Kitty, her mind more inquiring than his, looked suspiciously at Mr Penicuik, and demanded bluntly: "Why should we not, Uncle Matthew?"

"Never mind why you should not!" said Mr Penicuik irascibly. "Good God, girl, d'ye take me for a fool? Think I don't know you're playing deep?" He observed, with satisfaction, the flush that colored his ward's cheeks, and chuckled. "You're a good girl!" he approved. "I daresay, if you were tricked out in all manner of finery, you wouldn't look so ill, either. But, mind! I won't be left with that Fish for more than a month!"

On which valedictory utterance he dismissed his visitors, with the parting adjuration to make speedy preparations for their journey, because he had been put to enough expense already without having to provide dinner for Freddy that day.

Once out of earshot, Kitty clasped Freddy's arm, and said, in a rush of gratitude: "Oh, Freddy, how can I thank you sufficiently? I hope you may not dislike it excessively!"

"No, no!" said Freddy, always the soul of courtesy. "Thing was, thought it was time to give the old hunks the go-by! Never met such a cheese-paring fellow in all my life!"

✻ *Chapter VI* ✻

SINCE MISS CHARING'S WARDROBE WAS NOT EX-
tensive, the task of packing it was speedily accomplished, and it was not long after noon when the
betrothed pair set forward upon the journey to London. Miss Charing's almost dizzy delight at having so
easily won her guardian's consent to the visit was
marred only by fear that her hostess might not feel an
equal degree of pleasure at the treat in store; and by
the lachrymose conduct of Miss Fishguard, who wept
without restraint while she helped her charge to pack,
and asserted that she did not know what was to become of her, or how she was to look after Mr Penicuik
to his satisfaction. It did not console her to be reminded that no one had ever succeeded in doing this;
and the prospect of being separated from Kitty for a
month so wrought upon her sensibility that she suddenly declaimed, between sobs: " 'For all that pleased
in wood or lawn, While peace possessed these silent

bowers, Her animating smile withdrawn, Has lost its beauty and its powers!' "

Kitty, always of a more practical turn of mind than her governess, wrinkled her brow at this, and said: "Well, but it is so horridly damp and cold at this season that the woods and lawns don't please at all, Fish! And peace *cannot* possess Arnside when Uncle Matthew's gout is so painful!"

"Sometimes, Kitty," said Miss Fishguard tragically, "I wonder at you! Is 'the pang which parts us from our weeping friends' unknown to you?"

This reproach made Kitty feel so guilty that for the first stage of the journey her spirits were subdued, and she replied in monosyllables to such remarks as her companion addressed to her.

"Not feeling quite the thing?" inquired Freddy kindly.

"Oh, yes, but I feel a *wretch*, Freddy!" she confided. "Poor Fish asked me if I did not feel a pang at parting from her, and I do not!"

"I should rather think you wouldn't!" said Freddy, without hesitation. "Can't make the woman out at all, myself. Know what she said to me this morning? Asked me if I'd slept well, and when I told her that it beat me how anyone could sleep at all, with a dashed lot of cockerels crowing their heads off, she said that rural sounds exhilarate the spirit, and do something or other to languid nature!"

"Cowper," said Kitty, in a depressed tone. " 'Restore the tone of languid nature.' "

"Well, it's a bag of moonshine!" said Freddy. "What's more, I always thought so! Often hear of fellows ruralizing – going into the country on a repairing lease, y'know – but I never could see that it did 'em a particle of good. Well, if they're kept awake the better part of the night by a lot of cockerels, stands to reason it couldn't! It's my belief, Kit, the woman's touched in her upper works."

"No, she is merely addicted to poetry," explained Kitty.

"Well, that just shows you!" said Mr Standen reasonably. He abandoned the topic for one of more immediate importance. "How much did the old hunks give you in that roll?"

"Oh, Freddy!" exclaimed Kitty, awed. "Two hundred and fifty pounds! I am sure I can never spend the half of it! It is the greatest anxiety to me! I have it safe here in my reticule, but only think if I should chance to be robbed!" She untied the strings of this receptacle, and dragged out the roll. "Pray, will you take care of it for me?" she begged.

Mr Standen was just about to decline the office when a deep and cunning though entered his head. Having a very nice idea of the cost of feminine apparel, it did not seem to him that two hundred and fifty pounds would suffice to clothe a lady about to make her début in the first circle of fashion. He was a good-natured as well as an affluent young gentleman, and he now conceived a scheme whereby Miss Charing might be imposed upon entirely for her own benefit. Detaching a fifty pound bill from the roll, he handed it to Kitty, saying: "That's the dandy! You keep this one, and I'll give the rest to m'mother. Have all the bills sent to her, and she'll stand huff."

Except for a slight feeling of alarm at carrying as much as fifty pounds in her reticule, Miss Charing had no fault to find with this arrangement, so Mr Standen stowed the roll away in his pocket, and ventured to

speak of a matter which had been considerably exer-
cising his mind. "No wish to pry into what don't concern me," he said apologetically, "but can't help
wondering—Thing is, Kit, I'm dashed if I see what
your lay is!"

"My lay?" repeated Kitty, glancing sideways at him.

He blushed, and begged pardon. "Talking flash!"
he explained. "Forgot myself! What I mean is, good
notion to come to town for a spell! I'm not saying it
ain't. Only thing is, what's to come of it?"

Miss Charing, having foreseen this question, replied: "One should always seize opportunity, you
know. I am persuaded that once I am in London I may
easily discover an eligible situation. Or I might, if I had
pretty gowns, and Lady Legerwood is so obliging as
to introduce me to her acquaintance, even receive an
offer of marriage."

"No, dash it!" protested Mr Standen. "Not if you're
engaged to me, Kit!"

She became intent on smoothing the wrinkles from
her gloves. Her color considerably heightened, she
said: "No. Only—If there did happen to be some gentleman who – who wished to marry me, do you think
he would be deterred by that, Freddy?"

"Be a curst rum touch if he wasn't," replied Freddy
unequivocally.

"Yes, but—If he had a partiality for me, and found
I had become engaged to Another," said Kitty, drawing on a knowledge of life culled from the pages of
such novels as graced Miss Fishguard's bookshelf, "he
might be wrought upon by jealousy."

"Who?" demanded Freddy, out of his depth.

"Anyone!" said Kitty.

"But there ain't anyone!" argued Freddy.

"No," agreed Kitty, damped. "It was just a passing thought, and not of the least consequence! I shall seek a situation."

"No, you won't," said Freddy, with unexpected firmness. "That's what you said last night. Talked a lot of stuff about becoming a chambermaid. Well, you can't, that's all."

"Oh, no!" she assured him. "Upon reflection, of course I perceived that that wouldn't answer. And also I shouldn't wonder at it if Hugh was quite at fault, and I might do very well as a governess. To quite young children, you know, who don't need instruction in Italian or Water-color painting."

"Can't do that either," said Freddy.

"Well, really, Freddy!" cried Miss Charing indignantly. "Pray, what concern is it of yours?"

"Good God, Kit, of course it's my concern!" retorted Freddy, moved to express himself strongly. "You don't suppose I'm going to have everyone saying you'd rather go for a governess than marry me, do you? Nice gudgeon I should look!"

This aspect of the case had not previously occurred to Miss Charing, but she was a reasonable girl, and she at once perceived its force. "I suppose it would be disagreeable for you," she admitted. "Oh, well! I won't do it, then! If all else fails, I must just return to Arnside. Whatever happens, I shall at least have had one month in London!"

"Yes, but that's just it," said Freddy, knitting his brows. "Seems to me you've got a devilish queer notion of London! What do you suppose *will* happen?"

"Good gracious, Freddy, anything might happen! Well, at all events, much more than could ever happen to me at Arnside! You can't deny that that's so!"

"No, I can't," said Freddy bluntly. "That's what's worrying me. The more I talk to you, Kit, the more I wish I hadn't been such a sapskull as to let you persuade me into this business! You'll do something gooseish, and I shall get the blame for it."

"No, no, indeed I will not!" Kitty said coaxingly. "I promise I won't do anything you think wrong!"

"Dash it, Kit, *I* can't tell you how you should go on!" protested Freddy, horrified. "I ain't in the petticoat-line! Told you so at the start!"

"Of course not! You forget that your Mama will take care of me. Indeed, you have no cause to be uneasy!"

This reminder went some way towards allaying his fears, but a rare instinct for danger prompted him to demand: "Tell me this! Have you some scheme in your head I don't know about?"

"Yes," said Kitty, incurably truthful, "I have!" She observed the look of a hunted wild creature in his eyes, and clasped his hand in a sustaining way. "But it is nothing you would dislike!" she added. "I give you my word it is not, Freddy!" She saw that this very handsome assurance had not had the desired effect, and said reproachfully: "Freddy! Don't you believe me? When I have pledged you my word!"

"It ain't that I don't believe you, Kit," he explained gloomily. "Thing is, I'm dashed sure you don't know what I should dislike! Lord, I wish I were well out of it!"

It was now Miss Charing's turn to change color. "You don't mean – oh, you cannot mean to cry off?" she faltered.

"No, I don't!" responded Freddy, stung. "Never hedged off in my life! Play or pay, m'dear girl, play or pay! All I say is, wish I hadn't said I'd play! The next time I see that fat rascal of a landlord—!"

"Pluckley?" said Kitty, bewildered.

"That's the fellow," nodded Freddy, darling. "That bowl of punch! Never ordered it! Oughtn't to have had it. No, and, what's more, oughtn't to have let you have it either! No sense in wrapping it up in clean linen, Kit: must have been bosky, both of us!"

Nothing would move him from this standpoint, so Kitty, wisely abandoning the attempt, applied her energies to the task of reassuring him.

It was dusk by the time the post-chaise reached the outskirts of London, but there was still light enough for Kitty's eagerly straining eyes to discern such unaccustomed sights as a sedan-chair borne along by two stalwart carriers; a lamplighter mounted upon his ladder; a man with a tray of hot pies upon his head; an urchin sweeping a crossing for a portly old gentleman in a frock-coat and a Joliffe-shallow; carts, carriages, and coaches by the score; lights illumining fascinating wares in shop-windows; smart footmen sauntering on errands for their employers; beggars holding out cupped hands and dogging the footsteps of any benevolent-looking citizen; and, when the chaise drew towards the more modish quarter of the town, imposing mansions lining the streets, some with the flambeaux already kindled outside their doors.

Everything was strange to Kitty, everything wonderful. She called upon Freddy again and again to identify some building, dimly seen in the gathering darkness; or to explain the significance of a man in a scarlet coat and blue breeches; and she was so much excited and astonished by the many new sights and sounds that he tried his best to satisfy her curiosity. But although he could point out to her postmen, constables, and link-boys, and supply her with such interesting items of information as that nearly all chairmen were Irish, and that the unintelligible shout which had made her jump in her seat emanated from a stage-coachman, warning his roof-passengers to keep their heads down, as his coach swept under the arch of an inn, he was not very knowledgeable about the various large buildings which caught her attention. He explained that he was not familiar with the City, but engaged himself to show her all the landmarks farther west. However, by the time the chaise drew towards the more genteel part of the town it had become almost dark, and Kitty was feeling too much stunned by the noise and the bustle all about her to do more than blink at what seemed to her bemused gaze a myriad of dancing lights.

It was not until the chaise turned into the comparative quiet of Mount Street that it occurred to Friday that for anything he knew he might find his parents preparing to entertain guests to dinner. He refrained from making known this fear to his companion, and was relieved, when the chaise drew up outside one of the tall houses, to see none of the signs of projected hospitality. Nor, as he presently learned from the butler, were my lord and my lady dining out that evening. Ten minutes later, having left the shrinking Miss Charing to warm her chilled feet by the fire in one of the saloons on the entrance-floor, he discovered the reason for this departure from the normal.

He found his mama reclining upon a sofa in her dressing-room, a shawl spread over her feet, and a handkerchief redolent of aromatic vinegar clutched in one hand. She had removed her cap, and her carefully curled locks were in considerable disorder.

Lady Legerwood, the only surviving offspring of Mr Penicuik's third sister, Charlotte, was a fair woman, with more style than beauty, her large blue eyes being a little too prominent, and her chin showing a tendency to recede. The punctual presentation to her lord of six hopeful children had slightly impaired her figure, but she was generally considered to be a pretty woman; and, since she was as good-natured as she was foolish, she was almost universally liked. She was uncritically fond of her husband, doted upon her children, and was much addicted to what her uncle would unquestionably have termed extravagant frivolity.

The unexpected sight of her eldest son appeared to exercise a strange influence over her. She reared herself up on the sofa, her eyes dilating, and, throwing out a repelling hand, ejaculated: "Freddy! Have you *had* them?"

"Eh?" said Freddy, startled. "Had what, ma'am?"

"I *cannot* recall!" declared his parent, pressing the hand to her heated brow. "Meg has *not*! I remember that, because when poor Charlie had them we sent her to stay with Grandmama, for it was at the very moment when I was about to present her, you know, and only think how dreadful it would have been! I have been racking my brains to try to recollect whether you have had them, not that it signifies, I daresay, for you don't live here now, which is a thing I cannot like, for I am sure they cannot make you comfortable in those rooms of yours, only your papa would not let me say a word against it, and no doubt he knows what is best, only if they air the sheets properly it is more than I would bargain for! But heaven forbid, Freddy, that I should keep you tied to my apron-strings!"

"Yes, but what's amiss?" demanded Freddy, dutifully bending over the sofa to kiss one scented cheek.

Pausing only to clasp him to her bosom, and to return his salute with fervour, Lady Legerwood uttered fatally: "The measles!"

"Oh! Had 'em at Eton," said Freddy.

Lady Legerwood shed tears of thankfulness.

"Who's got 'em now?" inquired Freddy, mildly interested.

"All of them!" replied her ladyship dramatically. "Fanny and Caroline, and poor, poor little Edmund! I am quite distracted, for although I don't doubt Fanny and Caroline will speedily recover, Edmund is so full of them that I am in constant dread! I was up with him all the night, and am but now seizing a few moments upon my couch, as you see! You know how delicate Edmund has always been, my love!"

There were many elder brothers who might have cavilled at this statement; and certainly the Honorable Charles Standen, at present at Oxford, would have had no hesitation in giving it as his opinion that Edmund had been pampered from his cradle; but Freddy was as kind-hearted and as uncritical as his mother, and he only said: "Poor little fellow!"

Lady Legerwood squeezed his hand gratefully. "He will not suffer anyone but me to wait on him! I have been obliged to put off every engagement. We ought to be at Uxbridge House at this very moment – but I don't regret it, for I should think myself the most unnatural mother alive if I could go to parties when my beloved children were sick! But nothing could be more unfortunate, Freddy! You must know that Lord Amherst has taken Buckhaven off with him on this stupid Chinese mission, and now here is old Lady Buckhaven – and one can scarcely blame her, for I am sure Meg is so shatterbrained she should not be left alone! – declaring your sister must stay with her in the country until Buckhaven returns! It may be a year, or even more, and no one need think I do not feel for Meg in this predicament. But how could I reconcile it with my conscience, Freddy, I ask you, to bring her into this house of infection, when I *know* she never had the measles? I do not scruple to tell you, dearest, that she is expecting an interesting event in the autumn. So sad to reflect that Buckhaven must needs be from home upon the occasion, but your dear papa says it is a great honor that Amherst should have chosen to take him! So you must not wonder at it that you find me almost prostrate. My Benjamin so ill, not to mention his dear little sisters, and my eldest daughter – indeed, my eldest-born, for never shall I forget my disappointment when I learned I had given birth to a female, not that your papa ever spoke a word of blame to me, and only eighteen months later *you* were born, my dearest, so all was right! – Well, as I say, my eldest daughter requiring me to save her from her mama-in-law – an excellent female, of course, but so straitlaced, Freddy, that one's heart quite bleeds for poor Meg! And I cannot reconcile it with my conscience to uphold Meg in her determination to remain in Berkeley Square while Buckhaven is from home! If only she would consent to Cousin Amelia's going to live with her! But she will not, and I must own, my dear son, that I should not care for it myself, for you know what Cousin Amelia is! Yet what else can I suggest?"

Freddy made no attempt to answer this, but, fastening on to the most incomprehensible part of his mother's somewhat involved speech, demanded: "Why should Buck go to China? Silly thing to do!"

"Oh, Freddy, if I have said so once I have said it a hundred times! But Papa tells Meg she should be gratified to see her husband singled out for the mission. Do not ask me what it is about, for I am sure I cannot tell you! It is something to do with the injustice of those horrid mandarins to our traders, but for my part I think Buckhaven would have done better to have stayed at home. Why, he and poor Meg have not been married a year! But tell me, dearest, where have you been this age? You said you were going into Leicestershire, but I quite thought you told me you would be in town again before this."

"Very good sport," explained Freddy. "As a matter of fact, did come back, two days ago. Meant to wait on you, ma'am, but the thing was, found I had to go to Arnside."

"Arnside!" exclaimed Lady Legerwood. "Never tell me Uncle Matthew is dead?"

"Oh, no, he ain't dead!" said Freddy. "Pity, if you ask me! Sent for all of us."

"All of you?"

"Great-nephews. At least, Dolph would have it he didn't send for George, and I daresay he was right. No reason why he should have. Claud couldn't go, of course, and Jack didn't choose to."

"Freddy, is my uncle making his Will at last?" asked her ladyship eagerly.

"That's it. Ramshackle sort of a business. Leaving his fortune to Kitty, provided she marries one of us."

"What?"

"Thought you'd be surprised," nodded Freddy. "Poor girl didn't want to marry Dolph – stands to reason she wouldn't! Didn't fancy Hugh either. I wouldn't, myself. Prosy sort of a fellow! Long and the short of it is, ma'am, she accepted me!"

His mother's eyes started at him. "Freddy!" she said faintly. "*You* offered for Kitty Charing?"

Mr Standen perceived that his announcement was productive of more astonishment than delight, and blushed. "Thought you'd be pleased," he said. "Time I was getting married. Dash it, ma'am, told me so not a month ago!"

"Yes, but—Oh, Freddy, I believe it is a take-in! How can you be so—? Now, tell me it is untrue!" He shook his head, resolutely, adhering to his promise, made to Miss Charing, not to tell his parents any such thing. Lady Legerwood sank back against the sofa pillows, and pressed the vinegar-soaked handkerchief to her brow. "Oh, good heavens! What can have possessed you? *Surely* you have never—Freddy, do not tell me you have offered for Kitty for the sake of Uncle Matthew's fortune!"

"No, I haven't," replied Freddy. "It's what everyone else will tell you, though. Bound to!"

She stared at him. "But is it possible that you can have a *tendre* for the girl? I thought you had not been to Arnside above half a dozen times since you left school! How comes this about? I declare, you have set my poor head in such a whirl—! Heavens, what will your father say to this?"

"No reason why he should object, ma'am. Daresay he'll be glad of it. Very good sort of a girl, Kit: always liked her!"

This lover-like encomium caused her ladyship to give a gasp. " 'A very good sort of—' *Freddy!*"

"Well, ain't she?" demanded Freddy. "Thought you

was fond of her, ma'am! Often told me you pitied her, having to live cooped up with Uncle Matthew. Quite right! Never saw such an old curmudgeon in my life! What's more, that Fish of hers seems queer in her attic to me. Shouldn't wonder at it if between the pair of them they drove Kit into Bedlam. That's why I brought her up to town with me."

Lady Legerwood sat up with a jerk. "You did what? Freddy, you haven't brought her *here*?"

"Thought you'd like to see her," said Freddy feebly. "Engaged to me – present her to the family – show her the sights! Besides, nowhere else I could take her!"

Many thoughts jostled one another in Lady Legerwood's bemused brain; she uttered the most immediate of them. "With measles in the house!"

"It's a pity about that," agreed Freddy. "May have had 'em, though. I'll ask her."

"But it is impossible!" she cried. "What in heaven's name do you expect me to do with her?"

"First thing to do is to buy her some clothes. Can't have her going about like a dowd. Must see that, ma'am!"

"*I* am to buy clothes for her?" exclaimed her ladyship.

"Help her to choose 'em," amended Freddy. "Won't have to pay for 'em. Fact is, the old gentleman gave her a handsome sum for the purpose. Taking care of it for her. You tell me what the figure comes to, and I'll sport the blunt."

"Uncle Matthew gave her a handsome sum?" exclaimed his mother, momentarily diverted. "You don't mean it!"

"Surprised me too," murmured Freddy. "Surprised

me when he said she might come to town for a month, as well."

"A month! No, no, Freddy, indeed I cannot have her here! I would not for the world behave shabbily towards your betrothed, even though I cannot like this engagement, for I had hoped to see you make a much better match, and, indeed, I – not that that signifies *now!* And you are not to be thinking that I do not like Kitty, for I am sure she is an excellent girl, and I should be very glad to show her any kindness in my power! But I do not mean to entertain until the children are well again, and as for devoting myself to Kitty at such a moment, it is not to be thought of! Later, perhaps! She must return to Arnside for the present: I am persuaded she will understand how it is!"

"Won't do at all," said Freddy firmly. "Promised her she should spend a month in town. Can't break my word to her. Cruel thing to do. Set her heart on coming to London."

"Oh, dear, what is to be done, then?" sighed her ladyship, abandoning all attempt to grapple with the problem. "Where is she all this while?"

"Left her in the Blue Saloon. Said I'd break the news to you. Took a notion into her head you might not like it, and went into a quake. Wouldn't come upstairs with me."

"Well, I am sure I am not astonished at that! Poor child, I suppose she was so anxious to escape from that odious old man she was prepared to do anything to accomplish it! She must remain here for tonight, of course, and then we must consider what is best to be done. I will come down to her in a moment, tell her. And what your father will say when you break this news to him, Freddy, I dare not consider!"

But in the event Freddy was spared the necessity of having to break the news to Lord Legerwood. While he was closeted with his mama, his lordship had walked into the Blue Saloon, to find it inhabited by a damsel in an old fashioned bonnet and a drab pelisse, who turned an apprehensive and vaguely familiar face towards the opening door, and then rose to her feet, and dropped a shy curtsy. "How – how-do-you-do, sir?" she said, with a valiant assumption of ease.

"How-do-you-do?" responded his lordship politely.

"Perhaps," said Kitty, swallowing, "you don't remember me, sir. I am Kitty Charing."

"Of course!" he responded, coming forward, and shaking hands. "I thought I knew your face. But what a delightful surprise! Are you staying in London?"

"Well – well – I do *hope* so!" Kitty said, blushing vividly. "Only I am not expected, and perhaps it might not be quite convenient!"

Lord Legerwood's calm gray eyes took note of the blush; a twinkle came into them. "Can it be that you have come to stay with us?" he suggested.

She stood considerably in awe of him, for his cool, well-bred manners were quite unlike her guardian's, and made him seem immeasurably superior. He had an air of decided fashion, too, and an occasionally satirical tongue. The twinkle, however, reassured her. She smiled confidingly up at him, and said: "Yes, that is it! Freddy said you would not object to it, only, for my part, I did think we should have asked you first!"

"Freddy?" he said interrogatively.

She became a little confused. "Yes, sir. You see – Freddy brought me! He – he has gone to tell Lady Legerwood!"

That sapient eye caused her blushes to rise again.

"Indeed?" said his lordship. "Has Freddy been visiting his great-uncle? Dear me! But what am I about, to be keeping you standing! Do, pray, sit down again, and tell me how all this comes about!"

She obeyed the first part of this command (for such she felt it to be), but said: "I think, perhaps, Freddy ought to tell you, sir. In fact, I am quite sure he should!"

He drew up another chair, and seated himself in it. "Really? I am persuaded I shall much prefer to be told it by you. I always find it so difficult to follow Freddy when he tries to explain anything to me."

"Yes, but it wouldn't be the thing for me to tell you, sir!" objected Kitty.

"A delicate matter, I apprehend?" She nodded. "In that case, I cannot too strongly recommend you not to entrust the task of explaining it to Freddy," he said.

She drew a resolute breath. "Well, I must say it does seem hard that everything should fall on poor Freddy," she agreed. "The – the truth is, sir, that he has been so obliging as to – to offer for me!"

His lordship sustained this with fortitude, but there was a slight pause before he said: "This is very sudden!"

"I am afraid," said Miss Charing guiltily, "that it is a disagreeable surprise to you, sir!"

"Not at all!" he replied courteously. "I own to some slight feeling of surprise, but I assure you it is not disagreeable!"

Much cheered, Kitty said gratefully: "Thank you! I did not think of it at first, but while I have been waiting here I began to think that you might dislike it excessively, and to wonder if perhaps—"

"If perhaps—?" he prompted, as she broke off.

"I – we – should not have done it! Only – well, sir, it was all Uncle Matthew's fault! He has made an odious scheme to leave me his whole fortune if I will marry one of his great-nephews, and he sent for them to come to Arnside, so that he could tell them of it, and I might choose the one I liked the best." She added: "And however unbecoming it is in me to appear critical of one who is my benefactor, I must say that I think it was a most improper arrangement!"

"Most improper," he agreed. "But am I to understand that Mr Penicuik's great-nephews all obeyed this peculiar summons?"

"Jack did not," she replied. "And he knew why my uncle had sent for him, which makes me excessively glad to think that he had too much delicacy of mind to come upon such an errand!"

"The reflection must be of comfort to all his friends," said Lord Legerwood rather dryly. "May I know if they were all aware why they were sent for?"

"Dolph and Hugh seemed to know," she answered. "But Freddy had not the smallest suspicion of it. I daresay, you know, that if my uncle wrote in veiled terms he might not have understood what was intended."

"More than probable. But when the matter was made plain to him I collect that he was not backward in offering for your hand?"

"No, no, you must not be thinking that he offered for me because of the fortune!" Kitty said quickly. "I assure you, it is not the case at all! You must know that he – he had not previously supposed that his suit would be acceptable to Uncle Matthew!"

Lord Legerwood looked at her for a moment; then his gaze dropped to the snuff-box he held in one hand.

He flicked it open, took a delicate pinch of snuff, and said smoothly: "The – er – attachment between you is of longstanding, I apprehend?"

"Yes," said Kitty, pleased to find him so quick-witted. "We – we have always felt a – a decided partiality for each other, sir. So when he found that Uncle Matthew had pledged himself to give me to *whichever* of them I chose he – he was emboldened to Speak!"

Lord Legerwood dusted his fingertips with his handkerchief, and put away his snuff-box. "Really, a most romantic story," he remarked. "I must own I had not thought it of Freddy. How little one knows of one's offspring after all!"

She eyed him doubtfully, but was spared the necessity of answering him by the reappearance on the scene of her betrothed. Freddy came in with the news that his mother would in a few moments arrive to welcome her guest. He had prepared a glib speech assuring Kitty of Lady Legerwood's pleasure in the visit, but under his father's ironic gaze he faltered a little.

"Ah, Frederick!" said his lordship languidly. "I learn that I must offer you my felicitations."

"Oh – er – exactly so, sir!" Freddy responded. "Thought you'd be pleased! Time I was getting married. Brought Kit up to town, you see. Felt you'd wish to become acquainted with her. Before we puff it off in the papers."

"Oh, is the engagement not to be announced?" inquired his lordship, all polite interest.

"Uncle Matthew does not wish it to be announced quite immediately, sir," said Kitty. "There – there are reasons why it will be more convenient to wait for a few weeks, but I cannot well enter into these!"

"No, of course you cannot," said his lordship, as though he perfectly understood.

"Measles," said Freddy. "Not that the old gentleman knew about that, but it's a dashed good reason, come to think of it!"

Kitty looked at once anguished and bewildered, but Lord Legerwood seemed not to think the remark peculiar, agreeing, in the blandest way, that the measles afforded an excellent excuse for postponing the announcement of the engagement. Upon his wife's entering the room just then, looking perfectly distracted, he instantly said: "Ah, my love, no doubt Frederick has broken these delightful tidings to you! You have come to welcome our prospective daughter-in-law!"

She cast him a puzzled inquiring glance, but as his attitude clearly indicated his wish that she should receive Kitty with complaisance, and her own kindly disposition would have made it very hard for her to have repulsed the girl, she embraced Kitty, and said: "Yes, indeed! You must forgive me, if I seem surprised, my dear, for I had not the least suspicion, and—But you will explain it all to me presently! It is so unfortunate that you find us in such a fix, but you must come upstairs directly, and take off your bonnet, and be comfortable. Poor child, I am sure you must be tired and horribly chilled by the journey!"

She again looked for guidance towards her lord, but receiving nothing more helpful than one of his more enigmatic smiles took Kitty away to her dressing-room, murmuring quite audibly: "Oh, dear, I wonder what next will befall us?"

A silence followed the departure of the ladies. Freddy, quite as puzzled as his mama by Lord Legerwood's behavior, stole a cautious look at him, and waited.

"Quite a romance, Frederick," said his lordship, drawing out his snuff-box again.

"No, no!" disclaimed his blushing son. He added hurriedly: "What I mean is, shouldn't put it like that, myself!"

Lord Legerwood dipped his forefinger and thumb into the box, shook away all but a minute pinch of snuff and held this to one nostril. "It distresses me to reflect that you have been labouring under the pangs of what you believed to be a hopeless passion, and that I remained in ignorance of it," he observed. "I must be a most unnatural parent. You must try to forgive me, Frederick!"

Thrown into acute discomfort, Freddy stuttered: "N-never thought of such a th-thing, sir! That is – n-not as bad as that! Always very fond of Kit, of course!"

Lord Legerwood, a sportsman and a gentleman, abandoned the pursuit of unworthy game, shut his snuff-box with a snap, restored it to his pocket, and said in quite another voice: "In Dun Territory, Freddy?"

"No!" declared his unhappy son.

"Don't be a fool, boy! If you've steered your barque off Point Non-Plus, come to me for a tow, not to a chancy heiress!"

"It ain't that at all!" protested Freddy, much ha-rassed. "Mind, I knew that's what everyone would think, and so I told Kit!"

"I perceive that I have fallen into vulgar error," said his father. "Accept my apologies! I will refrain from embarrassing you with awkward questions, but may I know for how long I am to have the honor of entertain-

ing Miss Charing? And even – if it is permissible to
ask – what I am expected to do on her behalf?"

If there was a barb to this speech, it missed its mark.
Relieved to find his parent in so forbearing a mood,
Freddy replied gratefully: "Much obliged to you, sir!
Never a dab at explaining things! Thing is, Kitty took
a fancy to spend a month in London, and I promised
she should. Thought m'mother would take her about.
Pity I didn't know about the measles! Makes it all
dashed difficult." He scratched his nose reflectively.
"I shall have to hatch some scheme or other," he de-
cided.

"Do you think you will?" inquired Lord Legerwood,
regarding him with a fascinated eye.

"Bound to!" said Freddy. "Well, what I mean is,
must!"

❧ *Chapter VII* ❧

IT WAS FORTUNATE FOR MISS CHARING, WHO, from the moment of entering the Legerwood town house, had been stricken by feelings of remorse, that her hostess was so much preoccupied with the thought of her ailing children that as soon as she had installed her young guest in a comfortable bedchamber, and had rapidly explained to her the unhappy state of affairs, she felt herself impelled to go up to the nursery floor, to ascertain that no relapse had been suffered by any of the invalids, and that Nurse had not fallen asleep in her chair – a hideous dread which was as persistent as it was unjust. Miss Charing, left alone to the unaccustomed luxury of a fire in her bedchamber, and to the terrifying knowledge that she had but to pull the bell-rope to bring a handmaiden to her assistance, reviewed her situation with feelings of guilt. It had not previously occurred to her that the plot she had hatched might involve others besides the hapless Freddy. His parents, although known to her, had seemed to be but vague figures in the background, whose existence had no bearing upon her schemes. The entrance of Lord Legerwood into the Blue Saloon had banished such false notions; she had been within a hair's breadth of abandoning her whole project. She was restrained partly by an agonizing reluctance to confess so foolish an exploit to such an awe-inspiring personage; and partly by an even more agonizing fear that to do so would mean her instant return to Arnside. By the time Lady Legerwood had joined the party, she had contrived in some measure to soothe her conscience with the reflection that since she had no intention of marrying Freddy no lasting harm would be done by the imposture. But for all that, she looked forward with dismay to the questions Lady Legerwood must inevitably ask, and could only be thankful that maternal solicitude obliged her ladyship to postpone the dangerous *tête-à-tête*.

Having assured herself that Edmund, though sadly feverish, seemed inclined to sleep, Lady Legerwood descended the stairs again to her dressing-room. Out of consideration for Miss Charing, whose wardrobe she knew to be scanty, she had declared that she would herself sit down to dinner in her morning dress, but she would have thought it a very odd thing not to have made some alteration in her appearance. Not even her desire to seek counsel of her lord could be allowed to take precedence over the more pressing need to change her cap, and to repair possible damages to her complexion. She sent for her maid, discovered that her hair must be dressed again, and had just resigned herself to the impossibility of seeking his lordship out before the dinnerbell rang, when he most providentially walked into the room.

She greeted him with relief. "Oh, my love, I have been wanting to speak to you! Yes, the rose-point cap, Clara, and you need not wait! Stay, give me the orange-blossom scarf with the broad French border! No, perhaps that is a little too—The paisley shawl will do very well! You need not wait."

"Charming!" remarked his lordship, picking up the lace cap, and looking at it through his eyeglass.

"Yes, is it not? I knew you would be pleased! Not that I care a fig for such fripperies at such a moment! How can you be so provoking, Legerwood? What, I ask you, is to be done? I was never more taken aback in my life, and what must you do but stand there smiling as though you liked it!"

He laughed, and set the cap down. "Well, what would you have had me do? I could scarcely forbid the banns: Freddy is of age."

"As though that could signify! Not that I wished you to go to such lengths as that!"

"I wonder if he did?" said his lordship thoughtfully.

Her full blue eyes stared at him. "What can you possibly mean? *Freddy* wish it?" A dreadful suspicion smote her. "Legerwood! It cannot be that she has entrapped Freddy into this engagement?"

"Oh, no, most unlikely, I imagine!" he responded coolly. "Quite an innocent! – refreshingly so, I thought."

"Of course she is! Reared in such a way! But one is forced to consider whether she has not induced poor Freddy to offer for her only to escape from Arnside. And I am very, very sorry for her, and I am sure I know nothing against her, except that her mother was a Frenchwoman, which I cannot like, but it is *not* the match I hoped for! I hope I may not be an odious

schemer – and if I were, I should be delighted to know
that my dear son was to marry a fortune, which, I assure you, I am not, for of all things I detest anything
mercenary, particularly when it is not in the least necessary that he should do so! I should be very glad to
think that my uncle meant to leave legacies to the
younger boys, but as for Freddy, he is abundantly provided for, and I did hope to see him married to someone of consequence, and not to a little countrified girl
nobody ever heard of!"

"Do not despair!" recommended his lordship. "I
will own myself astonished if anything comes of this
engagement. My dear Emma, you are not such a
goose-cap that you can imagine either of them to be
in love with the other!"

Lady Legerwood was tying the strings of her cap,
but she let her hands fall, and turned in her chair to
confront him. "But if she has not entrapped him, and
they are not in love, in heaven's name why have they
become engaged?"

"That I don't yet know," he answered. "I am not
sufficiently well-acquainted with Kitty even to hazard
a guess. I suspect the existence of a plot—"

"Not of Freddy's making!" interpolated Lady
Legerwood, ruffling up in defense of her young.

"I am far too well acquainted with Freddy to make
it necessary for you to tell me that, my love. Certainly
not of his making. For some reason, as yet hidden
from us, Kitty wishes it to be thought that she is betrothed to Freddy. An interesting feature of the engagement – or so it seems to me – is that for reasons
equally mysterious no immediate announcement is to
be made."

"No announcement?" she cried. "But why not?"

"Measles," he said imperturbably.

"Nonsense!"

"Of course: it was Freddy's offering on the altar of parental curiosity. Kitty preferred to lay the blame at the door of your deplorable uncle's eccentricity."

"That might well be true," she said, considering deeply. "When my uncle made this disgraceful play you may depend upon it he meant Jack to benefit! I declare it serves him right to be so set-down! Perhaps he hopes it will all come to nothing. He could not refuse his consent to the engagement, of course, because he will never go back on his word. It is one of the things one so particularly dislikes in him! What should we do?"

"Do? Why, nothing! Except, perhaps, enjoy a diverting episode."

"For my part, I do not find it diverting!" she said tartly. "I think you should demand to know the whole!"

"Oh, do you? And for my part I think I should be foolish beyond permission to do anything of the kind. Freddy's efforts to concoct suitable lies for my delectation might, I daresay, be amusing, but I think I won't put him to so much mental fatigue."

"Oh, dear, I suppose he would lie to you! How very dreadful it is! And he expects me to dress Kitty, and to take her to parties with me—"

"No, you are mistaken. I collect that he has abandoned that scheme."

"Is she to return to Arnside?" asked her ladyship hopefully.

"Oh, no, I don't think so! Freddy is going to hatch another scheme."

"Legerwood, you know very well he will do no such thing! We shall be obliged to do something!"

"Nonsense, my love! Freddy assures me he is bound to think of something," said his lordship, at his most urbane.

But no one was more surprised than he when his heir, having sat throughout the second course at dinner wrapped in profound thought, announced suddenly: "Knew I should hit on something! Well, I have!"

Lady Legerwood, whose conversation during dinner had meandered between the sufferings of her younger children, and the predicament in which her married daughter found herself, looked doubtfully at him. "Hit on what, dear Freddy?"

"Meg," replied Freddy succinctly. "Going to visit her."

"Are you, my love? But—Oh, now you put me in mind of it I recall that she is going to Almack's tonight, with Emily Cowper!"

"Find her there," said Freddy.

"Well, of course, dear—But you are not dressed for Almack's!"

"Go back to my lodgings and change. Plenty of time!" said Freddy. "Must see Meg!"

"This brotherly devotion is most affecting," remarked Lord Legerwood. "May we know why it has so suddenly attacked you?"

"It ain't anything of the sort, sir!" said Freddy, justly indignant. "Told you I'd hit on something! Came to me with the cheese-cakes!"

"What a tribute to the cook!" said his father.

He looked at Freddy with an expression of patient resignation; but Miss Charing, who had been vainly trying, ever since the news of the epidemic raging in the house had been broken to her, to think of an alternative to returning to Arnside on the morrow, said anxiously: "Is it about me, Freddy?"

"Of course it is. Famous good notion! Meg don't want to stay with old Lady Buckhaven, don't want Cousin Amelia to keep her company, can't have Fanny, because she's got the measles – better have you!"

Lord Legerwood, in the act of raising his claret-glass to his lips, lowered it again, and regarded his son almost with awe. "These unsuspected depths, Frederick—! I have wronged you!"

"Oh, I don't know that, sir!" Freddy said modestly. "I ain't clever, like Charlie, but I ain't such a sapskull as you think!"

"I have always known you could not be, my dear boy."

"Kitty to stay with Meg!" Lady Legerwood said, considering it dubiously. "I must say—But would it answer? I am sure Lady Buckhaven wishes her to have some older female with her, and I own—"

"No need to tell her Kit's age, ma'am. Never leaves Gloucestershire, so she ain't likely to find out. Besides, couldn't kick up a dust! Affianced wife – can't stay here, because of the measles, stays with m'sister instead. Quite the thing!"

"Oh, Freddy!" exclaimed Miss Charing, eyes and cheeks glowing, "it is a splendid scheme! Only, will your sister like it?"

"Like anything that kept her away from old Lady Buckhaven," said Freddy. Upon reflection, he added: "Except Cousin Amelia. Well – stands to reason!"

So shortly after ten o'clock, just as Miss Charing

was climbing into bed after a quiet evening spent in poring over the fashion-plates in various periodicals, Mr Standen, beautiful to behold in knee-breeches and striped stockings, a blue coat with very long tails, a white waistcoat, and a neck-cloth which caused an acquaintance almost to swoon with envy, sauntered into the vestibule at Almack's Assembly Rooms. He handed his hat and his coat to an attendant lackey, gave a couple of twitches to his wrist-bands, and favored the great Mr Willis with a nod.

Mr Willis, according him the bow due to a Pink of the *Ton*, would not have dreamed of asking to see his voucher. Quite surprising persons might find themselves excluded from Almack's, but not the most capricious of its patronesses would have entertained for a moment the thought of excluding Mr Standen. He was neither witty nor handsome; his disposition was retiring; and although he might be seen at any social gathering, he never (except by the excellence of his tailoring) drew attention to himself. Not for Mr Standen, the tricks and eccentricities of gentlemen seeking notoriety! He was quite a pretty whip, but no one had ever seen him take a fly off the leader's ear, or heard of his breaking a record in a racing-curricle; he rode well to hounds, without earning the title of neck-or-nothing; and while he sometimes practiced single-stick in Jackson's Boxing Saloon, or tossed off a third of daffy in Cribb's Parlor, he was no Corinthian. Indeed, so far from aspiring to pop in a hit over Jackson's guard, or to stand up for any number of rounds with some Pet of the Fancy, he would have disliked either experience very much indeed. Nor could anyone have thought him an ideal cavalier-servente, for he was too inarticulate to pay charming compliments, and had never been known to indulge in the mildest flirtation. But a numerous circle of male acquaintances held him in considerable affection, and with the ladies he was a prime favorite. The most sought-after beauty was pleased to stand up with so graceful a dancer; any lady desirous of redecorating her drawing-room was anxious for his advice; no hostess considered her invitation list complete without his name. His presence did not, of course, confer on a party the distinction that Mr Brummell's did, but he was a much more agreeable guest, never arriving long after he had been despaired of and then departing within twenty minutes, and never startling the old-fashioned by uttering calculated impertinences. He could be depended upon, too. He would not stand against the wall, refusing to dance; and no hostess, presenting him to the plainest damsel in the room, had the smallest fear that he would excuse himself, or abandon his partner at the earliest opportunity. He was an excellent escort for any lady deprived at the last moment of her lord's attendance, for his appearance could not but add to her consequence, and he was always nice to a fault in every attention to her comfort. Nor was the most jealous husband suspicious of him. "Oh, Freddy Standen!" said these green-eyed gentlemen. "In *that* case, ma'am, very well!"

So Mr Willis, who did not condescend to chat with every visitor to the club, welcomed Mr Standen affably, and frowned at the footman who was trying to present him with a quadrille card. Whoever else might need instruction in the figures of the quadrille Mr Standen most certainly did not.

"Seen Lady Buckhaven tonight, Willis?" inquired Freddy, bestowing a final touch to his neckcloth.

"Yes, indeed, sir. Her ladyship came in with my Lady Cowper half an hour ago. Mr Westruther was one of her ladyship's party."

"Oh, he's here, is he?" said Freddy. "Much of a squeeze?"

"No, sir, we are a *little* thin of company, the season not having begun," replied Mr Willis regretfully. "But it wants forty minutes till eleven, and no doubt we may expect to see the rooms fill up tolerably well."

After this exchange, Freddy passed into the ballroom, and paused on the threshold, looking about him for his sister.

"Why, there is Freddy Standen!" exclaimed a bedizened matron. "I did not know he was in town again. Dear creature!"

She waggled a hand in a tight kid glove, but failed to attract his attention, this being claimed at that moment by a voice at his elbow.

"Hallo, my Tulip! Didn't you ruralize after all?"

The voice was full of lazy amusement, and it made Freddy turn quickly. It belonged to a tall man whose air and bearing proclaimed the Corinthian. Coat, neckcloth, fobs, seals, and quizzing-glass, all belonged to the Dandy; but the shoulders setting off the coat so admirably, and the powerful thighs, hidden by satin knee-breeches, betrayed the Blood, the out-and-outer not to be beaten on any sporting suit. The face above the starched shirt-points was a handsome one, with a mouth as mocking as its owner's voice, and a pair of intensely blue eyes which laughed into Freddy's. The sight of them might have caused Miss Charing's heart to flutter, but they awoke in Mr Standen quite different emotions. He opened his mouth to give utterance to a few of the sentiments which had been festering in his bosom for two days, and recollected with a sense of bitter frustration that he was pledged to utter none of them. He shut his mouth again, swallowed, and said merely: "Oh, hallo! You here, coz?"

"Yes, Freddy, yes: I am here, not my wraith! But what are *you* doing here? I thought to have heard of you at Arnside!"

"Got back today," said Freddy.

Mr Westruther's eyes quizzed him maddeningly. "What a short stay, coz! Didn't they make you welcome?"

Freddy had always rather admired and looked up to his splendid cousin, but he was not going to put up with this sort of thing. He replied, after only a moment's rapid consideration: "Oh, toll-loll, but it's a devilish uncomfortable house, and the old gentleman don't like me to take my man there. Besides, no need to stay longer!"

"No?" said Mr Westruther, amusement quivering in his voice.

It was seldom that Mr Standen, a peace-loving young gentleman, was conscious of a wish to come to blows with his fellow men, but a wistful desire to land his cousin a facer did for an instant flicker in his mind. Several circumstances rendered the gratification of this impulse ineligible, chief amongst them being the hallowed precincts in which they both stood, and the melancholy certainty that such violence could only lead to his own discomfiture. So instead of yielding to brutish instincts, he fell back upon finesse. Opening his snuff-box, he offered it to Jack, saying meditatively: "Queer start! Thought you were bamming me, and dashed nearly didn't go. Daresay you didn't know it,

but the old gentleman's going to leave his fortune to
Kit, provided she marries one of us."

Mr Westruther helped himself to a pinch from the
elegant gold box. "Some hint of this, I must own, coz,
had reached my ears," he said gravely.

"Surprised you didn't go to Arnside, then," said
Freddy.

Mr Westruther raised his brows. "But what made
you think me a gazetted fortune-hunter, Freddy?"

"Oh, I don't know about that!" said Freddy vaguely.
"Daresay people took it for granted you and Kit would
make a match of it. Thought myself the old gentleman
meant to leave the blunt to you. Well, you did too,
didn't you? Been living on the expectancy for years!"

Mr Westruther said appreciatively: "Well done,
Freddy! A hit! I didn't go to Arnside because I have
the oddest dislike of having my hand forced. Our revered great-uncle's whims are not unamusing, but this
one goes beyond the line of what may be tolerated.
When I go into wedded shackles it will be in my own
time, and in my own fashion."

"Good notion – if the thing comes off right," agreed
Freddy. "Trouble is, can't be sure it will!"

His cousin laughed. "I'll take my chance of that!"

Freddy was well aware of Mr Westruther's many
conquests. While he was far from understanding why
nine females out of ten were so foolish as to fall in love
with one who, if not a downright rake, was certainly
the most accomplished flirt in town, this was not a
question which had previously exercised his mind. Tonight, for the first time, he was nettled by Jack's assurance; and instead of thinking that it was rather cork-
brained of Kitty to hoax Jack, along with all the rest,
he suddenly realized that had he been free to tell the

truth he would not have done it. Time Jack had a set-down! A certain suspicion beginning to take shape in his mind, he said: "Wish you good fortune! Glad I met you tonight: wanted to tell you! Devilish grateful to you, coz! Never thought there was any chance for me in that quarter: shouldn't have gone to Arnside if you hadn't given me a nudge!"

If he had hoped to have confounded his cousin, he was disappointed. There was certainly an arrested look in Mr Westruther's face, but he only cocked an eyebrow, and said: "Can it be that I am to wish you happy?"

"That's it," replied Freddy. "Mind, we ain't puffing it off yet, because the old gentleman don't like it above half, but it's known in the family."

He had the satisfaction of seeing Mr Westruther's brows snap together, and the laugh quite fade from his eyes; but it was only for a second. The frown vanished as swiftly as it had appeared; Mr Westruther grinned at him, and said: "No, Freddy, no! Doing it too brown!"

"Ain't doing it brown at all," said Freddy stolidly. "Dolph, Hugh, and I all offered for Kit. Accepted me. Well, I knew she would!"

"What?"

"Dash it, Jack!" said Freddy, stung. "Any girl would rather marry me than Dolph or Hugh! No use saying Dolph's an Earl: he's run off his legs, besides being dicked in the nob! And as for Hugh – lord!"

"Just so," concurred his cousin. *"But, Freddy – but—!* I still say that you are doing it too brown! I will allow that Kitty might prefer you to Dolph or Hugh, but I'm not such a green 'un that I will swallow this hum that you – *you*, sweet coz! – offered your hand and heart to Kitty Charing! It conjures up an enchanting picture, but no, Freddy, no!"

Freddy toyed with the idea of presenting Mr Westruther with another picture, that of a long-standing but secret attachment, sketched by Miss Charing's reckless hand. Something told him that it would not be accepted; and he said instead: "Thought you'd be surprised. Fact is, been thinking for some time I ought to be married. Eldest son, you know: duty!"

"And your father so stricken in years besides!" said Mr Westruther helpfully.

"No," said Freddy. "He ain't stricken in years, but they've got measles in the house. No saying what might happen."

This flight into the realms of fancy was too much for Mr Westruther. "Enough!" he said. "This bubble was pricked before it was fully blown, coz. I hope you mean to regale me with the true story of what happened at Arnside. Did Dolph and Hugh indeed offer for Kitty?"

"Yes, they did, but anyone could have told 'em it wouldn't fadge. Couldn't expect Kit to like being asked only for Uncle Matthew's fortune. Knew I didn't want his blunt. Knew I was dashed fond of her, too. So I popped the question, and there we were. Got a notion we shall suit very well."

There was now a slight crease between Mr Westruther's brows, but he said, still in an amused tone: "Do forgive me! – But how came you, in these circumstances, to tear yourself away from your – er – betrothed so soon? And you always polite to a point!"

"Didn't tear myself away from her," replied Freddy.

"Brought her up to town with me. Wanted to present her to m'mother and father. She's in Mount Street."

He watched his cousin to see how this piece of corroborative information was being received, and was a little puzzled. There was a gleam in Jack's eyes, and the hint of a smile playing about the corners of his mouth. "I see," he said: He patted Freddy on the shoulder. "I felicitate you, coz: I am quite sure you will suit admirably! Of course I shall call in Mount Street to pay my respects to the future Mrs Standen, but in the meantime do, pray, assure her of my best wishes for her happiness!"

"Much obliged. Very likely she'll visit Meg, though."

"Then I shall call in Berkeley Square. What a charming surprise for Meg! Here she comes!" He paused, watching Lady Buckhaven, who had been taking part in the country dance which had just ended, trip across the floor towards them. "Dearest cousin, here is Freddy with such delightful news for you! I shall leave him to tell it to you, but I give you warning that when they strike up for the waltz you are mine, and I will by no means submit to being supplanted by him!"

Lady Buckhaven, a very pretty blonde, with her mama's large, rather full eyes, and a great deal of vivacity, cried out at this. "How can you, Jack? As though I would do anything so rustic as to stand up with my own brother! Freddy, where have you been this age? What have you to tell me?"

His eyes were on his cousin's retreating form; instead of answering, he said, in a disapproving tone: "What's he mean by calling you his dearest cousin?"

"Why, that I am, to be sure!" she retorted, laughing.

"Well, it ain't much to boast of," said Freddy, having passed his family under rapid mental review. "All the same, shouldn't encourage him!"

"Don't be so gothic, Freddy! He is the most enchanting flirt, and only think how ravishing it is to set odious creatures like Charlotte Kilvington there gnawing their nails with jealousy! I declare you are as stupid as Lady Buckhaven! Oh, Freddy, the most shocking thing! That antiquated old fidget insists that I cannot remain in London while Buckhaven is away!"

"Yes, I know. Thought of something, too. That's why I came tonight."

"Freddy, you have not? Oh, tell me this instant!" she cried, clasping ecstatic hands.

"Yes, but don't kick up such a dust!" said her censorious brother. "You'll have everyone gaping at us. Come and sit down! And, mind, now, Meg! you needn't set up a screech just because I've got something to say that'll surprise you!"

Thus admonished, Lady Buckhaven meekly accompanied him to two vacant chairs, placed between a pair of palms against the wall. Their progress was somewhat impeded by the determination of various acquaintances to greet them, but they arrived at their goal at last, and Lady Buckhaven said, disposing the diaphanous folds of her blue gauze overdress becomingly: "I can't conceive why you should be so mysterious! If it is all a take-in, I will never forgive you! Oh, Freddy, I must tell you the latest crim. con. story! You will be in whoops! Only fancy! – it is all over town that Lady Louisa Aldstone and young Garsdale—"

"Lord, I knew that before I went to Melton!" interrupted Freddy scornfully. "And you needn't tell me Johnny Eppleby fathered the last Thresham brat, because I know that too!"

"No!" exclaimed his sister.

Perceiving that he had over-estimated her new-found knowledge of the world, Freddy said hastily: "All a hum, I daresay! I wish you will stop chattering, and pay attention!"

She turned her blue orbs upon him expectantly, and, with all the air of one wearied with repeating an incredible tale, he disclosed his engagement to her. She was quite as astonished as Lady Legerwood had been, and much more exclamatory; but no sooner had he propounded to her his scheme for her own salvation and Kitty's entertainment, than she forgot every other consideration in wholehearted approval of a plan which bade fair to afford her with a reasonable excuse for eschewing the rural amenities of Gloucestershire. She retained the haziest memory of Miss Charing, having only once visited Arnside, and that some years previously, but she was sure she would like her excessively; and the intelligence that she would be expected without loss of time to superintend the purchase of a wardrobe she greeted with rapture. "And I am to introduce her into society? Oh, you may *depend* upon me, my dear brother!"

"Well, I do," acknowledged Freddy, "but I must say I don't feel easy! Never knew anyone with such a shocking eye for color as you, Meg! That underdress, or petticoat, or whatever you call it, that you have on! No, really, m'dear girl! It won't do!"

"Freddy!" cried Lady Buckhaven, stunned. "How can you say such a thing? This particular shade of pink is all the crack!"

"Not with this blue stuff it ain't," said Freddy positively.

"Jack," said Lady Buckhaven, tilting her chin, "said he had never seen me look more becoming!"

"Sort of thing he would say," responded Freddy, unimpressed. "Daresay you think *he* looks becoming in that devilish waistcoat he has on. Well, he don't, that's all! Take my word for it!"

Affronted, she exclaimed: "I never knew you to be so disagreeable! I have a very good mind not to invite Kitty to visit me!"

But this, as Freddy knew well, was an empty threat. Hardly had Lady Legerwood and her young guest left the breakfast-table than Meg swept in upon them, resplendent in a new pelisse of Sardinian blue velvet, and a bonnet with an audaciously curtailed poke and a forest of curled plumes; and displaying with ostentation the sables which had been her lord's parting gift to her. Between her dread that some germ of measles, wandering adventurously down from the nursery floor, might fasten upon her daughter, and her disapproval of sables and blue velvet, Lady Legerwood was for several moments too much occupied to present Kitty to the visitor. On the whole, it was her daughter's lack of taste which most exercised her mind, for her own eye for color, like Freddy's, was unerring. "Ermine or chinchilla with blue, Meg!" she said firmly. "Sables *never* show to advantage! Now, if only you had chosen to wear the Merino cloth pelisse I bought for you – not the earth-colored one, but the braided one in French green – it would have been unexceptionable!"

By the time this point had been fully argued, news was brought to Lady Legerwood that the doctor had arrived, whereupon, after hurriedly commending Kitty to her daughter's care, she hurried away, bent on convincing the worthy physician that certain unfavourable symptoms, which had manifested themselves during the night, made it advisable for him to call in Sir Henry Halford to prescribe for Edmund. As the family doctor, a rising man, was at daggers drawn with the eel-backed baronet, it did not seem probable that she would be seen again for some appreciable time.

Meg, as good-natured as her mother and brother, would have been amiable to anyone for whom her kindness had been solicited. Had she found herself confronted by a dazzling blonde she would not have spurned Kitty; but it could not be denied that the discovery that Miss Charing was a brunette immediately confirmed her in her conviction that she would like her prodigiously. Both were little women, but Kitty was built on sturdier lines than Meg, who was a wispy creature. One of her admirers had once labelled her ethereal, which so much delighted her that she ever after took great pains to live up to it, dressing her feathery curls à la Méduse, wearing gowns of the airiest materials, and cultivating a fluttering restlessness worthy almost of that still more ethereal beauty, Lady Caroline Lamb. As a débutante she had not been remarkable, for there were many prettier damsels, and her mother's sense of propriety allowed her natural liveliness little scope. But she had made an excellent marriage, and had speedily discovered that the wedded state exactly suited her. Matched with an affluent peer, a good many years her senior, she found that the world of *ton* had far more to offer a dashing young matron than ever she had suspected when she was demure Miss

Standen. Her husband regarded her with doting fondness; she had as much pin-money as she could spend; and she was able to gather round her a court of gentlemen who were far too wary to pay marked attentions to unmarried maidens. She had a considerable affection for her lord, and was very disconsolate to be obliged to part from him for perhaps as much as a year, even crying herself to sleep for three nights in succession; but since her disposition was volatile, she soon recovered from this state of despondency, and had now nothing to worry her but the dread of being obliged to live with her mother-in-law, and the certainty that her pregnancy would compel her to give up going to balls right in the middle of the London Season.

Most of this she poured into Kitty's ears, but as her conversation was even more inconsequent than Lady Legerwood's, Kitty was quite bewildered, and had great difficulty in uuraveling the thread of her discourse. However, Freddy arrived in Mount Street presently, and had no hesitation in putting an end to his sister's chatter by demanding to know if all had been settled between her and Miss Charing. When he learned that the matter had not yet been touched on, he was quite indignant, for he had hoped that no further strain need be placed upon his powers of contrivance. He now perceived that since he was cursed with a rattle for a sister he would be obliged to assume control of the affair. He spoke severely to both ladies, which drew a giggle from each, and provoked Meg into rallying him on his unloverlike behavior. Blushing deeply, he then bestowed a chaste salute on Kitty's cheek, saying apologetically: "Forgot!"

Fortunately for the deception, Meg was pondering

deeply, and took no note of this somewhat peculiar remark. She said suddenly: "No one must be allowed to see you until you are *gowned*, Kitty!"

Miss Charing, who had been miserably conscious of her outmoded raiment from the moment of setting eyes on Lady Legerwood's elegance, heartily assented to this.

"We will instantly go to Fanchon's!" announced Meg. "You trunks must be sent round to Berkeley Square – Mama's people will attend to that! Only pop on your bonnet, and we will be off directly! Freddy may come with us, if he chooses."

This offer being declined, Mr Standen providentially recollecting that he had an engagement at the other end of the town, the ladies fell into enthusiastic discussion of current fashions, Miss Charing showing Lady Buckhaven the picture of a ravishing Chinese robe of lilac silk which she had discovered in one of the numbers of *La Belle Assemblée,* and Lady Buckhaven arguing that a light puce would be more becoming to her new friend.

Freddy then took his leave; and as soon as the doctor left the house, Kitty sought out her hostess, to thank her for her hospitality, and to bid her farewell. Lady Legerwood embraced her kindly, bestowed upon her a handsome shawl of Norwich silk, which she had never even worn but which was going to cost her husband not a penny less than sixty pounds; and promised, as soon as she had the leisure, to find a more worthy betrothal gift for her. Kitty was thrown into dreadful confusion by this, and could only be thankful that there seemed at present to be little fear that Lady Legerwood would have any leisure.

She was borne off by Meg in a stylish barouche, and,

having miscalled it a landaulet, learned her first lesson. A barouche, Meg told her, was of the first stare of fashion; but a landaulet, for inscrutable reasons, was a dowdy vehicle, only fit for old ladies to ride in. "I will remember," she said. "I shall have a great deal to learn, because I have never been to London in my life. But I mean to apply myself!"

"Oh, you will be on the town in less than no time!" said Meg, adding naïvely: "Particularly if you are to stay with me, because I'm all the crack!"

"I can see that you are," said Kitty, in all sincerity.

❧ *Chapter VIII* ❧

IT WAS AS WELL FOR MR STANDEN THAT MISS Charing had been bred in the habits of the strictest economy, for his sister, entering wholeheartedly into his amiable plot to provide Kitty with a much more expensive wardrobe than had been contemplated by Mr Penicuik, would have had no scruple in recommending the purchase of at least half a dozen of the ravishing gowns displayed by Mme Fanchon. It had not occurred to her that Miss Charing might demand to be told the prices of the dresses she looked at, for it had already been agreed between them that the dressmakers and the milliners should be instructed to send in their bills to Lady Buckhaven, whom they knew so well; and nothing was more unlikely than that Mme Fanchon would of her own volition mention anything so ungenteel as a price. But from the moment of alighting from the barouche in Bruton Street, and entering the portals of one of London's most renowned modistes, Kitty was suspicious. Ushered into a showroom carpeted with Aubusson and furnished with gilded, spindle-legged chairs, and a multitude of tall mirrors, she felt unhappily certain that any gown exhibited in such opulent surroundings would be quite above her touch. She tried to whisper as much in Meg's ear, but Meg only laughed, and said: "Fiddle!" Then the great Mme Fanchon herself appeared, all smiles and curtsies, and, having been informed that she was to have the privilege of supplying her ladyship's cousin with several dresses, suitable for a young lady of quality about to come out into the world, at once went into conference with my lady, while Kitty stared with round, envious eyes at a grand ball dress of lace over white satin, which was displayed upon a stand at one end of the room. She had not fully assimilated its glories when Meg rejoined her, but Meg, observing the direction of her gaze, said: "Not lace! When you are married you may wear such a dress, but Mama would never allow me to do so when I came-out."

"Oh, no! I was only thinking how beautiful it is! I am sure it must be most dreadfully dear!"

"Well, yes!" assented Meg, with a tiny giggle. She had purchased just such a grande-toilette herself, not three months ago, and it had taken all the cajolery of which she was capable to reconcile the most indulgent husband alive to a staggering demand from Mme Fanchon for three hundred pounds. "Lace *is* a little dear! But girls who are just out, you know, always wear muslins, and cambrics, with perhaps one or two silken gowns for important occasions. Now, don't get into a pucker, Kitty! We shall contrive famously, I promise you! I thought it best to tell Fanchon you were my cousin, since you don't mean to advertise your engagement quite at once. And – you won't take a pet? – I said that you had lived very retired, with a strict and old-fashioned guardian, because I could see that she was staring to see such an outmoded bonnet and pelisse. She perfectly understands – and it is *quite true!* I don't mean that I wouldn't have said it had it not been true, for I hope I am not such a zany, but it gives one the most agreeable feeling to know that one really has spoken the truth!"

There was no time for more; Mme Fanchon, dispatching two underlings with certain instructions, came up to the ladies, and at once began to discuss with Meg such mysteries as French bead edges, worked muslin jaconet, spider-gauze, ribbon-braces, and Zephyr cloaks. And then Miss Charing tumbled headlong into the world of make-believe which had for so long beguiled her leisure hours; for the underlings came back carrying dresses – dresses for every occasion, figured, embroidered, flounced, and braided; adorned with blond lace, or knots of ribbon; some embellished with spangles, some with pearl rosettes, some with silver fringes. They were the garments Miss Charing had dreamed of, and never thought to wear; and it was small wonder that she released her clutch on the workaday world. The season had not begun, and no other clients had invaded the showroom: Lady Buckhaven decreed that the gowns should be tried on immediately. Kitty, standing before a mirror, first in an elegant walking dress of amber crape, then in a demie-toilette of mulled muslin, next in a satin ball dress, with a pelerine of fluted velvet cast over her shoulders, saw herself transformed, and lost her head.

But she came to earth too soon for Lady Buckhaven. Just as her ladyship was saying: "Then we are decided, are we not, love, on the sea-green, and the Berlin silk with the floss trimming? And the Merino pelisse, with the round cape?" she turned her head towards Madame, and said in a voice of strong resolution: "What, if you please, is the price of this dress I have on?"

Madame, unaware of Lady Buckhaven's frantic attempt to catch her eye, told her. The make-believe world collapsed in ruins; one last glance Kitty allowed herself at the mirrored vision of a modish young lady in rose-pink gauze; then she turned away, and said, with a quivering lip: "I am afraid it is too dear."

Madame, looking towards Lady Buckhaven too late, realized that she had vexed one of her more valued patronesses, read the message in those dagger-darting blue eyes, and exerted herself to make a recover. Gently turning Miss Charing to face the mirror again, she pointed out to her the many excellencies of the gown, and in a spate of volubility contrived to say that it was more economical to purchase one expensive dress than three cheaper ones, that the sight of mademoiselle in such a toilette must infallibly strike the beholder like a *coup de foudre*, that she believed she had confused its price with that of the cerulean blue satin which had not become mademoiselle, and, finally, that to oblige so good a customer as miladi she would make a reduction.

Kitty allowed herself to be persuaded. Though she must rigorously curtail further expenditure, she could not bring herself to spare one person at least this clap of thunder. If she went in rags for the rest of her days, Mr Westruther should see this lovely vision in rose-pink, and know what he had allowed to slip through his careless, cruel fingers.

And after that it seemed as though perhaps she

could afford to buy the sea-green walking dress, and the Merino pelisse to wear over it – neither as expensive as she had feared they must be. But she retained enough sanity to shake her head when it was pointed out to her that she would bitterly regret it if she neglected to buy a half-dress of Italian crape.

"Kitty," said Lady Buckhaven, struck by a brilliant idea, "if you do not mean to buy it, I will, because it is just what will suit me! Only I thought perhaps I ought not, because only last week I purchased one in bronze-green, which Mama says is a colour I should never wear, so of course I shan't, because no one knows better than Mama what truly becomes one. But I have just had the most famous notion! I will give you the bronze-green, and buy this one for myself, and that will make everything right!"

In this very reasonable way the problem was solved to everyone's satisfaction; Madame promised to deliver the hand-boxes in Berkeley Square that very day; and the ladies, each feeling that she had practiced a piece of clever economy, sallied forth to visit a series of milliners and haberdashers: Kitty, who had been thinking deeply, astonished her hostess by saying that if she might be put in the way of visiting a linen-draper she would buy such materials as she liked, and contrive to make herself gowns in imitation of what she had seen at Fanchon's. Like any other young lady of gentle breeding, Meg could embroider prettily, and had even been known to hem a seam, but the idea of making gowns for herself had never so much as occurred to her. When she learned that Kitty had been in the habit of doing so for years she began to think that life at Arnside must be bleak indeed, and in a rush of warm-heartedness said: "Well, you shan't do so in my house, you poor thing! Mallow – my dresser, you know! – shall find a sewing-woman to do it for you. The cost will be trifling – I know, because Mama employs one to make up dresses for Caroline and Fanny. Good gracious, she would be the very person! I will dash off a note to her directly we return home! Should you like to drive immediately to a linen-draper's, or are you tired? There is Layton and Shear's, or Newton's, in Leicester Square, which I believe is tolerably good. Or stay! Let us go to Grafton House! Emily Calderbeck told me that you would scarcely credit the things one may purchase there for the merest song! Poor creature, she is forced to embrace the most shocking expediencies, for Calderbeck, you know, is run quite off his legs! And the miserable thing is that *he* sets it down to Emily's want of management and economy, when all the town knows he has lost *thousands* at play! I must own that I am glad Buckhaven is not a gamester. Only think how uncomfortable it would be never to know whether you were rich, or ruined! I tell Jack that if ever he is married I shall pity his wife – just rallying him, you know!"

"Is Jack a gamester?" asked Kitty. "I – I didn't know! That is – Freddy said so, but—"

"Oh, yes! I don't mean to say that he is for ever in some horrid hell, like Calderbeck, but he plays at Watier's, where the stakes are shockingly high; and he bets on all the races – in fact, he is what Freddy calls a Go amongst the Goers! Shall we tell my coachman to drive to Grafton House?"

"Oh, yes, please – if you should not dislike it!" Kitty waited until the order had been given, and then said, in a disinterested voice: "Is Jack in London? I have not set eyes on him this age!"

"Of course, you must know him better than you know any of us," said Meg. "He is for ever visiting my great-uncle, isn't he? Do you like him? I hope you may, for he is often in Berkeley Square. Only pray don't say so to Mama! She would not like it above half, because he has *such* a shocking reputation! It is all nonsense, of course, and Buckhaven makes no objection. Naturally one knows where to draw the line, and, besides, it is perfectly proper to have one's cousin to visit one!"

Miss Charing was still digesting this when the barouche drew up outside Grafton House.

It had been one of Meg's schoolday amusements to visit the Pantheon Bazaar, under the careful chaperonage of her governess, and to spend her weekly pin-money in that astonishing mart; but ladies of high fashion did not commonly do their shopping at Grafton House, and she had never before entered its portals. She was inclined to be suspicious of an emporium patronized by such unfortunates as poor Emily Calderbeck, but after a very few minutes spent in looking at the wares for sale in the building she succumbed to the eternal feminine passion for Bargains, and became quite as enthusiastic as Kitty over silk stockings at only twelve shillings the pair, muslins at three shillings and sixpence the yard, and really elegant bugle trimming at the ridiculously low figure of two shillings and fourpence.

The only drawback to the shop was its popularity: it was crowded, customers being obliged to wait at the various counters for as much, sometimes, as twenty minutes before receiving attention. An overheard interchange between two women desirous of buying black sarsenet informed Lady Buckhaven and Miss Charing that more knowledgeable persons made a point of visiting Grafton House before breakfast; by eleven o'clock, it appeared, the emporium was always as full as it could hold.

"Shall we do that?" Meg whispered. "Only I don't think I could! Perhaps we had better stay, now we *are* here! My dear, look! Irish poplin, at six shillings the yard! Not that I should want poplin, but still—!"

It was while they were awaiting their turn to be served at one of the counters that Kitty's eyes alighted on the most beautiful girl she had ever seen. She could not help staring, for such gleaming golden ringlets, such deep blue eyes, so exquisite a complexion seemed to belong rather to a fairy-tale than to a stuffy and overcrowded shop. The child – for she did not look to be much more – was very elegantly dressed, in a swansdown-trimmed bonnet and pelisse of blue velvet that almost exactly matched her big eyes. From the wide, upstanding brim of her bonnet to the heels of her velvet half-boots all was perfection, except her expression. This was disconsolate, even a little scared. A stylishly gowned woman, who was turning over a pile of muslins on the counter, spoke to her, and, when she did not hear, spoke again, sharply, causing her to give a nervous start.

"For heaven's sake, Olivia, can you not pay attention?" the elder woman said, in a scolding tone. "How many times am I to tell you that these dawdling and languid airs of yours will not do? I am sure I may wear myself out, buying dresses for you, for anything you care, or any thanks I may get for it! Nothing is so disagreeable in a girl as that stupid sort of indifference, and so you will find!"

The girl flushed, and murmured something Kitty could not hear. She bent over the muslins, but apparently the choice she would have made did not suit her companion's notions, for Kitty heard the sharp voice say: "Nonsense – quite unsuitable! You have not the least notion! You put me out of all patience with you!"

The girl stepped back again, and making room for a stout matron to pass, brushed against Kitty. She looked round, begging pardon, in a shy, childish voice, and Kitty said at once: "It is dreadfully crowded, isn't it? Is it always so?"

"Oh, yes!" sighed the girl. "And Bedford House is worse!"

"I haven't been there. This is my first visit to London. Do you live here?"

"Yes – no! I mean, we used not to do so. I am just out, you see, so Mama has brought me to town."

"Why, it is the same – almost – in my own case! I have been shopping all the morning, and my head is in a whirl. It is all so big, and there is so much to see!"

"Do you dislike shopping?" asked the girl sympathetically.

"Gracious, no! I never enjoyed myself so much in my life, I think! Do you dislike it?"

"I liked it at first – having pretty dresses, and hats – but it is so tiring, standing still for hours, while they pin things round me! And being scolded for fidgeting, or tearing a flounce, or letting my best hat be spoilt in the rain."

The older woman, hearing her voice, had turned her head, and was keenly scrutinizing Kitty, in an appraising way which made Kitty feel that the cost of her clothing was being assessed to a halfpenny. She summoned the girl back to her side, but just at that moment Meg, who had been inspecting some Indian muslin handkerchiefs, looked round, and said: "My dear Kitty, do you think these pretty? Only three shillings and sixpence each! I have a very good mind to buy some."

The stylish woman stared very hard at her for an instant, and then, suddenly smiling with the utmost affability, spoke to the fair beauty in quite another voice, saying: "I did not perceive that you were engaged, my love! I only wished you to say whether you like this sprig-muslin." She then bestowed the smile upon Kitty, and added archly: "Has my daughter been telling you that she thinks shopping a dead bore? Such a naughty puss as she is, aren't you, pet?"

She glanced at Meg, as she spoke. Meg was looking inquiringly from Olivia to Kitty, and was considerably taken aback to find herself suddenly addressed.

"Good gracious! Lady Buckhaven, is it not? How do you do? I dare not hope that your ladyship recollects! – Mrs Broughty – I had the honor of meeting you at – lord, I shall forget my own name next, I daresay! I fancy you are acquainted with my cousin, Lady Batterstown. Dear Albinia! the sweetest creature! Your ladyship must allow me to present my daughter!"

This was uttered with such a gush of friendliness that Meg, not quite so well experienced in the ways of the world as she thought herself, was rather overwhelmed. She was certainly acquainted with Lady Batterstown, but she felt sure that she had never before encountered Mrs Broughty. But although she felt that Lady Legerwood, easy-going though she was, would unhesitatingly have depressed Mrs Broughty's pretensions, she found herself to be quite unable to do so. It seemed, moreover, that Kitty was acquainted with Miss Broughty: she had certainly been chatting to her, and it appeared that she regarded her with approval.

Mrs Broughty, voluble, and wonderfully assured, was talking of Kitty as though she knew her well, dextrously coupling her with Olivia, rallying both girls on their lack of interest in humdrum shopping, and saying that they must not be allowed to chatter to one another now, but might perhaps meet one day soon. She contrived to tell Meg that she was staying in Hans Crescent — quite out of the world, dear Lady Buckhaven would say! — and even to extort from Meg, stunned by this ruthless eloquence, the expression of a hope that they might become better acquainted. By this time her parcel had been made up, and she was obliged to move away from the counter. While she was taking leave of Meg, at much greater length than the circumstances warranted, Olivia, who had been standing all the time with downcast eyes, and heightened color, glanced fleetingly into Kitty's face, and said in a low, unhappy voice: "Pray, forgive—! I mean – I daresay we shan't meet again! I should not wish—"

Kitty interrupted impulsively: "Indeed, I hope we may!"

Miss Broughty clasped her hand gratefully. "Thank you! You are very good! I wish very much—You see, I have not any friends in London! Not *female* friends! Oh, Mama is waiting for me! I must go! Goodbye! – so happy to—!"

The sentence was left in mid-air; a tiny curtsy was dropped to Meg; and Olivia followed her mother towards the door.

"Well!" said Meg. "Kitty, who in the world are they? How do you come to know them?"

"But I don't!" Kitty replied. "I fell into conversation with Miss Broughty, but it was the merest nothing!"

"Good God, I thought they must be friends of

yours! Odious, pushing woman! I wish I had given her
a setdown! Depend upon it, if I see her again she will
claim me as a friend of long standing! I can't conceive
how Lady Batterstown comes to have such a vulgar
cousin, and I am positive she never introduced her to
me."

"Oh, dear, I am very sorry if I have got you into a
scrape!" Kitty said penitently. "But I felt so much pity
for Miss Broughty – I had been watching her, you
know, thinking how beautiful she was, and that horrid
woman spoke to her in *such* a way, and she looked
frightened, and unhappy! And then I could see she
was so much mortified by her mother's manners that
I could not but assure her that I should be happy to
meet her again. Meg, did you ever behold a lovelier
girl? She was like a fairy princess!"

"I suppose she was very pretty," acknowledged
Meg. "*If* her hair is naturally that color, which Mrs
Broughty's is *not!*"

Kitty could not allow the color of Miss Broughty's
hair to be called in question, and was about to defend
it when the assistant behind the counter providentially
intervened, desiring to be told Meg's pleasure. The
Broughtys were forgotten in the more absorbing business of deciding between a figured and a checked muslin.

Both ladies were considerably fatigued by the time
they reached Berkeley Square, but there were so many
parcels and bandboxes piled on the seat before them
that it was to be supposed that their labors had been
successful. The footman carried them all into the
house; and if Skelton, the austere butler, was surprised at his mistress's returning to her home with
bandboxes bearing the name of a far from modish

shop on their lids he was much too well trained to betray it.

The Buckhaven mansion was a large one, and furnished with a mixture of old and new taste, Meg having been unable, so far, to persuade her lord to replace all the antiquated chairs and tables which her predecessors had acquired. She conducted Kitty at once to a comfortable bedchamber, where a fire burned brightly in a modern grate, and a sofa, drawn up before it, invited repose. Someone had unpacked Kitty's trunk, and had laid out her dressing-gown. Meg recommended her to lie down upon the sofa for an hour, begged her to ring the bell if she desired anything to be brought to her, and tripped away to rest on her bed, in accordance, she told Kitty, with her doctor's advice.

Remembering that she was in a delicate situation, Kitty hoped very much that the day's shopping had not dangerously exhausted her. She herself was quite tired out, and had no sooner leaned her head back against the sofa cushions than she fell asleep. She awoke to a room lit only by the glow from the fire, and started up, wondering for how long she had been asleep. A knock on the door was followed by the cautious entrance of her hostess, who exclaimed in the voice of one by no means exhausted: "Oh, you have not rung for candles! Were you asleep? Did I wake you? I beg your pardon, but pray come to my dressing-room, Kitty! Mallow is there, and we have been looking out some things which I *never* wear, and perhaps you might like! You won't be offended? We shall be sisters, you know, and how stupid to stand upon ceremony! Do come!"

Kitty could only thank her, and be glad that there

was not light enough in the room for Meg to perceive her blushes. Almost she wished that the Standens had repulsed her, rather than have sunk her so deep in conscious guilt by their kindness. But the complications attaching to a belated confession were too numerous to be faced; lingering only long enough to allow her cheeks to cool, she followed Meg down one pair of stairs to her dressing-room. And here she found so many elegant things laid out for her inspection that she could scarcely be blamed for forgetting that she was an impostor. Meg's dresser, a middle-aged woman who had for many years been employed in the Standen family, knew all about Mr Penicuik, and so saw nothing remarkable, or worthy of her contempt, in Miss Charing's straitened circumstances. A little to Meg's surprise, she had thrown herself heart and soul into the task of deciding which of her mistress's gowns, and hats, and shawls could best be spared from her overflowing wardrobe. The modish Lady Buckhaven was not to know that her dresser, deep in Lady Legerwood's confidence, was at her wits' end to know how to restrain her dashing but inexperienced employer from appearing in public in garments which, however fashionable they might be, were quite unsuited to her fair prettiness. One glance at Miss Charing was enough to assure her that the greens and the ambers and the rich reds which Lady Buckhaven had so recklessly bought would admirably become this dark damsel. In her anxiety to be rid of garments the wearing of which by Meg would surely draw down upon her dresser's head reproaches from Lady Legerwood, she even offered to make such slight alterations as might be necessary to adapt them to Miss Charing's fuller figure. When Miss Charing shrank from accepting an opulent evening cloak of cherry-red velvet, ruched and braided, and lined with satin, she contrived to draw her a little aside, and to whisper in her ear: "Take it, miss! My lady – Lady Legerwood, I mean! – will be so very much obliged to you! Miss Margaret – Lady Buckhaven, I *should* say! – should *never* wear cherry!"

Kitty, who had a very fair eye for color, was obliged to acknowledge the justice of this. In the end, she returned to her own chamber, to dress for dinner, the dazed possessor of a costly evening cloak, a bronze-green half-dress, an amber robe of satin and lace, a round dress of lilac cambric, a bunch of curled ostrich plumes, dyed gold, and several scarves, reticules, and tippets.

On the following day, Meg's own hairdresser came to Berkeley Square, and, much hindered by the conflicting instructions of Lady Buckhaven and Miss Mallow, achieved a style for the hapless Miss Charing which succeeded in satisfying all parties. Miss Charing, staring wide-eyed into the mirror, saw reflected therein a stranger: a beautiful brunette, whose dusky curls, twisted into a knot on the top of her head, were allowed, at the sides, to fall on either side of her face in carefully careless ringlets. Meg being engaged with a party of friends, the rest of the day was spent by Miss Charing in judicious shopping, under the aegis of Miss Mallow. A large hole was dug into the fifty-pound bill handed to her by Freddy, but she felt that the money had been well spent, and was able to present herself that evening in Meg's drawing-room complete to a shade in the bronze-green robe bestowed upon her by her hostess, slippers of Denmark satin on her feet, a reticule of embroidered silk dangling from one wrist,

Lady Legerwood's handsome shawl draped negligently over her elbows, and the whole set off by the topaz set which, with a short necklet of pearls, were the only trinkets she had inherited from her French mother. Mr Penicuik, at the last moment, had disclosed the existence of these gauds, and had bestowed them upon her, bidding her to take care not to lose them. She had shown them to Meg that very morning, with the result that when her betrothed arrived in Berkeley Square to dine with the two ladies he brought with him a neat package from Jeffrey's jeweler to his Royal Highness the Prince Regent, which, when opened, revealed a very pretty pair of pearl earrings.

("If you were wondering what to give Kitty as an engagement present, Freddy, I can tell you what she chiefly needs!" had said Meg, encountering her brother in Bond Street, and unwittingly putting him in mind of his obligations.)

"Oh, Freddy!" gasped Miss Charing, gazing in mingled dismay and delight at these treasures. "Oh, no, no, no!"

"Kitty, how absurd you are!" Meg exclaimed, much entertained. "As though Freddy would not give you a present to commemorate your betrothal! It is such a pity that the circumstance of your not yet announcing it should make it ineligible for him to give you a ring! What do you mean to choose for her, Freddy? Diamonds, I suppose."

"You must not! *Indeed* you must not!" Kitty said earnestly, her countenance becomingly flushed.

"No, really, Kit!" protested Mr Standen, equally embarrassed. "The veriest trumpery! Assure you!"

He then turned to his sister, revolted by her suggestion that he was so lacking in taste as to choose an insipid diamond for a lady who should clearly be decked in rubies or emeralds. By the time the rival merits of these two stones had been argued out, Skelton had announced that dinner awaited her ladyship, and Kitty seized the opportunity afforded by Meg's leading the way to the dining-room to whisper agitatedly into Freddy's ear: "When it is at an end I shall give them back to you!"

"Good God, no!" Freddy said, shocked. "They ain't heirlooms, Kit! Sort of things anyone might give you!"

She was unable to accept this, but there was no time to say more: they had reached the dining-room, and Meg, as she took her seat at the table, was explaining that she had invited no guests because she believed that the engaged couple would prefer to be alone.

"Eh?" said Freddy. "Oh! Just so! Got something to say, now I come to think of it. Important."

He was naturally pressed to continue, but he only shook his head, looking so portentous that Kitty was alarmed, imagining various disasters, from a recall to Arnside to the loss of that precious roll of bills. However, when they went back to the drawing-room, Freddy explained himself, saying apologetically: "No sense in puffing off the business to the servants. Looked in at Almack's last night. Put me in mind of it. Can you dance, Kit?"

"Only country dances," Kitty replied anxiously. "Fish taught me the steps, but she does not know the waltz or the quadrille, of course."

Freddy nodded at his sister. "Caper-merchant," he said. "Thought as much!"

"Do you mean that she must hire a dancing-master?" demanded Meg. "Well, I think it is a great piece of nonsense, besides being a waste of time, for you know how much engaged M. Dupont always is at this season! Depend upon it, Kitty would be obliged to wait for days and days before he could find the time to come to her. Why don't you teach her yourself? For this I will say, Freddy! — however stupid you may be, you are by far the best dancer in London! And that, let me tell you, is what Lady Jersey says!"

"Does she, though?" said Freddy, moved by this tribute. "By Jove!" Doubt shook him. "Yes, but I couldn't teach Kit! Dash it all!"

"Oh, Freddy, please do!" begged Kitty, by no means anxious to spend any of her fast-dwindling substance on the services of a dancing-master.

"He *shall* do so!" declared Meg. "He shall teach you the waltz this very evening!"

The unfortunate Mr Standen protested in vain: he was no match for two determined females. Chairs and tables were thrust against the wall; and when, in a last, despairing effort to save himself, he pleaded that although he could do the thing he was dashed if he could explain it, Meg jumped up from the piano-stool, and very obligingly said that she would do it with him, so that Kitty might learn by observation. As Kitty could hardly be expected to watch the steps and to play the piano at the same time, Meg provided the necessary music by humming one of her favorite waltz airs, a performance which so lacerated the sensitive Mr Standen's nerves that he very soon declared that anything was better than to have such a devilish noise in his ear, and offered to give his betrothed a turn. Since Kitty had a natural aptitude, and Meg was able to come to the rescue when his verbal instructions became too incoherent to do more than bewilder his pupil, the lesson was very successful. In a remarkably short space of time, Freddy decided that she was sufficiently advanced to put his tuition into practice. He bade his sister play one of his favorite airs, took Miss Charing in his arm, and made her dance round the room with him. She was at first so much embarrassed that she made a great many false steps, for to stand so close to a man, and to feel his arm about her waist, positively constraining her to move in whatever direction he wished, was an unprecedented and rather alarming experience, and one, moreover, which she knew would have been violently disapproved of by her guardian and her governess. She kept her eyes shyly lowered, and could not help blushing a little. But as there was nothing in the least amorous in Freddy's light, firm clasp, and such remarks as he addressed to her were of an admonitory nature, she soon recovered her countenance, began to move with much more assurance, and even, presently, dared to raise her eyes.

"You know what?" Freddy said, when at last he released her. "You ain't a bad dancer at all, Kit. Dashed if I don't think you'll shine 'em all down!"

"Oh!" cried Kitty, a little out of breath, but triumphant. Do you think so indeed, Freddy?"

"Shouldn't be at all surprised. What I mean is, when you've rid yourself of this devilish trick you have of treading on me every now and then."

"You are a great deal too severe, Freddy!" said Meg, beginning to put the chairs back into their places. "She dances very gracefully! I am sure I should never have guessed she had never waltzed before!"

Freddy shook his head. "Would if you'd been dancing with her," he said simply.

"Well!" exclaimed Meg. "What an odious thing to

say! And you have been engaged to her only for three days!"

"Keep forgetting!" murmured Freddy, with a conscience-stricken glance at Miss Charing.

Thinking that she could not have heard aright, Meg was just about to ask him to repeat his remark when the door was opened, and Skelton ushered Mr Westruther into the room.

❧ *Chapter IX* ❧

LADY BUCKHAVEN GREETED THIS LATE-COMING visitor with unaffected pleasure. Mr Westruther, raising her hand to his lips, said: "My dear Meg, I can't express to you my delight at finding you at home – or my surprise! No sudden indisposition, I do trust!" He released her hand, and glanced, in his mocking way, at her companions.

It would have been too much to have said that he did not recognize Miss Charing in her elegant apparel, but she had the satisfaction of knowing that he was certainly surprised. His brows went up; he stood looking keenly at her for several moments before he spoke; and then he crossed the room towards her, and said laughingly: "Accept my sincerest felicitations, Kitty! Upon my word, I had almost made my most formal bow to my cousin's unknown, fashionable guest! What a fortunate dog you are, Freddy! Really, I can't feel that I congratulated you sufficiently!"

Freddy, who had regarded his entrance with marked

disfavour, said: "Well, it don't signify. Devilish queer times you choose to go paying visits!"

"Don't I?" agreed Mr Westruther, possessing himself of Kitty's hands, and holding them so that he could look her up and down. "Charming, Kitty! You are as fine as five-pence! Were you guided by Freddy's exquisite taste, or is this new touch all of your own devising?"

The bantering tone filled Miss Charing with a strong desire to slap him. Repressing so ungenteel an impulse, she replied affably: "Do you think I look well? I am so glad, but you should rather compliment Meg than Freddy."

"Then I do compliment Meg," he said, letting go her hands, and turning towards Lady Buckhaven. "Here you are, my little gamester! You came off all right."

She took the slim packet he held out to her, and gave a delighted crow of triumph. "I knew it must win! I am very much obliged to you! Have I ruined you quite?"

"Oh, run me off my legs! I must be rolled-up, or put a pistol to my head: I can't decide which fate to choose."

She laughed. "How sorry I am! Freddy, only fancy! There was a horse running today called Mandarin! And Jack laid me odds it would not win! So absurd of him, for how could it help but win, with my dear Buckhaven on his way to China?"

Freddy, who was inclined to view her sudden interest in the Turf with disapprobation, was just about to state his opinion in a few simple, brotherly words when he was interrupted by Miss Charing, who said, with a great deal of vivacity: "Oh, Jack, I must show you what Freddy has given me! See! Are they not pretty? The very ornaments above all others I so much wished for!"

Mr Westruther put up his glass to look at the earrings. Nothing could have been blander than the tone he used to express his admiration of the trinkets, but Kitty was quick to perceive a flicker of surprise in his eyes, and was satisfied that whatever suspicions he might nourish she had at least puzzled him.

The tea-tray was brought in just then. Meg pressed Mr Westruther to stay long enough to drink a cup with them, and Mr Westruther, at his most provoking, said: "Do you think I dare? I have the oddest feeling that Freddy wishes me to go away. I had no notion of his being so strict a brother! My dear coz, I do trust that the queer times I choose for paying visits have not misled you into thinking that my intentions are dishonourable?"

"Good gracious!" cried Miss Charing, much diverted. "As though he could be so stupid! I am persuaded you might visit at any hour you pleased, and the only thing anyone would say is, *Oh, it is only Jack!*"

She then wished that she had held her tongue, for Mr Westruther smiled approvingly at her, and said: "Well done, Kitty!"

He then proceeded, to her discomfiture, to inquire when he must set about the task of buying his wedding-gift, and, when she told him that the date of the ceremony was not yet decided, said: "Ah, exactly so! I was forgetting! The engagement is not immediately to be announced, is it? I wish you will tell me why you are keeping it a secret! I have been racking my brain to hit upon the reason, without the smallest success!"

Mr Standen, somewhat to Kitty's surprise, came un-
expectedly to the rescue. "Measles," he said.
"M'mother means to give a dress party for Kit. Can't
do it now. Better to wait a few weeks."

"Of course!" said Mr Westruther. "How could I be
so bird-witted? And where do you mean to spend the
honeymoon?"

"We – we have not made up our minds!" said Kitty.

"Yes, we have," interpolated Freddy. "Going to
Paris." He thought for a moment, and added: "Kit
wishes to meet her French relations."

"My dear Kitty, why did you not tell me so?" said
Mr Westruther, quite shocked. "Had I had the least
suspicion of this very natural desire—! But it is not too
late, I believe, to rectify my omissions! I have reason
to think that *one* of your French relations is even now
in London. Let me assure you that I shall lose no time
in bringing him to visit you! You will like him excessively – a man of the first rank and character, I am persuaded! Dearest Meg, I must tear myself away from
you – positively I must! Past ten o'clock, and I pledged
to present myself at the Rockcliffes' not an instant
later than half past nine! I must obviously make haste,
or I shall be guilty of unpunctuality. I kiss your hands,
my charmer, and Kitty's cheek. Oh, you have no occasion to blush, absurd child! Recollect that I was your
first love – in your nursery days, of course, so Freddy
must not take umbrage!"

Her color was indeed heightened, but she said,
stammering a little: "Yes, indeed you w-were, but
Freddy won't take umbrage at *that,* for you are precisely a schoolgirl's notion of what a romantic hero
should be, Jack!"

The laughter was back in his eyes. "A doubler!" he said.

Her own gaze fell; she said hurriedly: "But tell me! Who is this relation of mine, pray?"

"The Chevalier d'Evron. Rely upon me to make him known to you!"

A friendly nod to Freddy, and he was gone. Kitty said doubtfully: "Who can it be? I never heard of such a person, you know!"

"If you ask me," said Freddy, in a mood of dark skepticism, "it's a hum! Playing off his tricks, that's what *I* thought!"

"Why, whatever can you mean?" cried Meg. "He said the Chevalier was a man of the first rank and character!"

"Heard him," replied Freddy. "Might not have thought it was a bubble, if he hadn't said that. Dashed smoky, that's what it is! I know Jack! If this Chevalier of his is one of Kit's relations, willing to lay you a monkey he turns out to be a dirty dish!" He saw that he had alarmed and slightly offended Miss Charing, and added kindly: "No need to take a pet! Very likely thing to happen! Everyone has 'em in the family. *We* have. Well, you ask Meg if it ain't so!"

"Yes, very true!" corroborated his sister. "And they always arrive, without the least warning, to spend a long visit just when one is giving a *ton* party!"

"Under a cloud, and telling you there's an execution in the house," nodded Freddy.

"Oh, you are thinking of Alfred Standen, and poor Papa having to pay all his debts! But what is *much* worse, Freddy, is people like Cousin Maria, really *delighting* in being shabby-genteel! But there is not the

least reason to suppose that the Chevalier is not perfectly respectable!"

"Lay you a monkey he ain't," repeated Freddy obsti-
nately.

Neither lady accepted the wager, which, in the
event, was a fortunate circumstance for him. Nothing
was seen in Berkeley Square of Mr Westruther during
the succeeding two days, a defection on his part which
would have troubled Miss Charing much more had she
not been so sunk in dissipation as scarcely to notice
it. Lady Buckhaven might say that London in March
was as dull as could be, but in Miss Charing's eyes all
was wonderful, from Carlton House to an itinerant
vendor of hot pies. She was determined to see all the
sights, and to Mr Standen fell the task of escorting her
on an extensive and exhausting tour of the town. His
dismay at learning what was expected of him held him
speechless for a full minute, a space of time occupied
by Miss Charing in reciting a list of the historic edifices
she wished to see which made his eyes start from his
head with horror. He managed to utter an inarticulate
protest which made her pause and look inquiringly at
him. "No, dash it, Kit!" he said. "You can't think I'm
going to totter all over London looking at a lot of
buildings I don't want to see! Very happy to take you
driving in the Park, but that's coming it too strong, my
dear girl!"

Her face fell. "Meg thought you would take me,"
she faltered. "She says there can be no objection."

"Oh, she does, does she?" said Freddy, justly incensed. "Well, if that's what she thinks why don't she
take you herself? Tell me that!"

"But, Freddy, indeed, I think she should not, in her
situation! Might she not find it too fatiguing?"

"I should rather think she would! Anyone would!" said Freddy. "For the lord's sake, Kit, don't make such a goose of yourself! You'd be knocked into horse-nails!"

"No, no, I am persuaded I should not!"

"Well, I should!" said Freddy bluntly. "Besides, I don't know anything about these curst places you want to see! Couldn't tell you anything about 'em!"

"Oh, but that need not signify! Look, I purchased this book in Hatchard's shop this morning, and it tells one *everything!* It is called *The Picture of London,* and it says here that it is a correct guide to all the Curiosities, Amusements, Exhibitions, Public Establishments, and Remarkable Objects in and near London, made for the use of Strangers, Foreigners, and all Persons who are not intimately acquainted with the Metropolis!"

Freddy regarded the fat little volume with an eye of fascinated abhorrence. "Kit!" he ejaculated. "No, really, Kit! Not yourself! Can't be! Nice pair of flats we should look, going all over town with a dashed guide book!"

She looked wistfully at him. "Would you dislike it so very much? I won't tease you – only I have longed all my life to see St Paul's, and Westminster Abbey, and the Waxworks, and the Guildhall, and London Bridge, and the Tower, and perhaps I may never have the opportunity again!" Her voice broke on an unmistakable sob, but she swallowed resolutely, and laid the guide book aside, saying, with an uncertain smile: "I won't think of it any more, I promise you! I wouldn't have mentioned it if I had had the least notion it would be disagreeable to you, for *indeed,* Freddy, I am not unmindful of how *deep* I am in your debt!"

"Now, my dear girl!" expostulated Freddy. "Kit, for the lord's sake—! Oh, very well!"

A radiant face was turned towards him. "You will, Freddy!" Miss Charing cried joyfully. "You *will* take me? Oh, Freddy, how very good you are! I can never be sufficiently obliged to you!"

So Miss Charing, squired by Mr Standen, and armed with the *Picture of London* (Price Five Shillings, Bound in Red), set forth on a tour of the Metropolis in Lady Legerwood's town carriage, borrowed for the occasion by Mr Standen, who doubted his ability to discover the locality of the various places of interest his betrothed was desirous of visiting, and so, with rare acumen, decided to entrust this task to his mother's coachman rather than to attempt to find the way in his own natty tilbury.

Their first port of call was naturally Westminster Abbey. Had Mr Standen had his way, it would also have been their last. Fresh as paint, and full of enthusiasm, Miss Charing was determined to miss nothing, even dragging Freddy to the twelve chapels, where an attendant verger took them in charge, and imparted a great deal of information to them in a way that caused Freddy to whisper in Miss Charing's ear that he couldn't stand much more of this sort of thing, because it made him feel he was back at Eton. He conducted himself very creditably at Shakespeare's grave, saying that at all events he knew who *he* was, and adding a further touch of erudition by telling Kitty an interesting anecdote of having escorted his mother to the theater once to see Kean in *Hamlet,* and of having dreamt, during this memorable performance, that he walked smash into a fellow he hadn't set eyes on for years. "And, by Jove, that's just what I did do, the very next day!" he said. "Not that I wanted to, mind you, but there it was!" He admitted that he was glad to have seen the Coronation Chair; but the dilapidated effigies in the Henry the Seventh Chapel, in particular the ghoulish countenance of Queen Elizabeth, proved to be his breaking-point. He said that he had never seen such a set of rum touches in his life, and represented to Miss Charing in the strongest terms that another five minutes spent in the Chapel would make them both feel as blue as megrim. Miss Charing agreed that the effigies were horrid, and said she believed that Mme Tussaud's figures were superior. But when they reached the Hanover Square Rooms, where Miss Fishguard had once seen this famous collection, the luck favored Freddy: Mme Tussaud's exhibition had been removed to Blackheath years ago, and was now thought to be touring the country. Kitty was disappointed, but she bore up well, saying that they would instead visit the British Museum. However, reference to the *Picture of London* presented her with a piece of quelling information. "Spectators," stated this invaluable handbook, "are allowed three hours for visiting the whole, one hour for each of the three departments."

"Do you mean to tell me that if we go inside the place we shall have to stay for *three hours?*" demanded Freddy. "Why, I daresay we could do the thing in three minutes! What have we got to see there?"

"Well," said Kitty, in a daunted voice, "I must say it doesn't sound very interesting! The book says that there is one department devoted to Manuscripts and Medals, and one to Natural and Artificial Products, and the third is Printed Books."

"You don't mean it!" Freddy ejaculated. "The

thing's a dashed take-in! A pretty set of bubble-merchants they must be, the fellows that look after that place! I'll tell you what, Kit: it's a fortunate thing you brought that book! Why, if we hadn't had it we should have been done brown as a pair of berries! Wonder if m'father knows about it?"

"Well, I don't think we need visit it," said Kitty. She flicked over the pages of the guide book, but suddenly bethought her of her hostess's parting admonition. "Oh, Meg said I must go to see the marbles which Lord Elgin brought from Greece! She says *everyone* has seen them! They are at Burlington House, she told me."

Freddy said severely that it was a pity she had not remembered the marbles before they came to Hanover Square, but he gave the direction to the coachman, and confided, as the carriage wended its way southward again, that he would not object to taking a look at them. "Deuce of a dust kicked up about 'em!" he said. "Seem to be all the crack, though."

But when, having, as he put it, dropped the blunt for two tickets of admission and a catalogue, he confronted these treasures of ancient Greece, he was quite dumbfounded, and only recovered his voice when he was called upon to admire the Three Fates, from the eastern pediment. "Dash it, they've got no heads!" he protested.

"No, but, you see, Freddy, they are so very old! They have been damaged!" explained Miss Charing.

"Damaged! I should rather think so! They haven't got any arms either! Well, if this don't beat the Dutch! And just look at this, Kit!"

"*Birth of Athene from the brain of Zeus,*" said Kitty, consulting the catalog.

"Birth of Athene from *what?*"

"The *central* groups, which are the most important features of the composition, are missing," said Kitty, in propitiating accents. "And the catalog says that the metopes are *not* in good preservation either, so perhaps we should just study the frieze, which is excessively beautiful!"

But the disclosure that he had been maced of his blunt by a set of persons whom he freely characterized as hell-kites only to see a collection of marbles of which the main parts were missing so worked upon him that he could not be brought to recognize the merits of the frieze, but seemed instead to be so much inclined to seek out the author of this attempt to gull the public that Kitty hastily announced her wish to visit St Paul's Cathedral, and coaxed him out of the building.

During the drive to the City, Kitty diligently studied her handbook. She was conscious of a slight feeling of fatigue, so when she discovered that the guide thought poorly of the interior of St Paul's, likening it, in fact, to a vast vault, she fell in with Freddy's suggestion that they should content themselves with a view of the exterior. After this, she thought, they ought to drive to Cornhill, to look at the Bank of England, and the Royal Exchange. But here again the *Picture of London* came to Freddy's rescue. "It is unnecessary to describe minutely such architecture as that of the Royal Exchange," stated the guide austerely. "It is of a mixed kind, in bad taste."

"Well, there's no sense in going to look at that!" said Freddy, relieved. "What's it say about the Bank of England?"

" 'One of the wonders of commerce; and one of the abortions of art,' " read out Miss Charing.

"Is it, though? Well, that settles it! We needn't go to Cornhill at all. You know, Kit, that's a dashed good book! We can go home now!"

"Yes, for we should scarcely have time to visit the Tower, I suppose," agreed Kitty. "Only do you think we should see some of the prisons?"

"See the prisons?" exclaimed Freddy. "Why?"

"Well, I don't precisely know, but the book says that 'no stranger who visits London should omit to view these mansions of misery'."

But Freddy decided that they had had enough misery for one day, and bade the coachmen drive back to Berkeley Square, reminding Miss Charing, when she suggested that they ought, perhaps, to pause at the Temple on the way, that since she was accompanying Meg to an informal party that evening it would not do for her to be late in returning home. She agreed to this, consoling herself with the reflection that the Temple might easily be visited on their way to the Tower on the morrow.

Freddy groaned, but attempted no remonstrance. Any hope that he might have cherished that Miss Charing would be too weary to embark upon a second voyage of exploration was slain by her appearance on the following morning, dressed in a very smart habit, and obviously in fine fettle. She took her place beside him in the carriage, drew the *Picture of London* from her muff, and proved to him, by reading aloud from this book, that it clearly behoved her to see the Guildhall on the way to the Tower. This ordeal behind them, the rest of the day was spent more agreeably than Freddy had expected. He would not have chosen to waste his time in such a fashion, and he could only deprecate Miss Charing's determination to omit no corner of the various buildings from her tour; but he was pleasantly surprised to find that the Tower housed a fine collection of wild beasts; and he was even roused to real interest in the Mint, where they were allowed to watch the stamping of various coins. A tendency on Miss Charing's part to brood over the sufferings of such former visitors to the Tower as Lady Jane Gray and Sir Walter Raleigh he quelled, saying that there was no sense in falling into a fit of the dismals about things which had happened in the Middle Ages; and a moving account of the behavior of the Princess Elizabeth at the Traitors' Gate quite failed to impress him.

"Silly thing to do!" he remarked. "Shouldn't wonder at it if she caught a chill. I had an uncle who got soaked to the skin once. Had an inflammation of the lungs. Dead as a herring within the week. Come along, let us take a look at this Ladies' Line they talk about!"

It was upon their return from this expedition, and while Kitty was still describing to Meg some of the things she had seen, that Mr Jack Westruther paid a formal call in Berkeley Square, and brought with him the Chevalier d'Evron.

Any apprehensions engendered by Freddy's gloomy forebodings were put to flight on the instant. The Chevalier was a handsome young man, with a lively, intelligent pair of eyes, beautifully glossy locks of light brown, cut and curled *à la cherubim*, and an air and deportment worthy of the first circles. His long-tailed coat of bottle-green had obviously been fashioned for him by a master; his fawn pantaloons admirably became a pair of really excellent legs; his linen was meticulously starched; and his Hessian boots would have furnished anyone with a very tolerable mirror. If Mr Westruther, a careless beau, thought those cherubim ringlets a trifle effeminate; and Mr Standen, a high stickler, considered the Chevalier's waistcoat to be rather too florid, these were faults of style which the ladies were easily able to overlook. The Chevalier's bow almost put Freddy's to shame; air and address were alike distinguished; and when, to the advantages of a handsome face and a good figure, he was found to add a very slight foreign accent to his speech his success with the fair sex was assured.

Kitty, who had been staring at him while he bowed over Meg's hand, exclaimed suddenly: "But—You are Camille!"

He turned towards her, smiling. "But yes! I am Camille, little cousin! I did not dare to think that I could hold a place in your memory. Tell me, I beg of you! – did she long survive my surgery, that blonde beauty? Alas, that I should have forgotten her name!"

She laughed, warmly shaking hands with him. "Rosabel – and indeed she survived for many years! I am so happy to see you again! I hope my uncle, and your brother, are both well?"

"I thank you, very well. And your amiable guardian?"

"Yes, indeed. Are you upon a visit to England? Where do you stay?"

He told her that he was lodging in Duke Street, which, however little it might convey to country-bred Kitty, served to convince Meg that his domicile was as unimpeachable as his manners. Very well-pleased to add so personable a young man to her circle, she extended to him an invitation to a small rout-party she was holding three days later. He accepted with just the right degree of gratitude, and took his leave, after a visit lasting for a correct half-hour, in an atmosphere of general approval, even Freddy acknowledging that he seemed to be a tolerable fellow. It had transpired, during the course of conversation, that he, like Lady Buckhaven and the engaged couple, meant to be present at the Non-Pareil Theater that evening, to see a new play which was being put on there; he begged to be allowed to visit her ladyship's box during the interval, was accorded a gracious permission, and bowed himself out in a manner which led Meg to say that only a man accustomed to move in the world of *ton* could get himself out of a room with such ease and grace.

Kitty was so much delighted to have met again one of whom she cherished the kindest memories that her transports might have been expected to have cast her betrothed into agonies of jealousy. Mr Standen managed without effort to preserve his equanimity, a fact of which his cousin's amused eyes took due note.

"Seems a good enough sort of a fellow," Freddy said cautiously. "Mind, I didn't like his waistcoat, but, then, I don't like yours either, coz, so I daresay it don't signify. Where did you meet him? *I* haven't seen him before."

"But you have been in Leicestershire, Freddy," Jack reminded him. "I fancy the Chevalier has not long been amongst us, though I am told that he was reared in England."

"Yes, that is quite true," Kitty said. "I think my uncle came to England on account of the troubles in France, but Uncle Matthew so much dislikes French people that he would never invite my relations to Arnside. And so I never saw Camille more than once in my life, and that was when I was quite a little girl. But

I never forgot him, or how kind he was in mending the doll Claud sent to the guillotine!"

"I cannot tell you, my dear Kitty, how happy I am that it has been my privilege to bring you together again," said Jack, rising from his chair. "I must tear myself from you, Meg. How unkind it was of you, by the way, not to have invited me to go with you tonight! Our dear Kitty's first visit to the theater! It is an event – one which I would give much to witness. But you will tell me all about it, Kitty, won't you?"

"You would find that a great bore, I am persuaded!" she retorted.

"No, no! When have I ever been bored by your confidences?" he said, quizzing her.

"But, Jack, I will not be so wronged!" Meg cried. "It is Freddy's party, you must know, not mine!"

"Then it was very unkind of Freddy," he said, raising her hand to his lips.

"Thought you was promised to Stichill tonight?" said Freddy.

"I am, of course," admitted Mr Westruther. "But it was still very unkind in you not to have invited me!" He then took an unconventional leave of Kitty, pinching her chin, and bidding her enjoy herself, and went away.

"Never knew such a complete hand!" said Freddy. "I must say, I'm glad he ain't coming. For one thing, he'd very likely cut the piece up, and for another, five's an awkward number. Stonehouse is going along with us, and we'll have supper afterwards at the Piazza. You'll like that, Kit."

There could be no doubt of this; her eyes were sparkling already in anticipation of the treat. Mr Standen, returning to his lodging in Ryder Street, to change his dress for the evening's entertainment, nourished a faint hope that a visit to the theater might give her thoughts a new turn. He was perfectly willing to escort her to any place of amusement frequented by ladies of quality, but he was much inclined to think that any more expeditions such as those which had rendered the last two days hideous would send him into Leicestershire on a repairing lease.

The success of the evening was assured from the moment that Mr Stonehouse, a shy young gentleman afflicted with a slight stammer, made his bow, and showed plainly by his demeanour that he very much admired Miss Charing's style of beauty. To a girl who, besides having lived in rural seclusion, had never been used to think herself even tolerably handsome, the appreciative gleam in Mr Stonehouse's eye was as exhilarating to the spirits as a glass of champagne. When they took their seats in the box, they attracted some attention, and several persons, who had exchanged bows and smiles with Meg, looked very hard at Kitty, one foppish man even going so far as to level his quizzing-glass in her direction. She thought this very rude, but she was not altogether displeased until Freddy, observing the interest of the dandy, said in a resigned tone: "There's that fellow Luss. Thought he was out of town. Pity he ain't. Never knew anyone more inquisitive! Lay you odds we shall have him here in the first interval, trying to nose out who you are, Kit!"

"Is he staring so because I am a stranger?" asked Kitty, a trifle dashed.

"That's it. No need to put yourself about," Freddy said reassuringly. "It ain't that there's anything amiss: in fact, you look very becomingly."

This temperate praise exercised a rather damping effect upon her spirits, but these soon rose again, for Mr Stonehouse showed unmistakable signs of wishing to engage her attention. While Freddy and his sister exchanged desultory remarks about their various acquaintances in the audience, he drew his chair rather closer to Kitty's, and politely inquired if she was enjoying her visit to the Metropolis. He seemed surprised to learn that it was her first; and when she told him innocently that Freddy had been so obliging as to take her to Westminster Abbey and to the Tower, looked quite stunned.

"F-Freddy?" he repeated. "D-did you say *W-Westminster Abbey?*"

"Yes, and also the Tower. We meant to go into St Paul's as well, but the guide book seemed not to think highly of the interior, so we did no more than look at the outside. But we saw the Elgin Marbles!"

"N-not Freddy!" he said incredulously.

"Yes, indeed he did! Though I am bound to own that he did not care much for them."

"I shouldn't think he w-would," said Mr Stonehouse. "I c-can't imagine how he was p-prevailed upon to go!" He colored, and added apologetically: "No, I d-don't mean that! I c-can, of course, but it's very surprising! The best of good fellows, you know, b-but—" His voice broke. *"Elgin Marbles!"* he uttered. "Oh, l-lord!"

Freddy, overhearing, said severely: "Yes, but there's no need for you to spread it all over town, Jasper!"

"I c-couldn't resist it!" said Mr Stonehouse frankly. "D-didn't you admire 'em, Freddy?"

Since Mr Standen felt strongly on the subject, it was

fortunate that his sister created a diversion at that moment by calling Kitty's attention to a box on the opposite side of the house. "Look, Kitty! There is the Chevalier, just come in with Lady Maria Yalding and her sister! *Freddy!* If she has not brought Drakemire with her! Well!"

Kitty, following the direction of her eyes, saw a party of four people in the box. A stout woman, very fashionably dressed but neither beautiful nor in quite the first blush of youth, was disposing herself in her chair, assisted by the Chevalier, who held her fan and her reticule for her, and carefully arranged her elaborately trimmed cloak over the back of the chair. A thinner edition of herself, who bore more the appearance of a hired companion than of a sister, sat down beside her, somewhat perfunctorily attended by the fourth member of the party, a desiccated man with a misogynistic expression.

"Lady Maria is the fat one, and that's her elder sister, Lady Jane," explained Meg. "Annerwick's daughters, you know: he has five, and all as plain as puddings! No fortune, of course: Mama says that *old* Lord Annerwick ran through thirty thousand pounds before he was twenty-five years old even!"

"Good gracious!" said Kitty, looking in surprise towards Lady Maria's box. "I had supposed her to be very rich indeed! She wears so many jewels and feathers!"

"Oh, yes! For, by the luckiest chance, Mr Yalding wished to marry her, and although he was quite an ungenteel person – I believe, in fact, a *merchant!* – the Annerwicks could not but be thankful."

"Didn't want to marry her," interpolated Freddy. "Wanted to be in the *ton.* Offered for the Calderbank

girl first, but he smelled too much of the shop for
Calderbank. Queer old fellow! Didn't do him much
good, either. Nailed up a couple of years ago."

"N-no, but it d-did Lady M-Maria good," said Mr
Stonehouse. "He left his whole f-fortune to her. *She*
saw to that! D-dragon of a female!" He glanced across
the house. "Stupid, too. Who's the young b-blade
making—" He stopped abruptly, his question cut
short by a nip from Meg's fingers.

But Freddy, who had moved beyond the reach of his
sister's hand, answered it. "Cousin of Miss Charing's.
French fellow. Think he's dangling after her, Kit?"

"Oh, Freddy, surely he would not do so?" exclaimed Kitty, shocked.

"Might," said Freddy. "Wouldn't myself, but plenty
of fellows have. Well, bound to! Worth a hundred
thousand, they say. Trouble is, she's a dashed queer-
tempered woman. Uphall made a push to fix his interest with her. She'd have had him, too, but he couldn't
bring himself up to scratch. Told me he'd sooner be
rolled-up. Says it ain't so bad in a sponging-house –
once you get used to it. Good God! For the lord's sake,
don't look to the left, Meg! *Aunt Dolphinton!*"

With great presence of mind, Meg unfurled her fan,
and plied it so that it hid her profile. "Has she seen
us?" she hissed.

"Don't know, and I'm dashed well not going to look.
She's got Dolph with her, that's all I can tell you. We
shall have to take a stroll outside after the act, or she'll
start beckoning to us. You know what she is!"

Just then the curtain rose, and although Freddy's
enjoyment of the drama was marred by what he felt
to be the urgent necessity to evolve a scheme that
would enable them all to escape a compulsory visit to

Lady Dolphinton's box. Kitty instantly forgot the ordeal ahead, and sat throughout the act in a trance of rapt interest, her lips just parted, her gaze riveted, and her hands tightly clasping her fan. At the fall of the curtain Freddy made a creditable attempt to hustle the ladies out of the box before his redoubtable relative had had time to observe them; but owing to Meg's having lost her handkerchief, and to Kitty's having to be roused from her lingering trance, this failed. Before he could achieve his end, a knock fell on the door, and the Chevalier entered, so that the project had to be abandoned.

Kitty could not but be glad. That her handsome cousin should dangle after a fortune was a suggestion that distressed her. His prompt appearance in Freddy's box seemed to give the lie to it; and nothing in his demeanour betrayed the least desire on his part to return to Lady Maria's side. In full view of his hostess, he stayed chatting, very gay and debonair; and when Kitty, rendered quite uncomfortable by a fixed stare from the opposite box, told him that she feared he might be offending Lady Maria, his brows flew up in surprise, and he exclaimed: "But, no! How should it be possible? I have informed her that my cousin is present – my cousin whom for so many years I have not seen!"

"Well, she looks very cross," said Kitty.

"I am not very well acquainted with Lady Maria, but it seems that she suffers from bad humours," he said, with a droll look. "But I should not say so! I am, in effect, an ingrate! She has been most kind to one who is without friends in London, and – you understand my lips are sealed!"

"All very w-well," said Mr Stonehouse, when, by

tacit consent, he and Mr Standen withdrew from the box to take an airing in the corridor, "b-but if he hasn't any f-friends in London, w-why did he c-come here? N-not one of the Embassy people, is he?" He added hastily: "I don't m-mean to say that he isn't p-perfectly respectable! It just struck m-me that it was odd!" He became aware of a lanky figure in his path, and put up his glass. "Oh! Dolphinton! How d'ye do?"

Lord Dolphinton addressed himself to his cousin, briefly and to the point. "Mama says you are to bring Kitty to her box," he stated. "Freddy, I didn't know you were going to bring Kitty to town, did I?"

Mr Standen, though irritated by this peremptory command, was not deaf to the note of appeal in Lord Dolphinton's voice. "No, no!" he said soothingly. "At least, I don't know what you knew, Dolph, but no need to get into a taking, old fellow! Too late to bring Kit along to see my aunt now! You go back and tell her so! Bring her after the next act!" He then turned his relative gently round, and gave him an encouraging thrust, remarking to Mr Stonehouse, as Dolphinton ambled away: "Seven-months' child, y'know: daresay it accounts for it! Better go back and warn Kit!"

"Freddy!" said Mr Stonehouse, detaining him. "What *is* this? I m-mean, Elgin M-Marbles – W-Westminster Abbey—! Are you g-going to be *m-married?*"

"No, no!" Freddy said involuntarily. Recollecting himself, he added: "What I mean is – only betrothed! Keeping it a secret, Jasper! Family reasons!"

"Oh!" said Mr Stonehouse, much mystified. "Of c-course, if you d-don't want it known, I shan't s-say any-thing! But why—"

"Curtain's going up!" interrupted Freddy desper-ately, retreating into his box much in the fashion of a rabbit hotly pursued by a terrier.

❧ Chapter X ❧

CONSIDERABLY TO THEIR SURPRISE, AND NOT A
little to their relief, Lady Dolphinton received the engaged couple later in the evening with a degree of affability which was as rare as it was unexpected. She was
a hard-featured woman, with a predatory mouth, a
smile that never reached her eyes, and an air of consequence. At no time had she been popular with her de-
ceased husband's relations, for she was both proud
and ill-natured, insolent to persons whom she considered to be her social inferiors, tyrannical to her son,
and ruthless in the methods she employed to achieve
her ends. Even Lady Legerwood, always prone to take
the kindliest view of everyone, could not like Augusta.
In her eyes, Augusta was a bad mother, whose treat-
ment of her dull-witted son had, she maintained, done
much to increase his imbecility. She could say no
worse of anyone. The younger members of the family
were frightened of her when children, and avoided her
when they grew up. Mr Penicuik detested her. He

made very little secret of his belief that his nephew's untimely decease might be laid at her door; and none at all of his conviction that his great-nephew's peculiarities were directly inherited from her. He said that all the Skirlings were loose screws, adding darkly that he didn't blame them for setting it about that old James Skirling had been drowned while fishing on a Scottish loch. No one, he said, could be expected to advertise the fact that a member of the family had to be confined in a room at the top of the house, with a couple of attendants to see that he came to no harm.

Knowing how much she must have angered the Countess by rejecting Dolphinton's suit, Kitty went to her box in considerable trepidation, clutching Freddy's arm tightly enough to draw from him a remonstrance. She begged pardon, and expressed the hope that her ladyship would not say anything *very* dreadful. He seemed surprised, and said: "Lord, Kit, you ain't afraid of her?"

"N-no. At least – yes, I am a little! I think she is an *evil* person! And she can say such cruel things!"

"Go away if she does," said Freddy.

"Oh, Freddy, would you dare?" she asked, laughing a little.

"No question of daring: easy thing to do!"

"Freddy, she would be as mad as fire!" said Kitty, awed by the very thought.

But the practical Mr Standen refused to be intimidated. "Wouldn't make any odds to us if she was. Shouldn't be there to see it," he pointed out. "No need to be in a quake: I won't let her frighten you."

This unexpected sangfroid greatly impressed Miss Charing, but she could not be sorry that it was not put to the test. They found the Countess wreathed in smiles, arch felicitations to Freddy and broad compliments to Kitty issuing smoothly from between her thin, painted lips. Kitty was even permitted to kiss her ladyship's cheek; and learned, with incredulity, that nothing had more pleased the Countess than the news of her engagement.

While his mother was overwhelming Kitty with her goodwill, Dolphinton, having acquired a grip on Freddy's coat, was subjecting it to a series of tugs. Freddy, a wary eye on his aunt, was at first unconscious of this attempt to attract his attention, but when the tugs became imperative they attracted it to rather more purpose than Lord Dolphinton desired. "Stop it, Dolph!" he said indignantly. "First time I've had this coat on, and between the pair of you, you and Kit—" He paused, meeting his cousin's anguished look of entreaty, and said: "Oh, very well! What's the matter, old fellow?"

"Never told me you was bringing Kitty to town!" said Dolphinton imploringly.

"Of course I didn't! Why should I?" replied Freddy.

"He never told me!" said Dolphinton, addressing his parent.

She laughed, but in a way (as Miss Charing later told Mr Standen) that boded ill for him. "Good God, Foster, what is that to the purpose? I wish you will strive to be a little less foolish! And so you are staying with dear Margaret, Kitty? Such a sweet creature, but perhaps not quite the person to take care of you! Naughty girl! Why did you not come to me? I am sure, if I have begged poor Uncle Matthew once to send you to me for a season. I have done so fifty times! I promise you, I grudge you to Margaret! It was always the wish of my heart to bring out a daughter!"

She rattled on in this style until it became time for them to return to their own box, her eyes flickering all the while from Kitty's face to Freddy's, and back again. She inquired solicitously after Mr Penicuik, after the Legerwoods, after Mr Westruther, whom she had not seen for an age: could it be that he was still out of town? She wanted to know if Kitty was being tolerably well entertained in London: did Meg mean to procure a voucher for her, admitting her to Almack's? Had Freddy taken her driving in Hyde Park? But this was something Kitty must grant Dolphinton the pleasure of doing! She must know that he was an excellent whip: drove the prettiest turn-out. "You must take Kitty up beside you one afternoon, Foster: you will like to do that, I know!"

"Like to do that," he repeated obediently, but looking so miserable that Kitty was hard put to it to refrain from laughing.

"And, I must say," she told Freddy, once they were out of earshot, "I hope he does not offer to take me, for I am persuaded he would overturn me!"

"No, there you're wrong," replied Freddy. "Wouldn't think it, but he's a first-rate fiddler. Bruising rider too, if ever he had the chance! She don't let him hunt, but we had him down to stay in Leicestershire once. Never saw the poor fellow so happy! Dashed if he didn't lay his leg over the ugliest customer m'father ever had in the stables! Brute went like a lamb with him, what's more. You'd be quite safe. Not that I think he'll take you: looked devilish blue, didn't he?"

She agreed, but, knowing the Countess, she was not surprised when he came to pay a morning-call in Berkeley Square the following day, escorting that de-

termined lady. The Countess, graciously embracing
her niece, had come to congratulate her on her situation. She had been calling in Mount Street, to inquire
after the invalids, and had learnt from her dearest sister that Meg was increasing. But her ungrateful niece,
observing with amazement the affability she showed
towards Miss Charing, thought that she had come
rather to ingratiate herself with a girl whose adoption
by Mr Penicuik she had deplored for years. She heard
Dolphinton, acting under his mother's goad, make an
assignation to take Kitty for a drive in the Park that
very afternoon, and was quite at a loss to understand
the meaning of these strange tactics. "For what," she
argued, when these unwelcome visitors had left the
house, "can she hope to achieve, when she is apprized
of your engagement to Freddy? I perfectly understand
how greatly she must have wished you to marry Dolph,
when my uncle made you his heiress, for Mama says
that his estates are much embarrassed, and she, you
know, is shockingly expensive! Did you remark the
furs she was wearing! I could not but stare, and wonder how she contrived to rig herself out so handsomely on a jointure which Mama says cannot have
been large!"

"Well, she does not!" said Kitty. "Poor Dolph is so
foolish that you may depend upon it that it is she who
still holds his purse-strings! That is what Uncle Matthew says, at all events; and also that there is nothing
amiss but what a little management and economy
might well set to rights. Though I am bound to own,"
she added conscientiously, "that that is just what
Uncle Matthew would say!"

Meg laughed, but said: "It may be so, yet still I don't

see why she should think it worth while to encourage Dolph to take you driving!"

"Encourage! Poor Dolph! She *compelled* him!" exclaimed Kitty, unable to suppress a giggle.

"Well, I know she did, but I was never more surprised in my life than when I heard you say you would go with him! Why, Kitty?"

"Oh, Freddy assures me he won't overturn this phaeton of his!" said Kitty blithely. "I *could* not refuse, when I knew that odious woman would be so cross to him if I did! Besides, I mean to discover why she made him invite me! What should I wear, Meg, to go out driving in a phaeton?"

"To go out driving with Dolph, anything!"

"No, don't be provoking! Do, pray, tell me!"

"I will rather tell my poor brother how he is betrayed! The hair-brown pelisse, you goose, and the hat with the gold feathers!"

Lord Dolphinton arrived punctually in Berkeley Square, but Kitty's hopes of inducing him to explain his mother's odd conduct seemed likely to be blighted by the presence of a wooden-faced groom, who stood perched up behind them, well able to hear every word that was spoken. Indeed, when she ventured to suggest to Dolphinton that he was out of spirits, he shot a scared look at her, and followed this up by a series of grimaces which she correctly interpreted to be intended to convey a warning. She at once began to talk of trivialities, taking a great interest in everything about her, and trying to hit upon some means of detaching him from his guardian angel. It was a bright day, and a week of such spring-like weather had caused many buds to open. A glimpse of a path leading between flower-beds provided Kitty with the ex-

cuse she needed. She cried out in delight, and said:
"Primroses! Oh, how pretty! How much I should like
to explore that path!"

The hint failed. Lord Dolphinton shook his head.
"Not a carriage-way," he said.

"No, but do, pray, stop for a minute, Dolph! Would
you object to it if I were to run back, just to walk a very
little way down the path?"

"No," said his lordship, drawing his pair to a standstill. "Can't see why you want to look at primroses, but
I don't object. I won't keep the bays standing more
than ten minutes, though. Not disobliging, but won't
do that. Bad for them."

The groom, who had jumped down from the phaeton, and stood waiting to assist Miss Charing to
alight, gave a discreet cough, and said, touching his
cockaded hat: "I could walk the horses, my lord, if you
should wish to accompany Miss."

"Oh, yes!" instantly said Kitty. "Pray allow him to
do so, Dolph! I would dearly love to walk for a little
while in this beautiful park!"

Dolphinton appeared to be much struck by this suggestion. He said, with the first sign of animation he
had shown that day: "That's what I'll do! That's a
good notion. You think it's a good notion, don't you,
Kitty? Females don't walk alone in London. Finglass
shall walk the horses, and I'll go with you."

A fair-minded girl, Miss Charing realized that Lady
Dolphinton was not altogether to be blamed for treat-
ing her only child with impatience. She curbed her
own impatience, however, and waited until Dolphinton should have finished issuing his painstaking, and
somewhat repetitive, instructions to his groom. But
exasperation nearly got the better of her when his

lordship said, as they walked away together: "I'll tell you why I said it was a good notion. I don't want to look at primroses. Don't want to look at anything. Want to say something Finglass can't hear."

"Well, of course!" Kitty said. "That is why I said I should like to walk down this path!"

"You want to say something he can't hear?" asked his lordship, surprised. "Well, of all things! It's a – it's a – well, I forget the word, but there is one. Both of us wanting the same thing."

"Yes, Dolph, but never mind that!" said Kitty, taking his arm, and pressing it in a motherly fashion. "Tell me what it was you wished to say to me!"

"Wanted to say mustn't say anything with Finglass up behind. Tells my mother," explained his lordship.

Once again Miss Charing was obliged to exert considerable self-control. "Dolph, does that creature spy on you?" she demanded.

"Tells my mother where I've been. Tells her what I do."

"Why don't you turn him off?" she said hotly.

"She wouldn't let me."

She gave his arm a little shake. "She could not stop you! You are a man, Dolph, not a schoolboy!"

"Yes," he agreed. "But she could."

"Oh, I wish you were not so much afraid of your Mama!" sighed Kitty.

He paused to look down into her face, his own greatly astonished. "You do? It's that thing again. Thing I've forgotten. Because I do, too."

She perceived that it would be fruitless to pursue this subject. She said instead: "Why did your mother urge you to bring me for this drive?"

A deep sigh shook him. "Wants you to marry me," he replied. "Says I did the thing badly."

"But this is nonsensical!" she pointed out. "How can she think of such a thing when she knows I am engaged to Freddy?"

"Says you aren't. Says she suspected a bubble all along. Says she knew you wasn't when she saw you last night. Says she ain't to be deceived." He sighed again. "True!" he said, in a depressed tone.

Miss Charing's arm had stiffened. She said carefully: "She is quite out this time, however. Of course I am engaged to Freddy! Why should she suppose it is a bubble?"

Dolphinton wrinkled his brow in an effort of memory. "Something to do with Jack," he produced. "It don't make sense, which is why I can't remember it. I remember things very well in general, but not when I don't understand them."

"Well, it is a very good thing that you don't remember foolish things!" said Kitty warmly. "You may tell your Mama that she very much mistakes the matter! No, I suppose you would not dare to do so: I shall contrive a way of telling her myself."

He gripped her arm in great agitation. "No, no! You won't tell Mama I told you what she said!"

He was so much alarmed that her anger died. She said soothingly: "No, I promise you I will not, Dolph. I would never betray you: you know I would not! I wish very much that I could help you."

His grip shifted from her wrist to her hand, which he pressed gratefully. "I *like* you, Kitty!" he uttered. "I like you better than Freddy. Better than Hugh. Better than—"

"Yes, yes!" she interrupted hastily. "Better than any of them!"

They walked slowly on, Kitty lost in thought, Dolphinton content to remain silent. Suddenly Kitty spoke. "Dolph, I have been thinking, and it has occurred to me all at once—You don't *wish* to be married to me, do you?" He shook his head. "*Why* don't you?" she demanded straitly.

He swallowed once or twice. "Not – not good at explaining!" he said.

She paid no heed to this. "You like me, and you always do what your Mama bids you, and I must say it does seem to me as though you would be very glad to be married, if only to escape from your Mama. Dolph, can it be – are you—Dolph, do you wish to marry *someone else?*"

He turned quite pale, and almost dragged her round. "Go back to the carriage!" he said. "Keeping the horses standing!"

"No, that horrid groom is taking care of them for you. Tell me, Dolph! I won't tell your Mama! I won't tell anyone – upon my honor, I will not! It is some lady whom she does not like?"

"Never met her," he muttered. "Wouldn't like her."

"Come and sit beside me on that seat!" she coaxed.

"Take a chill! Better go back!"

"We will directly. It is so warm that I am sure it can do us no harm to sit for a few minutes in the sun. There! You see how pleasant it is! Pray don't be afraid to confide in me! I would like so much to be able to help you. What is her name?"

"Hannah."

"Hannah! Well – well, that is a very pretty name, I am sure! And her other name?"

"Plymstock. That's her brother's name," said his lordship, making the matter plain. "Lives with him. Lives with his wife, too. Mrs Plymstock. Don't like her. Don't like Plymstock either." He reflected for a moment. "Or the children," he said.

"Why don't you like Mr Plymstock?" asked Kitty, rather taken aback.

"He's a Cit," replied his lordship simply.

"Oh, dear! But perhaps he is perfectly respectable!"

"No, he ain't. He's a Revolutionary."

"Good heavens!"

He nodded. "Doesn't like me. Doesn't want me to marry Hannah. *She* says he don't like Earls. Shows you, doesn't it?"

She thought that it certainly threw a little light, but she refrained from saying so. "Tell me about Miss Plymstock!" she begged. "Is she pretty?"

"Yes," said his lordship. "Got the kind of face I like. Thought so the first time I saw her."

"When was that, Dolph?"

"Cheltenham, last year. Mama took the cure. Thought I was hacking about the country. Wasn't. Hoaxed her."

"A very excellent thing to have done!" approved Kitty. "I think you were very clever to have thought of it!"

"Hannah thought of it. I ain't clever: she is. But she don't bother me. Like to marry her," he said wistfully.

It appeared to Miss Charing that there would be little likelihood of his being permitted to do so. Only one circumstance could render such a match tolerable in Lady Dolphinton's eyes. She put a tentative question, and received in answer one of his melancholy headshakes.

"No. No fortune," he said.

"Oh, dear!" she said, thinking that it all seemed rather hopeless.

"I don't want a fortune. I want horses. Like to go and live at Dolphinton and breed horses."

"To Ireland! Well, and so you should! Does Hannah say that too?"

"Yes. She don't want to live in London either."

"I wish I could meet her!"

He looked surprised, but pleased. "You do? Wish you could meet Hannah?"

"Yes, but if she lives in Cheltenham—"

"Don't live in Cheltenham. Lives in Keppel Street. Not a good address. Mama wouldn't like it. Full of Cits and lawyers. Don't like it much myself. But I go there," said Dolphinton, in a burst of confidence. "Mama thinks I go to Boodle's. That's a hoax too."

It seemed to Kitty that this particular hoax was one which could only lead to disaster. She almost shuddered to think of what Dolphinton's fate would be if some chance discovered the deception to his parent. "Dolph, why should you not take me to visit Miss Plymstock?" she asked. "I wish very much to help you, but first I do think I should see her, because – well, I think I should!"

"Couldn't. Finglass would tell Mama."

"And so he may, for I have thought of an excellent scheme! Now, listen carefully, Dolph! When we go back to the carriage, I shall ask you where is Keppel Street. I think perhaps you should say you don't know – hoaxing Finglass, you see."

"I should like to do that," said his lordship, showing faint animation.

"Of course you would! Then you will ask Finglass

if he knows. And I shall say that I have a friend living there – what is the number of Miss Plymstock's house, Dolph?"

"Seventeen," he answered, watching her with rapt attention.

"Good! I will remember. I shall ask if you would object to it if I paid her a visit."

Lord Dolphinton, much stirred, had a flash of genius. "I'll say I don't object, and we'll go there!"

"Exactly so! Can you keep that in your head, do you think?"

He requested her to repeat it all; and when she had done so said that he could remember it very well. She did not feel hopeful, but it soon appeared that he had not been making an idle boast when he had told his cousins that he could remember things that were said to him two or three times. All passed precisely as had been planned, and it was not long before Miss Charing was seated in a drawing-room in Keppel Street, waiting for the manservant to bring Miss Plymstock to her. While she waited, she took stock of her surroundings. The house was respectable; the room in which she sat was furnished with propriety, if not with elegance; and she could perceive no signs of vulgarity, such as would render an alliance with Miss Plymstock quite ineligible. Then the door opened, and Miss Plymstock stood before her.

Miss Charing suffered a severe shock, and as she put out her hand realized that Dolphinton must have formed a greater passion than she had supposed to be at all possible. Only a man in love could have described Miss Plymstock as pretty. She was a rather stout young woman of about his own age, with sandy hair and lashes, and a florid complexion. While there was nothing repulsive in her appearance, few persons would have gone so far as to have said that she was even passably good looking. Upon Dolphinton's performing the introduction, which he did as soon as he had been prodded by Kitty, she shook Kitty's hand heartily, and said in a blunt but by no means ungenteel voice: "How do you do? I'm very happy to make your acquaintance, for I know of you from Foster here, and I can tell he likes you."

She then kissed his lordship's cheek, and patted him in a motherly way, told him to sit down and be comfortable, and turned again to Kitty. "He has told you about us, I don't doubt, and I can see you've not come here to tell me our marriage would be unsuitable. Well, I'm sure there's no need for anyone to do so, for I'm no fool, and I know it. But I mean to marry him, for all that, only how to bring it about is more than I can see."

Dolphinton, who had been watching her with an expression of dog-like devotion, sighed heavily.

"But his Mama cannot prevent the marriage, if he is set upon it!" Kitty said. "Dolph, you are twenty-seven years old! Could you not be *resolute?*"

He looked frightened, and began to stammer. Miss Plymstock took his hand, and sat patting it. "Don't be in a taking, Foster!" she said kindly. "Your Mama shan't know of it until I have you safe, and so I promise you."

The servant came in just then with a tray, which he set on one of the tables. Miss Plymstock rose, and said: "Now, you shall have a glass of the Madeira wine you like, and sit drinking it by the fire, while I take Miss Charing to my bedchamber. Sister's out, so no one will come in to disturb you, and if your Mama should ask you about your visit here you may say that Miss Charing and I went off together and left you alone, and she will be satisfied."

Kitty, feeling that in her own way Miss Plymstock was quite as masterful as Lady Dolphinton, meekly went with her up two pairs of stairs to her bedroom at the back of the house.

"You'll excuse my bringing you here," stated Hannah, putting forward a chair for her. "I was wishful to talk to you, and I don't care to speak out before Foster, because it makes him nervous, poor fellow!"

"If only one could prevail upon him to be firm with that odious woman!" Kitty exclaimed. "I own, I am a little afraid of her myself, but there is nothing she can do to him, after all!"

"Yes, there is, Miss Charing, and she don't scruple to hold it over his head. She and that precious doctor of hers! A pretty pair, and it would do me good, it would indeed! to tell them what I think of them! If he don't do what she bids him, she threatens she'll have him under lock and key, and tell everyone he's mad."

"Oh, no! She could not!" Kitty cried, horrified. "He is not! Not *mad!*"

"No, he's not, but no one could deny he hasn't all his wits," said Miss Plymstock dispassionately. "However, there's no harm in him, and I warrant you if he had me to look after him he would be a great deal better than he is now. For one thing, I don't mean to let his Mama come scaring him out of his senses; and for another, I think it will suit him much better to live in this Irish place of his than to be racketing about town, the way he's made to. He can have his horses, and though I daresay I shall find it a damp, ramshackle place, I don't care for that, because I've always had a taste for the country, and I don't doubt I shall soon set it in order."

Kitty did not doubt it either. Regarding her hostess with a fascinated eye, she faltered: "I beg your pardon, but – but do you *love* Dolph?"

The question in no way discomposed Miss Plymstock. She replied calmly: "I collect that you mean to ask me if I have *fallen in love* with him. Well, I have not, and I don't suppose anyone could. I like him very well, and I shall like to be the Countess of Dolphinton, and to be a married lady. My brother don't favor him, and he don't wish me to marry him, but I don't heed him. I'm not pretty, like you, and I have no fortune. It isn't likely I shall receive another offer." She met Kitty's eyes squarely, and said in her forthright way: "I'm not his equal in station, and I don't pretend I am; but you might say he wasn't fit to marry anyone. I promise you this: I mean to take good care of him, and to make him happy, poor Foster!"

Kitty stared at her, her brain working swiftly. Secluded though her life had been, she was well aware that there was perhaps no one amongst Dolphinton's relations who would not be shocked by such an alliance as this. Even Freddy, good-natured though he was, would frown upon it, she thought, recalling his disparaging remarks about the late Mr Yalding. In the eyes of society, Dolphinton's peculiarities were outweighed by his birth; the enjoyment of a substantial fortune was the only thing that could render Miss Plymstock eligible, and she had no fortune at all. But Kitty, looking at that homely countenance, could see poor, bewildered Dolphinton happily ambling round his Irish bog, ruled certainly, but kindly, and as certainly protected from his mother's disturbing influence. She drew a breath, and said: "I'll help you!"

Miss Plymstock's already high color deepened to a rich beetroot. "You're very obliging! I'm not one to wrap things up in clean linen, so I'll tell you I know how he was made to offer for you, and what you said when you rejected him, and it made me think you was a nice girl, and one I'd be glad to meet. Once his ring's on my finger I shall know what to do, for I'm not afraid of any of them; but the thing is, how to get it there? You must know, Miss Charing, that he's got a set of spies round him, that carry tales to his Mama. I don't doubt she's told them he's a trifle queer in his head. Well! If Sam – that's my brother! – would lend me his aid, I could maybe do the thing, but he won't, for he don't like Foster, and he would be glad to match me with a friend of his own, if he could do it. What he says is, an Earl's all very well if he's affluent, but one like Foster, with a weak head and no fortune, is a bad bargain. But to my way of thinking he's a better bargain than a tea-merchant, with snuff all over his waistcoat, and one foot in the grave – even if Mr Muthill was to offer for me, which I'll lay my life he don't mean to!"

"Exactly so!" said Kitty faintly.

"I've thought of Gretna Green," pursued Miss Plymstock, "because banns won't serve. If her ladyship didn't discover we had put 'em up, Sam would, for he keeps a close watch on me. I know it ain't the thing to be married across the Border—"

"No, pray do not do that!" Kitty interrupted, much shocked.

"I can't do it, because it would cost a deal of money, and her ladyship don't allow Foster more than a pittance. And it wouldn't be good for Foster to be chasing to Scotland for as much as three days, I daresay, thinking all the time his Mama was on his heels," replied Miss Plymstock, with unshaken calm.

"Oh, I am persuaded it would be very bad for him! We must think of a better scheme than that."

"But can you?" asked Miss Plymstock.

"Yes, between us we must be able to do so. I own, I do not immediately perceive how it is to be contrived, but I mean to think very particularly about it. It will be best if Lady Dolphinton believes him to be obedient, I think. She is the most absurd creature! I daresay you are aware that she has compelled him still to angle for me! Should we not turn this to account? Recollect, if she knows him to be in my company she will be satisfied! Something may suggest itself: it *must* do so! If you do not object, I will encourage him to be a great deal in my company; and – though it will go sorely against the grain with me! – I'll let her think I am not wholly averse from his suit."

"I'm agreeable," said Miss Plymstock. "But maybe this cousin Freddy of Foster's won't like it?"

"Freddy? It has nothing—I mean," Kitty corrected herself hastily, "he will have not the least objection, I assure you!"

❧ *Chapter XI* ❧

IN PURSUANCE OF HER AIMS, MISS CHARING AL-
lowed herself, with real heroism, to be inveigled by
Lady Dolphinton into visiting the Dolphinton house
in Grosvenor Place, a locality which her ladyship described disparagingly as quite out of the way, and this
in so scornful a voice that Kitty quaked to think of what
she might have said of so unmodish a quarter as Keppel Street.

There had been a time when Lady Dolphinton had
not spared to state her opinion of encroaching or-
phans, or her conviction that this particular orphan
was a sly little hussy. It seemed that that was now to
be forgotten. She was all amiability when Kitty presented herself in Grosvenor Place; and, since she
could be agreeable enough when she chose, soon had
the girl at her ease. She had the tact not to let Dolphinton appear, and the wit not to mention Mr Westruther;
and if she tacitly assumed that Kitty had accepted Mr
Standen's offer as a means of establishing herself cred-

itably, she did so with enough sympathy to make it hard for Kitty to be offended. The folly of the world in venerating the higher ranks of nobility was lightly touched upon; and also the advantages attached to a pretty young woman's allying herself with a complaisant man. "But *that* I should not say to you, my dear! Freddy – dear creature! – is a Standen! You will discover soon enough how straitlaced a family!"

Kitty could barely repress a smile, but by the time she had driven out with Dolphinton five times, and had twice accompanied him and his mother to the theater, Mr Standen surprised her by delivering himself of a protest. He said that she was making a cake of herself.

Kitty refuted the accusation with some heat. Mr Standen temporized. "Dashed well making a cake of me!" he said.

"Absurd!"

"Well, it ain't absurd. Here's half the town knowing you're engaged to me, and wondering if you're going to tip me the double. Mind, I wouldn't say a word if it weren't Dolph! Coming it a bit too strong, Kit, to prefer a fellow like that to me!"

"But, Freddy, we agreed that only your family should be told we were engaged! Surely you cannot have spread the news!"

"I should rather think I haven't! Now, for the lord's sake, Kit, don't be missish! You don't suppose we could tell m'mother and Meg without its leaking out! Besides, Jasper knows too: no use denying it when he'd asked Meg already. Sisters!" said Freddy, in a voice of loathing. He added, after a moment's reflection: "That cousin of yours knows, too."

"Camille? No, indeed, he does not! I have not said a word to him about it, I promise you, Freddy!"

"Told him myself," said Freddy.

She fixed her eyes on his face. "But *why?*"

"Thought it would be a good thing to do," replied Freddy vaguely.

"I can't conceive why you should have done so!"

"Oh, well! Cousin of yours!" said Freddy, his attention on his quizzing-glass, which he was polishing with his handkerchief.

"To be sure, yes! I do not object to his knowing, if he will not spread it about, for I have a particular kindness for him. He is a delightful man, don't you think, Freddy?"

"Very pleasant fellow," agreed Freddy.

"Meg says his manners have a truly Gallic polish. She is in transports over him! There is just that sportive playfulness, you know, which Englishmen, in general, have not. And a most superior understanding!"

"Shouldn't be at all surprised," said Freddy. "In fact, I'm dashed sure he has!"

She said, a little shyly: "You can't conceive how happy it makes me to have so respectable a relation! It is not quite comfortable, you know, to have *no one* of one's own family!"

"No, I daresay it ain't," said Freddy, his ready sympathy stirred. "Not but what you might have the better part of my relations, and welcome! However, I see what you mean, Kit. Thing is – no wish to interfere, but no use thinking you're up to snuff yet, my dear girl, because you ain't! Won't do for you to encourage the Chevalier to dangle after you. Don't want to be one of the *on-dits* of town!"

"Oh, no, indeed I don't!" she replied, laughing.

"But you quite mistake the matter, Freddy! Camille's behavior is unexceptionable! I daresay you may be thinking of Meg's having invited him to go with us to the Argyll Rooms, but I assure you that was quite an extraordinary happening! I could see you did not like it above half, but remember! we are first cousins, and had then but just met again after so many years! It was very natural that he should call rather frequently to see me, at the outset. I don't think I have met him, save in company, since that evening."

Freddy, who had taken his own simple measures to discourage the Chevalier's visits to Berkeley Square, looked faintly gratified. It had never before fallen to his lot to steer an inexperienced damsel past the shoals of her first London season, and it was not a task for which he felt himself to be fitted; but an intimate knowledge of his elder sister had not filled him with confidence in her discretion. He had a hazy idea that having brought Kitty to town it behoved him to keep an eye on her. He had taught her the steps of the quadrille; he had done considerable violence to his feelings by escorting both her and Meg to a masked ball at the Pantheon, so that she might, in this large and extremely mixed assembly, learn to dance creditably in public; he had requested his mother to procure a voucher for her, admitting her to Almack's, and had forbidden her straitly to accept any invitation to waltz there; he had dissuaded her from buying a jockey-bonnet of lilac silk, much admired by Meg; and he had taken strong exception to a pair of bright red Morocco slippers, saying in a resigned tone that it seemed to him that he would be obliged to accompany her the next time she went shopping. "And don't keep on telling me that they're Wellington slippers, because if

that's what they said in the shop they were bamboozling you!" he said, with some severity. "Dash it, the
Duke's a devilish well-dressed man, and he wouldn't
make such a figure of himself!"

There were small matters, and on all questions of
taste and fashion Mr Standen was well qualified to advise. Miss Charing's charming French cousin was a
more serious problem, and one which considerably
exercised his mind.

It was Mr Stonehouse who was responsible for
arousing certain suspicions in his breast. Mr Stonehouse had lately attended a rout-party at the French
Embassy, and could not recall that he had seen the
Chevalier at this select gathering. Those who most deplored Mr Standen's lack of scholarship would not
have called in question his worldly knowledge. He
knew that the scion of a noble French house should
have been present upon this occasion. There might be
several reasons to account for his absence; but Mr
Standen remembered that he had not liked the Chevalier's waistcoat, and he asked Mr Westruther where he
had met him.

"Now, where did I first meet him?" pondered Jack,
his mouth grave, and his eyes alight. "Was it at Wool-
er's, or was it in Bennett Street?"

Freddy, although he occasionally played hazard at
Watier's, was not a gamester, but he perfectly under-
stood the significance of his cousin's answer. Mr
Westruther had named two of London's gaming-hells.
With strong indignation, he demanded: "Good God,
Jack, is the fellow an ivory-turner?"

Mr Westruther laughed. "A very skillful one,
Freddy!"

"A Greek?"

Mr Westruther seemed surprised. "No, a French-man, surely?"

But Freddy was in no mood for such trifling. "That card will win no trick! Come, now! A Captain Sharp?"

"My dear Freddy, I have not the least reason to suppose it! Let us rather say, a first-rate player!"

Mr Standen's amiable countenance hardened. After staring fixedly at his cousin for a moment, he said with unusual dryness: "Playing a deep game, ain't you, coz?"

"Why, what can you mean?" said Jack, raising his brows.

"Not sure," said Mr Standen cautiously. "Don't know why you introduced the fellow to Kit."

"You must be a trifle disguised," said Mr Westruther, regarding him with concern. "You have forgotten that Kitty was desirous of meeting her French connections. Isn't she pleased with him? I was so sure she must be! A personable and a charming creature – you don't agree?"

"Yes, I do," Freddy replied. "Very pleasant fellow. Thing is, I've a notion there's something havey-cave about him, and I don't like it."

Mr Westruther's broad shoulders shook. "He offends your sense of the respectable, coz? Alas! Now, I find him so amusing! But I am not, of course, one of the stiff Standens."

"No, and you ain't engaged to Kit!" retorted Freddy, nettled.

"Very true. Are you?" said Jack sweetly.

"Seems to me," said Freddy, recovering after a moment from the effect of this undoubted doubler, "that it's you who are disguised!"

He thought it prudent to say no more to his cousin,

but to pursue his own investigations. These led him in due course to seek counsel of his father, whom he met one day in St James's Street, and who exhibited great surprise at seeing him, saying that he had supposed him to have gone out of town again. But this shaft went wide. Freddy eyed his satirical parent in mild bewilderment, and said reasonably: "Can't have thought that, sir! Dash it, met you at Meg's two nights ago!"

Lord Legerwood sighed. "You have your own armor, have you not, Frederick? Of course, I should have known better!"

"Offended you, sir?" asked Freddy intelligently.

"Not at all. How came such an idea as that into your head?"

"Notice more than you think," said Freddy, with simple pride. "Never call me Frederick except when I've vexed you!"

"Almost you encourage me to look forward to a brilliant career for you!" said his lordship, impressed.

"Shouldn't think so at all," said Freddy decidedly. "Wouldn't suit me. Besides we don't need two clever coves in the family. Mean to leave that sort of thing to Charlie. You going anywhere, sir?"

"Merely to White's."

"Come with you," said Freddy. "Been thinking lately I'd like a word with you."

"Surely not!" countered Lord Legerwood gently. "I do not live in the Antipodes!"

Freddy puzzled over this, and said after a moment: "Dashed if I see what that has to do with it, sir! You roasting me? I wish you won't, for I ain't in funning humor. Children going on well? Daresay you might not have noticed it, but I haven't been in Mount Street this age. Never seem to have any time to do anything but look after Kit! If it ain't seeing to it that Meg don't persuade her into buying a shocking bonnet, it's driving with her all over London and showing her a lot of tombs and broken-down statues you wouldn't think anyone would want to look at, let alone *pay* to look at!"

Fascinated, his father said: "Is that what you have been doing?"

"I should rather think it is! Yes, and that's put me in mind of another thing I wanted to say to you! This British Museum they talk so much about! You know what, sir? It's a dashed take-in! Ought to do something about it. Why, if Kit hadn't happened to have a deuced good book with her, we should have been bit, like a couple of green 'uns!"

"My dear Freddy," said Lord Legerwood, tucking a hand in his arm, "come into the club, and tell me about it!"

"Well, I will," Freddy replied. "Though that ain't what I chiefly want to say to you. Find myself in a bit of a fix – at least, shouldn't wonder at it if I do find myself in one. Had a notion I might do worse than consult you."

"You might – much worse!" said his lordship. "But first I must and will hear about the British Museum!"

He then led his son into the club, found a quiet corner in the morning-room, and bade him unburden his soul. He listened with rapt appreciation to Freddy's account of his ordeal, expressing himself so properly that Freddy was disappointed to find that he did not feel that it lay within his province to expose the several abuses discovered by his heir. When he further disclosed, apologetically, that the question of the acquisition by the nation of the Elgin Marbles was to come up before both Houses that very session, Freddy was shocked and incredulous, and for several minutes forgot the real purpose of this interview. It was not until he had been soothed by a glass of very dry sherry that he remembered it, and then he said, without the smallest preamble: "You know the Chevalier d'Evron, sir?"

"I have not that pleasure," responded Lord Legerwood.

"Thought as much," nodded Freddy. "It don't prove anything, of course, because he's a young man, and I daresay you might not know him. Ever hear of the family?"

"No."

"Smoky," said Freddy gloomily.

Lord Legerwood presently interrupted his meditations. "Who is this gentleman, Freddy?"

"Cousin of Kit's. She likes him. Mended a doll for her once, or some such stuff. Claud chopped its head off. Sort of thing he would do, come to think of it."

"Am I to infer that you don't share Kitty's liking for the Chevalier?"

"Wouldn't say that," replied Freddy, rubbing his nose. "Very pleasant fellow. But you know how it is: can't be on the town without learning to know a flat from a leg!"

"I am happy to hear you say so. Tell me more of this – leg?"

"No, no, he ain't a leg! At least, I don't know that he is. Shouldn't think it's as bad as that. Jack's too downy to play cards with a leg. But he ain't a flat either. Daresay you might not have noticed him, but he was at Meg's party t'other evening."

"Are you talking of a handsome young exquisite in a coat of pronounced cut, and an over-large tie-pin?"

"That's the fellow," said Freddy. "Good air, good address, talks of his uncle the Marquis. But they don't seem to know him at the Embassy."

"Disquieting," agreed his lordship. "One must bear in mind, however, the late disturbed times in France. Possibly one of the new nobility?"

"That's what Jasper says, but it don't make it any better. Seems to me that fellow Bonaparte ennobled a lot of devilish queer fish. Thing is, this Camille of Kit's looked to me as though he meant to dangle after her. Told him we was engaged. Told him the terms of this Will Uncle Matthew means to make. Then he stopped haunting the place. Dangling after the Yalding fright instead."

"In fact, an adventurer! I imagine Annerwick will take good care that his daughter doesn't marry to disoblige him. Isn't there a sister living with Lady Maria, as dragon?"

"Yes, but she's a poor dab of a female. The *on-dit* is that Lady Maria means to have the Chevalier. Wouldn't surprise me at all: handsome fellow, very popular with the ladies. No use saying it ain't my affair. Seems to me it might be. What I mean is, if Annerwick took fright, very likely to set a lot of dashed awkward inquiries afoot. If the fellow's an impostor, disagreeable situation for Kit. Besides, she don't like not having relations. Told me so. Said it made her comfortable to have a respectable cousin. Ought to do something about it."

Lord Legerwood, who had been listening to him with much more interest than he was wont to accord him, said: "I expect you ought, Freddy, but precisely what you should do I confess I don't immediately perceive."

Freddy looked surprised. "Don't see any difficulty about that, sir. If he's a loose-fish, nothing for it but to get rid of him."

Lord Legerwood's eyes widened a little. "I trust you are not proposing to fight a duel, Freddy?"

"Lord, no! Cork-brained thing to do. Pack him off to France again: that's the dandy!"

"An excellent scheme – if you can bring it about."

"Daresay I shall think of a way," said Freddy. He observed a curious expression on his father's countenance, and said with slight concern: "Anything amiss, sir?"

"No – oh, no!" replied Lord Legerwood, recovering himself. "I almost believe that you will think of a way, for I perceive that you have depths hitherto unsuspected by me, my dear boy. Tell me, if you please, if I am correct in assuming that my part in this is to discover for you, if I can, who and what is your Chevalier?"

"That's it," said Freddy, gratified by such ready understanding. "Very much obliged to you if you would, sir."

"I will do my poor best," bowed his lordship. "Meanwhile, permit me to congratulate you upon the change you have wrought in Kitty's appearance! I collect that yours has been the guiding hand: alas, I knew when I saw her the other evening that my poor Meg could have had little to say in the choice of her apparel!"

Freddy looked pleased. "Elegant little thing, ain't she?" His brow clouded. "Shouldn't have worn those topazes, though. Wouldn't let me give her a set of garnets. Pity!"

Lord Legerwood, although noting this peculiar re-

luctance on Miss Charing's part to receive gifts from
her betrothed, refrained from comment. He merely
said, polishing his eyeglass: "Oblige me, Freddy, by
telling me if Jack Westruther is often to be found in
Berkeley Square?"

Freddy's brow darkened. "Too dashed often for my
taste. No need for you to trouble yourself, though.
Keeping my eye on Meg!"

Lord Legerwood, sustaining yet another shock, said
faintly: "You are?"

"To be sure I am. What's more, got my own notion
of what's in the wind." He nodded portentously, but
added: "Don't mean to say anything about that: not
my affair! Trouble is – beginning to think he's too
damned loose in the haft!"

"I have thought that any time these past seven
years," said Lord Legerwood.

"You have?" said Freddy, regarding him with affectionate pride. "Always say you're the downiest man I
know, sir! Up to every rig and row in town!"

"Freddy, you unman me!" said his father, profoundly moved. "No one, I believe, has yet called me
a slow-top, but I own I am happy to learn that you are
– er – keeping an eye on your sister."

"Yes, but no need to fear there'll be any brats coming through a side door," said Freddy bluntly. "For
one thing, can't, with Meg increasing; for another –
Jack's got his eye on a devilish prime article. Don't
think he would, either: dash it, not such a rum touch
as that!"

With this assurance Lord Legerwood had to be content, for his son's confidences were at an end. Freddy
saw no reason to inform his parent that he had been
thunderstruck to discover that Miss Charing had, by

means unknown to him, become acquainted with the damsel whom he had no hesitation in designating a prime article. He had already viewed with disapprobation her friendship with an ill-favored female of obviously plebeian origin; his feelings when he called in Berkeley Square and found his affianced bride entertaining Miss Broughty held him spellbound upon the threshold, his jaw dropping, and his eyes starting from his head. When Miss Broughty presently took her leave, he nerved himself to expostulate with Kitty, representing to her that to be striking up an acquaintanceship with the daughter of a lady whom he did not scruple to call an Abbess, if ever he saw one, could in no way add to her consequence. "It won't do, Kit! Take it from me!"

To his intense discomfiture he came under the beam of Miss Charing's wide-eyed, inquiring gaze. "What does an Abbess signify, Freddy?" she asked.

He was thrown into disorder, and replied hastily: "Never mind that! Wouldn't understand if I told you! Thing is, the woman's putting that girl up to the highest bidder. Oughtn't to say such things to you, but there it is!"

"I know she is," responded Kitty calmly. "She is quite the most odious woman imaginable! I am so sorry for poor Olivia! Indeed, Freddy, you would pity her if you knew the whole!"

"Yes, I daresay I should. No harm in being sorry for her, but it won't do to be making a friend of her."

"But, Freddy, surely there can be no objection! Though we may dislike Mrs Broughty, Olivia's birth is respectable for she is related to Lady Batterstown, and she, I know, is a friend of your Mama's!"

Freddy sighed. 'Trouble is, Kit, you ain't been on

the town long enough to know the ins and the outs! Oliver Broughty was a dashed loose screw, by all I've ever heard, and it don't make a ha'porth of odds if he was some kind of a third cousin to Lady Batterstown, or if he wasn't. In fact, he was, but it's what I was telling you t'other day: every family has its scaff and raff! *We* have! Thing is, don't foist 'em on the *ton!*"

Kitty wrinkled her brow. "It is true that Lady Batterstown seems not to have been very kind to the Broughtys. One cannot but feel that had she but befriended Olivia the poor girl might have achieved a very creditable alliance, for you cannot deny, Freddy, that she is most beautiful!"

"That ain't enough," said the worldly-wise Mr Standen.

"Well, but it seems as though sometimes it is!" argued Kitty. "Olivia has been telling me about the beautiful Miss Gunnings, who were no better connected than she is, and yet, when their Mama brought them to London, they took the town by storm, and one of them married two Dukes!"

"No, really, Kit!" protested Mr Standen. "Doing it too brown! Couldn't have!"

"But indeed she did! First she was married to the Duke of Hamilton, and when he died she married the Duke of Argyll!"

"Oh, when he *died!*" said Freddy, glad to have this point elucidated. "No reason why she shouldn't. Not but what this little ladybird won't marry a Duke, let alone a couple of 'em. Well, I put it to you, Kit! I don't know how it was when these Gunning-girls of yours were on the town, but the only Duke I can think of who hasn't been married for years is Devonshire, and it's not a bit of use laying lures for him, because it's common knowledge he tried to fix his interest with the Princess Charlotte, and it ain't likely he'd take Olivia Broughty instead!"

"Of course I don't mean that she should marry a Duke!" replied Kitty. "Only it would be too dreadful if she was *sold* – for one can call it nothing else! – to such a creature as Sir Henry Gosford!" She saw that these words had made a profound impression, and said triumphantly: "You are shocked, but I assure you—"

"I should dashed well think I am shocked!" interrupted Freddy. "You aren't going to tell me that fellow visits Meg?"

"No, of course not—"

"Then where the deuce did you meet him?"

"I didn't meet him! Meg pointed him out to me once, when we were driving in the Park, but she only said that he was a horrid old rake, and she did not even give him a common bow in passing! It is Olivia who has told me all about him, and I do think you must have felt for her, Freddy, had you been here! She is being quite persecuted with his attentions, and because he is so rich, and Lady Batterstown has not put Olivia in the way of receiving more eligible offers, Mrs Broughty encourages his advances! Indeed, she positively forces him upon Olivia! How it will end I dare not think, for Olivia regards him with the greatest repugnance, and yet she is so much afraid of her Mama that she knows not what to do, and says that she fears sometimes that she may be compelled to do something desperate – though *what* this could be I don't know. I cannot think that she would take the terrible step of putting a period to her existence!"

"Well, there ain't any need for you to think it," said

Freddy, quite unmoved by this flight. "No wish to vex you, but Gosford ain't the only buck throwing out lures to the girl!"

She said innocently: "No, no, she has received not one offer, Freddy!"

Mr Standen, feeling himself quite unequal to the task of explaining to her the precise nature of the offers likely to be received by Miss Broughty, gave it up. He might have pointed out that dazzling beauties, unaccepted by the *ton,* and permitted to appear in public accompanied only by a cousin of unmistakable vulgarity who showed only too ready a disposition to efface herself if a modish buck ogled her charge, did not commonly achieve brilliant alliances, but, on the contrary, were more in the habit of being offered *cartes blanches* by such connoisseurs as Mr Westruther. Freddy was well aware of his cousin's pursuit of the fair Olivia. He did not think that the attentions of such a notable Corinthian were distasteful to her; but he was very sure that however ardent Jack's passion for her might be it would not carry him to the altar in her company. Whether he would succeed in mounting her as his latest mistress was a question which had not hitherto exercised Mr Standen's mind, since it had in no way concerned him. He now hoped very much that Mr Westruther's circumstances were not affluent enough to tempt Mrs Broughty, for he perceived, nebulously but with dismay, that such a liaison would be attended by quite hideous complications. Mr Standen, being blessed with sisters, entertained not the slightest doubt that Kitty, befriending Olivia, would be the recipient of all the secrets of her bosom. At the best, a certain crusading instinct in Miss Charing would undoubtedly lead her to kick up the devil of a dust, he

thought. At the worst – but here Mr Standen's powerful reasoning broke down, and he floundered in a sea
of conjecture.

He had not forgotten that Kitty confessed to him,
on the road to London, that in coming to town she
had a scheme in mind which she preferred not to disclose. There were moments when he thought he had
a very fair idea of what this might be. He had been
faintly surprised to learn from her that she hated Mr
Westruther, for her youthful adoration of so magnificent a personage had been common knowledge in the
family. As far as he could be said to have considered
the matter at all, Freddy had supposed that the childish passion had worn itself out. But having been privileged to observe Kitty's demeanor when Mr
Westruther chanced to be present he no longer felt
very sure of this. His Aunt Dolphinton, yielding to an
uncertain temper, had informed him waspishly that
Kitty had accepted his offer in a fit of pique; and while
he paid very little heed to this at the time he soon
began to think that it might be the truth. He could not
otherwise account for Miss Charing's affectionate demeanour towards him when, and only when, Mr
Westruther was present. Jack had accompanied them
to the ball at the Pantheon, but so far from evincing
any desire to dance with him, Kitty had accorded him
one only of the waltzes he demanded, and had excused
herself from attempting to perform the steps of the
quadrille under his guidance. "No, the next country
dance, if you please!" she said.

"But I do not please! How can you be so impolite?"

She laughed. "Oh, must I stand on ceremony with
you? No, I have known you for too many years, and
I don't scruple to tell you that I daren't trust myself

to you in a quadrille, for you know, Jack, I made sad work of that waltz with you! To own the truth, I don't care to dance waltzes or quadrilles with anyone but Freddy."

So Mr Westruther, bowing in mock humility, allowed himself to be fobbed off with a country dance; and was presently afforded an excellent opportunity, had he cared to avail himself of it, of observing how merrily Miss Charing twirled about the hall with Mr Standen. But as he chose rather to flirt outrageously with Meg, Miss Charing could not be sure that he did observe it. When they stood up together in the country dance, she no longer sparkled, and three times answered him at random. Called to order, she begged pardon, and said she had not been attending.

"Thinking of Freddy, no doubt," said Mr Westruther sardonically.

"No, I can't plead that excuse. My mind was merely wandering."

Since the ladies whom Mr Westruther chose to honor with his attentions did not commonly allow their minds to wander when he was talking to them, he was momentarily taken aback. Recovering, he laughed. "A heavy set-down! Can it be that I have had the ill-fortune to offend you, Kitty?"

She was not obliged to reply to this, as they were separated just then by a movement of the dance. When they came together again, she asked him if he did not think Freddy a beautiful dancer.

"Certainly: the best in town," he responded. "One might say that it is his only accomplishment – unless you hold his tailoring to be an accomplishment?"

"That is not a proper mode in which to speak of Freddy to me!" she countered forthrightly.

"Don't be absurd, Kitty!"

She disregarded this, but said seriously: "I think Freddy has what is better than accomplishments – a kind heart!"

"Or do you mean a yielding disposition?" said Mr Westruther, quizzing her. "Poor Freddy!"

She flushed. "He is your cousin, and you may sneer at him if you choose, but you shall not do so to me, Jack!"

"You are mistaken: the emotion that fills my breast is not contempt, but compassion."

For the second time in her life, Miss Charing was conscious of a strong desire to slap that handsome, mocking face. She controlled it, saying in a repressive tone: "I believe that he may yet surprise you."

"He *has* surprised me," replied Mr Westruther.

Miss Charing could only be glad when the dance ended.

❧ *Chapter XII* ❧

KITTY, HOWEVER MUCH MR WESTRUTHER might disconcert her, was not ill-pleased by the results of her strategy. She had certainly arrested his attention. If he disbelieved the story of the engagement (and he gave every sign of disbelieving it), the tacit refusal of both parties to it to own the truth, coupled with Kitty's apparent lack of interest in his activities, compelled him to alter his tactics. He did not doubt his ability to put an end to the comedy at any moment of his own choosing, for he was well aware that she had adored him for years; but he did not mean to let her, or his Great-uncle Matthew, dictate terms, or force his hand. Nothing in his life had annoyed him more than Mr Penicuik's ultimatum. He certainly meant to marry one day; he as certainly meant country-bred, innocent Kitty to be his wife, believing that either to him or to her would Mr Penicuik's fortune be bequeathed; but he was not a pawn on any chessboard of Mr Penicuik's making; and, for he was a gamester, he would have forgone every penny of that considerable fortune rather than have obeyed such a summons as he had received. Moreover, he was betting upon a certainty: Kitty was his for the lifting of a finger. He feared no competition from any one of his cousins, and if he had been surprised to learn of her engagement to Freddy it had been momentarily: an instant's reflection showed him what must have been her reason. He was amused by it; he could even appreciate it; and although he meant to punish her a little, he bore her no ill-will for such a flash of spirit. But however negligible a rival Freddy might be, Mr Westruther was not so lost in self-esteem that he did not recognize the danger of Kitty's succumbing to the flattery of other and more personable suitors. A pretty girl – and Mr Westruther had been surprised to discover how very pretty Kitty could be when she was tricked out in all the elegancies of fashion – presented to society by the Standens, carrying with her the aura of large expectations, would not lack admirers. However much Mr Penicuik might pride himself on abiding by his pledged word, Jack would not have wagered any considerable sum on the chance of his abiding by it, were Kitty to present herself at Arnside on the arm of a really brilliant suitor. Mr Westruther, introducing the Chevalier d'Evron to her in a spirit of pure mischief, had his own reasons for discounting danger from that quarter; her encouragement of Dolphinton's absurd attentions he did not understand but was able to shrug away; there were other bachelors, by far more eligible, whom it would be unwise to despise. One, in particular, a youthful peer, had shown unmistakable signs of developing a *tendre* for so lively and unaffected a damsel, and a noted connoisseur, not indeed in the first blush of his youth but none the less attractive for that, had not only solicited her to dance upon the occasion of her début at Almack's, but had followed up this mark of his approval by sending her flowers upon the next day. It was time for Mr Westruther to move, even though he had no intention of dancing so easily to the tune of Miss Charing's impertinent piping. It was one thing to be amused by the schemes of a child he had known from her cradle-days; quite another to yield to them. He could sympathize with her desire to visit London, but he would have been better pleased had she remained, rather like a Sleeping Beauty, at Arnside. Marriage in the immediate future he wished to avoid; but if Kitty doubted his intention to make her ultimately his wife it would be as well to fix his interest securely with her. None knew better than he how to charm and to tantalize until his victim had no eyes for another than himself. His conquests were many; and if no lady had actually died of unrequited love, one at least (but it was generally acknowledged that her sensibility was immoderate) had suffered a decline on his account. The appearance on her horizon of an even more captivating admirer had happily arrested the fell disease; but anxious parents took inordinate pains to shield their susceptible daughters from the fleeting attentions of a most destructive flirt.

Sustaining two set-downs from Miss Charing, who twice found excuses for refusing invitations to drive out with him in the curricle drawn by his famous chestnuts, Mr Westruther sent her, by the hand of his groom, a ravishing fan of ivory, pierced, gilded, and painted with delicate medallions by the hand of Angelica Kauffman. Accompanying this gift, was a letter so adroitly phrased that Kitty knew not how to refuse the fan. It was the betrothal present, Mr Westruther wrote, of her oldest friend, who dared to subscribe himself by affection, if not by blood, her ever-loving cousin, Jack.

"Well!" exclaimed Meg, not quite pleased. "I am sure he has never given *me* anything one half as pretty! He must certainly have had a run of luck! The most *expensive* trifle, my dear Kitty!"

Pressing her hands to her hot cheeks, Kitty said: "I must not accept such a valuable gift!"

"Good gracious, why should you not? You can scarcely refuse it, my love! Quite unexceptionable, I assure you! 'Your ever-loving cousin'—! Very prettily phrased, upon my word!"

So when Mr Westruther renewed his invitation to his cousin-by-affection to drive with him to Richmond Park, to see the primroses there, bursting into pale flower under the shade of immemorial trees, it seemed to Miss Charing that she could only accept, with becoming pleasure. The luck favored Mr Westruther; the appointed day was one of bright sunshine. It encouraged Miss Charing to wear a Villager-hat of satin straw, with flowers at one side, and an apple-green ribbon passed beneath her chin, and tied in a skittish bow under her ear; and to carry a frivolous parasol, bestowed upon her by Meg. Mr Westruther found himself thinking, as he handed her into his curricle, that her appearance was such as must satisfy the most exacting of men.

It was his custom to drive abroad with a diminutive Tiger perched up behind him, but on this occasion he had dispensed with the services of this youth. He told Kitty, with the flicker of a smile, that such chaperonage could not be thought necessary for such near relations (by affection) as themselves. She agreed to it, but warily. Yet not the most querulous critic could have called in question Mr Westruther's conduct from start to finish of this expedition. He was the big cousin who had enchanted her childish fancy; he might laugh at her, but he refrained from laughing at Freddy; if he never once referred to her engagement, at least he gave no sign of disbelieving it. Only at the end of an afternoon for which Kitty thanked him with real gratitude did he lower the mask for an instant. The laugh sprang to his eyes; he looked down into her face for a moment, lightly pinched her chin, and said, the words a caress: "Foolish, doubting, little Kitty! There, in with you, my child! I cannot leave my horses to go with you!"

The color rushed up under his careless fingers; she glanced fleetingly into his face, lowered her eyes gain, and with a stammered: "Th-thank you! It was very agreeable!" ran up the steps, and into the house. He drove away, very well satisfied; thinking, too, that the country cousin was unfurling new and charming petals.

He let two days pass, and then called one morning in Berkeley Square to invite both ladies to go with him to Sadler's Wells on the following evening, so that Kitty might see the great Grimaldi in a revival of his very successful pantomime, *Mother Goose*. Though Meg might cry out against so unsophisticated an entertainment, Mr Westruther knew Kitty well enough to be sure she would revel in it. Had it been possible, he would unhesitatingly have taken her to Astley's Amphitheater, and would himself have derived a good deal of amusement, he thought, from watching her awe and delight at Grand Spectacles, and Equestrian

Displays. But the Amphitheater, like its rival, the Royal Circus, never opened until Easter Monday, by which time, Mr Westruther trusted, Kitty would have returned to Arnside.

Meg's butler, admitting him into the house, informed him that her ladyship had driven out, but that Miss Charing, though about to take the air with a friend, was in the Small Saloon. He then escorted Mr Westruther to this apartment, and, all unwitting, subjected him to a severe shock. "Mr Westruther!" he announced, and went away, leaving Mr Westruther on the threshold, a little rigid, the lazy smile frozen on his lips.

There were three people in the room. There was Kitty, in a mulberry bonnet and pelisse, engaged in working her fingers into a pair of new gloves; there was Freddy, standing with his back to the fire; and there was Miss Broughty, radiant in pale blue merino, with swansdown trimming, and a swansdown muff.

It was only for an instant that Mr Westruther was shocked into immobility. Before Kitty, turning to greet him, had time to observe his stupefaction, he had recovered himself, and had moved forward, saying with perfect sangfroid: "I collect that I have not chosen my moment well: you are going out! Never mind! my errand is soon discharged."

"Yes, Miss Broughty is so kind as to give me her company," she replied, shaking hands with him. "We mean to walk in the Park, and see how the daffodils and the crocuses come on. Olivia, pray allow me to introduce Mr Westruther to you!"

"Unnecessary," he said coolly, advancing towards Olivia, and holding out his hand. "I already have the honor of being acquainted with Miss Broughty. How do you do?"

This announcement was productive of only the mildest surprise in Miss Charing; but when she glanced towards her friend she was astonished to see her face suffused with blushes. Miss Broughty looked up, and looked down, stammered something inaudible, and barely permitted Mr Westruther to touch her hand before tucking it away again in her muff. Such conduct, even in a girl unused to society, seemed strange. Kitty wondered if Jack could in some way have offended Olivia. She knew him to be occasionally arrogant and had just decided that he must have wounded Olivia's susceptibilities with some slighting look or remark, when she chanced to catch sight of Freddy. The elegant Mr Standen bore all the appearance of one who had been stuffed, his gaze being so glassy, and his face so totally devoid of expression, that one glance in his direction was enough to convince Kitty that she had stumbled upon a mystery he would have been very glad to have kept hidden from her. Only a short time earlier she would certainly have demanded an explanation, but her little stay in London had already taught her to command her tongue. Seeming not to notice Olivia's confusion, she said: "And what is your errand, Jack?"

It was soon disclosed; she could not answer for Meg's willingness to go to Sadler's Wells, but she said that for herself she would be all happiness to accept. She then shook hands with both gentlemen, unmistakably dismissing them, and swept Olivia off for their proposed walk in the Park.

Alone with Mr Standen, Mr Westruther said sweetly: "Would you care to explain to me, my very dear coz, how I come to find that charming ladybird on terms of intimacy with Kitty?''

"Yes, I didn't fancy you'd like it overmuch," replied Freddy. "Nothing to do with me. Don't imagine I introduced her to Kit, do you?"

"The notion, I own, had presented itself to me," said Mr Westruther.

"Well, I didn't," said Freddy. "Dashed bacon-brained notion to take into your cockloft! For one thing, not acquainted with the girl myself; for another, not the sort of girl I would introduce to Kit." He thought this over for a moment, and then said scrupulously: "What I mean is, won't be, if she pays any heed to the lures you've been throwing out to her this age past! Looked to me as though she well might. Pretty little bit of muslin, but hen-witted."

"I thank you!" Mr Westruther said sardonically. "If not to you, Freddy, to whom are my thanks due for this clever touch?" He perceived that he had bewildered his cousin, and added impatiently: "Well? Who made Kitty known to the girl her perfidious cousin Jack has made the object of his attentions?"

"Don't think anyone did," replied Freddy. "Met her by chance. Know what I think? Good thing if you was to take a damper! Not engaged to Kit, coz!"

Those very blue eyes glinted at him. "I might make the obvious retort, Freddy, but I won't!"

The two ladies in question, meanwhile, were treading briskly down one of the paths in the Park, their hands tucked in their muffs, and their pelisses fastened tightly up to their throats, for although the sun shone, encouraging daffodils to burst from their sheaths, an east wind blew strongly.

"Dear Miss Charing, if you knew the solace it is to

me to be in your company!" Olivia said. "I should not repine – I know that Mama has made many, many sacrifices to make this visit to the Metropolis possible, but, oh, I was happier by far at home, with my sisters!"

Kitty was already aware of the existence of Amelia, and Jane, and Selina, and she uttered a murmur of sympathy. She was not of an age fully to comprehend the anxieties of a mother indifferently blessed with four daughters, but she understood from Olivia that these were acute. Dear Papa, it seemed, had not left his family in affluent circumstances; but he had certainly endowed them with good looks, a commodity in which they had been bred from earliest youth to trade to the best advantage. Only Jane, they feared, was bookish; and Amelia showed a dreadful tendency to freckles. Olivia, the loveliest as well as the eldest of the sisters, did not question that it was her duty to make a good match. She had come to London with that object; but whenever her maiden fancy had speculated on the good match it had always come to her in the guise of a young and handsome suitor, and never in that of an elderly roué. She had supposed too that Dear Papa's grand relations in Brook Street would welcome her and Mama to their house; but here again reality had fallen sadly short of expectation. Repulsed by the Batterstowns, Mama had been obliged to accept the hospitality of her sister, living in Hans Crescent; and however good-natured Mrs Scorton might be, she had no entrée into the world of fashion, and was undeniably vulgar. Not for Miss Broughty the select gatherings at Almack's, the *ton* parties, the box, when the season began, at the Italian Opera. Mama, skirmishing round the fringes of society, had achieved one or two genteel invitations for her daughter, but none of them

led to the triumphs she had so confidently predicted.
As for taking the town by storm, as the beautiful Gun-
ning sisters had done, sixty-five years earlier, either
times had changed, or there was some peculiar virtue
attached to pairs. "But Amelia is not yet sixteen,"
Olivia explained seriously, "and the expense, besides,
could not have been met."

It seemed to Kitty a pity that her new friend's mind
was set so irrevocably upon marriage, but her suggestion that Olivia might seek an eligible situation as a
governess met with no favor at all. Olivia stared at her
with dismay in her big eyes, and unequivocally stated
her preference for death. Upon reflection, Kitty was
obliged to own that she was scarcely fitted for such a
post. Her intellect was not superior, and her education
was scanty. She had great sweetness of temper, a biddable disposition, and sufficient refinement to shrink
from the machinations of her Mama and her cheerful,
loud-voiced cousins; but the more Kitty saw of her the
less was she able to believe that that lovely exterior
hid the slightest strength of character. She thought it
surprising, too, that so beautiful a girl should have had
no suitors at home for whom she appeared to have felt
any partiality. Olivia explained that the neighborhood
was restricted. "I am sure no one could like Ned
Bandy, and the Wrays, you know, are horribly vulgar.
There was only Mr Sticklepath, and of course *that*
would not do."

"He was not eligible?" Kitty ventured to ask.

"Oh, no! I daresay he has not twopence to rub together, poor man!"

"But you liked him, perhaps?"

"No, but he would have been very glad to have married me, even though I have no fortune, because his

housekeeper is lately dead, and he does not know how to go on, and I can dress meat neatly and cheaply, besides being able to sew, and to iron better than the washerwoman."

The vision of an impoverished but romantic young lover died still-born. Daunted, Kitty said: "And was there no one else? No one at all? I declare, it must be as dull as my own home, and I had thought that nothing could be!"

"Only young Mr Drakemire," said Olivia. "He is rather stout, but *very* genteel. He stood up twice with me at the Assembly, but the Drakemires, you must know, live at the Big House, and Lady Drakemire did not at all like his seeming to admire me, so he did not take me out driving as he said he would. Mama scolded, but indeed it was not my fault! I said everything she told me to, but it wouldn't serve."

"I have sometimes thought," said Kitty, tentatively, and after a short pause, "that nothing could be more disagreeable than to marry a gentleman for whom one feels no strong attachment."

"No, indeed!" Olivia sighed.

"I could not do it. In fact, I would liefer by far die unwed!"

"Would you?" said Olivia wistfully. "But, then, dear Miss Charing, our circumstances are so different! You have all the comfort and consequence of fortune—"

"No, I assure you I have not! I am wholly dependant upon the generosity of my guardian! I do not exaggerate when I say that I have not a penny in the world!"

"Yes, but your guardian is rich, is he not? Mama, you see, is not rich at all, and I have three sisters," said Olivia unanswerably. "I must be married. Oh, how vexed Mama would be if she was obliged to take me home again, and all the money she saved for this visit spent to no purpose!"

She looked so really frightened that Kitty said quickly: "Of course you will be married, and to a man you can esteem, too! Good gracious, don't tell me you have not a great many admirers already, for I shall certainly not believe you! Indeed, I think everyone who sees you must admire you, for you are by far the prettiest girl in London!"

Olivia colored, and averted her face. "Don't – pray! Gentlemen do sometimes admire me, but – but they do not offer to marry me. Situated as I am – the manners of my cousins – so very free! – I have met with a want of propriety in – in some whom I believed to be so *very* gentlemanly!"

"I know what you mean, I daresay," said Kitty, wisely, but in blissful ignorance of Miss Broughty's meaning. "You are now and then judged by your company, and you find yourself treated with that kind of high-bred insolence which I have frequently noticed in London, and which *I* do not consider high-bred at all, but, on the contrary, excessively ill-bred!" She added frankly: "Forgive me, but I could not but notice that you were not quite pleased to meet Mr Westruther in Berkeley Square! If you should have thought that he was not civil to you when you met him previously, I assure you he does not mean to offend! He has sometimes a little height in his manner: Lady Buckhaven rallies him on it, saying he sets up people's backs. He is never formal, you know – indeed, I fancy he treats no one with particular distinction!"

"Oh, no!" breathed Olivia. "I did not mean – I should not have mentioned—Such a very distinguished man! His air and address so exactly—" She broke off in confusion, and quickly directed Kitty's attention to a clump of purple crocuses.

Some inkling of the truth began to dawn on Kitty. It was apparent to her that the magnificence of Mr Westruther had had its inevitable effect upon Miss Broughty. She did not wonder at it; she would indeed have found it hard to believe that any female could be ten minutes in Mr Westruther's company without falling under the spell of his charm. But her sojourn in London, short though it had been, had convinced her that those who called Jack a shocking flirt spoke no less than the truth. It was, of course, reprehensible, but the failing did not diminish his charm: rather, it added to it, Kitty admitted to herself, a little guiltily. Nor was it just, she thought, to censure him too heavily, for the many ladies who blatantly set their caps at him gave him every encouragement to persist in his evil ways. But Kitty had quite a shrewd head on her shoulders, for all her country innocence, and somewhere, at the very back of her mind, not consciously acknowledged, lurked the conviction that Jack would never marry to his own disadvantage. None knew better than she what havoc he could create in female breasts; it would be dreadful if he (unwittingly, of course) scarred Olivia's tender heart. She said impulsively: "Yes, Freddy – Mr Standen – calls him a buck of the first head! He is precisely the hero every schoolroom-miss dreams about – as I have told him! I have known him all my life, you must understand: we have been as cousins."

"Yes," Olivia said, still with her eyes fixed on the crocuses. "I collected, when he came in – I was not previously aware of the relationship."

"Oh, in fact there is none!" Kitty interrupted. "I call

all my guardian's great-nephews my cousins! Yes, what a splendid patch of color, to be sure! Another day will see them in full bloom, but we shall take cold if we stand still in this sharp wind!''

They walked on, the path soon leading them to the promenade flanking the carriage-way. It was not long before a most unwelcome sight assailed Miss Broughty's eyes. She said, under her breath: "Sir Henry Gosford! I implore you, dear Miss Charing, do not desert me!"

Kitty had not the smallest intention of deserting her, being wholly unacquainted with the tactics adopted by her cousins, the Misses Scorton; but she had no time to reassure her: that time-worn beau, Sir Henry Gosford, had already swept off his hat, and was executing a bow before them. "Venus, with Attendant Nymph!" he uttered.

An involuntary gurgle of mirth drew his eyes towards the Attendant Nymph. He raised his quizzing-glass with an air of hauteur, but speedily allowed it to fall again. No quizzing-glass, however magnifying its lens, could avail against Miss Charing's clear, unwavering gaze. From the crown of his jauntily poised beaver to the toes of his polished boots, Miss Charing surveyed him, critically, but with indulgence. For a horrid moment it seemed to him that she detected the tight corsets he wore; and knew that the glowing chestnut hue of his curled and oiled locks could only be ascribed to the exertions of his barber. In the agitation of this moment, he failed to assimilate the introduction stammeringly performed by Miss Broughty. A lifetime of self-satisfaction came to his rescue; he realized that the Attendant Nymph's rapt gaze could only spring from admiration of so complete a Bond Street

Lounger; favored her with a nod, and a smile not pronounced enough to disturb the maquillage which so cleverly hid the wrinkles in his face, and turned his attention to Miss Broughty. "Fair Amaryllis!" he said. "It is not too much to say that you adorn the spring! All our beauties are cast into the shade, I protest!"

"No, that's not right, sir," said the well-read Miss Charing, painstakingly helpful. " 'To sport with Amaryllis in the shade,' and *quite* ineligible!"

Sir Henry sustained a severe shock. His jaw dropped, and he groped again for his quizzing-glass, and raised it, this time with every intention of depressing pretension. Miss Charing's wide dark eyes observed this maneuver with interest. The glass dropped; Sir Henry said, showing all his excellent, if not genuine, teeth in an unloving smile: "Very witty, Miss – er – Scorton!"

"You cannot have been attending, sir," said Kitty reprovingly. "I am Miss Charing, not Miss Scorton."

"Oh. I beg pardon! I did not immediately perceive—! Ah, exactly so! You are not Miss Broughty's cousin, ma'am! Ten thousand pardons! My dear Miss Broughty, you are unattended – you have no footman no maid! You must allow me to escort you!"

Olivia, thrown into the greatest discomfort, knew not how to counter this. Her companion was made of sterner stuff. "Unattended, Sir Henry? When you yourself knew me for an Attendant Nymph!" exclaimed Miss Charing. "Indeed, we shall not put you to so much trouble!"

He protested that he could know no greater pleasure, talked archly of the distinction of having a lovely lady on either arm, and interspersed these compliments with broad hints to Kitty to take herself off, so

that there seemed to be no possibility of getting rid
of him. But when they had walked a few hundred yards
salvation appeared in equestrian guise. Kitty, idly
looking at the carriages and the horsemen, suddenly
perceived her French cousin, trotting towards them
on a brown hack. She waved; he saw her; and at once
drew up, sweeping off his hat, and bowing. "My cousin! But what a *coup de bonheur!* They tell me that to
be *gent du monde* in England I must ride in the Park,
so behold me, mounted, *à grands frais,* upon a slug! I
have my reward, *cependant quoi qu'il en soit!"* He laughed
down into Kitty's eyes, saw in them an unmistakable
message, glanced at Sir Henry, and at once swung
himself lightly out of the saddle, twitching his bridle
over the hired hack's head, and saying: "You will permit me to go with you, cousin?"

Much pleased with this swift, Gallic comprehension,
Kitty said: "Oh, we shall be delighted to have your escort, Camille! Sir Henry here – oh, let me make you
known to my cousin, the Chevalier d'Evron, Sir
Henry! – has been so obliging as to turn his steps aside
to accompany us, but now that you are come we need
no longer trespass upon his good nature!" She then
turned, and held out her hand to Sir Henry, adding
brightly: "Goodbye! It was so kind in you!"

There was nothing for him to do but to take his dis-
missal with what grace he could muster. The Chevalier, having discovered Miss Broughty, averted his
eyes from her countenance with an effort, and bowed
again, saying with mechanical civility: *"Au plaisir de vous
revoir, m'sieur!"*

Sir Henry executed a bow, glared for a moment at
the handsome young Frenchman, and walked away,
jauntily twirling his cane. Kitty, observing that the

Chevalier's gaze had returned to her blushing friend's face, hastily repaired an omission. "My dear Miss Broughty, you must allow me to present to you my cousin, the Chevalier d'Evron!"

"How do you do?" whispered Olivia, putting out her hand, and blushing more furiously than ever.

"Mademoiselle!" breathed the Chevalier, taking the little hand reverently in his, and holding it as a man might hold a rare bird.

❦ *Chapter XIII* ❧

NEVER HAD THERE BEEN A CLEARER CASE OF love at first sight! As the Chevalier stood, tenderly holding the little gloved hand in his, while his gaze devoured the flower-like face, Olivia raised her eyes to his in a look of wonder, as though she had been an enchanted maiden awakened from long, dreamless sleep. Kitty, interestedly watching, thought that they exchanged hearts in that moment, and was quite sorry when a recollection of their surroundings made each look away. Olivia recovered her hand, and the Chevalier began at once to talk in his vivacious style to Kitty. He walked beside them, leading his horse, and when they would have parted from him at the Stanhope Gate, declared that he had been on his way to the livery stables when he had encountered them, and wished to ride no more. He escorted them along Mount Street; and Kitty, much enjoying her first efforts at match-making, begged them to stroll on towards Berkeley Square while she paused at the

Legerwood house, to inquire after the invalids. When she presently overtook them, they were conversing with the ease of long friendship, or perfect understanding; and the Chevalier had begged leave to stable his horse, and to return immediately to Lady Buckhaven's house, that he might have the privilege of driving Olivia back to Hans Crescent. Kitty could only admire such ready address. The Chevalier certainly had no carriage in England, but she did not doubt that he would contrive to beg, borrow, or hire a suitable vehicle. Nor was she disappointed: in a surprisingly short space of time he presented himself in Meg's drawing-room, leaving a groom from the livery stables he patronized in charge of a neat phaeton-and-pair.

He arrived to find the elder Miss Scorton sitting with Kitty and Olivia, and Kitty could have laughed aloud to see the look of chagrin that flickered in his eyes. But Olivia's cousin Eliza, a kind, vulgar spinster of uncertain age and romantic disposition, had no notion of spoiling sport. She had indeed come to bear Olivia company on her way home, but one glance at the Chevalier's excellent riding-dress and indefinable air of affluence was enough to convince her that here was a possible *parti* for her beautiful little cousin who combined wealth with attributes still more alluring to the female mind; and she lost no time in breaking into a voluble explanation of the several reasons which made it inconvenient for her to take Olivia back to Hans Crescent for at least an hour. She then took leave of Miss Charing, and departed, but not, rather unfortunately, before Lady Buckhaven came in. Meg received her protestations with civility, but coolly; and when she and Kitty were presently left alone she said, in a pet, that she wished Kitty would not invite such vulgar creatures to her house.

Kitty was contrite, but she was able to assure her hostess that Miss Scorton had no notion of encroaching. "She came only to escort Olivia home, you know. But, Meg, did you observe my cousin? I declare to you he no sooner clapped eyes on Olivia than he had no eyes for anyone else! It is the most famous thing!"

But Meg did not think it a famous thing at all. "Of course I observed your cousin, and I must say, Kitty, I think it is foolish beyond permission to encourage such a thing! The Chevalier and a girl with such low connections? You must be mad to think of it!"

"Oh, fiddle!" Kitty said. "You will own that her birth is respectable, and as for her connections, why, Camille will take her away to France, and they need never be troubled by Mrs Broughty, or the Scortons!"

"You can know nothing of relations if that is what you think!" said Meg tartly. "Good gracious, I wonder that Freddy will let you make such a goosecap of yourself!"

Miss Charing refrained from explaining that it was not in Mr Standen's power to control any of her actions. She guessed that Meg would lose no time in telling Freddy, and was fully prepared to counter opposition from that quarter. But Freddy, rubbing his nose as he always did when at a stand, merely said in a thoughtful voice: "Shouldn't wonder if you were to catch cold at that, Kit."

"Why, what do you mean?"

"Don't think it'll fadge," said Freddy.

"Oh, you are thinking of those dreadful Scortons, I daresay! I own, if Camille were an Englishman it might not do, but consider! – he is here only upon a visit, and it is not to be supposed that Mrs Broughty or her sister will for ever be journeying into France! Indeed, I should be astonished if they went there at all! To Olivia herself there can be not the least objection!"

"Got a notion Mrs Broughty won't like it," said Freddy.

She stared at him. "But why should she not? Besides, I have learnt that Camille was received by her when he drove Olivia to Hans Crescent that day, and nothing could have exceeded her affability!"

Freddy looked vaguely distressed, and rubbed his nose harder than ever.

"But, Freddy—!"

In Freddy's pocket there nestled a brief note from Lord Legerwood, informing him that he could discover no noble French family bearing the patronymic of Evron. *"Of 'my uncle the Marquis,'"* wrote Lord Legerwood, *"there is no discoverable trace. One feels that the creation of this peer was a mistake. One is further tempted to hazard the conjecture that your Chevalier may well prove to be a* chevalier d'industrie. . . .*"*

Freddy looked at Miss Charing, whose innocent eyes were fixed inquiringly upon his face, and colored. "French, y'know!" he said. "Been at war with the Frogs so long—!"

Miss Charing was satisfied, and laughed away such doubts. Freddy, foreseeing that Mrs Broughty, as well as himself, might be inspired to make certain inquiries, perceived shoals ahead, and looked unhappier than ever. His sister would have been glad had she been able to persuade him to remonstrate with his betrothed on her friendship with Olivia; for although Mrs Broughty, content to have insinuated her daugh-

ter into the genteel stronghold of the Buckhaven mansion, did not herself attempt to gain the entrée there,
Meg lived in constant dread that she would one day
do so. She told Freddy that she feared to be dragged
into the Scortin-set: if Mrs Broughty presented herself
in Berkeley Square she would not know how to refuse
her admittance. Freddy replied, in a practical spirit,
that such knowledge was unnecessary. "Only have to
tell Skelton you ain't at home: he'll do the rest. Dash
it, that's what butlers are for!"

"Oh, well, if you don't care for *me*," said Meg
crossly, "I wonder you should not care for Kitty's getting herself into a scrape, as she very likely will!"

"Don't see why she should," responded Freddy ob-
stinately.

Meg was in low spirits, suffering from the little *mal-
aises* of pregnant women, which made her say with a
fretfulness alien to her character: "How can you be so
stupid? *That* sort of thing always leads to trouble! It
is all kindness, and I am sure I am quite as sorry for
Miss Broughty as anyone, but one cannot make a
friend of everybody in distressing circumstances! Only
Kitty has been about the world so little she does not
understand, and you do not make the least push to set
her right!"

"Yes, I do!" said Freddy, stung by this unjust remark. "If it hadn't been for me, she'd have been going
all over town in that devilish hat *you* told her was all
the crack!"

"It *was* all the crack!" exclaimed Meg, sitting upright on the sofa in her indignation. "Only you are so
gothic and stuffy! You would not let her purchase it,
just because you had never seen one of the new

jockey-bonnets before! So *I* did, and it has been very much admired, let me tell you!"

"What?" ejaculated Freddy, roused to real dismay. "Good God, Meg, you ain't such a sapskull as to put a lilac coal-scuttle on that yaller head of yours?"

"A great many persons of *exquisite* taste," his sister informed him in trembling accents, "have told me that I look excessively becoming in it!"

"A great many gapeseeds!" said Freddy witheringly. "It's time m'mother left the young 'uns to Nurse to look after, and stopped you making a figure of yourself! No, really, Meg! Might consider me, you know! Might consider Mama, too! Do us credit!"

"Like Kitty! Permitting you to tell her what she may wear, and what she may not! I wonder she will listen to you!"

"Sensible little thing, Kit," said Freddy. "Does do me credit! M'father was saying so only the other day."

"Well, she does look remarkably well, I own," said Meg, "but in *one* way, Freddy – and I don't say it out of spite, for I love her dearly! – she doesn't do you any credit at all. And Mama has heard of it, for she is *not* still looking after the children, and she asked me if it were true, and what could be the meaning of it? Of course I turned it off, and indeed I don't believe a word of it, but – *why* does she let Dolph attach himself to her so particularly?"

But here Freddy felt himself to be upon acutely assailable ground, and he beat a retreat. A visit to Mount Street the following day did nothing to heal the wound to his *amour propre*, for although Lord Legerwood made no reference whatsoever to the intrusions of Dolphinton, Lady Legerwood was not similarly reticent. In deep concern, she informed him that the few

particular friends to whom she had confided the news
of his engagement were quite in a puzzle to know what
to think of Miss Charing's predilection for Lord Dolphinton's society. It was not, therefore, surprising that
when, a few days later, Mr Standen, bowling along Piccadilly in his tilbury, reached the bottom of Old Bond
Street in time to see Miss Charing, accompanied by
Lord Dolphinton, enter the portals of the Egyptian
Hall, upon the south side of the street, he should have
been moved to pull up abruptly, to consign his carriage to the care of his groom, and to cross Piccadilly
in a purposeful manner.

The Egyptian Hall, which had been erected four
years previously, was otherwise known as Bullock's
Museum, and contained curiosities from the South
Seas, from North and South America; a collection of
armoury, and works of art; and had lately received, as
an additional attraction, the Emperor Napoleon's
traveling carriage. Its cognomen was derived from the
style of its architecture, which included inclined pilas-
ters ornamented with hieroglyphics. It was an imposing edifice, but it had not previously tempted Mr
Standen to inspect its many marvels. Nor, when he had
penetrated beyond the vestibule, did he waste time in
studying the exhibits tastefully arranged around the
walls. The only object in which he was interested was
found seated primly upon a chair, a catalogue in her
gloved hands, and her gaze fixed thoughtfully upon
the model of a Red Indian chief in full panoply of war.
Of Lord Dolphinton there was no sign, a circumstance
which caused Mr Standen to exclaim, quite contrary
to his intention: "Well, if this don't beat the Dutch!
First the fellow brings you to a devilish place like this,
and then he dashed well leaves you here!"

"Freddy!" cried Miss Charing, jumping almost out of her skin.

"And don't you say *Freddy* to me!" added Mr Standen severely. "I told you I wouldn't have it, Kit, and I dashed well meant it! Have the whole town talking!"

Kitty looked very much bewildered, but as it was plain that Mr Standen was filled with righteous wrath she refrained from protest, merely saying in a small, doubtful voice: "Frederick? Should I, in public, call you Mr Standen?"

"Call me Mr Standen?" said Freddy, thrown quite out of his stride. "No, of course you should not! Never heard such a silly question in my life! And it ain't a bit of use trying to turn the subject! Not one to take a pet for no reason, but this is the outside of enough, Kit!"

"I wasn't trying to turn the subject! You *said* I must not call you Freddy!"

Mr Standen stared at her. "Said you wasn't to call me Freddy? Nonsense!"

"But you did!" replied Kitty indignantly. "Just this moment past! I must own, I think it was very unkind in you, for I had no notion it was wrong!"

"It's my belief," said Mr Standen, with austerity, "that you're trying to fob me off, Kit! Well, it won't fadge! *I* saw you walk into this place on Dolph's arm! Seems to me there's something deuced havey-cavey going on between the pair of you. Time I had a word with Dolph! Where the devil is he?"

Enlightenment dawned on Miss Charing. She gave an irrepressible gurgle of mirth. "Oh, Freddy, is *that* what brings you here?"

"Yes, it is, and it ain't anything to laugh at!" said Freddy. "Good God, you don't suppose I'd come to a place like this for no reason, do you? I'd as lief visit Westminster Abbey again!" He levelled his glass, and swept a condemnatory glance round the room. "In fact, liefer!" he added. "I don't say those effigies weren't pretty devilish, but they weren't as devilish as this freak you was staring at when I came in. You know what? – you'll start having nightmares if you don't take care! Lord, if it ain't just like Dolph to choose a place like this for his dashed flirtations! Shows you he's queer in his attic."

"He did not bring me here to flirt with me!"

"Now, don't you tell me he wanted to look at curiosities from the South Seas!" said Freddy warningly. "I ain't a big enough bleater to swallow that one! Just a trifle too loud, Kit!"

"No, of course he did not. Oh, dear, how awkward this is! I wonder what I should do?"

"Well, I can tell you that!" said Freddy. "You can stop making a cake of me. What's more, if you let Dolph go on hanging round you for ever I'll tell everyone that our betrothal is a hum!"

"Freddy, you would not!" exclaimed Miss Charing, turning pale. "What can it signify to you, after all?"

"Does signify. Here's m'mother wanting to know what I'm about to let you go all over town with Dolph! Never felt such a flat in my life!"

"Oh, I am so very sorry!" said Kitty contritely.

"Yes, I daresay, but I'm dashed if I see what your lay is! If you wanted Dolph, why the deuce didn't you accept his offer? No need to have dragged me into the business at all."

Kitty laid an impulsive hand on his arm. "Freddy, you *could* not think that I would ever marry poor Dolph?"

"Well, no," admitted Freddy. "In fact, I'll take dashed good care you don't!"

"I don't want to! Though, I must say, Freddy, it is not in the least your affair!"

"That's just what it *is*," said Freddy bitterly. "No good saying I ain't responsible for you, because I am. Mind, I didn't think I should have to be at the outset – well, stands to reason I didn't! Wouldn't have let you talk me into this! – but the more I think of it the more I see that if you go and do something cork-brained there ain't a soul who won't say it was my fault for not taking better care of you."

"Oh, no, Freddy!" she cried, shocked. "How could people say such a thing?"

"Well, they would. What's more, quite true! Daresay I'd say it myself. Can't bring a girl to town like this, and then let her do something bird-witted. Not the thing!"

"I *promise* you I won't do anything bird-witted!" Kitty said earnestly, clasping his hand. "Indeed, Freddy, I don't mean to tease you, for I am so very much obliged to you! And I never, never meant to be a charge on you!"

Much discomposed, Freddy made inarticulate noises. Miss Charing, still holding his hand, thought profoundly. Recovering himself, Freddy said: "No need to talk like that, Kit: happy to be of service! Fond of you! Proud of you, too."

She turned her eyes towards him, astonished. "Proud of me? Oh, no! how could you be? You're hoaxing me!"

"No, I ain't. You've got taste, Kit. Always look just the thing! Credit to me!" He paused, and added, his brow creasing: "At least, except when you wear the

wrong jewels. Ought to let me give you that garnet-
set! No reason why you shouldn't: the merest trumpery! Assure you!"

"There is every reason!" she responded, pressing
his hand tightly, her eyes swimming. "Oh, Freddy, you
are so very good to me, and I see what a Wretch I am
to have put you in this fix!"

"No, no!" he said, horrified to see tears in her eyes.
"Now, for the lord's sake, Kit—! Nothing to cry about!
Besides, can't cry here! Have all the fools gaping at
us! I ain't in a fix. Only thing is, won't have you attach-
ing Dolph to you." He looked round the room.
"Where the deuce *is* the fellow?" he demanded.

"In one of the other rooms. Oh, Freddy, dare I trust
you?"

"Well, upon my word!" he exclaimed, affronted.
"Seems to me that if you didn't know that when you
made me become engaged to you you must be as badly
dicked in the nob as Dolph!"

"Yes, yes, but this is not my secret, and I promised
I would betray it to no one!"

"What secret?" said Freddy, blinking.

"Well – Freddy, you are fond of Dolph, are you
not?"

"No," replied Freddy. "What I mean is, sorry for
the poor fellow, of course. Dash it, couldn't be fond
of him!"

"No, I suppose—At all events, you wouldn't harm
him, would you, Freddy?"

"Of course I wouldn't harm him!"

"Even if you could not quite like what he meant to
do?" Kitty said anxiously.

Suspicion gleamed in his mild eye. No one could
have called Mr Standen quick-witted, but the posses-

sion of three sisters had considerably sharpened his instinct of self-preservation. "Depends what that is," he said cautiously. "If it has anything to do with you, Kit—"

"No, I promise you it has not!"

"Sounds to me like a smoke," he said, by no means convinced. "Because if it hasn't anything to do with you—"

"Only that I am going to help him!"

Mr Standen thought this over, and came to the conclusion that there was only one way in which his unfortunate relative could be helped. "If you're hatching a scheme to poison Aunt Augusta, I won't have anything to do with it!" he said.

"How can you be so absurd? Of course I am not!"

"Good thing, if one could do it," said Freddy handsomely. "Thing is, bound to be a scandal. If it ain't that, what do you mean to do?"

"Let us go and find Dolph!" said Kitty. "Mind, Freddy! even though you may not approve of it, you won't breathe a word to your Aunt Augusta!"

The suggestion that he could be thought capable either of enacting the rôle of informer, or of bandying unnecessary words with Lady Dolphinton, so much revolted Mr Standen that he was moved to expostulate. Kitty begged pardon hastily, and dragged him into the adjoining room. Here Lord Dolphinton and Miss Plymstock were discovered, seated side by side upon a plush-covered settee in the middle of the room, his lordship plunged in gloom, and Miss Plymstock soothingly patting his hand. When they perceived Miss Charing and her escort, they both rose, Dolphinton looking frightened, and Miss Plymstock pugnacious.

"I think, Hannah, that you have already met Mr

Standen," said Kitty. "I have told him *nothing*, but I think we ought to admit him into our confidence, and I have come to ask your permission to do so."

"How d'ye do?" said Miss Plymstock, extending a hand sensibly gloved in York tan. "Miss Charing was so obliging as to say that you would not take exception to Foster's being a good deal in her company, but I thought to myself that she was very likely mistaken. You're Foster's cousin Freddy, ain't you?"

Considerably taken aback, Freddy admitted it. His hand was crushed in a hearty grip; Miss Plymstock said in her blunt fashion: "I daresay you won't like it above half, but I mean to marry Foster, and you don't look to me like one who would try to throw a rub in the way!"

"No, no!" uttered Freddy feebly, casting a wild glance in Miss Charing's direction.

"Miss Charing is being so kind as to lend us her aid," pursued Miss Plymstock. "For my brother don't like the match any more than the Countess would, I can tell you, and how to meet Foster, with the spies we both have set about us, is more than either of us knew how to do. But Sam – that's my brother – only knows I bear Miss Charing company on some of her expeditions; and the Countess is pleased enough to think Foster is fixing his interest with her; and if she knows I go along too, as I don't doubt she does, she don't think any more than that Miss Charing takes me for propriety, which is what anyone would expect; and if she saw me she wouldn't spare me a second glance, I'll lay my life, for I'm no beauty, and never was."

Mr Standen, reeling under the impact of this forth-right speech, had scarcely recovered himself suffi-ciently to murmur a polite rejoinder, when he received (as he afterwards expressed it to Miss Charing) a floorer from Lord Dolphinton, who said: "Yes, you are. Very beautiful. Kind of face I like."

Mr Standen took another look at the homely countenance confronting him, realized that his unfortunate cousin was of unsounder mind than he had supposed, and said kindly: "Exactly so!"

"Well, that's all a hum," said Miss Plymstock bracingly. "What's more, my brother's in trade, and so was my father before him, and I've no fortune. I'm telling you so to your head, because no good ever came of hoaxing people. If you think I ain't fit to match with an Earl, why, I know that as well as anyone, but I shall make Foster a better wife than any of the grand ladies he might offer for, and so I assure you!"

Much alarmed by the unmistakably belligerent note in Miss Plymstock's voice, Freddy hastened to say: "Nothing to do with me! Not my affair, y'know!"

"You would not try to intervene, would you, Freddy?" Kitty asked.

"No, no! Word of a gentleman! In fact, rather not have anything to do with it!" said Freddy, in a burst of candor.

But Miss Charing was not at all inclined to permit him to adopt this craven attitude. She obliged him to sit down between herself and Hannah upon the settee, while she poured into his unwilling ear the full tale of his cousin's difficulties. Miss Plymstock punctuated the recital with corroborations and occasional emendations; and Lord Dolphinton stood before the group, watching Freddy with very much the look of an anxious spaniel doubtful whether he was to receive a pat or a kick. Freddy found his intent gaze unnerving, and several times begged him to sit down. Lord Dolphinton shook his head. "Mean to marry Hannah," he said.

"That's right, old fellow," responded Freddy. "No need to stand there staring at me, even if you do."

"Keep an eye on you," said his lordship. "See what you're thinking. Hannah says you won't like it. *I* don't think you won't like it. Been watching you. Don't look to be in a miff. You ain't in a miff, are you, Freddy?" Reassured on this head, he regarded his cousin with fond gratitude, and said: "You know what, Freddy? I like you. Always did. I like you better than Hugh. Like you better than Jack. Better than Biddenden. Don't like him at all. Don't like Claud much either."

"Yes, well, much obliged to you, Dolph!" said Freddy patiently. "But it ain't a bit of use thinking I can help you in this fix, because I dashed well can't!"

"Kitty's going to help us," said Dolphinton, with simple faith.

"That's as may be," interposed Miss Plymstock. "There is no need for you to tease yourself, Foster, for we shall contrive in some way or another; but it seems to me it's for Mr Standen to say whether Miss Charing may stand our friend or not. And if you don't choose she should, sir, there's no one could blame you, for I don't doubt that Foster's Mama will kick up a rare dust, and behave mighty unpleasantly to her."

"It don't signify what my Aunt Augusta does," replied Freddy, for the second time in his career astonishing Kitty by a display of courage which seemed to verge on foolhardiness. "Can't do Kit a mischief: shouldn't let her. Daresay she'll set up a screech. Thing is, Kit don't live with her, and nor do I. Shan't have to listen to anything she says."

Miss Plymstock, listening to this eminently practical

speech with warm approval, was moved to grasp Mr Standen's hand again. "You're a sensible man!" she said gruffly. "Now, you listen to what your cousin says, Foster, and think if it ain't what I've been drumming into your head this age past! Once the knot's tied between us, and I have you safe, there's nothing your Mama can do to hurt you, and so I promise you! You tell him that's true, Mr Standen!"

"Yes, I daresay it is," agreed Freddy, recovering his hand, and hoping very much that she would not feel herself impelled to wring it a third time. "The thing is, the knot ain't tied, and I'm dashed if I see how it is to be, if Dolph's being spied on all the time."

"We shall think of a way," said Kitty.

Her betrothed regarded her with misgiving. "Yes, but it won't do if you think of sending 'em off to Gretna Green, or anything like that, Kit. Not one to throw a rub in your way, but that's coming it too strong!"

"Yes, indeed! In any event, Miss Plymstock thinks it would not answer, so you may be easy!"

Mr Standen, however, was not at all easy; and he took the earliest opportunity of telling Kitty so. "Shatterbrained, that's what you are, my dear girl!" he informed her, with some severity. "First it's one thing, and then it's another! Told me you wanted to come to town to establish yourself, but all you do is to mix yourself up in affairs that don't concern you. Shouldn't wonder if you were to find yourself at a standstill."

"But, Freddy, you would not have me refuse to help poor Dolph?"

"Well, I would," he said. "Mind, it don't matter to me if he chooses to marry that shocking fright, because he ain't a Standen, for one thing; and for an-

other he's so badly touched in his upper works there's
no saying but what he might not do something a
dashed sight worse than marry a tradesman's daughter. Thing is, bound to be a rare kick-up if the thing
comes off, and I'd as lief have nothing to do with it."
He met Miss Charing's slightly reproachful eyes manfully, and added: "Tell you what, Kit! Got too kind a
heart!"

A smile swept across her face. "Oh, Freddy, how absurd you are! When you have a much kinder one than
I have!"

"No, really, Kit!" protested Freddy, revolted.
"Haven't got anything of the sort! Been on the town
for years!"

"Yes, you have," averred Kitty, lifting his hand to
her cheek for a brief moment. "And when I consider
how dreadfully I have imposed upon you—Oh, well!
At least, I promise I won't embroil you in *this* business!
You won't object to it if I help them? For it is the most
shocking thing, Freddy! – I could not speak of it with
Dolph standing by, but Lady Dolphinton holds him in
subjection by threatening to have him shut up as a lunatic! And *that* he is not!"

"You don't mean it?" exclaimed Freddy, much
struck. "Of course he ain't a lunatic! Got no brains,
that's all. Well, I ain't got any either, but you wouldn't
say I was a lunatic, would you?"

"No, and you have got brains, Freddy!" said Kitty
indignantly.

Mr Standen, already shaken by having his hand
rubbed worshipfully against a lady's cheek, goggled
at her. "You think I've got brains?" he said, awed.
"Not confusing me with Charlie?"

"Charlie!" uttered Miss Charing contemptuously.

"I dare say he has book-learning, but you have – you have *address*, Freddy!"

"Well, by Jove!" said Mr Standen, dazzled by this new vision of himself.

❧ *Chapter XIV* ❧

MEANWHILE, that noted Corinthian, Mr Jack Westruther, was rapidly passing from a state of amused tolerance to one of slightly puzzled exasperation. That Kitty should cajole Mr Standen into a counterfeit betrothal with the object of arousing jealousy in the breast of the man she really loved was something Mr Westruther could understand, and even appreciate. That she should decline his invitations for no better alternative than a few hours spent in Dolphinton's company was something he was very far from appreciating. She could not, he was persuaded, hope to awaken one spark of jealousy in him by such absurd tactics. He did not think so poorly of her as to suppose that she might seriously be encouraging his lordship's advances, for he held Dolphinton in utter contempt; but a chance meeting with his cousin Biddenden, in Boodle's Club, certainly sowed a seed of doubt in his mind.

"So Kitty Charing has a fancy to become a Countess!" said Biddenden, with a short laugh. "Well! I am not at all astonished! I'm sure I hope you are satisfied, Jack! A rare bungle you have made of it, you and Hugh between you!"

"Don't you mean a Viscountess, George?" suggested Mr Westruther amiably.

"No, I don't. She'll be Countess of Dolphinton before the year's out, mark me! Much good may it do her!"

"Would you care to hazard a bet on the chance?"

"You'd lose!" said his lordship brutally. "You thought the girl was head over ears in love with you, didn't you? Well, I thought it too, and nicely bubbled we have been! It's my belief she's a deep 'un, and had her eye on Dolphinton from the outset."

"I do hope, my dear George, that you mean to explain to me why, if this is so, she did not take him when she had the chance offered to her? I seem to be remarkably dull-witted today, for the reason is hid from me," said Mr Westruther, with unabated amiability.

"You'd know fast enough had you been at Arnside," replied Biddenden. "The girl was in such a pet she was ready to throw a fortune to the wind, and took Freddy merely to spite the rest of us."

"No: only to spite me!" said Mr Westruther, laughing.

"Much you know! If Dolphinton had gone about the business like a man of sense, instead of as good as telling her he hoped she'd refuse his offer, she'd have accepted him! Good God, Jack, you never heard anything to equal it! The fellow's as mad as Bedlam, and ought to be shut up!"

"Undoubtedly. May I know whence you culled this

farradiddle? If you came to town only two days ago you have certainly been busy!"

"Oh, I had it from my Aunt Augusta!" Biddenden replied. "*She* is in high croak, I can tell you! And well she may be! When I think of Dolphinton's inheriting Uncle Matthew's fortune—Upon my soul, Jack, I had a great deal rather it was you!"

"Handsome of you!" said Mr Westruther, grinning at him.

"Ay, well, it won't be you!" said Biddenden crossly. "You can lay your life to that! Kitty has shown her hand plainly enough. Either she meant to have Dolphinton all along, and took Freddy merely because she could scarcely accept such an offer as that idiot made her – with Hugh and me standing by, too! – or she fancied a Viscount to be as good as an Earl, until she came to town, and learned her mistake!"

"What a foolish fellow you are, George!" said Mr Westruther gently. "Whatever else Kitty may have learnt in town, she has not learn to think that beggarly Earldom superior to the title Freddy will inherit."

"Very true! An Irish title, too! I would not give a groat for it myself. But an Earl is always an Earl, you know, and ten to one my aunt has stuffed the girl's head full of nonsense about the great position she would occupy if she were to marry that dolt." He pursed up his mouth, and sat twirling his quizzing-glass on the end of its riband. "I fancy Kitty is not the innocent we took her for," he said, after a pause. "It occurs to me that she may very likely have come to the realization that marriage with Dolphinton would carry with it certain compensations. A complaisant husband, my dear Jack, is not altogether to be despised!"

Mr Westruther got up out of his chair. "No? But you are, George! Believe me, you are!"

Lord Biddenden flushed, and half started to his feet. Mr Westruther, observing him with a good deal of mockery in his eyes, said: "I shouldn't, George: really, I shouldn't! Your credit would never survive a vulgar brawl in Boodle's; and although I daresay you would like to plant me a facer you must know very well that it is quite beyond your power to do it."

"Upon my word!" Biddenden said explosively. "You're very squeamish all at once! A new come-out for you to be taking exception to a complaisant husband!"

"You mistake, George: no man sets a greater value on these gentry than I. My contempt is roused by the blubber-headedness that leads you into such gross error. Kitty had never such an idea in her mind. What a clodpole you are, dear coz! You have rusticated for too long – indeed, you have!"

He left Biddenden fuming and speechless; but although he was smiling, the seed of doubt had been sown. The suggestion that Kitty wished for a complaisant husband he was able to dismiss with as much contempt as he had shown George; a suspicion that she might succumb to the lure of a high title lingered uncomfortably. He met her at Almack's Assembly Rooms on the following evening, claimed her hand for the boulanger, and chose to sit out the dance with her. The involuntary giggle which escaped her when he complimented her on her new conquest informed him that his suspicion had been unworthy. He said curiously: "I wish you will tell me, my pretty one, what is this deep game you are playing?"

She turned her wide, disconcerting gaze upon him inquiringly.

"Well?" he said, holding the gaze, a challenge and a laugh in his eyes. "Such an eligible suitor as you have acquired, my dear! They tell me you are for ever in his company. I wonder that Freddy will permit it!"

She sipped her lemonade. "Freddy knows all the games I play," she replied tranquilly.

"Does he? Poor Freddy! He has my most profound sympathy.' He took her fan from her, and spread it open. "Very pretty. Did he give it to you? *I* did not!"

"Oh, no! The one you gave me would not do with this dress. Though it is very pretty too, and I frequently carry it," said Kitty, in a kind voice.

"I am honored," he bowed, giving it back to her. He spoke smoothly, but there was a spark of anger in his eye. The little girl who adored him was learning too many town tricks, and needed a lesson. If she imagined that he could be brought to heel by such tactics as these, it would be well for her to discover her mistake. For a cynical moment, he found himself thinking that it would really have been better for him to have swallowed his annoyance at Mr Penicuik's arbitrary conduct; to have gone to Arnside; and to have become formally betrothed to the heiress. He knew well that Mr Penicuik, concerned first and last with his own comfort, would not have pressed for a speedy marriage, but would have been glad to have kept Kitty with him, safely engaged, but free to wait upon him while he had need of her services. Mr Westruther, who never tried to deceive himself, was forced to acknowledge that Kitty's riposte had taken him by surprise. He had been amused at first; but the more sophisticated she became the less was he pleased. Nor was her visit to London well timed. Mr Westruther, pursuing another quarry, found her presence at first tiresome; and, when she became acquainted with the lovely Miss Broughty, disastrous. He had done what he could to bring that friendship to an end; but although he had been easily able to inspire Meg to protest against it, he could not feel that Kitty was very likely to pay much heed to her featherbrained hostess. It was plain that such a friendship must lead to undesirable complications. Olivia seemed not to have admitted Kitty into her confidence; she would certainly do so if the acquaintance were allowed to ripen; and although Mr Westruther had conferred no right on Kitty to censure his morals or his conduct, and was by no means averse from allowing her to see that she was not the only woman in his life, this was not the moment he would have chosen for such a disclosure as Olivia might make. When he had found Olivia in Berkeley Square, he had been conscious of a feeling of unaccustomed annoyance. He was a man of even temper, regarding his world with an amused and a cynical eye, able nearly always to shrug away irritations with a laugh; but the discovery that Kitty had made a friend of the pretty creature on whom he was prepared to bestow everything but his name aroused real anger in his breast. He thought savagely that it was just like her; and remembered with unaffectionate clarity the many occasions when she had seemed to him to be an extremely tiresome little girl. He could almost have believed that she had done it to vex him. But that would have involved Freddy in the affair, who must have told her the truth; and although, in momentary exasperation, he had accused Freddy of this treachery, he knew that he had done his amiable cousin an injustice. He might mock at Freddy, but he was carelessly fond of him, and he knew him to be wholly incapable of making so unhandsome a gesture. The acquaintanceship had indeed sprung from a chance meeting; and for one of its unfortunate repercussions he had no one but himself to blame. It had been he who had introduced her fascinating French cousin to Kitty. Nothing, he ruefully acknowledged, could have been more natural than Kitty's subsequent presentation of the Chevalier to her new friend.

Calling in Hans Crescent with every intention of taking Olivia out in his curricle to Richmond, he had found the Chevalier very much at home in the drawing-room, captivating Mrs Broughty as much as her daughter. This circumstance was easily explained: everything about the Chevalier bespoke the man of birth and fortune. If his handsome face, and sweetness of manner, attracted Olivia, it was his air of affluence which made him acceptable to Mrs Broughty. No one could have accused him of boasting of his aristocratic connections, but in his conversation he betrayed an intimate knowledge of the French world of fashion; while a passing, careless reference to his uncle, the Marquis, and another to a château in Auvergne, had the effect of impressing Mrs Broughty strongly in his favor. A young Frenchman, visiting England for his pleasure, and related to the lady who was betrothed to Lord Legerwood's eldest son, bore all the outward appearance of a desirable *parti;* and if he was not perhaps as wealthy as Sir Henry Gosford he was no doubt quite wealthy enough to come to agreeable terms with Olivia's Mama.

But Mr Westruther, ushered into the drawing-room, and dominating the company with his height, and his

air of easy assurance, received a sufficiently warm welcome from Mrs Broughty. She stood a little in awe of
him; she was flattered by his attentions to her daughter, for although she might be in some doubt of the
Chevalier's position she had no doubt at all of Mr
Westruther's. He was an acknowledged leader of fashion; he belonged to that select world which haughtily
refused to admit her into its ranks; and he was so much
petted and courted that to have won his favor was a
triumph for any lady. She was uncertain of only two
circumstances: the size of his fortune, and the precise
nature of his intentions. Mr Westruther, well aware of
this, made no effort to enlighten her on either point,
the first of which, he guessed, was the one of para-
mount importance. Mr Westruther had his own notion
of the circumstances under which the enterprising
lady had induced the late Oliver Broughty to marry
her; and he did not suppose that she would scruple
to sell any of her daughters into elegant prostitution,
provided that the price offered were high enough.
Probably she would prefer to marry Olivia to the aged
Sir Henry Gosford; but if Olivia were to prove intrac-
table it was not likely that her Mama would repulse
other, less respectable, offers. Not that Mr Westruther
had the smallest intention of negotiating any kind of
bargain with a woman whom he comprehensively despised. He found Olivia enchanting, but he wanted no
unwilling mistress. He was not the only man casting
out lures to the lovely creature, but until he found the
Chevalier ensconced in the drawing-room in Hans
Crescent he knew himself to be without serious rival.

He paused for a moment on the threshold, raising
his quizzing-glass, smiling at Olivia, raising an eyebrow at the Chevalier, sweeping Mrs Broughty with

the indulgent, mocking glance which both enraged
and impressed her. "Ma'am!" He made his bow to Mrs
Broughty. "Your very obedient! Miss Broughty, your
slave! Chevalier!" A nod sufficed for the Chevalier,
but when Olivia held out her hand he took it, and held
it, saying laughingly: " 'Most radiant, exquisite, and
unmatchable beauty,' can I persuade you to drive out
with me?"

Miss Charing, had she been present, would undoubtedly have been able to have supplied Olivia with
the context of these mock-heroics; Olivia, by far less
well-read, was cast into adorable confusion, looking
at once flattered and frightened, and murmured: "Oh,
pray—! How foolish of you! It is so very obliging of
you, but it is not in my power to accept! We are in the
expectation of receiving friends."

"Alas!" he said lightly. "My luck is quite out. Shall
I go away at once, or may I sit with you for a few minutes?"

Mrs Broughty, crying out against the suggestion
that he should depart, pressed him to take refreshment. He declined it, but sat down, stayed talking la-
zily for a quarter of an hour, and then rose, saying that
he must no longer keep his horses standing. "How
came you here, d'Evron? Can I offer you a seat in my
curricle? You have not set up your own carriage, I
fancy?"

"No; it seems not worth the pain. In general, I hire
a vehicle; today I came here in what I am informed I
must call a hack. I have that correctly?"

"Oh, perfectly! Your command of the English
tongue compels one's admiration. If you came in a
hack, you must certainly allow me to convey you back
to Duke Street. Farewell, sovereign cruelty! I shall

hope for better fortune the next time I come to visit you!"

The Chevalier, perceiving that Mr Westruther had no intention of leaving him in possession of the field, submitted gracefully, bowed over the ladies' hands, and accompanied his ruthless benefactor out into the street. A compliment to Mr Westruther on his horses was indifferently received, and failed to divert him from his purpose. "Yes, a match pair," he replied. "And how have you been going on since I last saw you, my dear d'Evron? You contrive to amuse yourself tolerably well in London?"

"Indeed, I shall not know how to tear myself away! I have met with such kindness, and feel myself quite at home in consequence."

"Your charm of manner has swept all before it," said Mr Westruther. "I am for ever being asked who is my delightful French acquaintance, and where he comes from."

"Ah, this is some of the *taquinerie* for which you are famous, I think!"

"Not at all. I am sure the friends you have made in England are legion. Now, who was it who wished to know only the other day where you had hidden yourself? Hoped you had not fallen a victim to the influenza—Yes, of course! It was Lady Maria Yalding! To have made such a conquest as *that* is something indeed!"

"I cannot flatter myself so grossly," responded the Chevalier quietly. "But you remind me of my obligations, sir: Lady Maria has been most kind, and I must not neglect her."

"Just so," agreed Mr Westruther. "One sees the

temptation, of course, but it would be folly not to with-
stand it."

"I understand you, I suppose," the Chevalier said
after a moment, and in a mortified tone.

"I feel sure you do: so quick-witted, you French-
men! You must forgive my meddling: since I had the
pleasure of bringing you and your cousin together I
must think myself in some sort responsible for you.
I should dislike excessively to see you tumble into one
of the pitfalls with which society is so amply provided.
Always so difficult for a foreigner to recognize them,
isn't it?"

"Do you mean to indicate, sir, that we have just left
one of these pitfalls?" asked the Chevalier, taking the
bull by the horns.

"Why, yes!" said Mr Westruther, pulling up for the
turnpike. "Charming, of course – quite the most rav-
ishingly lovely little ladybird in town! – but no fortune,
my dear d'Evron, and a mother who is a veritable
harpy!"

"I am aware."

"Naturally. She should have been an Abbess – ah,
an *entremetteuse*, Chevalier! The fair Olivia is for sale
to the highest bidder."

"Sir Henry Gosford? The thought revolts!"

The pike was open, and Mr Westruther set his pair
in motion again, keeping them rigidly to a sedate pace,
unusual in him. "Gosford, if Olivia will have him," he
agreed. "He is wealthy – a matter of primary importance to Mrs Broughty; and he is besotted enough to
offer marriage – not, I fancy, so important, but still desirable."

"You appal me!" the Chevalier exclaimed. "It cannot be that the woman would allow that beautiful innocent to become a man's mistress!"

Mr Westruther laughed softly. "Unless I miss my bet, d'Evron, Mrs Broughty, until she entrapped the late Broughty into marriage, was herself what we call a prime article – of Covent Garden notoriety, you know! I should suppose that that way of life may not appear to her so undesirable as it seems to appear to you."

"Horrible! It is horrible to think of such a thing in connection with that girl!" the Chevalier said vehemently.

"My dear young friend, are you picturing the fair Olivia in the Magdalen?" said Mr Westruther, with a touch of impatience. "There is not the least reason to suppose that she would not enjoy a varied and luxurious career, and, in all probability, end her days in a state of considerable affluence. We do not all of us cast our mistresses naked upon the world, you know!"

"Sir!" said the Chevalier, trying to control his agitation. "You have been frank! I shall ask you to pardon me if I too speak without restraint! Is it thus that you desire mademoiselle?"

"It is certainly not as my wife," replied Mr Westruther, rather haughtily.

"I would do all within my power to prevent it!"

A slight smile crossed Mr Westruther's face. "But, then, there is really so little within your power, is there? If I were you – and this is the friendliest advice I can give you! – I would strive to forget Olivia, and continue to besiege Lady Maria's citadel. I wish you very well at that, and will engage not to cast the least rub in your way. But you must not trespass upon my ground, you know. Not the smallest good can come

of it, I do assure you. I am persuaded you did not come
to London with the intention of marrying a penniless
girl. Nor do I think you have sufficiently appreciated
the determination of Mrs Broughty. Perhaps you have
no objection to the inquiries she will certainly make
into your precise circumstances; but do, my dear
d'Evron, consider what might be the consequences if
some malicious person were to breathe into the lady's
ear a doubt – just a doubt!"

The Frenchman stiffened, and paused for a moment
before replying: "In effect, you are offensive, sir!"

"Oh, no, no!" Mr Westruther said gently. "You mistake!"

"I must believe you to be my enemy!"

"Again you mistake. I am sufficiently – how shall I
put it? – an *âme de boue!* – to derive considerable enjoyment from watching your progress, Chevalier! It com-
mands my admiration. Indeed, I should be sorry to see
it blighted, and I wish you all success with the Yalding.
There will be certain difficulties, of course, but *she* is
both headstrong and obstinate, while *you* are adroit,
and I am persuaded you will overcome them, carrying
her off, as it were, in Annerwick's teeth. That will afford quite a number of persons enjoyment. You are
not acquainted with Lady Maria's papa? You are to be
felicitated: an unlovable man! And here we are at Duke
Street!"

"I must thank you, sir, for bringing me here!" said
the Chevalier formally, preparing to alight.

"A pleasure, believe me!" smiled Mr Westruther.
"Au revoir, my dear sir!"

Two days later, when driving Kitty in the Park, at
the fashionable hour, he was able to observe the fruits
of his encounter with her cousin. London was still a

little thin of company, but the unusually clement weather, which had brought the hunting season to an early close, had tempted many to return to town. Quite a number of notabilities were to be seen, riding or driving in the Park, and Kitty was kept very well entertained by Mr Westruther's pithy descriptions of their identities, their manners, and their foibles. It was when they were approaching the Riding House on their second circuit that they met Lady Maria Yalding's barouche. A press of vehicles had brought both the barouche and the curricle momentarily to a standstill, and they stood alongside each other for long enough for the occupants of each to have time for recognition, and greetings. Beside Lady Maria's buxom form, splendidly attired in purple, above which her high-colored face rose triumphant, sat the Chevalier, listening with an air of absorbed interest to what she was saying. Upon the lady's hailing Mr Westruther in her bluff, rather loud-voiced way, he glanced up quickly, met Mr Westruther's eyes, and at once turned his attention to Kitty, saying, as he took off his hat, and sketched a bow: "Ah, well met, my dear cousin! I do not know, Lady Maria, if you are acquainted with Miss Charing?"

The protuberant eyes stared at Kitty. Lady Maria said: "Oh, yes! Met you somewhere, I believe, Miss Charing. Staying with Lady Buckhaven, aren't you? Lovely weather, isn't it? I say, Westruther, do you see the Angleseys are back in town? Just met Anglesey, with his girls. My dear Camille, what is holding us up for so long? Some fool trying to lionize, I daresay, with a badly broke horse! Oh, now we are off! Goodbye! Happy to meet you again some day, Miss – can't remember names!"

Mr Westruther allowed his pair to have their heads a little, and as they were on the fret Kitty was whisked off before she could reply to this brusque speech. She said, in a tone of strong displeasure: "What very odd manners, to be sure!"

"You need not regard her: all the Annerwicks are famed for their rudeness," responded Mr Westruther. "They are convinced, you see, that they are vastly superior to the rest of mankind, and so have no need to waste civility."

"I am astonished that Camille should be so often in her company," Kitty remarked, wrinkling her brow. "He escorted her to the play last night, you know: I saw him, for I was there with Freddy, and the Legerwoods. It is quite impossible that he should like her! But they must be upon excessively friendly terms for her to call him Camille in that odious way! It doesn't seem to me at all the thing."

"It should perhaps be explained to you that Lady Maria is a very rich woman."

"That is what Freddy said, but I will not allow it to be true that Camille is a fortune-hunter!"

He was amused. "What a high flight!"

"It is odious, Jack! Surely you must perceive that!"

"Not at all. Think of the offers you yourself received when it became known you were an heiress!"

She colored. "Indeed, I thought them odious too!"

"Dear me! Even Freddy's?"

She knew not how to reply to this; and, after a moment, said rather lamely: "He did not offer for that reason."

"Or at all?" suggested Mr Westruther.

She put up her chin. "Of course! You may ask George and Hugh if you don't believe me! They were both present! Besides – what an absurd thing to say! Pray, how could I be engaged to him if he had not offered for me?"

"Well, you might have offered for him," said Mr Westruther thoughtfully.

She was now very much flushed, and answered with some difficulty: "I wish you would not talk such nonsense!"

"And I wish that you would stop behaving so nonsensically, foolish child! Freddy, indeed! As well ask me to believe that you mean to marry Dolphinton!"

Her eyes flashed. "How dare you say such a thing, Jack? To compare Freddy with poor Dolph—! It is the most infamous thing, and I won't endure it!"

His brows rose. "But what heat! It does you the greatest credit, my dear, but it is quite uncalled for. I intended no comparison: merely the one is as unlikely a suitor as the other. Am I forgiven?"

"I am sure it is of no consequence," she said stiffly. "Oh, there is Miss Broughty, walking with her cousins! Pray, will you pull up for a moment?"

"No," he said. "I have no wish to talk to Miss Broughty, or her deplorable cousins, and I would advise you, my love, to be a little more careful what friends you make in London. *This* connection cannot add to your credit, believe me!"

"I have no patience with such stupid pride!" she said. "It is all folly and self-consequence!"

He glanced down at her, a glint in his eye. "You are becoming remarkably hot at hand, my child, are you not? No: Freddy is decidedly not the man to control your spurts! However, don't let us quarrel! I want to talk to you of quite another matter. Have you had any news lately from Arnside?"

She turned her head, surprised. "Why, yes! Fish writes to me every week!"

"Have you any notion that all is not well there?"

"Not the least in the world!" she replied. "To be sure, poor Fish could do nothing but bemoan her lot at first, but she is such a good creature she has made the best of it, and, indeed, is not, I think, managing so very ill. Uncle Matthew's gout is less painful, which must make it not so disagreeable for Fish. Why should you suppose something is amiss?"

"Merely that I have had no word from him. In general, he is a regular correspondent of mine, as you may know. However, I daresay I am in disgrace with him."

She knew that this was true, but said nothing. Mr Westruther turned his head, and she saw that his eyes were laughing again. "For not obeying his peremptory summons," he explained.

"He did not quite like it, perhaps," she acknowledged. "He has the oddest notions! For my part, I was thankful that you did not come. I knew you would not, of course."

"Why, yes, I imagine you might," he said. She looked up quickly, and he added, smiling: "I never supposed, Kitty, that you would wish me to offer for you at my great-uncle's bidding."

"Most certainly not!"

"Like Dolphinton, and Hugh – and *not* like Freddy," he said. "I, too, have the oddest notions, and one of them is that I will be neither bribed nor coerced into a proposal of marriage. Really, I think my uncle should have known me better. You too, dear Kitty."

"I knew you very well indeed, and I never thought you would come!"

"You did not know me at all, my child, or you would not be in London today," he replied calmly.

It was fortunate, since she was at a loss for an answer, that a diversion was just then created. Kitty perceived Lady Legerwood's barouche, and desired Mr Westruther to pull up. He drew up alongside the barouche; greetings were exchanged, inquiries made after the progress of the convalescents; and by the time the curricle was again in motion the awkward moment had passed, and Kitty was able, quite naturally, to inaugurate a different topic of conversation. Mr Westruther permitted this; but when they drove out of the Park presently he referred again to his great-uncle. "In spite of this very gratifying intelligence, that his gout is paining him less, I find I cannot be entirely easy in my mind," he said. "However, I collect that you will shortly be returning to Arnside?"

"I? No!" Kitty said.

He looked down at her, slightly frowning. "Surely you informed me that you had come to town for one month?"

"Why, yes! But Meg has so very kindly invited me to remain with her for the present that I need not go home again. With little Edmund still so poorly, and Lady Legerwood being determined to take him to the seaside, Meg is quite in a fix, for she says that Margate always makes her bilious, besides being shockingly flat at this season. So I am to remain, to bear her company, which is a piece of great good fortune for me."

"Does my uncle give his consent to this?" he demanded.

"Yes, and I believe I have to thank my dear, good Fish for it! Only fancy, Jack! Actually she persuaded him to send me a draft for twenty-five pounds! His

gout must be very much better, I think: Fish says it is
all due to a remedy which she discovered in some old
household book! At all events, I was never more grateful for anything, because although Freddy is for ever
begging me to let him be my banker, that I will not
do!"

"You astonish me!" he said sardonically. "I had
supposed him to have been franking you all this
while."

"No, indeed!" she cried. "How could you think such
a thing? Uncle Matthew bestowed a very handsome
sum on me, upon my betrothal!"

"Handsome indeed, if it has paid for all your finery,
my dear!" he said dryly. He saw that she was looking
startled, and laughed. "Never mind! But I wish you
will go back to Arnside, Kitty. I believe you have been
guilty of a great piece of folly in leaving my uncle in
this way."

They had reached Lady Buckhaven's house by this
time, and Kitty was preparing to alight from the curricle. She paused. "Nonsense! Why did you laugh like
that? It is true that Freddy has paid all my bills, but
he has done it with the money Uncle Matthew gave me
for the purpose!"

"Oh, is that how it has been?" said Mr Westruther
gravely. "I begin to think I have underrated Freddy!"

❧ *Chapter XV* ❧

SINCE FREDDY, ACCOMPANIED BY HIS STAMMER-
ing friend, Mr Stonehouse, was dining in Berkeley
Square that evening, before escorting both ladies to
Almack's, Miss Charing was easily able to find an opportunity of taking him apart, for the purpose of prob-
ing to its depths Mr Westruther's strange remark. But
Freddy, who had long foreseen that he would sooner
or later be called upon to render an account of his
stewardship, was prepared, and instantly confounded
her by assuming all the air of one unjustly accused of
dishonesty. He said that he had faithfully discharged,
through his sister's agency, all milliners' and mantua-
makers' bills; that a small sum still remained in his possession; and that perhaps Kitty would wish him to
hand this over to her? In her anxiety to disabuse his
mind of its quite dreadful misapprehension, Kitty lost
sight of the real purpose of her inquiry. She did once
try to explain to him what this was, but as he only said
severely that she was doing it rather too brown, and

added, with awful irony, an assurance that his circumstances made it unnecessary for him to rob her, she was obliged to devote her energies to the task of smoothing his apparently ruffled sensibilities. "In fact," Freddy told his sister, later in the evening, "brushed through the thing tolerably well! That is, as long as you don't make a muff of it, Meg! Daresay she'll ask you for a sight of the bills. Better say you gave 'em to me."

"Why should I have done that?" she asked, willing but puzzled.

"Dash it, you must be able to think of some reason!" said Freddy, with asperity. "Seems to me no one but me can think of anything in this family! Getting to be devilish fatiguing. Even my father said he didn't know how to – well, never mind that! You tell Kit I'm keeping the bills to show to the old gentleman. Come to think of it, shouldn't be at all surprised if he asked to see 'em: sort of thing he would do!"

"Well, it is to be hoped he does not," observed Meg practically. "Depend upon it, he would be as mad as fire. When do you mean to make your engagement known, Freddy? It seems so odd of you not to put an announcement in the *Gazette!* I am sure at least a dozen people must know of it!"

"Can't announce it till m'mother comes home from Margate," replied Freddy firmly. "Must give a dress party! Season not begun: no one in town yet!"

"You are the strangest creature! I declare, you will be well served if Kitty takes Dolph instead of you!"

"Well, she won't."

"Much you know! My dear brother, Dolph veritably *haunts* us! It is occasioning a good deal of remark, let me tell you!"

"Know all about that. You let Kit alone!" said Freddy.

"Oh, very well, but if you don't take care she will fall into a scrape!" Meg said, shrugging her pretty shoulders.

However, when Freddy demanded what kind of a scrape Kitty could fall into, she was unable to think of one, and was obliged to refer in a mysterious manner to the unfortunate friendship with Miss Broughty and her relatives, hinting at dire, if unexplained, consequences. Freddy said, in a fair-minded way, that he thought the Broughtys a dashed nuisance. "What I mean is, encroaching! No saying where it will end. You remember that female m'mother was kind to in Bath? Rum touch that used to come and cry all over the lodging m'father took in Laura Place? Took m'mother the better part of a year to be rid of her."

"Good gracious, yes! Depend upon it that is just what will happen with this Olivia! She will impose upon Kitty's good nature in precisely the same way. But will Kitty listen to what I tell her? No! Oh, Freddy, that odious Mrs Scorton has invited her to dine in Hans Crescent, and she says she shall go, because she cannot bear to be thought proud!"

"Lord, Meg, I should have thought you might have prevented her!" exclaimed Freddy, quite disgusted. "Easy enough to have hatched up an engagement, and said you depended upon her to be at home that evening! I'll tell you what it is: you've a deal more hair than wit!"

"Oh, well!" Meg said, looking a little conscious. "I could not do that, as it chances, for I am going out myself that evening. One of Buckhaven's old aunts: I would not subject Kitty to her odious, quizzing ways for the world!"

Freddy looked suspiciously at her, but she was rearranging her scarf, and did not meet his eyes. "Sounds to me like a hum," he said.

"Good gracious, why should it be?"

"Don't know. Thing is, know you! Well, stands to reason! Bound to! However, Kit ain't likely to get into a scrape, dining in Hans Crescent. Come to think of it, might serve pretty well. You ever seen those Scortons, Meg? Well, I have! Nothing but a parcel of vulgar dowds! Very likely to give Kit a distaste for the whole business. Don't you go kicking up a dust!"

So, on the appointed day, the Buckhaven town coach conveyed Miss Charing to Hans Crescent; and when the coachman asked her at what hour she would wish him to call for her again, Mr Thomas Scorton, the son of the house, informed him that he would charge himself with the agreeable duty of conveying Miss Charing to Berkeley Square. She demurred a little, but was overborne, Mr Scorton telling her, with a wink, that they had a famous scheme arranged for the evening. She was obliged to acquiesce therefore, and to allow herself to be ushered into the house. Here she was met by Olivia, who led her upstairs to take off her cloak, chattering all the way. Kitty knew already that Mrs Broughty was spending a night at her own home, but she was scarcely prepared for the rest of Olivia's news. Olivia, whose eyes were shining like stars, told her that her cousin Tom had been so obliging as to hire a box at the Opera House, for the masquerade, and that her dear, dear Aunt Matty had said that if they were all determined to enjoy a frolic she would escort them, for she knew what it was to be young, and in her day she had hugely loved a frisk of this nature.

"And, oh, dear Miss Charing, was it dreadfully fast of me? – I wrote to your cousin the Chevalier, telling him that we hoped for the honor of your company, and asking him if he would go with us! And he is even now talking to my aunt in the drawing-room! Oh, have I done amiss?"

"No, no, but – a masquerade! I am not dressed for a ball. And if it is a masquerade, should one not be dressed in character? I wish you had told me earlier, Olivia!"

"Oh, it doesn't signify! None of us mean to wear historical costumes, but only dominoes and masks, and I have procured a domino for you, my aunt warning me that very likely you would not be permitted to go with us, if Lady Buckhaven knew of it. She says that members of the high *ton* despise these masquerades amazingly. I knew you would not care for that! We shall be masked, of course, and no one will know us."

Kitty recollected that a mask and a domino had been her only disguise at the Pantheon masquerade, and was satisfied. She would have preferred not to have gone to a large ball under Mrs Scorton's chaperonage; but she felt that she was perhaps refining too much upon trifles. A refusal on her part to go to the Opera House must necessarily break up the party, and spoil Olivia's pleasure. She schooled her countenance to an expression of gratification, and secretly hoped that she would not be obliged to dance very frequently with Tom Scorton.

As the two ladies descended the stairs to the drawing-room on the first floor, Olivia said, shyly, but as though sudden happiness made it impossible for her to resist a little gush of confidence: "Do you know, Miss Charing, it is the most absurd thing, but I fancied – that is, I had an apprehension – that something had occurred to vex the Chevalier? He had not visited us for such an age! At least, it was only ten days, of course, but I supposed – I was in the expectation—But it was all nonsense, for he was very glad to come to-night. You will say I am a goose!"

Kitty, who was preceding her down the stairs, looked back, saw her blushing, and said laughingly: "No, but do, pray, tell me! Have you fallen in love with Camille? I could see, upon his first setting eyes on you, that *he* was very much struck, I assure you! When must I wish you happy?"

Discomposed, Olivia turned away her face, faltering: "Do not—! It would be so very unbecoming in me—! He has not spoken, and if I thought that he might do so, lately I have been afraid, when there seemed to be no continued observance, that I had imagined the whole, or – or perhaps that he felt I was not grand enough!"

"If he is such a coxcomb as that, you would be very well rid of him!" Kitty replied.

"No, no, how can you say such a thing? So perfectly the gentleman! Indeed, I am fully conscious of the difference in our stations – scarcely dared to entertain the hope that *his* affection was animated towards me, as *mine*, dear Miss Charing, was animated towards him!"

They had by this time reached the landing, and there was no opportunity for further discussion. Kitty, with the uncomfortable recollection in her mind of having on a number of occasions observed her cousin dancing attendance on Lady Maria Yalding, could not but be glad of it. Olivia opened the door into the drawing-room, a babel of voices smote their ears, and Kitty entered to find the rest of the party already assembled. It so happened that the Chevalier was seated in a chair that faced the door, and as Kitty paused for an instant, looking for her hostess in what seemed to be a crowd of persons, he glanced up, his eyes alighting upon Olivia. There was no mistaking the ardent expression that sprang to them, or the tenderness of the smile which touched his lips. The next moment he was on his feet, and was bowing to his cousin. She smiled, and nodded to him, and moved forward to greet Mrs Scorton, who had surged up from the sofa, her bulk formidably arrayed in purple satin, and upon her crimped locks a turban embellished with roses and feathers.

No one could have doubted Mrs Scorton's good-nature; and very few would have denied her vulgarity. She shook Kitty warmly by the hand, embarrassed her by thanking her for her condescension in coming to Hans Crescent, and said, with a jolly laugh: "Olivia would have it I should not invite you, but 'Nonsense, my dear,' I said. 'I warrant Miss Charing is not so high in the instep she won't enjoy a frolic as well as anyone!' I daresay Almack's may be very well, though I don't know, for I was never there in my life, but what I say is it sounds mighty stiff and dull to me, and I was always one for a little fun out of the ordinary, as I'll be bound you are too! Now I must introduce everyone to you, and we can be comfortable. Not that I need to introduce my girls, and I hope I'm not such a simpleton as to present your own cousin to you! But this is Mr Malham, my dear, that's promised to Sukey here, as you may have heard. A fine thing to have Sukey going off before her sister, ain't it? Not that I want to lose my Lizzie, as well she knows, but we all roast her about it – just funning of course! And this is Mr Bottlesford. We call him Bottles."

Kitty knew that she was not going to enjoy the party. As she curtsied slightly to both gentlemen, Mrs Scorton outlined for her benefit the plan for the evening. After dinner, she said, they would play at lottery tickets, or some other jolly, noisy game, for an hour, and then drive to the Opera House. "And Tom shall escort you home in good time, I promise you, for I don't mean to let any of you girls stay much after midnight, and so I warn you, for although I'm as fond as you are of a masquerade it don't do to be lingering on when things get a trifle too free, as very likely they will."

After this she begged Kitty to take a chair near the fire, and Miss Scorton, who had been much impressed by as much of Lady Buckhaven's house as she had been privileged to see upon her one and only visit to it, began to ply her astonished guest with questions which were as artless as they were impertinent. She wanted to know how many saloons there were in the house, how many beds her ladyship could make up, how many covers could be laid in her dining-room, how many footmen she employed, and whether she gave grand parties every night, and had a French maid to wait upon her. There seemed to be no end to her interrogation, but after about twenty minutes she was interrupted by the dinner-bell, and the company trooped downstairs to the dining-room.

Here they were joined by the master of the house, of whose existence Kitty had previously been unaware. He was quite as stout as his wife, but by no means as good-natured. When he shook hands with Kitty, he grunted something which she might, if she chose, understand to be a welcome; and his wife explained, as though it were a very good joke, that he disliked parties, and never joined them except to eat his dinner. With these encouraging words, she directed Kitty to the chair at his right hand, disposed her own ample form at the foot of the table, beckoned the Chevalier to sit beside her, and said that she hoped all her guests had brought good appetites with them.

They were certainly needed. Mrs Scorton was a lavish housewife, and prided herself upon the table she kept. When the soup was removed, the manservant, assisted by a page and two female servants, set a boiled leg of lamb with spinach before his master, a roast sirloin of beef before his mistress, and filled up all the remaining space on the board with dishes of baked fish, white collops, fricassée of chicken, two different vegetables, and several sauce-boats. Everyone but Mr Scorton, who applied his energies to the tasks of carving and of eating, talked a great deal; and Tom Scorton, who was seated beside Kitty, entertained her with a long and boring story of a horse he had bought, and subsequently sold at a very good price, and without a warranty, upon the discovery that the animal was for ever throwing out a splint.

When Mrs Scorton had unavailingly pressed everyone to take another helping, the dishes were removed, and the second course was laid on the table. This consisted of a roast chicken, some pigeons, a large apple pie, an omelet, and a chafing-dish piled high with pancakes. After that, a dessert was set out, which included, besides what seemed to Kitty every imaginable variety of cake and sweetmeat, a large assortment of preserved fruits, and two dishes full of roasted chestnuts.

Observing that Miss Charing seemed to fancy nothing but a French olive, Mrs Scorton begged her to take a meringue, or a slice of Savoy cake; and Eliza asked her how many courses Lady Buckhaven in general sat down to. When she learned that her ladyship contented herself with a very much lighter diet, she exclaimed at it; and Mrs Scorton blessed herself to think that she should keep a better table than a baroness.

After this passage, the company returned to the drawing-room, where a card-table had already been set out; and as soon as the box containing all the fish had been found, everyone but Mr Scorton, who had retired to some fastness of his own, settled down to a game of lottery tickets. Since the consumption of dinner had occupied nearly two hours, the excitements of the game had scarcely had time to pall before it was decided that it was time to leave for the Opera House. Kitty was provided with a loo-mask, and a cherry-red domino, and accorded the seat of honor in her hostess's carriage. As nine persons had to be conveyed into town in two carriages, she was uncomfortably crowded, but this disadvantage was more than compensated for by the reflection that she had not been condemned to travel in the landaulet with Eliza and Mr Bottlesford, both of whom enjoyed local reputations as wits of the first order, and were consequently embarrassing companions. Having been seated at dinner on the opposite side of the table to her cousin, she had had ample opportunity of observing him during the interminable meal, and it had struck her forcibly that he was ill at ease. His gaiety seemed mechanical, and an indefinable air of trouble hung about him. She determined that by hook or by crook she would contrive to engage him in a *tête-à-tête* before the evening was out. The suspicion that he had come to London with the intention of winning a rich bride insensibly grew upon her; and she hardly knew whether most to blame her own imprudence in having introduced him to Olivia Broughty, or his mercenary ambitions, which made it possible for him to pursue Lady Maria when his heart was plainly lost to Olivia.

Upon her first entrance to the Opera House, which she happened never to have visited before, Kitty was quite dazzled by its magnificence. It was adorned with a painted ceiling, and lit by clusters of candles in crystal chandeliers. Besides a gallery, and a roomy pit, there were four tiers of boxes, hung with crimson draperies, and their fronts tastefully decorated in white and gold. The stage, where the ball was already in full swing, was large, extending past the first six boxes; and to add to the festivity of the scene, a fanciful backcloth had been let down, so that English country dances, Viennese waltzes, French quadrilles and cotillions were all danced against a rich eastern background. Although it was some time before midnight, the house was already crowded, and every costume from the simple domino to the magnificence of Tudor doublets was to be seen. Nearly everyone was masked, but several bold-eyed damsels, and a number of gentlemen, had dispensed with this disguise, and were behaving with what, to country-bred Kitty, seemed a strange lack of decorum.

By means which he was only too ready to impart to anyone who could be induced to listen to him, Tom Scorton had procured a box on the lowest tier, a cunning stroke on which he invited his mother and her guests to congratulate him, but which Kitty soon discovered to be an unenviable position. They were

much exposed to the advances of beaux on the look-
out for trim figures that gave promise of youth and
beauty behind the masks; and as a number of these
gentlemen were slightly foxed they were difficult to repulse. Neither of the Misses Scorton appeared in the
least discomposed by this nuisance, Eliza going so far
as to bandy witticisms with a pertinacious buck, im-
probably attired as Charles I; and Susan consenting
to dance the boulanger with a dashing Harlequin. The
Chevalier soon detached Olivia from the rest of the
party, and led her on to the floor; and Kitty was
obliged to bestow her hand upon Tom for a set of quadrilles which was just then forming. When they presently returned to the box, they found it deserted, and
Tom said cheerfully that they might depend upon it
that his mother had gone off to the Saloon, in search
of refreshment. To be left unchaperoned at a gathering of this nature was not at all what Kitty had bar-
gained for, and she began to feel uncomfortable, and
to wish that she had had the resolution to decline the
evening's treat. However, Susan and Mr Malham
sooned joined them, which made her feel less conspic-
uous; and she tried her best to join in their ecstasies
over the ball.

It was indeed an experience she thought she might
have enjoyed very well under such protection as
Freddy or Jack would have afforded her, for she had
never seen anything comparable to it before, and
could have sat happily enough, watching the glitter-
ing, shifting throng, had she been assured that no
questing buck would dare to accost her. But however
innocent she might be she was no fool, and a very little
time sufficed to convince her that Opera House masquerades were not commonly frequented by ladies of

quality. Conscience-stricken, she reflected that Freddy had been quite right when he had said that intimacy with Olivia's relations would lead to undesirable results. This was one of them; and although she was far too warm-hearted to regret having befriended Olivia, she did regret that she had allowed herself to be drawn into the Scortons' set. She was aware for the first time of the cogency of Meg's arguments, and was much inclined to think that she owed her shatterbrained hostess an apology.

It was some time before anything more was seen of Olivia and the Chevalier; and when they did reappear it at once struck Kitty that they did not look as though they were enjoying the masquerade. Where the mask ended, Olivia's cheek was seen to be very pale, and the Chevalier's smiling mouth was oddly tight-lipped. Olivia at once sank into a chair at the back of the box, saying in a disjointed way that the heat was insufferable; and the Chevalier, after a moment's hesitation, solicited Kitty's hand for the next waltz. But when he presently led her towards the dancing floor, his air of gaiety was so forced that she said impulsively: "Should you dislike it, Camille, if we strolled in the corridor, instead of dancing? I have had no opportunity to speak to you all the evening – and Olivia is quite right! It is dreadfully hot here."

He said mechanically: *"A volonté!"* and took her out of the crowded auditorium into the comparative coolness of the corridor. Here they found two chairs placed against the wall, and, for the moment, unoccupied. As she seated herself, Kitty said: "I wish you will tell me, Camille! Has anything happened to vex you?"

He dropped his head in his hands for an instant, and replied, as though the words were wrenched from him: "I was mad to have come! But the temptation – overmastering! I desired – oh, *à corps perdu!* to yield to it! Madness! *C'en est fait de moi!*"

Startled, she exclaimed: "Good God, what can you mean?"

He stripped off his mask with an impatient movement, and ran a hand across his brow, saying with a shaken laugh: "I must suppose that you, my little cousin, know the truth! It is not possible that I should win the hand of that angel. I am a villain to have permitted the affair to march so far! For me, it is *adieu paniers!*"

"You know, Camille, it is true that I am half a Frenchwoman," said Kitty, quite bewildered. "But I never learned to speak the language with the least fluency, and I must own that I don't *perfectly* understand what that may signify."

"Farewell hope!" uttered the Chevalier.

Kitty found this dramatic phrase so strongly reminiscent of Miss Fishguard in her more sentimental moments that she was nearly betrayed into a giggle. After a short struggle with herself, she asked bluntly: "Why?"

He replied, with a hopeless gesture: "I have been permitted a glimpse of paradise! It is not for me!"

"I do wish, Camille, that you will speak more plainly!" said Kitty, rather exasperated. "If you mean that Olivia is paradise, and that it is she who is not for you, pray why should you say such a thing? Have you quarrelled with her?"

"A thousand times no!" he declared vehemently. "Would I quarrel with an angel from heaven? The very thought is a blasphemy!"

"Yes, very true, but Olivia is not an angel from heaven," Kitty pointed out. "Is it that her lack of fortune makes her ineligible, or that you fear she would not be acceptable to your family? I own that Mrs Broughty is a dreadful woman, but—"

"It is I who cannot be acceptable to Mrs Broughty!" he interrupted.

A suspicion that he had been drinking crossed her mind. She looked anxiously at him, and said: "Come, you are talking nonsense, cousin! Perhaps you are not as wealthy as that odious Sir Henry Gosford, but I am persuaded, from what Olivia has told me, that Mrs Broughty is inclined to look upon you with the utmost complacence!"

He gave a short laugh. "Without doubt! *C'est hors de propos, ma chère cousine!* It is the Chevalier she looks upon with complacence. You, of all people, must know that there is no Chevalier!"

She was now more than ever convinced that he had been drinking deeply, and said in some concern: "Camille, I think you don't know what you are saying! No Chevalier? But – are you not the Chevalier d'Evron?"

He looked intently at her, and made a fatalistic gesture. "I am in your hands, in effect! But you are my cousin! I thought – it did not seem to me possible that you should not know the truth. I have been grateful to you for your silence. When the so-obliging Mr Westruther told me that you desired to renew your acquaintance with me – eh, that was a moment indeed! But always I am a gamester: it is my profession. Impossible to refuse the offered introduction! I came to Madame la Baronne's house, risking all upon one throw of the dice." A hint of his dancing smile appeared in his face; he said ruefully: "Ah, I will be frank, my dear cousin! Trusting in – in – oh, in *mes agréments!*

You were silent: I believed I had once more succeeded! *Quel fat!* You did not know the truth!"

"My guardian has never talked to me of my mother's
family," she faltered. "I thought, when Mr Westruther
brought you to Berkeley Square – that is, I did not
question—"

"My credentials? But had you known that our family
is not a noble one—? Would you have betrayed me?"

"Oh, no!" she said quickly. "How could I do such
a thing? But – but *why,* Camille? What can it signify?
Jack – Mr Westruther – has no title, but he is at the
very top of the *ton,* I assure you!"

"Ah, he has birth, *ma petite!* For me, a title is a necessity. I shall not deceive you: I am, as well Mr Westruther knows, an adventurer! I have said: I am in your
hands!"

This dramatic finish to his speech went wide of the
mark. Ignoring it, Kitty said: *"Jack* knows?"

"Be sure! He is no fool, that one! Also, he is dangerous. I have had the effrontery to love the object of his
desire, you must understand. With my rich widow, he
wishes me all success: ah, bah! what do I care, when
I have seen that angel? I shall love her *à jamais,* but
I know well she is not for me!"

He sank his head in his hands as he spoke, and so
did not perceive the effect of his remarks upon Miss
Charing. Much that she had not previously understood now became plain to her. Opening and shutting
her fan, and staring with unseeing eyes at the medallions painted on its leaf, she wondered, in a curiously
detached way, how it came about that her most pronounced emotion was a feeling of disgust. "Jack
wishes to marry Olivia?" she said slowly.

"Marry! No!" he returned. "Pardon! You know him

well! You have perhaps a kindness for him! I should not have allowed myself to speak!"

She remembered remarks made by Olivia which had puzzled her. Drawing an audible breath, she said: "It does not signify. I understand you, I suppose. Jack wishes her to be his mistress. And you – loving her as you say you do! – will permit this?"

He raised his head, saying hotly: "What can I do? Do you imagine that madame her mother would for one little instant entertain my suit, if she knew the truth? That I have neither title nor fortune! That my father is the proprietor of a *maison de jeu* – what you call a gaming house!"

"Good God!" said Kitty, rather faintly. "D-does Olivia know this?"

"She knows all! Could you believe me capable of deceiving one whom I worship? Of stealing her from her mother *à la derobée?* No! I am not so infamous! I do not conceal from you that I came to England an adventurer! It is known that if one is of – of *bonne tenue, bien né, riche,* and above all French – *c'est drôle, ça!* – one may be *bien-venu* in London! To be French, that bestows upon one a *cachet!* – It is known, then, that with these qualities one may do very well in England." He spread out his hands *"De plus,* in my childhood I lived here. I know England; I can speak the language with fluency. Perhaps I have not always the right idiom, or the accent, but that, *chère* Kitty, is regarded by the English as *fort attrayant!"*

"Yes, but I don't understand. Did you – did you come to England to marry an heiress?" asked Kitty wonderingly.

"To seek my fortune, let us say."

"Lady Maria? Camille, was it to pay your addresses to her that you came?"

"Ah, no! My meeting with Lady Maria was a *coup de bonheur*. Naturally, I am interested in ladies of large fortune, but of her existence I did not know until I was presented to her."

This frank exposition of his aims very much shocked Miss Charing. She uttered a protest. "Oh, pray do not—! Surely you cannot mean to offer for Lady Maria! How could you *bear* to be married to her? I cannot believe it of you!"

"Marriage!" he said, smiling. "My dear little cousin, do you think that that would be permitted? If she would consent – *eh bien,* one must resign oneself! But I find her a woman insufferably proud, and I think she could not support the mortification of having so plainly encouraged the advances of one who is not – how shall I say? – *a chevalier d'honneur,* but a *chevalier d'industrie.*"

She gazed at him uncomprehendingly. "No, indeed! I think she would die of shame! But—"

"She would wish the so-fascinating Chevalier to depart from England without scandal, is it not so? Well, that could be arranged."

She was by this time so much shocked and distressed that she could only find voice enough to say: "Olivia *knows* this? You have told her?"

"I have told her!" he said, with a groan. "But just now! It was necessary: I could not continue—! You must understand that I have for her a passion, a devotion, which makes it impossible that I should deceive her!"

"Oh, I wish to heaven I had never made you known to her!" Kitty exclaimed. "This is dreadful! I perceived, when she came back to the box, that she was suffering from some agitation, but that it could be as bad as *this* I had not the least apprehension!''

"Believe me," he said earnestly, "it was not *à dessein* that I engaged her affection! When first I saw her I was carried beyond myself – I did not consider – I had never imagined to myself that I should ever meet one who so exactly fulfilled the dreams a man of sensibility must make for himself! *Bécasse!* I should have acted with resolution. I allowed myself to be transported. When I tore myself away, I believed I was the only sufferer. But when, after so many days of misery, I received her billet, and yielded to the temptation of seeing her again, it was made plain to me that I had wounded her. She asked me, as you did, if I was troubled. What would you? I told her that I was not what she thought me to be, but a gamester, one on whom she would never be permitted to bestow her hand! She saw that there could be no hope for either of us. You may say that we have received our death-blows!''

She was easily able to refrain from making any such remark. In a tone of considerable censure, she said: "Good God, Camille, how could you distress her so? Surely you would have done better to have held your tongue – to have made up your mind not to see her again?''

"I could not!" he replied. "Would you have had me allow her think that she had bestowed her heart upon a mere *coquet?*"

"Yes, indeed I would!" said Kitty. "I daresay she would very soon have forgotten all about you. But now—! Oh, what a shocking tangle it is! I don't know what to say! I wish you will take me back to the box!"

He rose at once. "I will do so. And you? I am at your mercy!"

She said crossly: "If you mean, shall I tell the world that you are an – an *impostor,* no, I shall not! You must perceive how reluctant *I* must be to see my own cousin exposed in such a way. In fact, I expect you were very well aware of that when you disclosed the truth to me!"

He replied, with a faint smile: *"C'est ce qu saute aux yeux, enfin!"*

"You are quite abominable!" she told him.

He began to walk with her down the corridor. "I know it, alas!"

She was too much mortified to make any reply. They proceeded in silence for a moment or two, and might have exchanged no further remarks, had not a most unwelcome sight suddenly presented itself. Strolling towards them, a masked lady in a black domino on his arm, his own mask dangling by its strings from his hand, was Mr Westruther. "Oh, good God!" Kitty exclaimed involuntarily. "Put your mask on, for heaven's sake Camille!"

"It is too late: he has seen me," he responded quietly. "It is no matter: he will not recognize you. Do not speak!"

The advancing couple halted before them. "My very dear friend the Chevalier!" said Mr Westruther. "Now, what an agreeable surprise!" His penetrating eyes ran over Kitty's form, and remained fixed on her face. His brows lifted a little, and to her annoyance she knew herself to be blushing. "Dear me!" he said, a note of amusement in his voice. "May I hazard a guess, or would that be indiscreet?"

The Chevalier returned a light answer; but Kitty was

staring at the lady on Mr Westruther's arm. She had
untied the strings of her black domino, and it fell apart
to reveal a gown of lilac silk and gauze which Kitty
knew well. The discovery that Mr Westruther had
brought his cousin Meg clandestinely to the masquerade seemed to her to set the crowning touch to an evening of unalleviated mortification. She lost her
temper. "Indiscreet? No, how should it be?" she said,
with unusual asperity. "To be sure, it is quite a family
party! For goodness' sake, Meg, keep your domino
closely tied, if you don't wish to be recognized! I daresay half London must know that dreadful lilac dress,
for nothing that Freddy, or Mallow, or I can say to you
serves to convince you that it is not at all becoming
on you!"

"*Kitty!*" gasped Meg, clutching Mr Westruther's
arm. "Good God, what can have possessed you to
come to this place? It is most improper in you!"

"I am sure that if *you* feel no scruple in coming *I*
need not!" returned Kitty swiftly. "*I*, after all, came
under the protection of Mrs. Scorton!"

"Fine protection!" said Meg, with a little angry tit-
ter.

"Very true, but better than none!" flashed Kitty.
"Nor did I tell lies about dining with aunts!"

"You did! You said you were dining in Hans Crescent!"

"It was the truth! I *did* dine there, and I hadn't the
least notion *this* was intended!"

The Chevalier, considerably alarmed by these signs
of brewing storm, tried at this point to intervene, saying: "*Ma chère cousine,* we must return to our box, or
Mrs Scorton will become anxious!"

Neither lady paid any heed to this foolish interruption. Meg said: "Let me tell you that I am under the protection of my own cousin!"

"*Fine* protection!" instantly replied Kitty.

Mr Westruther began to laugh. "End of Round 1!" he said. "Largely cross-and-jostle work, though both opponents appeared full of gaiety, ready to sport their canvases. We shall see some flush hits in the next round, Chevalier."

"How dare you?" exclaimed Meg furiously. "I think, of all the *odious* people—"

"No, no, my love, you must not start sparring with me! I am your second!" said Mr Westruther.

"I beg of you, my cousin, only consider!" said the Chevalier. "Already we attract notice!"

"I am perfectly ready to return to Mrs Scorton, I assure you."

"What a spoil-sport you are, Chevalier!" drawled Mr Westruther. "Mere flourishing so far! We have not yet arrived at the lilac gown, which I take to be the crux of the matter. Come now, Meg, rattle in!"

But this mocking encouragement had the effect of turning his principal into a stiff figure of outraged propriety. "Pray take me back to our own box!" said Meg, in freezing accents. "We are keeping dear Kitty from what I am persuaded must be a most agreeable party. I am myself returning to Berkeley Square in a very few minutes, but no doubt Mrs Scorton will convey you there when the masquerade is over, Kitty."

She then swept a dignified curtsy, took Mr Westruther's arm again, and walked away with him down the corridor.

A good deal concerned, the Chevalier began to express his contrition at having been imprudent enough to have removed his mask. Kitty cut him short, saying that it did not signify; and in silence they went back to Mrs Scorton's box.

The next half hour passed for Kitty like a species of nightmare. She was obliged for civility's sake to dance several times, but the masquerade was fast developing into a romp, and, as though to make matters even more disagreeable, two total strangers had been added to the party, and were contributing their mites to its success by flirting in an inebriated and very ungenteel way with the Misses Scorton. Their sallies were received with shrieks of mirth, and playful raps across the knuckles from furled fans, and the only person, besides Kitty herself, who seemed to deprecate their inclusion in the party was Mr Malham, who several times informed Kitty that he had a very good mind to call that fellow in a Spanish costume to book. Since the fellow in question was behaving extremely freely with Miss Susan Scorton, Kitty could only be surprised that he did not do it. She was herself subjected to a good deal of annoyance; and since her cousin had once more spirited Olivia away from the box, and Mrs Scorton, much flushed, and refreshing herself with sips of champagne, took it all as a very good joke, she felt herself to be wholly unprotected. She excused herself from waltzing with Tom Scorton, and, when the rest of the party surged out of the box to take the floor, was thankful to find herself alone, Mrs Scorton having gone off with Eliza, to pin up her daughter's torn flounce. She withdrew to a chair at the back of the box, trying to compose her disordered nerves, but was startled, a few minutes later, by feeling a touch on her shoulder. Such had been the experiences of this disastrous evening that she uttered a cry, and shrank away from the hand. A familiar, and most welcome, voice smote her ears. "No, really, Kit!" it said. "No need to screech! Only me!"

"Freddy!" she cried, turning sharply in her chair. "Oh, how thankful I am! How in the world did you know I was here?"

"Happened to be in Berkeley Square when Meg's coachman took her off." he replied. "Said young Scorton meant to bring you home. Didn't like it above half, so I took a hack to Hans Crescent. Thought I'd bring you home myself. Servant said you wasn't there. So I saw old Scorton – very rum touch! He told me where you were: told me the number of the box. So I came to fetch you away. Thing is, Kit – *not* the thing!"

"Oh, Freddy, I know it!" she said clasping his hand between both of hers. "Pray believe that I would never have consented to have come had I the smallest notion how it would be! But what could I do, when it was all arranged? It has been so very dreadful! You do not know the half! Will Mrs Scorton be offended if you take me home? I would give anything to escape from this vulgar place!"

"Don't signify if she is," he replied, patting her shoulder in a soothing way. "No business to bring you here! you leave it to me!"

"Oh, yes!" she sighed gratefully. "You will know just how to do!"

She was perfectly right. Upon Mrs Scorton's reappearance, she found herself confronted, not by the fool of his family, but by the Honorable Frederick Standen, a Pink of the Pinks, who knew to a nicety how to blend courtesy with hauteur, and who informed her, with exquisite politeness, that he rather fancied his cousin was tired, and would like to be taken home. One of the uninvited guests, entering the box in

Eliza's wake, ventured on a warm sally, found himself being inspected from head to foot through a quizzing-class, and stammered an apology.

The eye, hideously magnified by the glass, continued to stare at him for an unnerving moment. "Ah, just so!" said Mr Standen, letting the glass fall at last. "Come, Kit! Your very obedient, ma'am!"

He allowed his betrothed only time enough to utter a civil word of gratitude for a delightful party, and then bore her away, saying, as he shut the door of the box: "Obliged to take you home in a hack, Kit! Nothing for it!"

"You are welcome to take me home in a wheelbarrow!" she assured him.

"Wouldn't do at all!" said Mr Standen decidedly. "Sort of thing that would be bound to set people's backs up. Besides, haven't got a wheelbarrow!"

She gave a shaken laugh. "Oh, Freddy, how can you be so absurd, when you are so *wise?*"

Much struck, he said: "You think I'm wise? *Me?*"

"Of course I do! You *always* know just what one should do, and if only I had attended to you, when you warned me what would come of it, if I allowed myself to be drawn into poor Olivia's set, I should not have fallen into this scrape. Are you very much displeased with me, Freddy?"

"No, no! Not your fault! Just not up to snuff!" he assured her.

"You are a great deal too kind to me!" she said, pressing his arm. "*Indeed* I am sorry, and so very grateful to you for rescuing me! I was in flat despair! Oh, but, Freddy, I could not help wishing you had been present at that dreadful dinner-party! Only, if you had been, and we had exchanged glances, I know I must have gone into whoops, so perhaps it is as well you were not! I sat beside Mr Scorton, and he barely spoke a word, but ate and ate, until his face shone, and I don't think he *could* speak!"

"Told you he was a rum touch," remarked Freddy. "Able to speak by the time I arrived, though. Queer set of company, wasn't it? Who was that fellow I set down just now?"

"I haven't a notion, and I doubt if the Scortons have either, for he was not of our party at the start of the evening. And I must say, Freddy, you did it beautifully! It was almost enough to make up for all the rest!"

"Very happy to have been of service!" murmured Mr Standen, gratified. "Fellow been annoying you?"

"He was quite odious, but no, it wasn't *that!*"

"Something else?" said Mr Standen encouragingly.

Kitty nodded, biting her lip. "Yes, but I think perhaps I should not speak of it, even to you. I am in such a fix, and don't know what to do!"

"Don't do anything until we've got a hack!" recommended Freddy. "Tell me then!"

Kitty was glad to follow the first part of this eminently sensible advice; but when she sat beside Freddy, in the darkness and mustiness of the hackney-coach, and he bade her tell him the whole, she hesitated.

"Much better do so," he said. "Might be able to help you."

"Freddy – it is *most* secret!"

"Well, dash it, Kit, you don't suppose I'm going to blab it out to anyone, do you?"

She sighed. "No. Of course you would not. The

thing is, my cousin, the – my cousin Camille was there tonight."

"Thought very likely he would be."

"Yes, but – Freddy, what do you know of him?"

"Don't know anything," replied Freddy firmly. "Seems a very pleasant fellow!"

"Has Jack said anything to you about him?"

"Said he was your cousin. Told us so one evening at Meg's place. Must remember that, Kit!"

"Is that *all* Jack knows?"

"Lord, how should I—Dash it, Kit, I'm not going to answer a lot of questions, when I don't know what the deuce you've got in your head! Silly thing to do! Bound to land myself in the basket! What's Jack been saying to you?"

"Nothing! It was Camille himself, who – who made a – a shocking disclosure to me this evening. Freddy, it seems that he is not a Chevalier at all, but a – I must say, an *adventurer!*"

"Is he, though?" said Freddy. "Thought he was an ivory-turner myself. Comes to the same thing."

"Good God, did you know this?" she exclaimed.

"Didn't *know* it. Just a notion I took into my head. Fact is, asked m'father to discover who he was. No wish to distress you, Kit, but he ain't known at the Embassy, and this precious uncle of his don't seem to exist. At least, very likely he may have a dozen uncles, but there ain't a Marquis amongst 'em. No need to get into a taking over that! Don't *have* to have Marquises in the family! Quite respectable not to. Well, what I mean is, think of us! *We* haven't any!"

"But I cannot think that Camille is at all respectable," said Kitty, in a small voice. "I very much fear, Freddie, that he is a gamester!"

"He is?" said Freddy, rather pleased. "Just what I said! Tell you so?"

"Yes. He said also that his father runs a *hell!*"

"No, does he? Shouldn't wonder if it was in the Palais Royale," said Freddy knowledgeably. "Find all the best ones there, so m'father tells me."

Taken aback, Kitty said: "But, Freddy, is it not very shocking?"

"Well, it ain't precisely what one wants in the family," admitted Freddy. "Dashed awkward, if your uncle ran a hell in London, of course, but he ain't at all likely to, and if only we can hit on a scheme to get rid of this Camille of yours – not that I've anything against the fellow, except that it's as plain as a pikestaff he might easily become a deuced nuisance – we shall be all right and tight."

"I have the greatest apprehension that there will be some dreadful scandal!" said Kitty. "I see that I must tell you the whole. Freddy, it appears that he has fallen desperately in love with Olivia!"

"No harm in that," said Freddy. "In fact, good thing! Don't mind telling you, Kit, that it's his dangling after the Yalding widow that made me take fright. Bound to lead to trouble! Needn't think old Annerwick won't make a lot of dashed awkward inquiries, because that's just what he will do. Anyone would!"

"Oh, Freddy, I fear you do not understand!" said Kitty unhappily, and began, in a halting voice, to tell him just what the Chevalier had said to her.

He listened to her attentively, but his comment, at the end of her recital, was not just what she had expected. "Do you mean to tell me the fellow said all this to you, Kit?" he demanded incredulously. "Well, if that don't beat the Dutch! Why the deuce couldn't he have kept his mouth shut? French! Never knew such a set of gabsters!"

"I must own, I did rather think that myself," she confessed. "Indeed, I was aghast to learn that he had disclosed the truth to Olivia."

"I should think you would be!" he agreed. "No doing anything with such a gudgeon! Think she'll spread the tale?"

"Oh, no, I am persuaded she would not! But only think of the pain she must have suffered!"

"No use thinking of that. Got enough to think about on our own account. Nothing for it but to pack the fellow off to France again, Kit. Dashed if I'll have him causing you embarrassment! Devilish unpleasant situation, if the truth leaked out, y'know."

"Oh, yes, and how shocking it would be if poor Lady Maria were to be taken in, when I know the whole, and should have warned her! Only, how *can* I, Freddy?"

Rather alarmed, he said: "Lord, no! Now, for God's sake, Kit, don't you do anything buffle-headed! Only make bad worse! Got to think of a way to be rid of him. Daresay I shall hit on something."

"Would he go, do you suppose, if you threatened him with exposure?" she asked doubtfully.

"Not unless he's a regular flat, which we know he ain't," he replied. "Must know I wouldn't do any such thing! Nice scandal to start in the family!"

"Would – would Jack?" she asked. "That is what I can't help being afraid of! I – I fancy Jack may have a good reason for wishing Camille otherwhere."

"Fellow tell you that too?" demanded Freddy. "Well upon my soul!"

"Is it true, Freddy?" asked Kitty shyly.

"No use asking me. For one thing, dashed improper! and for another, wouldn't tell you, if I knew, which I don't. Got something better to do than to pry into what don't concern me."

"Well," said Kitty, with fortitude. "I have learnt a great deal since I came to town, and I think very likely it is true."

"It don't signify whether it is or whether it ain't. Point is, Jack won't expose your cousin any more than I will. Coming it a trifle too strong! What I mean is, if he rumbled the fellow's lay, what the devil did he mean by presenting him to you, let alone a lot of other people? Yes, by Jove! Brought him to m'sister's house! Spiked his own guns, Kit! He's a bruising rider, but he don't over-face his horses. He'll keep his mouth shut."

"Freddy, if he knew – or even suspected – that my cousin was not what he pretends to be, why – why did he bring him to Berkeley Square?"

"Because it's the sort of thing he would do!" said Freddy tartly. "Same reason he tried to hoax me into going down to Arnside. Got a dashed queer sense of humor."

"Yes, I see," said Kitty. "I expect he wanted to punish me a little. Why didn't *you* tell me what you suspected, Freddy?"

"Because I ain't a French gabster!" said Freddy.

❧ *Chapter XVI* ❧

UPON THEIR ARRIVAL IN BERKELEY SQUARE, they were admitted into the house by the porter. Freddy was just about to take formal leave of his betrothed when his sister, attired in a flounced and frilled dressing-gown of rose-pink silk, appeared at the head of the staircase, and began to deliver herself of a dignified request to Miss Charing to come to her bedroom before she retired to her own. As the speech had been carefully composed and conned, it was a pity that the greater part of it remained unuttered. Her ladyship, perceiving Kitty's escort, broke off in sudden dismay, and clutched the banister-rail. *"F-Freddy?"* she said faintly.

"Oh, Meg, is that you?" cried Kitty, nobly coming to her rescue. "I wish you had not sat up for me! Was it very tedious, your party?"

A speaking look of gratitude was cast down at her. Meg recovered her color a little, and replied: "Oh, yes, a dead bore! Do, pray, come to my room! Goodnight,

Freddy! Don't keep Kitty standing down there, prosing on for ever!" She waved an airy hand, and disappeared again from view.

Freddy, who had been surveying her with an expression on his face of strong disapproval, said despairingly: "*Pink!* Dashed if I know why it is, but a female's only got to have a yaller head, and nothing will do for her but to wear pink! Can't be surprised poor Buckhaven's gone to China, can you? Now, mind, Kit! not a word to her about your cousin!"

"No, I promise I will be utterly silent on that head!" Kitty assured him, giving him her hand, and clasping his warmly. "Goodnight! And *indeed* I thank you, Freddy!"

He kissed her fingers gracefully. "No, no! Pleasure!" he stammered.

He then departed, and Kitty sped up the stairs to her hostess's room. Their quarrel was forgotten: Meg said without preamble: "Kitty, how in the world came Freddy to bring you home? Good God, I was ready to sink!"

"He went to fetch me from the Scortons' house, learned where I had gone, and came there in search of me. What a goose you are, Meg! I was in agonies lest you should betray yourself!"

"He didn't suspect?" Meg said anxiously.

"No, of course he did not!"

"What an escape!" shuddered Meg. "I have been quite sick with apprehension, for he doesn't like it when I go out with Jack, and if he knew of *this* I daresay he would tell Papa, and you may depend upon it I should be packed off to stay with Lady Buckhaven on the instant! I must say, it was excessively handsome of you not to have told him, Kitty!"

"As though I would do anything so shabby!" exclaimed Kitty. "But whatever possessed you to go to the Opera House? How *could* Jack have taken you there? I saw at once that it was not at all the sort of party one ought to go to, and surely he must have known that?"

"Oh, yes! He said that Freddy would have his blood, if he came to hear of it, but there was not the least harm, you know! I have always so wished to go to one of those masquerades, and of course Buckhaven will never take me, and nor will Freddy, so I teased Jack to! He took very good care of me, I assure you, and it is not as though I was unmasked. We came away at midnight, but I should like to have remained, for I thought it was very good sport, though, of course, shockingly vulgar! Did you enjoy it?"

Kitty shuddered. "It was quite the worst evening I have ever spent!" she said. "I was never more thankful in my life than when I saw Freddy!"

"Was he very much vexed?" inquired Meg. "He has such stuffy notions!"

"No, no, he was so kind that I almost burst into tears! And he *might* have reproached me! I do think," said Kitty fervently, "that Freddy is the most truly chivalrous person imaginable!"

Freddy's sister, regarding her with awe, opened her mouth, shut it again, swallowed, and managed to say, though in a faint voice: "Do you, indeed?"

"Yes, and a great deal more to the purpose than all the people one was taught to revere, like Sir Lancelot, and Sir Galahad, and Young Lochinvar, and – and that kind of man! I daresay Freddy might not be a great hand at slaying dragons, but you may depend upon it none of those knight-errants would be able to rescue one from a social fix, and you must own, Meg, that one has not the smallest need of a man who can kill dragons! And as for riding off with one in the middle of a party, which I have always thought must have been extremely uncomfortable, and not at all the sort of thing one would wish to happen to one—What is the matter?"

Meg raised her head from the sofa-cushions: "He w-would say it was n-not at all the th-thing!"

"Very well, and why should he not?" said Kitty, refusing to share in her hostess's unseemly mirth. "If you were to hear of such a thing's happening, you would think it most improper, now, wouldn't you?" A sudden thought occurred to her, and she choked, and said, in an uncertain tone: "As a matter of fact, he said that Lochinvar sounded to him like a d-dashed loose-screw!"

A wail from the depths of the cushions proved to be too much for Kitty's command over herself. Both ladies then enjoyed a very hearty laugh; after which they embraced, and parted company for the night without exchanging any further confidences.

The following day passed uneventfully, the only excursion undertaken by two rather weary ladies being a walk to Mount Street, whither they went to take leave of Lady Legerwood, who was conveying the nursery party to Margate that day. As this included Fanny and her governess, her ladyship's own maid, and two damsels hired to wait on the nursery and the schoolroom, it was an impressive cortège which set out from London, Lady Legerwood carrying Edmund in her own post-chaise; Miss Kendal and the two unmarried daughters of the house following in a second chaise; and Nurse, with the attendant abigails, and a mountain of baggage, bringing up the rear in a large traveling coach. Lord Legerwood, who was escorting his family, and remaining with them for a few days, had taken one look at the pile of invalid comforts destined for the chaise that bore his ailing youngest son, and had said that he preferred to ride.

Lady Legerwood, although flustered by all the bustle of departure, found time to sit for a few minutes with the visitors, inquiring anxiously after Meg's state of health, giving her a great deal of good advice, charging Kitty to take care of her, and loading both young ladies with conflicting admonitions on what they should do in the event of accident. She said worriedly that she very much disliked being obliged to leave them unprotected, but derived a certain modicum of comfort from the reflection that it would not be many days before Lord Legerwood was back in town.

"Meanwhile, my love," said his lordship, taking snuff, "you may safely leave them in Freddy's care."

These bland words caused his heir, who had joined the party, very natty in a new coat of blue superfine and pantaloons of a delicate dove-shade, to eye him with acute suspicion. Perceiving it, he laughed, and said: "Pray do not look at me as though I was a coiled snake, Freddy! I am sure you will take excellent care of the girls. My dear, I do not wish to hurry you, but it is time we were setting forward."

Everyone then went out to where the carriages waited; a footman was sent to fetch another rug for the invalid; Nurse and Miss Kendall dissuaded her ladyship from unpacking a valise to assure herself that Edmund's medicine had not been forgotten; farewells were spoken, kisses exchanged, and at last the steps of the carriages were let up, and the doors shut. Kitty, who could never see Lady Legerwood without suffering a smart of conscience, and was particularly discomposed by having received a very kind embrace from her, found that Lord Legerwood was at her elbow, and was thrown into still worse confusion by his holding out his hand to her, and saying, with a smile: "For the present, goodbye, my child. I look forward to having you under my own roof at no very distant date now."

A blush flooded her cheeks; she stammered she knew not what; and cast an almost frightened look up into his face.

"Don't run away, will you?" he said quizzically. "I like Freddy's engagement very well, you know. It has done him a great deal of good."

"Sir – Lord Legerwood!" she said desperately. "I cannot—"

"You cannot talk to me in the open street. Very true! You shall tell me all about it next week, when I return to town. I must go now."

He gave her hand a pat, and released it, bade farewell to his son and daughter, mounted his horse, and rode off in the wake of the carriages.

"What can Papa have meant?" wondered Meg. "What are you to tell him, Kitty. Why do you look so oddly?"

"I don't think I have anything I need tell him," replied Kitty, in a hollow tone. "Do you, Freddy?"

"No," said Freddy, "but there's something he might have told me! Dash it, I ought to have thought of it before! When does term end?" He saw that he had mystified his audience, and added impatiently: "Oxford!"

"Good gracious, I don't know!" said Meg. "What does it signify?"

"It may not signify anything to you, but it dashed well does to me!" said Freddy, with feeling. "Because if m'father's gone junketing off to Margate, and I've to take care of Charlie, it's the outside of enough! The last time Charlie was in town he was pounded by the Watch, and I had to go and bail him out at three in the morning, because he'd spent his last groat! Yes, you may laugh, Meg, but you know very well that if Charlie comes down from Oxford, and finds m'father away, he'll be bound to kick up some lark or other! I don't say it ain't a natural thing to do, but the thing is I shall get the blame for it. I must go and take a look at the calendar at once."

"Freddy, you will come to see me later, won't you?" Kitty begged. "You know we have something important to discuss!"

"Yes, I'll come tomorrow," he said. "Must make sure Charlie don't catch me napping first!"

Kitty was a good deal amused, but as she and Meg began to walk back to Berkeley Square, Meg said: "Poor Freddy! He is for ever being obliged to get Charlie out of a scrape, you know!"

"But I thought Charlie was the clever one!" objected Kitty.

"Oh, yes, indeed he is! He took a great many prizes at Eton, and never finds the least difficulty in learning anything! Only, of course, Freddy is the eldest, besides being on the town, and so it is not to be wondered at that Charlie depends upon him in all his absurd fixes. Charlie," said Meg, with simple pride, "is very wild, you see."

Upon the following morning, while she waited for

Meg in the barouche, outside a shop in Bond Street, Kitty heard her name spoken, and turned her head from the contemplation of a hat in a milliner's window across the street to find that Mrs Broughty and Olivia had paused beside the carriage.

She saw at once that Olivia was looking pale and unhappy, and realized, as soon as Mrs Broughty began to speak, that that lady was very much incensed at the knowledge that she had been to the masquerade. The most profuse apologies to Miss Charing tripped off her tongue; she dared not hope that she would forgive Olivia for having drawn her into such a scrape; feared she must have been very much disgusted; scarcely knew how she herself could ever venture to look dear Lady Buckhaven in the face again.

Hoping very much that Meg would not suddenly appear to put her in this necessity, Kitty said everything that was proper, even going so far as to assert mendaciously that she had passed a very agreeable evening.

"I would not have had such a thing happen for the world!" Mrs Broughty declared, a flush of annoyance in her cheeks. "Opera House masquerades indeed! I cannot conceive how Olivia can have consented to such a vulgar scheme, for you are not to be thinking, Miss Charing, that I have not taught her better, as I don't doubt you must be. Fine doings for a gentleman's daughter, as I have been telling her ever since I heard about this start! If she does not destroy all her chances, it will be no fault of hers, I am sure! I was never more put out in my life!"

"Oh, pray, hush, ma'am!" begged Kitty, perceiving that Olivia was on the brink of tears. "There was no harm done, I do assure you! Have you some errand in Bond Street? I am awaiting Lady Buckhaven, and should be so much obliged to you if you will permit Olivia to bear me company for a few minutes!"

"I am sure the obligation is all on my side, dear Miss Charing, for I was prepared for you to cut the connection, and never have another word to say to Olivia! I am bound for Hookham's Library, and I shall be very happy to leave Olivia with you, if you will be so condescending as to overlook her conduct."

"If Olivia will be so good as to stroll with me down the street, I will bring her to Hookham's in a few minutes," promised Kitty, descending from the barouche. Addressing the footman who had jumped down to open the door for her, she said: "If her ladyship should return before I do myself, please inform her that I shall not be gone above fifteen minutes!" She then bowed civilly to Mrs Broughty, and bore Olivia off in the opposite direction to Hookham's, saying, as she slipped a hand in her arm: "We cannot talk freely in the carriage, so I thought you would not object to walking a little way with me. My dear, pray do not look so cast down! Indeed, there is not the least need! I am sorry your Mama should be so much vexed, and fear you have been having a sad time of it, poor little thing!"

"It has been so dreadful!" Olivia said, in a trembling voice. "I thought we must have packed our trunks yesterday, for Mama quarrelled quite shockingly with Aunt Matty – I daresay you might have heard them half a mile away, particularly when my poor aunt fell into strong hysterics. However, it is now made up between them, only Mama says that I have ruined all my chances, besides having behaved ill from the start, in not making a push to avail myself of all the opportunities that have been put in my way. But, oh, my dear

Miss Charing, I *did* try to do just what she bid me, and I should have been very glad to have caught a rich husband *then*, for I had not met Camille! Only now it is all changed, and the only hope I have is that I shall go into a decline, and die!"

Slightly startled by this peculiar ambition, Kitty said: "Good God, don't speak of such a thing! May I talk frankly to you? My cousin disclosed the whole to me, as I daresay he may have told you. You may guess how shocked I am, and how distressed to think that it should have been I who made him known to you! Believe me, had I had the smallest suspicion of the truth, I would never have done so! I have been an ill friend to you, Olivia. I am fully conscious of it!"

"Oh, no, no, never!" Olivia exclaimed. "We loved one another at first sight! Whatever becomes of me, I cannot regret that I have known him! But even hope is denied us: it is useless to suppose that Mama would give her consent, for although Camille's Papa, you know, is in a very good way of business – he is the proprietor of *several* gaming establishments in Paris, and all of them of the first style of elegance! – Mama is so determined I should make a grand match that I know it would not *do* for her. Then, too, how would Camille's Papa regard it? I have no fortune, and it is precisely that which Camille came to England to seek! Oh, Miss Charing, when I consider that *I* must be the unwitting cause of perhaps destroying all *his* chances, I declare I could almost cast myself into the river!"

Kitty had been prepared for reproaches, but scarcely for this. It was a moment before she could collect her wits enough to answer: "But you could not wish to marry one who is – alas! – an imposter? Worse! It pains me to say it, for I too had the greatest kindness

for Camille! but I fear, Olivia, he is an *adventurer!* He
has deceived us all! The shock to me has been severe,
to *you* how much more so it must have been!"

"Oh, yes, for I knew on the instant that Mama would
dislike it extremely! But he has not deceived *me,* dear
Miss Charing! Nothing could be more noble than his
conduct!"

"Olivia!" said Kitty, trying to reassemble her
thoughts. "You cannot mean that you would be willing
to ally yourself with him!"

"Oh, if it were possible!" sighed Olivia. "I am sure
I do not know why a man should not be a gamester,
if his talents make it an eligible profession for him!
Can it be that you suspect him of employing cheating
tricks? I assure you, it is unjust! He says that Greeking
methods never answer, and that he never uses them,
save in the direst straits! His Papa's houses are patronized by all the grandest people, and they *never* use
loaded dice, or buy inferior wines! *That,* Camille says,
is a very false economy. Everything should always be
of the best, so that one's clients may be pleased, and
come again and again. Of course, it costs a great deal
of money at the outset, but the returns are enor-
mous!"

Kitty could think of nothing better to say than: "Are
they, indeed?"

"Yes, although there are, as one can readily perceive, great hazards. Only fancy! A run of luck may
break the bank at any moment! How exciting it must
be! I had previously no notion!"

"No?" said Kitty, quite stunned.

"No, for I knew nothing of such matters." Olivia
sighed, and relapsed into a mood of dejection. "But

it is all to no avail! Mama would never give her consent."

"You must love my cousin very much!" Kitty said.
"Oh, dear, I wish—But that's to no purpose! Do you
think, if Camille were to engage upon some respectable occupation—? No, I suppose it would not answer."

"Oh, no, for how should he succeed? He was bred
to his profession, you see, and you must perceive that
with his air and address, and his great skill, it is the
very thing for him! Moreover, it is very romantic to
be for ever pitting one's wits against everyone, and I
could not endure it if I were to be the means of thrusting him into some occupation which he would think
a dead bore! I must put him out of my thoughts,
though of course I never shall, for how shocking it
would be if I were to ruin his whole career? Besides,"
added Olivia, on a sob, "it is out of the question that
I should be able to do so! Mama says I must make up
my mind to it to accept Sir Henry, if he should be so
obliging as to offer for me!"

They had turned, by this time, and were retracing
their steps. "That," said Kitty decidedly, "you must
never do! My poor Olivia, it is the most shocking coil,
and I don't know what to say, except that it would be
quite wicked of you to marry that odious old man!"

"Indeed, I would much rather die!" Olivia said earnestly. "The very thought of it casts me into such despair that I am sure it would be better for me to be
dead! But Mama says that he cannot live for ever, and
in the meantime I may have as many lovers as I please,
provided only that I am discreet. But I do not want
many lovers!"

"Good God, I should hope not!" exclaimed Kitty.

"I shall never love anyone but my Camille!" said Olivia, showing an alarming tendency to dissolve into tears.

"For heaven's sake, Olivia, don't start to cry!" begged Kitty. "Recollect, it is not in your Mama's power to force you into a distasteful marriage! Oh, if only I could see what was best to be done, but I am wholly at a loss!"

"Oh, Miss Charing, will you help me?"

"Yes, yes, to the utmost of my power, but it is all such a dreadful tangle – Olivia, pray dry your eyes! We are approaching the library!"

Olivia obediently produced her handkerchief, saying gratefully: "I knew you would stand my friend!"

Since Kitty, though anxious to befriend her, had no idea how this was to be done, she felt very much conscience-stricken, and was glad to be able to restore her to Mrs Broughty before she was called upon to outline some scheme for her relief. The only course that offered itself to her was to confide the whole to Freddy; but as he had sent a message to Berkeley Square that he would dine with his sister that evening, she had a good many hours to while away before she could seek his advice. These were spent by her in concocting and immediately discarding a number of quite unsuitable stratagems, and in blaming herself bitterly for her part in the affair. A diversion was created midway through the afternoon by Mr Westruther, who came to pay a morning visit. As Meg had retired to lie down upon her bed, Kitty received him alone, and would not have received him at all had she had the least warning of his arrival. But he was ushered into the drawing-room, where she sat brooding by the fire, so that she had no opportunity to deny herself.

She accorded him a somewhat cool welcome, but he was quite impervious to such snubs, merely laughing at her, and saying, with a quizzical lift of one eyebrow: "Vexed with me, Kitty? For taking Meg to the masquerade? Now, consider how unjust! Am *I* vexed with *you* for allowing your fascinating cousin to be your cicisbeo? Certainly not! I hope you enjoyed an excellent evening's entertainment."

She ignored the greater part of this speech. "No, I did not enjoy it, and I am astonished that you could have taken Meg to such an improper party!"

"Little prude!" he said, amused. "Did not the dashing Chevalier take good care of you? I had thought him to have been quite in his element!"

"I collect," said Kitty, boldly confronting him, "that you have taken my cousin in aversion. Will you be so good as to tell me why?"

"My dear Kitty, what in the world can I have said to put such a notion as that into your head? You wrong me, really you do! So far from taking the Chevalier in aversion, I admire his address profoundly, and quite envy him his assurance. Such delightful Gallic polish, and so skilled a card-player! It is a privilege to have met him. Indeed, I hope he may be going to do me the honor of visiting me this very evening, to pit his skill against mine. I am myself a gamester, you know, and I have a great desire to measure myself against one whom I have reason to think a past master in the art."

She was dismayed, but summoned up enough courage to reply: "I wish you may not have cause to regret it!"

"Ah, well!" he said, his eyes glinting down at her. "Perhaps he may have the advantage of me in some respects, but in others I venture to think that I have the advantage of him."

She was silenced, and he presently left her a prey to uneasiness. There could be no doubt that he knew that Olivia had been at the masquerade, for she recalled that she had herself told him that she was there with the Scortons; and she could not rid her mind of its suspicion that his invitation to her cousin to visit him must have some bearing on this circumstance.

When Freddy arrived in Berkeley Square that evening, she could scarcely restrain her impatience to take him apart, and pour her apprehensions into his ears; but as it lacked only a few minutes to the dinner-hour, and Meg had already joined her in the drawing-room, this was clearly ineligible. Moreover, it immediately became apparent that grave cares were pressing upon Freddy's soul, for upon his sister's demanding of him, in a rallying tone, whether Charles had already descended on the town, he replied: "No, term don't end for another ten days. It's worse than that! Dashed if I didn't receive a letter from him this morning! Yes, and what's more, I had to pay sixpence for it, which I'd as lief not have done. It ain't that I grudge sixpence, but what I mean is, why the deuce should I have to give sixpence for a thing I'd as soon not have?"

"Oh, heavens, is he in a scrape?" exclaimed Meg.

"Well, of course he is! Knew that as soon as I saw the letter! Stands to reason! What would he want to write to me for, if he hadn't made a cake of himself in some way or another? Never knew such a fellow! Mind, I daresay it's only some snyder dunning him, but there's nothing for it: I shall have to take a bolt to Oxford tomorrow."

"Going out of town *now?*" cried Kitty.

"Yes, but I shan't be gone above one night. Dashed inconvenient, but the thing is, if Charlie's landed himself in the basket, must pull him out! Fond of him," he added, on an explanatory note. "Besides – wouldn't do for it to come to m'father's ears!"

"No, indeed! Of course you must go! I hope you may not find that anything very serious is amiss."

"Yes, I hope so too," said Freddy. "Because if it's anything that means I must go and talk to the bag-wig – what I mean is, the Dean – it's no use going to Oxford at all, because I don't suppose he'd listen to me. Never did when I was up myself, and dashed well *had* to talk to him. Not that I wanted to, mind you, but there it was: obliged to!"

"Could it be that Charlie has become *entangled?*" suggested Meg, looking anxious.

Freddy rubbed his nose. "Got into the muslin company? Might, of course, though he ain't one for the petticoats. Oh, well, if that's all it is, nothing to worry about! Buy her off!"

On this comforting thought, they all went in to dinner. The lighthearted insouciance which characterized the Standens had its effect upon Kitty; and her desponding mood soon changed to one of hope. She was still quite unable to see any way in which she could help Olivia to overcome her troubles, but the cheerful nonchalance with which Freddy confronted the task of rescuing his graceless junior from whatever dire straits he had fallen into insensibly made her feel that the tangle caused by her cousin's descent upon London would not be beyond his power to unravel.

When Meg kindly, but (as she pointed out to them) reprehensibly, left the betrothed couple to their own devices, later in the evening, it could not have been said that Freddy's ingenuity was displayed to any marked degree. He explained, when asked if he had thought what was best to be done, that he had had no leisure in which to examine the problem. "Must see I haven't, Kit! Had a great deal on my mind. Gave me a nasty jar, I can tell you, when it struck me Charlie might be coming down any day. Dashed calendar of mine don't tell one the dates of the terms, either. Took me the better part of the day to find 'em. And now, just as I thought all was right, I've got to go jauntering off to Oxford, and I daresay I shall have to do a lot of thinking when I get there. The thing is, Charlie's a dashed clever fellow, but he ain't got a particle of common sense. No use asking me to get rid of the Chevalier until I come back to town. Do it then."

"Get rid of him? But how can we, when you yourself said it would be useless to threaten to expose him unless he went away?"

"I don't know, but very likely I shall hit on something. Well, dashed well must! He hasn't been calling here, has he?"

"No, oh, no! But I met Olivia today, and I very much fear that it has gone deeper with her than I knew. I own that what she said astonished me! It seems as though the only thing she cares for is that Mrs Broughty would never countenance such a match. You may imagine my surprise when I discovered that Camille's disclosure has not shocked her, as it shocked me!"

"Daresay it wouldn't," responded Freddy, after giving the matter some thought. "Come to think of it, Kit, bit of an adventuress herself!"

"Freddy!"

He gave an apologetic cough, but said firmly: "No

use wrapping the thing up in clean linen. I don't say it's her fault, but she told you herself she came to town to catch a rich husband. Well, nothing to say against that! Point is, that Broughty woman would play any havey-cavey trick to bring the thing off. Unscrupulous, that's the word!"

"*She* is, yes! But not Olivia!"

"Very likely not, because she hasn't the wit for it. No wish to offend you, Kit, but she sounds a cork-brained girl to me. Always did! I don't say she ain't goodhearted, but if she's got the sort of principles you have yourself I'd like to know where she learned 'em!"

Kitty stared at him in a little dismay. "Must one *learn* to have principles?" she faltered.

"Lord, yes! Well, I put it to you, Kit! How the deuce would you know the right way to go on if you was never taught anything but the wrong way?"

She digested this for a moment in silence. "I fear there may be much in what you say," she said reluctantly. "It has sometimes seemed to me that poor Olivia's thoughts have not a proper direction, and I have wondered at it, for, indeed, Freddy, she is a good, kind girl! But however it may be it would be wicked to see her thrust into marriage with such a person as Sir Henry Gosford, and make not one push to save her! And when I consider what the alternative might be, and how much I am to blame for her present distress, I feel that I *must* try to help her! I am persuaded you must enter into my sentiments upon this occasion!"

Mr Standen was far from doing any such thing, but he was never one to engage in fruitless argument, so he held his peace. He perceived, however, that Miss Charing's large charity would not permit her to abandon her unfortunate protegée, and eyed her with a good deal of misgiving.

She had risen from her chair, and was walking restlessly about the room. "*Something* must be done for Olivia!" she said. "She depends upon me to help her, which makes it so particularly dreadful that I cannot! And then there is poor Dolph! All this business has almost made me forget him and Hannah! What wretched work I am making of it!"

"Know what I think, Kit? Good thing if you did forget 'em! What I mean is, very sorry for the poor fellow, but got enough on our hands without him."

"Oh, no! When I pledged them my word I would assist them!"

Freddy sighed.

"And then there is myself!" Kitty said. "I can't tell how it has come about, but I have done nothing of what I intended! Kitty, we must not continue in this fashion! It was very wrong of me ever to ask such a thing of you! Wrong, and so foolish that I am amazed at myself! Only see what has come of it!"

"Dash it, Kit, thought you was enjoying yourself!" said Freddy, a little hurt.

She turned impulsively towards him. "Oh, it has been the most delightful thing that ever happened to me!" she said. "I shall remember it my whole life long! I never was so happy! But it must end. On *that* I am resolved! We must consider what is best to be done."

"Talk it over when I come back from Oxford," said Freddy.

"Perhaps," said Kitty, "the thing would be for us to quarrel."

"No, dash it! I don't want to quarrel with you!"

"And I am sure I could never quarrel with you, Freddy!" said Kitty warmly.

"There you are, then! No sense in it."

"I meant only that we should pretend to quarrel."

"Wouldn't answer at all," said Freddy. "Everyone knows I ain't quarrelsome. Tell you what, Kit: good notion if we don't tease ourselves about that till we've packed your cousin off to France. Got to pack Dolph off to Ireland, too."

"But you said you wished I would not!"

"Oh, well!" said Freddy, in a temporizing spirit. "I'd liefer you did that than started quarrelling with me! Come to think of it, it ain't such a bad notion. Might as well be rid of Dolph while we're about it. Mind, I don't dislike the poor fellow, but it ain't what I'd choose, having a cousin who's queer in his attic loose on the town!"

"No, indeed! Oh, dear, I cannot help wishing that you were not obliged to go to Oxford tomorrow!"

"No need to worry about that," said Freddy kindly. "Shan't stay above one night there, and I don't mean to dawdle on the road. Hired a chaise-and-four. Won't take me much above four hours to get back to town. Make an early start, and be in London by noon. No time for anything to go amiss here. Besides, no reason why anything should. Wouldn't go if there was."

⚘ *Chapter XVII* ⚘

SINCE LORD BUCKHAVEN WAS A MAN OF AFFAIRS, he paid for an early delivery of the post at his town house. Consequently, Kitty found a letter addressed to her in Miss Fishguard's spidery handwriting lying beside her plate on the breakfast table next morning. She broke the wafer that sealed it, and opened it, but was soon knitting her brows over it. It was evident that it had been written in considerable agitation, for although the opening lines, which expressed Miss Fishguard's hope that her charge was in good health and continuing to find her stay in town agreeable, were perfectly legible, the writing soon became little better than a scrawl. As Miss Fishguard, in a conscientious determination to save Kitty the cost of receiving a second sheet, had crossed her lines closely, the task of deciphering the whole was very nearly impossible. After poring over it for some minutes, Kitty exclaimed: "I declare I don't know what can be the matter with Fish! In general, she writes such a very neat hand, and here she is sending me a letter I cannot make head or tail of! I do *hope* Uncle Matthew has not driven her out of her wits!"

"I should think he would drive anyone out of her wits," observed Meg, sipping her coffee. "He must be the most odious person imaginable!"

"Yes, but in her last letter Fish wrote that he was behaving quite amiably. Besides, she is really so much accustomed to his odd ways that she would not make a fuss only because he had thrown his stick at her, or something of that nature. But there can be no doubt that something is amiss, for she begs me to return so that she may tell me what has happened."

"But you cannot!" said Meg, putting down her cup.

"No, and she seems to feel that, for there is something here which I think is *spare you for one day.* That must mean you, Meg. Oh, yes! Now I see! That word, which I took to be *Ladybirds,* must be *Lady Buckhaven!* Then there is something I cannot read, and *being thought a cockatrice.*"

"Who?" demanded Meg. "If she means me, I think it is excessively uncivil of her, besides being unjust, for I never saw her but once in all my life!"

"Perhaps it isn't cockatrice. Yet it certainly looks like it. However, here, on the very next line, is something about Henry VIII, so I don't think it can be."

"She cannot be writing to you about Henry VIII!" objected Meg.

"Well, one would think not, but you see for yourself!" replied Kitty, showing her the sheet.

The fair head and the dark were bent over it. "I must say, it does *seem* to be Henry VIII," admitted Meg. "Perhaps she is likening Uncle Matthew to him! He was very disagreeable too, wasn't he?"

"Yes, so he was! He had rages, and cut off people's heads. No doubt that is it! But who can this Katherine be?"

"Katherine of Aragon!" said Meg brilliantly.

"No, I am sure it's not Aragon. Besides, how absurd! They must have been obliged to turn one of the maids off, and hire a new one. Perhaps Uncle Matthew has taken a dislike to her. He usually does."

"I cannot conceive why Miss Fishguard should beg you to go home only because she has engaged a new servant."

"Oh, no, and it seems not to be that at all, for I can distinctly make out *unable to write it,* and, a little farther on something about my generosity. Then there is a word which looks like *treason,* so it can have nothing to do with this Katherine. It must be Henry VIII again, and yet—You know, Meg, I think I shall be obliged to post down to Arnside, if Freddy will be so good as to take me when he comes back to town, for there can be no doubt that poor Fish is in great distress!"

Meg agreed to it, though rather reluctantly. She said that she feared that Kitty would be persuaded to remain at Arnside; and Kitty, once more stricken by the warm kindliness of the Standens, forbore to tell her that the day was rapidly approaching when she must for ever lose her young chaperon. The only salve Kitty could find to apply to her unquiet conscience was the knowledge that she had really been of use to Meg.

Soon after breakfast, Meg, arrayed in a blue velvet pelisse, and the only one of her hats which she thought likely to escape the criticism of the censorious, went off to pay a dutiful call on her husband's Aunt Maria, with whom she had untruthfully announced her intention of dining, on the night of the masquerade. Kitty

offered to accompany her, but Meg thought that it
would be better if Aunt Maria did not set eyes on her.
Having contrived to convey to the formidable lady,
who, mercifully, disapproved so strongly of frivolity
that she rarely went into society, the impression that
Kitty's betrothed was a very sober girl, of strict upbringing and rigid principles, it would clearly be an
act of madness to present a dashing young female, rav-
ishingly attired in a morning dress of twilled French
silk, and with her hair cut and curled in the very latest
mode. "Besides, Aunt Maria would be bound to say
you were fast, because she thinks all pretty females
must be."

"I?" gasped Kitty. *"Pretty?"*

"Now, Kitty, don't be missish! You know you are!
Papa was saying only the other day that you have a
great deal of countenance. Of course, the thing that
particularly pleases Mama is that you have such excellent taste. She sets the greatest store by that, you
know, and says she shall be very glad to take you about
with her as soon as she is able, because you will do
us all such credit! Shall you be going out? If you are
in Bond Street, I wish you will take back *The Pastor's
Fireside* to Hookham's – unless you mean to read it
yourself, but I do not at all recommend it!"

She then departed, leaving her guest to peruse the
morning papers before sallying forth on her errand.
She had just put on her hat and pelisse, and was descending the stairs to the hall when Lord Dolphinton,
having tugged violently at the bell and banged the
knocker several times for good measure, was admitted
into the house.

"Miss Charing!" uttered his lordship, in agitated accents.

"I fancy, my lord, that Miss has but this instant stepped out, but I will inquire," bowed Skelton.

"Wait for her!" said Dolphinton, thrusting his hat and cane upon the slightly startled butler. "Must see her! Important!"

"Good gracious, Dolph, whatever is the matter?" exclaimed Kitty, hurrying down the stairs.

Dolphinton clutched her hand, and said in a gasp: "Must see you!"

"Yes, yes, of course!" said Kitty. "Come into the breakfast-parlor, and tell me all about it!"

He allowed himself to be led into this apartment; but when she had shut the door, and pushed him gently into a chair by the fire, he seemed to find the greatest difficulty in enunciating a word. He sat opening and shutting his mouth for some moments, staring at her with such an expression of misery on his face that she became alarmed, and begged him to tell her if anything terrible had happened to Miss Plymstock.

He swallowed convulsively. "Not Hannah. Me! Don't know what to do. Obliged to offer for you again!"

She could not help laughing. "Now, Dolph, don't be absurd! I collect that your Mama has been teasing you?"

He nodded. "Says I must sweep you off your feet. I don't want to. Don't want to sweep anybody off her feet. Not even Hannah. Don't know how. Besides, Freddy wouldn't like it. Might call me out. Not going to fight a duel with Freddy! Won't do it! I *like* Freddy! Like him better than Hugh, or—"

"Yes, yes, you like him better than any of your cousins!" said Kitty. "He won't call you out, I promise you!"

"Mama says he won't but I don't know. Mama says you won't marry him. Says she knew it all along. Says if I do the thing right you'll marry me. Says—"

"She says that I shall like to be a Countess, and you have only to tell me of all the advantages which would be mine, if I married you, for me to accept your offer!" interrupted Kitty. "But this is all nonsense, Dolph, and there is nothing to put you in this taking! You may tell your Mama that you did her bidding, and I refused to listen to you."

He shook his head. "Don't understand. Haven't *thought!* I have. People may say I can't think, but I can. Often think for hours and hours. Thought about this. See it all. You refuse me – can't come here any more – shan't see Hannah – put a period to my existence! Only thing is, able to swim! shouldn't like to put a pistol to my head. At least," he added, "don't think I should. Got peppered in the leg by a careless fellow once. Didn't like it above half."

Considerably frightened, Kitty knelt beside his chair, and took his hand, and patted it. "No, no, Dolph! Pray do not talk in that wild fashion! I do understand! – I understand perfectly! It is all my fault for not having thought of a way to help you all this time! But I will get you out of this fix!"

"You will?" said his lordship anxiously.

"I will!" she declared. "Oh, dear, it seems as though everything has come upon me at the same time! First, Camille, and then Fish, and now—" She broke off, as an idea occurred to her, and suddenly raised her eyes to his lordship's face, staring fixedly at him.

"You think you can get me out of it?" he said, a glimmer of hope in his eye.

"Wait!" said Kitty. She sat back on her heels, her brows knitted, and her gaze intent upon the wall.

His lordship waited obediently, watching her with very much the air of an expectant dog. All at once, her face broke into smiles, and she turned to him, seizing both his hands, and saying impulsively: "I have it! How can I have been such a goose as not to have thought of it before? My poor, dear Fish! It is all her doing! You shall marry Miss Plymstock, and I can contrive it so that Freddy shall incur not the smallest blame for it! The only thing is – Dolph, should you object to deceiving your Mama?"

"You think I could do that?" he asked intently.

"You could, if I showed you how it may be done, and told you several times what you must say to her."

"Yes, I could," agreed his lordship, pleased to find his powers recognized. *"Like* to do it!"

"To be sure you would! Now, listen carefully, Dolph! I find myself obliged to go to Arnside, and you shall take me! You will tell your Mama that you did just as she bade you, and I said that I was willing to marry you, if Uncle Matthew would consent to it, only I must see him face to face, to explain the matter to him. Have you understood that, Dolph? Very well! You will tell her that you mean to take me to Arnside tomorrow – Oh, Dolph, will she let you take me in your own carriage? I believe the post charges are shockingly dear, and I daresay you would find it as hard to lay your hand upon a large sum of money as I should!"

"Take you in my own carriage," he repeated, showing his comprehension, and keeping his eyes fixed on her face in a painful effort of concentration.

"Yes, I think she will raise no demur," decided Kitty. "And there can be no fear of her coming with us, because Uncle Matthew has sworn he will not allow her to enter his house again, and she must know he meant it, because the last time she came he made Stobhill bolt all the doors, and shouted to her out of the window of his dressing-room that she was to go away. Poor Fish had one of her worst spasms, and I must own that it was shockingly uncivil of Uncle Matthew! Well, then, Dolph, you shall bring your carriage here tomorrow morning, quite early, remember, because I particularly wish to be gone out of town before noon! And I will arrange for Hannah to be here, as though she came with me to bear me company, you know, and we will drive away, all three of us! And we shall not go to Arnside, but to Garsfield Rectory!"

"Go to Garsfield Rectory," agreed his lordship, puzzled but trusting.

She gave him a little shake. "To *Hugh,* Dolph! You know he is the Rector! He can marry you to Hannah and then you will be safe, and Hannah will not permit your Mama to tease you ever again! And your Mama will not question the propriety of your taking a valise with you, because she will expect us to remain at Arnside for the night! It is the most famous scheme, and the best of it is that Freddy need have nothing to do with it! It will be all my fault, and no one will be able to blame him in the least degree!"

It took time and patience to instil his rôle into Lord Dolphinton's slow mind, but once he had thoroughly grasped the ramifications of the plot he became so enthusiastic that he was with difficulty dissuaded from accompanying Kitty upon a visit to Keppel Street. She thought it wiser that he should not go with her, however, having little dependence on his discretion, and a lively apprehension that his presence would set Hannah's sharp-eyed sister-in-law very much upon her guard. Having assured herself that he did indeed understand what he was expected to do, and promised to send him word if some accident should prevent Miss Plymstock from playing her part in the affair, she saw him off the premises, and at once sped forth to Keppel Street.

She had the good fortune to find Miss Plymstock alone, and had no difficulty in making her understand what was purposed for her benefit. Miss Plymstock heard her in calm, attentive silence, shook hands with her in a very painful way, and said gruffly: "Don't know how to thank you, but I daresay you can guess what I should wish to say to you, Miss Charing. You may depend upon me! If her ladyship has taken to frightening Foster again, there ain't a moment to be lost. I won't have her driving him out of his wits, that's certain! You don't need to tease yourself, wondering what will happen when I've married him: I'll take care of that! Only let me get his ring on my finger, and I shall know how to do! I ain't afraid of her ladyship, nor of anyone, and I don't mean to let her come next or nigh poor Foster. I daresay there will be a great deal of botheration, not to say unpleasantness, over his money, and that, but I'm prepared for it, and I have a smart lawyer in my eye, who will very likely settle it all in a trice. And if she thinks to make that nasty doctor of hers say that Foster's mad, we'll see what *my* doctor, that's an honest, sensible man, will say to that! He ain't mad! And if he were, why, it's the business of his lawful, wedded wife to take care of him, and so my lady will discover before she is much older!" She nodded her head in a determined way, but after dwelling for a moment or two, in brooding silence, upon the prospect of utterly confounding her future mother-in-law, brought her thoughts back to the immediate present, and said briskly: "I shan't breathe a word to my brother, Miss Charing. Time enough to tell him what's become of me when I'm Lady Dolphinton! But it won't do for me to be seen walking out of here tomorrow with a portmanteau, or some such thing. If I was to put up what I shall be needing at once, before Sister comes back, do you think, Miss Charing, you could be so obliging as to carry it away with you to Berkeley Square? You must know that commonly I go shopping for Sister in the mornings, so that any little thing I might be needing tonight I can pop into my basket tomorrow, and none the wiser."

Kitty readily acquiesced in this scheme, and accompanied Miss Plymstock upstairs to her bedchamber to assist her with her packing. She soon found, however, that Miss Plymstock needed no assistance. Having unearthed from an attic at the top of the house a modest valise, she dumped this on the floor of her room, took a rapid survey of her wardrobe, and made an instant and practical selection of the garments to take with her. These were swiftly bestowed in the valise; Miss Plymstock carried it downstairs herself; and, having made sure the servants were not within sight, let herself and Kitty out of the house, saying briefly: "I'll carry it till we find a hack, if you please!"

This was soon done; Miss Plymstock once more wrung Kitty's hand, said fiercely: "Wish I knew how *I* could be of service to *you!*" and walked off before Kitty could reply.

It was not to be expected that Meg would accept without question Kitty's sudden decision to go to Arnside before Freddy's return to town, nor did she do so. After listening with astonishment to Kitty's manufactured explanation, she demanded to be told the truth, saying that she had never listened to such a bamboozling story in her life.

"But, Meg, indeed I think that I should go to Fish at once! And Freddy will scarcely wish to leave town again so soon after his journey from Oxford!"

"Kitty, I *know* this is a take-in! I warned Freddy that you would run off with Dolphinton, if he did not take care, but I didn't really believe you would! But—"

Kitty laughed. "I should hope not indeed! How can you be so nonsensical? I promise you I will never do that! Now, Meg, you may be perfectly easy, because I have asked my friend, Miss Plymstock, if she will go with me – to lend me countenance, you know, and make everything quite proper!"

"You don't mean that odd-looking creature who came here one day, and took you out walking?" gasped Meg. "Well! I'm sure I don't wish to offend you, but I must say, Kitty, that you have the strangest friends! And as for needing her to make it proper, fiddlesticks! One would imagine you meant to go on a journey to Scotland, instead of to Arnside! I wish you will tell me what you are about! I have a strong notion I ought not to let you go. Freddy will say so, depend upon it, and I shall be quite in disgrace with him."

"No, that you will not, for he won't be vexed," Kitty assured her. "He knows, in part, already and I will write a letter, which you may give him when he comes to see you tomorrow, explaining the rest. I promise you, Meg, I don't mean to do anything he would not like. I *could* not!"

"If you think he will not object, why must you be so secret?" asked Meg reasonably.

"Because it will be better for you not to know anything about it," explained Kitty.

Meg gave a moan of protest. "Oh, heavens, I have
never had a Spasm in my life, but I shouldn't be at all
surprised if I have one now! You are going to do
something dreadful!"

"No, I am not. At least, *some* persons may say so, but
Freddy will not, and I am sure you will not either. Only
consider, Meg! How could I do anything dreadful,
when Miss Plymstock goes with me? And I will faithfully promise to return here the very next day!"

Meg was a little reassured by this. She made several
attempts, during the course of the day, to coax the secret out of Kitty, but Kitty would do nothing but shake
her head, and giggle. This was exasperating, but it did
not seem likely that she would have giggled had she
been bent on some desperate action, so Meg gave it
up at last, shrugging her shoulders, and saying: "Oh,
very well, though I think it is very disagreeable of you,
and I beg you will not blame *me* if you find yourself
in a scrape!"

"No, that I won't!" Kitty said, in the throes of com-
posing a letter to Freddy.

This missive soon covered several sheets of Meg's
elegant, gilt-edged writing-paper, for it seemed a very
natural thing to tell Freddy the whole story, not omit-
ting any detail which she felt sure he would enjoy, such
as the clever arrangement she had made for the journey in the carriage Lady Dolphinton doubtless considered to be her own, and poor Dolph's woebegone face
when he said that he had come to sweep her off her
feet.

She could not help feeling a trifle anxious, next day;
and she would not have been altogether surprised had

she received a visit from Lady Dolphinton. To have entrusted so important a share in the arrangements to Dolphinton did indeed seem a hazardous thing to have done, and made her fearful of the issue. However, when Miss Plymstock arrived in Berkeley Square, shortly after ten o'clock, and heard of these qualms, she said confidently that all would be well. "He don't understand things quickly, Miss Charing, but once you fix a thing in his head, which I don't doubt you did, he don't forget it. The only thing is that he may be in a sad pucker, what with the excitement, and being scared his mother will find him out."

She was right on both counts. Twenty minutes later, a traveling-carriage drew up outside the house, Lord Dolphinton alighted from it, and, after casting around him a glance suggestive of a hare hotly pursued by hounds, hurried up the steps to the front door. He was soon ushered into the Saloon where Kitty and Hannah were sitting, and barely waited until Skelton had withdrawn before gasping: "Did it! Got the carriage. Told a lot of lies. Remembered everything you said!"

"That's right," said Hannah, in a motherly voice. "You've done very well, Foster, just as I knew you would, and now you may be easy."

"No, I mayn't," he said, wiping his pallid countenance with a crumpled handkerchief. "Afraid she'll come after me!"

"Well, she will do no such thing, my dear, because there's no reason why she should."

His lordship looked at her with terror in his eye. "Got Finglass with me!" he uttered. "Spies on me! Didn't dare say I wouldn't have him. Thought she might suspect."

"And a very good thing too," said the redoubtable

Miss Plymstock calmly. "I'd just as lief he was under my eye, for he can't work any mischief if we keep him with us."

"Yes, and you may employ him afterwards to carry the news that you are married back to your Mama," interpolated Kitty encouragingly. "You must not be afraid of him, Dolph, for although he may spy on you, he cannot *do* anything, you know. He is obliged to obey your orders; and now that you have escaped from your Mama you do not care what tales he may carry to her."

He looked doubtful, but Hannah told him that Kitty was quite right, and he seemed to accept this assurance, and to become less agitated. But just then Meg's voice was heard, and Kitty was obliged to remind him hastily that Meg was not in the secret, which threw him back into disorder. Fortunately, Meg thought him at all times so very odd that she was unlikely, Kitty hoped, to notice any additional peculiarity in his bearing.

She entered the room, shook hands with Miss Plymstock, and civilly invited her to partake of a little refreshment before setting out on the journey.

"Like to start now!" said Dolphinton, in a hoarse whisper, and plucking at Kitty's sleeve.

"My dear Dolph, there can be no need for such haste!" said Meg. "I daresay it will not take you above two hours to reach Arnside."

This made him look so anguished that Kitty made haste to say that she particularly desired to reach Arnside in good time. "Because Uncle Matthew shuts himself up in his bookroom all the afternoon, and so I shall be able to enjoy a comfortable talk with Fish," she explained.

"I shan't have to see Uncle Matthew, shall I?" said Dolphinton, a fresh terror raising its head.

"No, no, you need not see him! I think, Miss Plymstock, that perhaps we had better go immediately."

"I'm agreeable," responded Hannah, picking up her basket.

Meg, eyeing the basket in a fascinated way, and wondering what could be in it, made no further attempt to detain the travelers. She accompanied them to the front door, and stood on the top step to wave goodbye, calling after Dolphinton to be sure to bring Kitty back in good time the next day. This adjuration made him pause, just as he was about to climb into the carriage. He looked over his shoulder in a harassed manner, and was just about to say that he was not coming back to London when two small but resolute pairs of hands seized his coat and dragged him into the carriage. The door was shut on him, and his groom mounted on to the box beside the coachman. "Drive fast!" said his lordship, putting his head out of the window. "Spring 'em!"

❧ Chapter XVIII ❧

MR STANDEN, ARRIVING IN BERKELEY SQUARE
just after noon, allowed Skelton to help him out of his
many-caped driving-coat, laid his hat and gloves on
a side-table, and paused under a large Venetian gilt
mirror to adjust his cravat. "Ladies at home, Skelton?"
he inquired.

"Her ladyship is partaking of luncheon in the
breakfast-parlor, sir. Miss Charing went out of town
this morning, and will not be back, I understand, until
tomorrow."

Freddy looked mildly surprised. "Did she, though?
What made her do that?"

"I couldn't say, sir."

"Queer start!" remarked Freddy. "No need to announce me."

Skelton bowed, but opened the door of the parlor
at the back of the house for him. Freddy wandered into
the room, and accorded his sister a brotherly greeting.

"Hallo, Meg! What's this Skelton tells me about Kit? Where has she gone to?"

"Oh, Freddy, is that you?" exclaimed Meg. "How quick you have been! Kitty might just as well have waited for you! Not that I believed a word of that story, for I hope I am not such a dummy! She has gone off to Arnside, but she means to return tomorrow."

"Old gentleman taken ill, or something?" inquired Freddy, seating himself at the table, and selecting an apple from the dish of fruit in the middle of it.

"No, I don't think that was it. She had a most peculiar letter from Miss Fishguard yesterday, all about Henry VIII, and she said it was plain to her that something must be amiss at Arnside."

"All about Henry VIII?" repeated Freddy incredulously. "What's he doing at Arnside? Well, what I mean is, can't be doing anything! Fellow's been dead for centuries. Good thing, if he's the one I'm thinking of."

"Well, that is what we couldn't discover, for the stupid creature wrote so wildly neither of us could read her letter. There was something about a cockatrice, and a girl called Katherine, whom Kitty thinks must be a new servant, and then, a little farther down the page, something about treason. There was no understanding it at all!"

"Plain as a pikestaff!" said Freddy, delicately peeling his apple. "Touched in her upper works. Thought as much, when I was down there."

"Yes, but that is not all, Freddy. First, Kitty said she should ask you to take her home, to discover what was the matter. And then, that very same morning, she said she would not wait for you, but would ask Dolph to take her instead! I assure you, I tried to dissuade

her, but she wouldn't listen to me, and she *has* gone
with Dolph!"

Mr Standen, having peeled his apple, now quartered
it. "Shouldn't have done that," he said, shaking his
head. "Much better have waited for me! No use taking
Dolph: he's touched in his upper works too. Won't
know what to do, if that Fish turns out to be violent."
He ate one of the quarters, and added reflectively:
"Come to think of it, shouldn't know what to do myself. Still, might make a push to do something, which
he won't."

"Upon my word, Freddy, you take it very cooly!"
cried Meg. "Here's Kitty, running off in this mysterious way with Dolph, and you seem not to care a but-
ton!"

"Well, I don't," replied Freddy. "She won't come
to any harm with Dolph."

"For anything you know she may have eloped with
him! You are the most extraordinary creature!"

"I know dashed well she hasn't eloped with him, and
if you weren't so bird-witted you'd know it too."

"Well, I do know it, but you must own that after the
way he has been dangling round her it would not be
surprising! But, in fact, she took that very odd friend
of hers as well – Miss Plymstock."

Freddy was subjecting the dish of fruit to a close
scrutiny, but at these words he let his eyeglass fall, and
said: "Did she, though! Then that explains it! At least,
don't quite see why she's gone to Arnside, but I daresay there's a very good reason."

"So you *do* understand it!" said Meg. "To be sure,
Kitty said you would, but I thought she was hoaxing
me. Freddy, what is she doing? Not one word would

she vouchsafe to me, except that it would be better if I didn't know, which nearly sent me into hysterics!"

"Daresay she was right," said Freddy, considering the matter. "Might be the devil of a dust over it – if she's doing what I think she is, which, mind you, I ain't sure of."

"You had better read the letter she wrote to you," said Meg, suddenly remembering the existence of Kitty's letter, and producing it from her reticule.

"I should dashed well think I had!" said Freddy indignantly. "If it ain't just like you, Meg, to sit there prosing on for ever instead of giving it to me at once!"

"I had forgot I had it," apologized Meg, giving it to him.

He cast her a look of scorn, broke the wafer, and spread open the sheets. His sister sat in growing impatience while he slowly perused the whole, every now and then turning back to consult some phrase on a previous page. Restraining her ardent wish to demand enlightenment, she waited until he had come to the end before saying: "Well?"

Mr Standen, who appeared to be wrestling with some knotty problem, paid not the smallest heed to this interjection, but, to Meg's intense annoyance, began to read the letter all over again. He then said cryptically: "If you ask me, she's made a muff of it!"

"Well, I do ask you!" said Meg, pardonably incensed. "Made a muff of *what*?"

"It don't signify," said Freddy, rising to his feet. "Good thing she wrote to me, though. Might have caught cold at this!"

"Freddy!" shrieked Meg. "You don't mean to leave me without telling me what has happened?"

"Yes, I do," he replied. "Tell you all about it presently! For one thing, haven't time just now: got something important to do! For another, Kit don't want me to."

"Oh, it is the most infamous thing!" Meg cried.

"No, no, it ain't as bad as that!" said Freddy earnestly. "Don't say there won't be the deuce of a dust kicked up, because there will be. *I* can stand the huff, but you wouldn't like it."

On these tantalizing words, he left the room, bestowing a kindly pat on his sister's shoulder as he passed her chair. He shrugged himself into his driving-coat again, picked up his curly-brimmed beaver, set it on his head with nicety and precision, took his gloves in his hand, and let himself out of the house.

It was his intention to walk to the nearest thoroughfare, there to find a hackney-coach; but as he paused on the top step to consult his watch, one of these useful vehicles rounded the corner of the Square, and, in another minute, drew up outside the Buckhaven house. Freddy, restoring his watch to his pocket, descended the steps, vaguely wondering who might have come to visit his sister in a common hack. The answer to this problem then burst upon his vision: Miss Broughty almost tumbled out of the coach, and began to search in her reticule for the recompense needed to satisfy the demands of the Jehu seated on the box. These appeared to be beyond her means, for she embarked on a somewhat agitated argument with her creditor. Freddy was not one of Miss Broughty's admirers, but an inner voice warned him that his affianced bride would certainly expect him to befriend any protegée of hers, so he stepped forward, removing his hat, and bowing with his peculiar grace. "Beg you will allow me!" he murmured.

"Oh!" gasped Olivia, startled, and dropping her reticule. "Mr Standen!"

He restored her property to her. "How do you do? Very happy to be of assistance! Shocking robbers, these jarveys!"

The gentleman on the box began indignantly to recite the lawful charges for the hire of hackney vehicles, but when he discovered that the swell in the sixteen-caped coat had not the slightest intention of disputing these with him, changed his tone, and said that if he could have his way he would never drive any but a member of the Quality. He then pocketed the handsome sum handed up to him, winked expressively, and drove off, with a twirl of his whip.

"Oh, Mr Standen!" faltered Olivia. "You are so very obliging! I do not know what to say! I had no notion—! My one thought was to reach dear Miss Charing, and I just hailed the first coach I saw, and jumped into it!"

The inner voice which seldom added anything to Mr Standen's comfort now warned him that trouble loomed in front of him. He said: "You want to see Miss Charing?"

"Oh, yes, for I am in the greatest distress, and she said that she would help me!"

"Very sorry to be obliged to disappoint you: gone out of town!" said Freddy apologetically.

This time, Miss Broughty dropped her muff as well as her reticule upon the flagway. "Gone out of town!" she repeated, looking perfectly distraught. "Oh heavens, what shall I do?"

Freddy once more retrieved her belongings. Taking Miss Broughty's exclamation in its most literal sense, he replied with great civility: "Very difficult for me to say. Happy to do anything in my power, but not in possession of the facts. No use asking for Miss Charing today: call again tomorrow!"

"Too late!" uttered Miss Broughty, in tragic accents. "I am lost, for there is no one I may turn to, except Mr Westruther, and I cannot, I cannot!"

Mr Standen now knew that his inner voice had not deceived him. His instinct was to extricate himself with what dexterity he could summon to his aid from a situation which bade fair to plunge him into the sort of embarrassment his fastidious soul loathed; but an innate chivalry bade him stand his ground. He said, with a deprecatory cough: "Very understandable! Shouldn't turn to him, if I was you. Better tell me! Do my best to assist you: betrothed to Miss Charing, you know!"

She stared wildly up into his face. "Oh, yes, but— How could I? You are not to be teased with my affairs, I am sure! Besides – oh, I could not!"

"Not at all!" he said. "Pleasure! Collect it concerns Miss Charing's cousin: very delicate matter, but no need to conceal anything from me: know all about it!"

"You do?" she cried. "But it does not concern him! At least—Oh, what shall I do?"

Mr Standen, deftly catching her muff, which she released as she began to wring her hands, restored it to her, and said very sensibly: "Take a turn about the Square with me. Can't stand here: have all the fools in town gaping at us!"

Miss Broughty, a biddable girl, weakly accepted the support of his proffered arm, and allowed herself to be led along the flagway. She was at first unable to do more than utter disjointed and inexplicable ejaculations, but soothed by Mr Standen's unintelligible but consolatory murmurs she was very soon pouring her troubles into his ear.

It might have been supposed that Freddy, whose intellect was not of the first order, would have found it impossible to grasp the gist of an extremely tangled and discursive story, but once more the possession of three volatile and excitable sisters stood him in good stead. Recognizing at a glance, and as swiftly discarding, all the irrelevant details with which Miss Broughty obscured her tale, he very soon mastered the essential fact, which was that Sir Henry Gosford had requested her Mama's permission to solicit her hand in marriage, and that if she refused to bestow this upon him, her Mama would kill her.

Well aware that to bring the voice of sober reason to bear upon the exaggerations of agitated females was both fruitless and perilous, Freddy wisely let this pass, and listened in sympathetic silence to an enumeration of the various hideous fates Miss Broughty considered preferable to marriage with Sir Henry. If he did not feel that she was made of the stuff that could face with fortitude the prospect of being crucified, or boiled in oil, he did realize that she was in very great distress, and making sincere efforts to escape a somewhat sordid destiny. At the first opportunity, and emboldened by her many references to her Camille, he asked her if the Chevalier knew of this disaster. Two large tears trembled on the ends of her lashes, and she replied: "Oh, no, no, for what would be the use? Mama will never, never consent to my marrying him, and it would cast him into such agony!"

It was at this point that his brilliant stroke of policy came into Freddy's head. He was so much dazzled by it that he was obliged to hush Miss Broughty, who was distracting him with her monologue. "Can't think, if you keep talking," he explained. "Very important I should think: got a notion!"

She was obediently silent, looking up every now and then into his face, but not venturing to address him again. They had come within sight of Lady Buckhaven's house once more before he emerged from his abstraction, and said abruptly: "Going to take you to m'sister. Your Mama likely to come seeking you there?"

She trembled. "Oh, if she were to guess—! But she will not miss me directly, for she is in town herself, and she does not know I ran away from my uncle's house as soon as she went out. But—"

"It don't signify," said Freddy. "Tell m'sister's butler to say you ain't there. Very reliable fellow, Skelton."

"But how can I intrude upon Lady Buckhaven?" protested Olivia. "*She* cannot help me, and indeed I would not ask it of her!"

"No, but must leave you somewhere while I settle the thing," explained Freddy.

She clasped both hands round his arm, crying breathlessly: "Settle it! Oh, sir, *can* you?"

"Told you I'd got a notion," he reminded her. "Mind, not sure the thing will come off right, but no harm in trying!"

There were those who might have doubted Mr Standen's ability to bring anything off right, but Miss Broughty was not of their number. In so elegant a gentleman, and one, besides, who was engaged to her dear Miss Charing, she could not but repose the utmost confidence. She attempted no further remonstrance, but accompanied him meekly up the steps of Lady Buckhaven's house.

Skelton, looking slightly surprised, admitted them into the house, and volunteered the information that her ladyship had just ordered her carriage.

"Never mind that!" said Freddy, handing over his hat and gloves. "Where is she?"

"I fancy, sir, that her ladyship is in her dressing-room. I will inform her that you have returned."

"Needn't do that. Take Miss Broughty into the Saloon! And mind this, Skelton! – if anyone comes here asking for her, she ain't here, and you haven't seen her!"

In the course of a long and successful career, Skelton had gathered much experience of eccentric young gentlemen. He had not previously included Mr Standen in this fraternity, and he was both grieved and shocked to find that his judgment had been so much at fault. But he concealed his feelings, and led the shrinking Miss Broughty to the Saloon, what time Mr Standen trod lightly upstairs to his sister's dressing-room.

"Good gracious, Freddy!" exclaimed Meg, when she saw him. "What now, pray?" A gleam of hope shone in her eyes. She cast aside the hat she was just about to set on her head, and said eagerly: "Oh, do you mean to tell me the secret after all?"

"Not that one," responded Freddy. "Tell you another instead!" He perceived that she was looking affronted, and added: "Not bamming you! Wish I was! Dashed awkward business! Fact is, need your help."

A little mollified, but still suspicious, she looked an inquiry.

"Got the Broughty girl downstairs," said Freddy. "Put her in the Saloon."

"Then I wish you will take her away again! I don't want her!" said Meg, with asperity.

"That's just it: I don't want her either. Been thinking for some time I should have to get rid of her. Think I can do it! You knew that cousin of Kit's was trying to fix his interest with her, didn't you?"

"Oh, I know that Kitty was attempting to make a match between them, but I think it was most unsuitable!"

"No, it ain't: best match she could make, if you ask me!"

"She! And what of the Chevalier, pray?"

"Now, listen, Meg! Going to tell you something I don't want you to repeat. Got to trust you."

"As though you did not know I would never breathe a word to a soul of anything you told me in confidence!"

"Well, see you don't, because it ain't a story I want to find flying round the town!" said Freddy, unimpressed. "You remember what we were saying about the Chevalier before Jack brought him here?"

"No," said Meg mystified.

"Yes, you do! Told Kit he'd very likely turn out to be a dirty dish."

"Oh, that! Yes, why?"

"Exactly what he has turned out to be," said Freddy. "Not a Chevalier at all: deuced loose fish, in fact! Just what I thought: a dashed ivory-turner!"

"Freddy, *no!*" cried Meg, turning quite pale. "Oh, poor Kitty! Does she know?"

"Stupid fellow told her. Thing is, Meg, must get rid of him too!"

"Good heavens, yes! Only think of the scandal, if anyone should discover the truth!"

"Exactly so! Dashed awkward situation. Queered me how to settle it, I can tell you. Hit on a notion just now. Get rid of them both!"

Meg stared at him. "Both? Do you mean Miss Broughty as well?"

"That's it. Poor girl's in the devil of a pucker! Gosford offering for her, and she won't have him. Ran off to beg Kit to help her. Met her in the Square, and she told me all about it. Very fortunate circumstance, because it gave me a notion. Pack 'em both off to France!"

"You must be mad!"

"No, I ain't. In love with one another. At least, the girl is: keeps talking on about her Camille till you can't but feel queasy! Kit says d'Evron is too. Shouldn't be surprised: seems to be more of a gudgeon than you'd think. Trouble is, knows his case is hopeless."

"I should think so, indeed! If ever I saw an odious, scheming woman—"

"Got to elope with her. Going to tell him so," said Freddy.

"*Freddy!*" gasped his scandalized sister.

"No need to screech," said Freddy. "Dashed good notion!"

"It is quite *shocking!* And when I think that you are for ever telling me *I* am bird-witted, I declare I could slap you! She had very much better marry Sir Henry!"

"No, she hadn't," contradicted Freddy bluntly. "For one thing, not the sort of fellow anyone would do better to marry. For another, getting to be a trifle crack-brained – well, stands to reason he wouldn't offer to marry this little article of virtue if he weren't! If she married him, sure as check she'll be kicking up larks all over town within the twelve-month, because it ain't to be expected she'll know how to do the thing neatly."

"Well, it is no concern of yours if she does!" argued Meg.

"Dashed well is my concern!" said Freddy. "Nice thing if a friend of Kit's was to be one of the *on-dits* of town, and very likely drawing Kit into her scrapes! If you think Kit wouldn't be for ever trying to pull her out of 'em, you don't know Kit!"

Impressed by this eminently practical point of view, Meg said doubtfully: "Yes, but – an elopement! I cannot like it!"

"I should hope you would not," said Freddy, with a touch of austerity. "Dash it, you're a Standen! Point is, the Broughty girl ain't! Mind, I don't know yet how Kit's cousin will take it, so I haven't said anything to the girl. If he ain't willing, I shall be at a stand. Going to visit him. Leave Miss Broughty here."

"Freddy, I won't be a party to it! Only fancy how displeased Buckhaven would be, if it came to his ears! Besides, what a fix I should be in if Mrs Broughty knew that I had helped her daughter to do anything so improper!"

"Won't know it: told Skelton to say she wasn't here, if anyone came asking for her," replied Freddy. "Can't stay longer: devil of a lot to do!"

He waited for no further expostulations, but left the dressing-room, and ran down the stairs. Pausing only to look into the Saloon, and to tell Olivia, nervously seated on the edge of a chair, that he would be back presently, he again left the house, and set off in the direction of Duke Street.

He was fortunate enough to find the Chevalier at home. The Chevalier, in fact, had risen at a late hour, had partaken of breakfast at noon, and received his unexpected guest in a magnificent dressing-gown, for which he made rueful apologies.

"You find me *en deshabille!* I have had last night what I think you call a pretty batch of it!"

He set a chair for Freddy as he spoke. He was smiling, but his bright eyes were wary, and there was a suggestion of tautness about him. He would have assisted Freddy to divest himself of his long coat, but Freddy shook his head, saying: "Don't mean to make a long stay: got a great deal to do!"

The Chevalier bowed, and turned away to produce from a cupboard a bottle and two glasses. "You will, however, take a glass of madeira with me?"

"Do that with pleasure," said Freddy. "Come to see you on a devilish ticklish business, d'Evron. Daresay you know what it is."

"In effect," said the Chevalier, after a momentary silence, "my cousin has told you certain things?"

"Knew 'em already," replied Freddy. He added apologetically: "Been on the town for some time, y'know!"

"*Quoi?*" ejaculated the Chevalier, flushing. "There is, then, something in my *ton*, my *tenue*, which betrays me?"

"No, no, nothing like that!" Freddy assured him. "No need to take a pet! Thing is – well, it's what I was saying to m'father t'other day: can't be on the town without learning to know a flat from—" He broke off in some slight confusion, as the infelicitous nature of this reminiscence occurred to him.

The Chevalier burst out laughing. "Ah, I can supply

the word! I become very much *au fait* with your idioms. You would say "from a leg", I think!"

"Well, I would," owned Freddy. "It ain't your *ton*. Dashed if I know what it is! Just thought you was a trifle smoky."

"It is to be hoped that others are not so – how shall I say? – intelligent! Or have you come to threaten me with exposure?"

"Must know I haven't," replied Freddy. "Cork-brained thing to do! Engaged to your cousin: don't want her to be uncomfortable; don't want any scandal either. What's more, don't wish you any harm."

The Chevalier made him a mock bow, and began to pour out the wine. "I thank you! Well, and so I am a leg! I live, in fact, *d'invention!* I take risks, yes, but not, perhaps so great risks as some have thought. I will tell you, Mr. Standen, that if you had come to threaten me I would have snapped my fingers in your face, so! As I have snapped them in the face of your so-amiable cousin!"

"Which one?" inquired Freddy. "What I mean is, got a lot of cousins! Quite safe to snap your fingers in my cousin Dolphinton's face, but if you mean my cousin Jack, which I fancy you do, silly thing to have done! Dangerous fellow to cross."

"Be content! He will not expose me, for he dare not!"

"Might not do that," agreed Freddy. "Wouldn't lay a groat, though, against the chance of his doing you a mischief. Very seldom seen him queered on any suit. However, it ain't any concern of mine." He sipped his wine, a thoughtful expression on his face. "Come to think of it, might be able to put you in the way of serving Jack a back-handed turn," he remarked.

The Chevalier shrugged his shoulders. "*A quoi sort de le faire?* If I chose to do it, I would remain in England. I do not fear him, believe me! That he knows! It is a little amusing that he should have put himself to such pains to persuade me to return to my own country. It has been my intention to do so, since – several days. That gave me to laugh *sous cape!* Will he flatter himself I went away because he bade me? No, I think – but it matters nothing! Did you come to visit me to tell me to go, sir? *Cela n'en vaut pas la peine!*"

"Came to tell you Miss Broughty's in the devil of a fix," said Freddy calmly.

The Chevalier had walked over to the window, but he turned swiftly at this. "You would say that Miss Broughty is in trouble?"

"That's it," nodded Freddy. "Run away from Hans Crescent. Not the thing, but can't blame her. Never saw such a set of rum touches in my life as those relations of hers! What's more," he added, considering the matter dispassionately, "not a good part of the town. Wouldn't like to live there myself."

"For the love of God—!" cried the Chevalier impatiently. "What has happened to her? Where is she?"

"Left her with m'sister," Freddy replied. "She came to ask Kit to help her."

"Ah, she has a heart of gold, this Kitty, and she will do so!" the Chevalier exclaimed, his brow lightening a little.

"Daresay she might, but she ain't there," said Freddy stolidly.

"Not there! Where then is she?"

"Gone down to my great-uncle's. Poor girl's at a standstill: don't know what to do! Seemed to me I'd best come and tell you about it. Thing is, she can't stay in Berkeley Square. First place that Broughty woman will think of, when she starts searching for her."

"But tell me, I beg of you! It is not – *mon Dieu*, it is not that madame has discovered—? It is not I who am the cause—?"

"Oh, no, nothing of that nature! You know Sir Henry Gosford? Offered for her."

"That ancient!" the Chevalier said contemptuously. "I know well the intentions of Madame Broughty, but Olivia will laugh at the *vieillard!*"

"Wasn't laughing when I saw her. Said her mother would kill her if she didn't do as she was bid. Shouldn't think she would, myself, but no use telling Miss Broughty that: in the deuce of a pucker, y'know! Trembling all over."

"Ah, *la pauvre!* it is a *dragon de femme*, that one, but she cannot force that angel to the altar, after all! She will scold, she will threaten, but she will not harm her own daughter! This Sir Henry will be forgotten – I too must be forgotten! – and one day, I am assured, she will meet another – *un brave homme!* – and she will be happy. To think of it is to tear the heart from my body, but I must wish it for her sake – I must accustom myself to the thought!"

"Well, it ain't a particle of use accustoming yourself to it," said Freddy, unimpressed. "Won't happen."

"She will not consent to marry that *radoteur!*"

"No, very likely not. Seems to me she'll accept a carte blanche from my cousin Jack," said Freddy brutally.

"No! no!" ejaculated the Chevalier, turning pale. "You shall not say such a thing!"

"Have said it. Very understandable thing to do. Frightened of her mother: won't return to her. *You* go off to France: nothing else she can do! Must know Jack would treat her devilish handsomely: at least, he would while she was living under his protection. Trouble is, these little affairs don't commonly last long. Mind, I don't say Jack would turn her off without a shilling, because he wouldn't. Shabby thing to do, and he ain't shabby. But—"

"Stop! stop!" said the Chevalier hoarsely. He cast himself into a chair by the table, and buried his face in his hands. "Every word you speak is torture! Ah, why did I cross her path? I have brought misery upon her!"

"Don't see that at all," objected Freddy. "Dashed good thing you did cross her path! Able to rescue her."

The Chevalier's fingers, writhing amongst his glossy brown locks, were fast ruining what had been an admirable example of the Brutus, made fashionable by Mr Brummell. Freddy watched this with pained disapproval. It did not seem to him to serve any useful purpose: it was, in fact, a work of quite wanton destruction.

"You do not understand!" groaned the Chevalier. "I would give my life, my all, but I am helpless! I cannot help her, I, of all men! You may say I am *au bout de mon Latin!*"

"Well, I shouldn't say anything of the sort, because I ain't at all easy in the French tongue, and I'm dashed if I know what it means. Daresay m'father would: they used to talk the devil of a lot of French in his day. Italian, too. Went junketing about all over the Continent, y'know. That fellow Bonaparte put a stop to that, which is why I never made the Grand Tour. Not that

I'm complaining. Never thought I should have liked it above half, to tell you the truth."

The Chevalier stared at him rather wildly. "Ah, what are you saying? It is *hors de propos!* You bring me news which kills me, and talk to me of the Grand Tour! It is entirely English, *en effet!*"

"Well, what the deuce should it be?" said Freddy reasonably. "Just told you I don't speak French!"

The Chevalier once more sank his head in his hands, saying with a bitter laugh: "Oh, you are without sensibility, you!"

"I may be without sensibility, but I'm dashed if I'd sit tearing my hair out when a man came to tell me Kit was in trouble!" retorted Freddy. "Much good that would do her!"

The Chevalier raised his head, and flung out his hands. "But can you not understand that I am without power? Never would that woman permit me to marry Olivia! Ah, do you imagine that I do not care, that I do not desire with all my heart to call her my own, to take her to France, far, far from such as her mother – that Gosford – that *roué*, your cousin?"

"Well, why the devil don't you do it?" demanded Freddy. "Never saw such a fellow for making speeches!"

The Chevalier's hands dropped. He sat staring at Freddy, as though thunderstruck. "Do it?" he repeated. "You would say – *an enlévement?*"

Freddy sighed. "No, I wouldn't. Keep telling you I don't speak French."

"*Pardon!* A – a flight – a – I do not know the word!"

"Daresay you mean an elopement," said Freddy helpfully. "That's it: carry her off to France before her mother finds her."

The Chevalier's eyes flashed. "Ah, you believe me to be altogether base!" he exclaimed.

"Well, you're out there, because I don't. Seems to me you're altogether bacon-brained!"

"But—It would be an infamy! I tell you, I have for that angel a respect, an adoration beyond your comprehension! To steal her in that manner – I, a gamester, an adventurer! – is a villainy too great!"

"Shouldn't call it a villainy myself," said Freddy. "It ain't the thing, of course: not saying it is. Mind, if you didn't mean to marry her, it wouldn't do at all!"

"If it were possible, I would marry her at this instant!" the Chevalier said impetuously.

"Well, it ain't possible. Marry her when you get to France."

The Chevalier began to pace about the room. "I would take her to my mother. *She* is not such a one as Madame Broughty, rest assured!"

"Very good notion," approved Freddy.

"My father – ah, if at first he was a little angry with me, would he not relent when his eyes alighted upon my angel?"

"Bound to," agreed Freddy.

The Chevalier faced him. "Tell me, then, you who are of a family of the most distinguished, the most correct, should I do this thing?"

"Dash it, just what I *have* been telling you!" said Freddy. "What's more, there's no time to be lost."

A doubt shook the Chevalier. "Can it be that she would trust me? So young, so innocent!"

"Why shouldn't she? What I mean is, no reason at all, if she's an innocent. Ought to know that!"

The Chevalier drew a deep breath, and flung open his arms. "*La tête me tourne!* But one little half-hour

past, behold me, *plongé dans le désespoir!* Then you come
to me, *comme ange tutélaire,* and you transport me to Paradise!"

"Very happy to be of service," murmured Freddy,
rising, and setting down his empty glass.

The Chevalier gave a shaken laugh. "Ah, I am without words! *Je n'en suis plus!*"

"Are you, though?" said Freddy hopefully. "Good
thing: no time to waste in speechifying! Fact is, never
one to talk much: not clever, y'know!"

"*You—!*" uttered the Chevalier, in throbbing accents. "You will permit me at least to thank you!"

Freddy's eyes started from his head with horror, for
it seemed, for one hideous moment, as though the
Chevalier had every intention of embracing him. However, the excitable Frenchman contented himself with
seizing both his hands, and exclaiming in a voice of
profound emotion: "My benefactor!"

"No, no, assure you, nothing of that sort!" said
Freddy. "At least – put me in mind of something!
Don't know how you may be fixed for the ready! Happen to have a large sum about me: thought I might
be needing it, but it turned out I didn't. Beg you won't
hesitate to tell me if it ain't quite convenient to you
to lay down your blunt just at present!"

"Ah, you are the soul of generosity!" the Chevalier
said, pressing his hands fervently. "But no! I too have
about me a large sum of money!" An imp of mischief
leaped into his eyes. "Shall I tell you? Yes, for could
I withhold from you any secret? Your cousin did me
the so-great honor to invite me to his *logement,* having,
as he told me, an *envie* to pit his skill at piquet against
mine. *Eh bien!* he has some skill, that one, but I was
perhaps a little enraged – *pour raison à moi connue!* – and

I did not choose that he should win. *C'est du genre comique, n'est-ce pas?*"

"Fuzzed the cards, did you?" said Freddy. "Hope you haven't knocked him into horse nails! However, no concern of mine. Daresay he'll make a recover: never known him to be rolled up yet! Thing is, ought to hire a chaise! Won't want to travel by the Mail. Got a notion it don't leave the General Post Office till after nightfall. Dashed uncomfortable business, traveling by night! Besides, ought to leave town immediately."

Soyez tranquil! I go to hire a post-chaise on the instant! One night we must be in Dover, for the packet, you must know, leaves at a little after eight in the morning. Have no fears! My angel shall be as a queen, and I her slave!"

Since Freddy was grappling with thoughts of his own, this chivalrous utterance drew from him only an abstracted nod. The Chevalier, at last releasing his hands, began to stride about the room, formulating his plans for flight. Freddy interrupted him without ceremony. "Tell you what!" he said. "Bring her to you! Won't do for her to set out from m'sister's house. Better not be seen here either. You know the Golden Cross? Very tolerable house, at Charing Cross. Meet you there, in an hour's time. Not likely to see anyone we know, which we should, sure as check, if you set out from the Bear, in Piccadilly. Going back to Berkeley Square now: don't want to waste any more time! Got important business to settle on my own account."

He then picked up his hat, and his ebony cane, and departed, cutting short the Chevalier's thanks and protestations.

Arrived once more in Berkeley Square, he found his sister civilly, if unenthusiastically, entertaining Miss

Broughty in the drawing-room. From the wan look in one face, and the expression of long suffering in the other, it was to be inferred that Meg's attempts to divert her visitor's mind had not been crowned with success. Upon Freddy's entrance, Olivia started up, clasping her hands at her palpitating bosom, and exclaiming: "Oh, what have you done, sir?"

"Fixed it all right and tight," responded Freddy. "Taking you to meet d'Evron at the Golden Cross in an hour's time: be in Dover in time for dinner, I daresay. Packet to Calais tomorrow morning."

This laconic explanation had the effect of momentarily stunning the ladies. Meg, the first to recover her power of speech, cried: "An elopement? She must not! Freddy, have you run mad?"

But Olivia, after gazing in a rapt manner at Freddy for several speechless moments, threw him into great embarrassment by seizing his hand, and kissing it. "Oh, Mr Standen, how can I ever thank you?" she stammered. "Oh, how kind you are! Oh, I am so happy!"

"Thought you would be," murmured Freddy, recovering his hand. "D'Evron very happy too. Means to take you to his mother immediately. Begs me to assure you – can place the utmost confidence in him! Going to be a queen, or some-such thing: wasn't attending very particularly, but got a notion that's what he said."

"But, Freddy, does she know the truth?" demanded Meg. "That he is not what we have believed him to be? That he is—"

"Oh, indeed, ma'am, I know *everything!*" Olivia assured her. "Oh, pray do not say I must not go to my Camille!"

"But—"

"Here, Meg, must have a word with you!" interrupted Freddy, gripping her arm, and propelling her towards the door. Outside the room, he released her, but said in a tone of strong censure: "If it ain't just like you to be trying to throw a rub in the path, the very moment we are in a way to going on like winking! You hold your tongue, now, or you'll plunge us all back into disorder!"

"Yes, but, Freddy, I have been thinking, and—"

"Well, I wish you won't, because I never knew any good to come of it when you started thinking. Very likely to find ourselves in queer stirrups if we was to listen to you."

"I declare you are the most odious creature alive!" said Meg indignantly. "Pray, have you considered what a situation I shall be in when that horrid woman discovers that I helped her daughter to elope?"

"Won't discover it. Mean to warn her not to mention the matter. When Skelton tells her the girl ain't been here – which reminds me: must remember to slip a couple of Yellow Boys into his hand! – well, when he tells her that, she's bound to think of d'Evron. Won't find him at his lodging. Paid his shot – at least, I hope he will – and gone! Plain as a pikestaff! Now, you be a good girl, Meg, and don't for the lord's sake, try to think! Something more important to be done. Can't let Miss Broughty go off without her nightgown! Must give her what she'll need till she gets to Paris."

"What, are you expecting me to give that wretched girl my own clothes?" demanded Meg.

"Won't miss a nightgown, dash it! Better give her a shawl too."

"If I do, will you promise never to tell Mama I had the *least* knowledge of this shocking business?"

"Promise anything!" said Freddy recklessly.

"Oh, very well, then!" Meg said, and went back into the drawing-room to invite Olivia to go upstairs with her to her bedchamber.

Some little time later, Freddy handed Miss Broughty into a hackney-coach, directed the coachman to drive to the Golden Cross, and took his seat beside his charge. At their feet reposed a modest valise, and over one arm Miss Broughty carried a folded shawl. Her cheeks were delicately flushed, her eyes were softly sparkling, and she appeared to be floating in some pleasurable dream. She was recalled by Freddy's voice, addressing her, and turned towards him with a start. "Oh, I beg your pardon! I was not attending!"

"Just wanted to be sure all was right," said Freddy. "M'sister give you everything you should have?"

"Oh, yes, she was so very kind, and she packed the bag with her own hands! I was quite overcome!"

"Did it herself, did she? Then I'll lay a monkey she forgot something!"

"No, I am sure she did not! Only fancy! She *would* have me take such a pretty dress, to wear when I reach Paris, because she says this one I have on will be sadly crushed by the journey!"

A gleam of hope shone in Mr Standen's eye. "The lilac one?" he asked.

"No, it is not lilac, but green, and of the finest cambric!"

He sighed. "Thought she wouldn't part with the lilac one," he said mournfully. He passed under rapid mental review such articles as he supposed must be necessary to a female setting forth on a long journey, and suddenly said: "Hairbrush and comb. Tooth-brush."

Miss Broughty turned a stricken gaze upon him. "Oh, dear! I don't think—Whatever shall I do?"

"Stop and purchase 'em," replied Freddy with decision. "Good thing you told me m'sister packed the bag. Where do you commonly buy such things?"

"I don't know," faltered Olivia. "I have not had occasion to buy them since I came to town. Oh, I am sure they can be had at Newton's, in Leicester Square, only I – I have only a shilling or two in my purse, and I dare not go into Newton's in case Mama might be there!"

"Get 'em for you," said Freddy, putting his head out of the window to shout the new direction to the coach-man.

"Oh, Mr Standen, you are so very—! No, no, you must not!"

"Yes, I must," said Freddy. "Can't go off to France without a toothbrush. Wedding present!"

Olivia saw nothing incongruous in this, but thanked him earnestly. While he braved the dangers of New-ton's Emporium, she remained cowering in her corner of the coach, dreading every instant that her mother's face would appear at the window. But no such terrible sight assailed her eyes; and in a short space of time Mr Standen rejoined her, placing on her lap a neat parcel; and the hack rumbled on towards Charing Cross.

Here, in the yard of the Golden Cross, pacing up and down, his watch in his hand, and on his face an expression of anxiety, they found the Chevalier. When he saw Olivia peeping from the window of the coach, he thrust his watch back into his pocket, and sprang forward to wrench open the door, exclaiming: "*Mon ange, ma bien-aimée!*"

"My Camille!" squeaked Olivia, almost falling out of the coach into his arms.

They embraced passionately. Mr Standen, descending more soberly from the aged vehicle, observed these transports with fastidious pain, and felt that some explanation was due to the interested coachman. "French!" he said briefly. "Don't you drive off! I shall be needing you. Er – no wish to meddle, d'Evron, but daresay you may not have noticed: couple of waiters looking at you over the blind! That your chaise? Get into it, if I were you!"

"Ah, my friend!" said the Chevalier, turning to him. "What can I say to you? How can I repay you?"

"No need to say anything at all," replied Freddy firmly. "Pressed for time! Easily repay me! Very much obliged to you if you won't visit London again!"

The Chevalier burst out laughing. "Ah, have no fear! Present, if you please, my compliments to my cousin – my regretful farewells!"

"Oh, yes, Mr Standen! Pray, will you explain to dear Miss Charing how it was, and tell her that I shall never, never forget her kindness?" said Olivia. "And, oh, Mr Standen, I am so very grateful to you for all—"

"Yes, yes!" said Freddy, shepherding them to where a postchaise stood waiting. "Beg you won't give it a thought! Pleasure!"

He then handed her up into the chaise, shook hands with the Chevalier, and waved goodbye as the horses began to move forward. After that, he turned back to the hackney. "Doctors' Commons!" he commanded. "And don't dawdle!"

🌿 *Chapter XIX* 🌿

IT WAS NOT A VERY LONG DISTANCE FROM LON-
don to the Reverend Hugh Rattray's parish of Garsfield, but the time spent on the road was more than
enough to reduce Lord Dolphinton's nerves to rib-
bons, and to place a great strain upon Miss Charing's
patience. Not all her representations served to convince him that his mother was not hard on his heels;
and when a broken trace necessitated a wait of several
minutes it really seemed as though any further check
would wholly overset his slender reason. As for pausing to partake of refreshment, when the horses were
changed, he would not hear of it. Neither Finglass nor
the coachman showed any surprise at his twittering
impatience, so Kitty could only suppose that such
moods were not uncommon in him. She herself had
not been prepared to find him so much tortured by
apprehension, but after traveling only five miles in his
company she could readily understand why Miss Plym-

stock had so unhesitatingly stated that a journey all the way to Gretna Green would not have done for him.

Miss Plymstock, to Kitty's abiding admiration, maintained throughout her air of stolid calm, talking to his lordship in a matter-of-fact way which seemed to soothe him, and never for an instant betraying a hint of exasperation. Indeed, Kitty was tempted to believe that she felt none, and was quite ashamed of herself for wishing on several occasions to speak sharply to him.

Garsfield, a very respectable parish, was situated less than ten miles from Arnside, and comprised, besides the village, several farms, one or two handsome houses, perhaps a dozen smaller ones, occupied by the lesser gentry, and a number of picturesque cottages. The Rectory, whose garden abutted on to the Churchyard, was a comfortable, squarely built house, situated at one end of the village street. Everything about it, from its front door, set precisely between two pairs of sash windows, to its tidy flower-beds, was neat and symmetrical. Miss Plymstock admired it very much, and said, as she alighted from the carriage, that it was just such a house as she would like to live in herself. This observation momentarly diverted his lordship's mind from its cares, but also caused him to feel an added anxiety. He said, looking earnestly into her face: "Like Dolphinton House better!"

"Yes, I am persuaded I shall," she replied.

"Not like this," said his lordship, closely watching for the effect of his words upon her. "Bigger. Much bigger. Bigger than George's place. Bigger than Arnside." He reflected, and added, with a certain amount of dissatisfaction: "Not as big as Legerwood."

"Legerwood would be too big for me, and Arnside

too small," said Miss Plymstock, never having visited either house.

He was much pleased with this answer, and turned back to inform Kitty, who had stayed to direct the coachman to drive the carriage round to the stables, that Hannah preferred Dolphinton to either Legerwood or Arnside. He then perceived that his carriage was driving away, and was at once attacked by a dread that Finglass, suspecting that he had been hoaxed, would, by means unknown, hasten back to London to carry the news to Lady Dolphinton. He seemed to think that it was by no means impossible that Finglass should have the effrontery to ride off on the Rector's hack; and was much inclined to summon the man back.

"No, no, that *would* make him suspicious!" said Kitty. "Depend upon it, he is thinking of nothing but going off to the Green Man! I told him that we should remain for at least an hour."

"Come, Foster!" said Miss Plymstock, putting a hand in his arm. "You know he believes Miss Charing has a message to give your cousin from Lady Buckhaven! You may be sure he sees nothing odd in our having come here before going to Arnside. Now, haven't you told me how often you have been visiting the Reverend in the past?"

He admitted it, and consented to be drawn on towards the house. But here a stunning disappointment awaited them. Hugh's housekeeper, who herself opened the door to the visitors, exclaimed in dismay that the Reverend was away from home.

A moan broke from Lord Dolphinton, and, for once, Miss Plymstock was at a loss. She looked at Kitty, her eyes round with horror.

"Away!" said Kitty. "Oh, dear, what a—Is he at Arnside, perhaps, Mrs Armathwaite?"

"No, miss. He has gone to Biddenden for two nights," replied the housekeeper. "He *will* be put out to think he was away, when you and his lordship came to visit him!"

"We must send for him!" said Kitty resolutely. "It is most important that I should see him. Someone must ride to Biddenden with a letter!"

Mrs Armathwaite looked very much astonished; and ventured to point out to her that since Biddenden Manor was situated quite fifteen miles distant from Garsfield the Rector could scarcely be fetched in time to reach his home before dusk.

"Must be fetched!" said Dolphinton urgently. "Important!"

"Well, of course, my lord, if you say so," replied Mrs Armathwaite doubtfully. "I suppose Peter could take the cob."

"Peter take the cob," nodded his lordship.

"Yes, my lord. If you will come into the parlor, I'll have a taper put to the fire immediately."

She looked a little curiously at Miss Plymstock as she ushered the party into the parlor on the left of the front door, so Kitty, perceiving this, at once made Hannah known to her, describing her as a friend who had been kind enough to bear her company on the journey. This explanation seemed perfectly to satisfy Mrs Armathwaite, and she curtseyed, and went away to procure refreshment for the uninvited guests.

The two ladies then held a consultation in undervoices, as a result of which Miss Plymstock begged Lord Dolphinton to show her more of the Rector's garden, and Miss Charing went off to his study to find pens, ink, and paper.

The composition of a letter to Hugh she soon found to present her with certain difficulties. After writing *My dear Hugh,* she sat for some time tickling her chin with the end of the quill, wondering how best to phrase her need. A very little earnest cogitation was enough to convince her that the story of his cousin Dolphinton's love-affair would be better conveyed to him by word of mouth, since she could place no dependence on his withholding it from Biddenden, who, she felt sure, would heartily disapprove of such an alliance. In the end, the letter which Hugh's man, Peter, was instructed to carry to his master with all speed was extremely brief, containing nothing more than the intelligence that his affectionate Kitty was at the Rectory and in urgent need of his help. It seemed probable that this communication would bring him home as fast as his horse could carry him.

In the meantime, Mrs Armathwaite had been busy. By the time Peter had been sent off on his errand, a cold collation had been set out in the dining-parlor. Miss Plymstock having diverted his thoughts successfully, Dolphinton was able to attack the remains of a sirloin of beef with gusto. He and Kitty made hearty meals; it was, curiously enough, Miss Plymstock who seemed not to fancy more than a mouthful of any dish offered to her. She disclosed to Kitty at the earliest opportunity the reason for her lack of appetite.

"I don't know how it is, Miss Charing," she said, "for you may believe I am not in general a vapourish creature, but I won't deny that I can't be easy in my mind. It ain't only this mischance of finding your cousin away from home, but it came to me when Foster was showing me the orchard that in all the bustle and the excitement not one of us took the least thought to where him and me was to go once the knot has been tied between us. What's more, I daresay it won't be possible for this Reverend to marry us now until to-morrow."

Such a mundane consideration as this had not crossed Kitty's mind, but she instantly perceived the force of it, and was inclined to blame herself severely for her lack of practical foresight.

"However, there can be no difficulty about tonight, for this house is very commodious, you know, and you may be sure Hugh will be pleased to have beds made up for you," she said. "Of course, I *could* take you to Arnside, but I fear you might not be quite comfortable there, on account of my Uncle Matthew's disliking strangers excessively. But afterwards! I own I had not thought of that. Oh, dear, I wish it had been possible for me to have consulted Freddy, for it is just the thing he could have advised us on! You will not like to stay at some respectable hostelry?"

"Lord, it ain't that!" said Miss Plymstock. "But until I can settle things betwixt Foster and that mother of his we shan't have more than a few guineas between the pair of us, for I daren't take him back to London, you know, and if I don't do that, how is he to reach his bank?"

"He must borrow some money from Hugh," said Kitty. "Oh dear, how stupid it was of me not to tell him to draw a large sum out yesterday!"

"It wouldn't have answered. Let me tell you, Miss Charing," said Hannah grimly, "that it's his Mama that draws the money, and doles it out to him as she chooses! I don't doubt she's gone beyond her rights, but what I say is, things won't be put in the way they should be in a trice. However, I don't mean to be teasing you with such matters. The chief thing is for us to be married as soon as may be. It won't do to be keeping Foster in the suspense he's in now. He's sensible enough if he's kept happy and quiet, but all this botheration and excitement ain't good for him, and I don't doubt I shall have a rare task to keep him occupied until his cousin returns."

She had not understated the case. During the hours which followed, the task of keeping Dolphinton occupied taxed their ingenuity to snapping-point. Garsfield village was intersected by a busy cross-country road, and during the course of the afternoon a great many vehicles passed the Rectory. Every time the sound of approaching hoof-beats penetrated to the parlor, Dolphinton became obsessed by the idea that his mother had discovered his clandestine intentions and would, in another instant, descend upon him. Happily, there was a large cupboard in the parlor, filling the recess on one side of the fireplace. His lordship remembered its existence when a vehicle was heard to draw up outside the gate, and with rare presence of mind dived into it. The vehicle, which turned out to be a sporting curricle, belonged to one of the young Churchwardens, who called at the Rectory merely to leave a note for the Reverend Hugh; but nothing would induce Dolphinton to leave his hiding-place until the ladies could assure him that the visitor had driven away. A backgammon board being discovered, he was persuaded to sit down to play this mild game with Miss Plymstock. It served, in some measure, to restore the balance of his mind, but any unexpected noise outside the house had the effect of making him take precipitate refuge in his hiding-place, until he began to remind Kitty of nothing so much as a jack-in-the-box. Miss Plymstock made no attempt to dissuade him from bolting into the cupboard, saying very sensibly to Kitty that if it made him happier to do so she was sure he was doing no harm to anyone.

When Hugh arrived, it was past five o'clock, and he took his uninvited guests by surprise, walking up from the stables through the garden, and entering the house by a side door. The sound of a firm footstep approaching the parlor so much alarmed Dolphinton that he forgot the existence of the cupboard, and sought refuge instead under the table. So the Rector, standing transfixed upon the threshold, was confronted by the unusual spectacle of two ladies on their knees, trying to coax something or somebody to emerge from behind the screen of a fringed table-cloth. One of the ladies looked over her shoulder towards him, and he recognized, not without difficulty, his great-uncle's demure ward, Kitty Charing. When he had last seen her, she had worn a sober green gown, and her hair had been arranged in neat bands. He beheld her now in what seemed to him a very much too dashing driving-dress, which was not only of a frivolous shade of pink, but was also embellished with mannish epaulettes. The dark locks, of whose neatness he had formerly approved, had been cut and curled and arranged in a style which, however becoming it might be, could scarcely have been called demure; and he could not doubt that the high-crowned bonnet with two curled ostrich feather plumes, and very long satin strings, which reposed upon a chair against the wall, belonged to her.

"My dear Kitty!" he said, surprise and disapproval blended in his voice.

"Thank goodness you have come at last!" she returned. "Now, Dolph, don't be so foolish! It is only Hugh!"

The Rector now perceived that his somewhat feeble-minded cousin was peeping at him from under the tablecloth. His astonishment grew. "Dolphinton! You here? I hope you mean to explain to me what this means, Kitty!"

"Well, of course I do!" she replied. "Only first, do, pray, persuade Dolph to come out!"

"Come, Foster!" said Hugh, with grave authority. "You must not sit under the table, you know. You are not a child."

His lordship crawled out of cover, and rose sheepishly to his feet. "Had a fright," he explained. "Frightened of my mother. She'll bring Foulstone after me. I know she will. Shut me up."

Miss Plymstock took his hand, and patted it. "No, she will not, Foster. Now, didn't you tell me you would be safe with your cousin? Besides, she believes you to be at Arnside, and very well pleased she is. You tell him, sir, that he's safe here?"

The Rector, who had been looking at Miss Plymstock with a good deal of surprise and no very marked degree of approbation, said rather frigidly: "Foster knows that he has nothing to be afraid of under my roof, ma'am. Come, Foster, sit down in this chair, and straighten your neck-cloth! This will not do at all, my dear fellow! Such foolish conduct, is not suited to your position, you know."

"I wish I wasn't an Earl," said his lordship wistfully. "I could do a lot of things if I wasn't. I could breed horses. Sit under the table, if I wanted to. But I don't want to sit under the table. I don't want to hide in the cupboard either."

"Certainly not!" said his cousin.

"If I wasn't an Earl I shouldn't have to. Shouldn't have to offer for Kitty, either."

Hugh patted him kindly on the shoulder, but said to Kitty, with some severity: "I do not know what you can have been about to have upset the poor fellow like this! It was wrong, and thoughtless in you, my dear Kitty."

"It was not I who upset him, but that wicked, cruel mother of his!" cried Kitty, stung by this unmerited reproof. "I should have supposed you must have known that, for you are very well aware how she uses him!"

He said, in a voice of still graver censure: "Whatever may be my aunt's faults, such language is quite improper, and, indeed, uncalled for."

"Well, it certainly ain't that!" interposed Miss Plymstock, in her downright way. "I was never one for mealy-mouthed talk: don't believe in it! What Miss Charing says is the plain truth: wicked and cruel she is, and so I shall tell her, when *I* meet her ladyship!"

The Rector stiffened. "May I request you, Kitty, to present me to your friend? I fancy I have not the pleasure of her acquaintance."

"Good gracious, what can I have been thinking about?" exclaimed Kitty. "Pray forgive me, Hannah! This, as you have guessed, is Mr Rattray. And, Hugh, this is Miss Plymstock, who is betrothed to Dolph!"

He bowed, but said: "Indeed! I must suppose that the engagement is of very recent date, since this is the first intimation I have received of it."

"No, it is of long-standing date, but secret."

"Secret," repeated Dolphinton, nodding his head, and looking anxiously at the Rector. "Going to marry Hannah, Kitty says I shall. Kitty said I should hoax my mother, and I did. I got the carriage, too. Did it well, didn't I, Hannah?"

"To be sure you did, my dear," she told him, sitting down beside him.

"Do you tell me that you have contracted an engagement without my aunt's knowledge?" demanded Hugh sternly.

Dolphinton looked frightened; Kitty said impatiently: "Of course he has! How can you be so absurd, Hugh? As though you were not very well aware that she wishes him to marry me! You know how it is with him! He has been obliged to keep his engagement a secret. And that is why I have brought him and Miss Plymstock to you, so that you may marry them!"

He looked quite thunderstruck. "Are you telling me, Kitty, that this is why you are here, and sent me so urgent a message that I found myself constrained to respond to it, in spite of the fact that my leaving Biddenden in such haste put my brother and his wife to considerable inconvenience? I went to Biddenden upon family affairs of some moment, and all must be at a stand until I return there."

"Well, I am sure I am very sorry, Hugh, but you may return as soon as you have performed your part here, you know!" said Kitty reasonably.

"That," he said. "I am by no means inclined to do! I do not know under what circumstances Dolphinton has contracted his engagement, but it is plain to me that it is not one of which my aunt would approve. You would not else be here! I cannot lend myself to anything that savours of the clandestine."

"Hugh!" gasped Kitty. "I had thought you poor Dolph's friend!"

"I am his friend, as I hope he knows."

"You cannot be, for you would not stand there talking in that heartless way if you were! Dolph and Miss Plymstock love one another!"

Miss Plymstock, who had been stolidly staring at the Rector, interposed, to say bluntly: "Seems to me it ain't in your power to refuse to marry us, sir, for all this fine talking. Foster's of age, and so am I. You're thinking, I daresay, that I ain't good enough for your cousin. Well, I don't pretend to be any better born than what I am, but what I do say is that I shall make Foster a better wife than many a one that has a title."

"Yes, you are good enough for me!" said Dolphinton. "I won't let you say you ain't. Won't let anyone say it!"

"That's right, Dolph!" said Kitty approvingly.

Emboldened by this encouragement, his lordship went further. "I won't let Freddy say it, and I *like* Freddy. Like him better than Hugh. If Hugh says it, I'll draw his cork. Do you think I should do that, Kitty?"

"Well, I don't precisely understand what it means, Dolph, but I daresay it would be an excellent thing to do."

"Lord, my dear, it don't matter to me what anyone says of me!" said Miss Plymstock. "Let 'em say what they choose, for it won't vex us. Don't you start picking a quarrel with the Reverend! He's bound to think you're marrying beneath you, for I can see he's a proud kind of a man; but maybe, if he likes to come and visit us in Ireland, he'll own he was mistaken."

Dolphinton's face brightened. "I should like Hugh to visit us. Like Kitty to visit us. Like Freddy to visit us too. I shall show them my horses."

Kitty took advantage of this interlude to pull the Rector over to the window, and to say to him in an urgent undervoice: "Hugh, upon my word I promise you that you cannot do Dolph a greater service than to marry him to Hannah! She is the kindest, most practical creature! She means to take him to Ireland, and let him breed horses, so that he may be perfectly happy and busy. You must own it would be the very thing for him!"

"Certainly, I have always been an advocate for his living quietly in the country. It is noticeable that whenever he has been staying here with me he is perfectly rational. I do not say that his intellect is strong, but he is by no means an imbecile."

"Indeed, he is not! But are you aware, Hugh, that his Mama threatens to have him locked up?"

He cast a quick glance over his shoulder, but Dolphinton was engaged in enumerating to Miss Plymstock the various attractions of his Irish house. "You must be mistaken! She could not do such a thing. It is quite unnecessary."

"I don't know what she is wicked enough to do, but I do know that that is what terrifies poor Dolph so. As for that doctor of hers, Dolph is thrown into a quake whenever he thinks about him. Why, she even sets his servants to spy on him! He told me so himself, and how they tell her all he does and where he goes!"

"You shock me very much!" he said. "I had not believed it to have been possible. But to be eloping in this fashion, and to expect me to abet him in conduct which is quite improper—"

"I see what it is!" she interrupted, a sparkle in her eye. "You are afraid to do it! You are afraid of your aunt, and of what people may say! I think it very poor-spirited of you, Hugh, but I am very sure it is not in your power to refuse to marry two persons, when there is no – no impediment!"

He said, flushing a little: "There is no occasion for you to speak with such unbecoming heat. I am certainly not afraid to do what I conceive to be my duty. But in this instance there are considerations of family involved, which—"

"If Freddy does not regard such considerations, I am sure you need not!" she interrupted.

He looked rather taken aback. "Does Freddy, then, know of this affair?"

"Yes, indeed he does!"

"I can only say that I am surprised. However, I cannot allow Freddy to be a guide to *my* conduct."

She was stung by his tone of superiority into retorting: "I do not know why you should not, for *he* is a Standen, after all!"

At this moment, Miss Plymstock touched Kitty's arm. "Beg pardon, but I'll be glad to know what you have decided," she said. Sinking her voice, she added: "It won't do to be keeping Foster in suspense, for he's had a very exciting day, which ain't good for him." She glanced from Hugh's rigid countenance to Kitty's angry one. "I collect you don't mean to oblige us, sir," she said. "Well, if you won't you won't, but I'll tell you to your head I'll not let Foster go back to be driven crazy by his mother. If I'm driven to it – though I own it ain't what I like, partly because I was reared to be respectable, and partly because it don't put me in a strong position when it comes to dealing with her ladyship – I'll take Foster away, and live with him as his mistress until I can find a parson that *will* marry us."

The Rector looked down from his impressive height into her homely but resolute countenance, and said stiffly, and after a moment's pause: "In that event, ma'am, I am left with no alternative. I cannot perform the ceremony at this hour, but if you will have the goodness to show me the license, I will marry you to my cousin tomorrow morning."

A stricken silence greeted these words. Both ladies stood staring up at him. "L-licence?" Kitty faltered at last.

"The special license to enable persons to be joined in wedlock without the calling of banns," explained the Rector. "Surely, my dear Kitty, you were aware that this is necessary for what you propose I should do?"

"I have heard of special licences," she said. "I didn't know – I thought—Oh, what have I done? Hannah I am so very sorry! I ought to have asked Freddy! *He* would have known! I have ruined everything!"

"It's my blame," said Miss Plymstock gruffly. "The thing is we've never had anything but banns in my family, and it slipped my mind."

Kitty turned, laying a hand on the Rector's arm. "Hugh, it can't signify! You would not stick at such a trifle as that!"

"If you have not obtained the necessary license, it is quite out of my power to perform the ceremony," he said.

Lord Dolphinton, who had been trying to follow this, now joined the group by the window, plucking at Miss Plymstock's sleeve, and demanding: "What's this? Does he say I cannot be married? Is that what he says?"

"I am sorry, Foster, but unless you have with you a special license it is impossible for me to marry you."

His lordship uttered a moan of despair. Miss Plymstock drew his hand through her arm. "Don't you fly into a pucker, my dear!" she said calmly. "We shall find a way to brush through it, don't fear! We—"

She broke off, for the door had opened, and a beam of lamplight shone into the darkening room. Mrs Armathwaite came in, carrying a lamp, which she set down upon the table, saying: "I've brought the lamp, sir, and there's no need for you to worry yourself about dinner, for it happens that we have a nice shoulder of mutton, which I've had popped into the oven, and a couple of spring chickens, which will be on the spit in another ten minutes. Good gracious, what ails his lordship?"

Dolphinton, in the act of disappearing into the cupboard beside the fireplace, paused to say in anguished tones: "Not here! Not seen me!"

Kitty, who had also heard the sound of a vehicle drawing up, peered out into the dusk. "Dolph, don't be afraid! It is not your Mama! It is only some gentleman – why – why, I do believe—It is Jack! Good God, what can have brought him here? Oh, I am persuaded he will be able to help us! What a fortunate circumstance! Come out, Dolph! it is only Jack!"

❧ *Chapter XX* ❧

IN A VERY FEW MOMENTS, MR WESTRUTHER, admitted to the house by Mrs Armathwaite, strode into the Rector's parlor, and stood for a minute on the threshold while his keen, yet oddly lazy eyes took in the assembled company. They encountered first Miss Charing, who had started forward into the middle of the room. An eyebrow went up. They swept past the Rector, and alighted on Miss Plymstock. Both eyebrows went up. Lastly, they discovered Lord Dolphinton, emerging from the cupboard. "Oh, my God!" said Mr Westruther, shutting the door with a careless, backward thrust of one hand.

The Rector's parlor was of comfortable but not handsome proportions, and with the entrance of Mr Westruther it seemed to shrink. The Rector was himself a large man, but he neither caused his room to dwindle in size, nor seemed out of place in it. But he did not wear a driving-coat with sixteen capes, which preposterous garment added considerably to Mr

Westruther's overpowering presence; he did not flaunt a spotted Belcher neckcloth, or a striped waist-coat; and if the fancy took him to wear a buttonhole, this took the form of a single flower, and not a nosegay large enough for a lady to have carried to a ball. He had a shapely leg, and took care to sheathe it, when he rode to hounds, in a well-fitting boot; but he despised the white tops of fashion, and his servant was not required to polish the leather until he could see his own reflection in it.

Mr Westruther moved forward, the big mother-of-pearl buttons on his driving-coat winking in the lamplight. He put out his hand, and with one long finger tilted Kitty's chin up. "What a charming gown, my dear!" he remarked. "You should always wear pink: did the estimable Freddy tell you so? He has his uses! May I kiss you?"

"No, you may not!" said Kitty, pushing his hand away.

He laughed. "Ah, just so! Far too many persons present, are there not? Am I correct in supposing that you are here on precisely my own errand? Did you bring Dolphinton? A mistake, I feel – but I cannot believe that he had the wit to come of his own volition."

He spoke lightly, but she had the impression that under his air of mockery he was angry. This puzzled her, and had the effect of diverting her own annoyance. She said slowly: "No, I am not here on any errand of yours, Jack. To be sure, I have no notion of what your errand may be!"

"Have you not? Then I will tell you, my love!" He rounded suddenly upon the Rector. "I am so happy to have found you at home, coz! Do, pray, inform me! – Are you aware of what has been going on under your

saintly nose, at Arnside, or has it escaped your notice?"

The Rector's eyes flashed. "I will rather inform you,
Jack, that I find your manners offensive!"

"Do you? I am glad to hear it – quite enchanted, in
fact! You become almost human. In general, you
know, I find you as dead a bore as any waxwork."

The Rector's hands clenched involuntarily, and his
austere mouth tightened. Mr Westruther, observing
these unclerical signs of wrath, laughed. "Do you
mean to have a turn-up with me? I should not advise
it. You were a first-rate boxer once, but you have let
yourself get sadly out of condition, I fancy."

"Don't try my patience too far!" said the Rector, his
breathing a little quickened.

"Oh, to the devil with you!" Mr Westruther said impatiently. "Give me a plain answer! Do you know what
has been going forward at Arnside, or are you sand-
blind?"

Lord Dolphinton, whose eyes had been going from
one to the other of his cousins, now saw fit to explain
the situation, in so far as he was able, to his betrothed.
"That's my cousin Jack," he informed her. "Told you
about him. He's vexed with Hugh. Hugh's vexed with
him. I don't know why, but I wish he hadn't come. I
don't like him. Never did."

"Let it console you, sapskull, to know your sentiments are reciprocated to the full!" said Mr Westruther, with a snap.

"I'll thank you, sir, to keep a civil tongue in your
head!" said Miss Plymstock, entering the lists in steely
eyed defense of his lordship. "If there's anything you
are wishful to say in Foster's disparagement, say it to

me – if you dare! I've heard a deal about you, and not a word that wasn't true, by what I can see!"

This unexpected attack successfully arrested Mr Westruther's attention. Up flew his mobile brows; genuine amusement set his eyes laughing again; he lifted his quizzing-glass and through it inspected Miss Plymstock from head to foot. "A formidable opponent!" he remarked. "Diminutive, but pluck to the backbone! May I have the honor of knowing who you are?"

"Oh, Jack, pray will you stop behaving in this odious way?" begged Kitty. "It is Miss Plymstock, who is going to marry Dolph, and we are in such a dreadful fix! Only I do think that perhaps you could help us out of it!"

"I feel sure you are mistaken."

"No, no, I know you could do it, if you would! What in the world has made you so cross? What is it that has been happening at Arnside?"

"So you don't know! Then let me inform you, my love, that while you have been cutting capers in town, your dear Fish has entrapped my great-uncle into offering to bestow upon her his hand, and his not inconsiderable fortune?"

"What?" almost shrieked Kitty. "Uncle Matthew marry Fish? You must be mad?"

"Whoever else is mad, it is certainly not I!" he replied. He looked at the Rector with narrowing eyes. "I observe, coz, that these tidings do not come as a surprise to you!"

"No. They do not," said the Rector coldly. "I have been aware for some weeks of my uncle's intentions. I may add that I have also been admitted into Miss Fishguard's confidence."

"Have you indeed? It did not occur to you, I must assume, to warn either Kitty or me of what was looming before us?"

A slight, contemptuous smile curled the Rector's lips. "You are correct in your assumption," he said. "It does not appear to me that my uncle's schemes are any concern of yours, my dear cousin!"

"But, good God, how has this come about?" cried Kitty. "Uncle Matthew and my poor Fish! Why, she goes in terror of him, while as for him, whenever his gout troubles him it is fatal for her to enter his room! *Surely* you are mistaken!"

"Oh, no, I am not mistaken!" he replied grimly. "My uncle did me the honor to write to me, informing me of his purpose. I am but just come from Arnside. My only mistake has been in thinking that my saintly cousin might, for once in his life, allow his commonsense a little rein!"

His cousin was goaded into making a very unsaintly retort. "Not quite your only mistake, I fancy!"

For an instant Mr Westruther looked quite murderous; then he uttered a short laugh, and said: "As you say!"

Kitty, who had been staring at him in blank astonishment, suddenly exclaimed: "Can that have been why Fish begged me to return? And yet—Jack, how is this *possible?*"

"You, my dear Kitty, made it possible when you so unwisely left Arnside. So far as I am privileged to understand the matter, the Fish has been busy! She has learnt to play chess so that he may beat her every night; she has prevailed upon him to believe that the pangs of his gout have been alleviated by some antiquated remedy of her finding rather than by the clemency of the weather; and finally she has instilled into his mind the famous notion that since it will not suit his comfort to dispense with her services it will cost him less to marry her than to continue to pay her a wage!"

Kitty turned her eyes towards Hugh, in a mute question. He said gravely: "I cannot deny that I believe my uncle to be influenced by motives of economy."

"But Fish—! Can it be that she will consent? When I recall her dismay, upon learning that I was going on a visit to London, I cannot believe it!"

"Very true, but you must recollect, my dear Kitty, that Miss Fishguard's future, were she to leave Arnside, cannot be other than precarious. Moreover, since you went away, and she has been obliged to fill your place in the household, she has discovered, in some measure, how to make herself agreeable to him. Indeed, I have seldom known him to be in more amiable spirits!"

"Very adroitly has she discovered how to make herself agreeable!" struck in Mr Westruther. "We have underrated her, my dear Hugh – let us own as much! Has she bamboozled you with her tears, and her vapours, and her protestations? What a bleater you must be!"

"Then that must have been what she meant by *treachery!*" exclaimed Kitty, unheeding. "How foolish of her! As though I could think such a thing of her! If she does indeed wish to marry Uncle Matthew, it is an excellent scheme!"

"I hope you may think as much when you find yourself cut out of my uncle's Will by a brat in her image!" said Mr Westruther viciously.

"An unlikely contingency!" said the Rector.

"On the contrary, nothing could be more likely! My uncle is not in his dotage, as well we know; and if the Fish is much above forty, I have been strangely misinformed!"

Kitty could not repress a giggle. "Oh, dear, how ridiculous it would be! I must go to Arnside as soon as I may."

"Let that be immediately!" said Mr Westruther.

"It cannot be immediately, Jack! I told you that we were all in an uproar here! I have been so *stupid,* and if poor Dolph's plans are overset through it I shall never, never forgive myself!"

"That ain't so," interrupted Miss Plymstock, who had been engaged in quietly explaining to Lord Dolphinton the meaning of a dialogue that was rather too swift for him to follow. "It's my blame, Miss Charing, and don't you think I shall be trying to lay it at your door, for that I shall never do!"

"Oh, Jack!" said Kitty distressfully. "Never mind about Uncle Matthew for a moment! I brought Dolph and Miss Plymstock here, so that Hugh might marry them, and I was such a *goose* that I forgot – at least, I never knew, and that is stupider than anything! Hugh says they must have a special license, and they have not got one!"

"In that case," said Mr Westruther, "you have wasted your time. May I suggest that you waste no more time, but that you turn your mind instead to—"

"Jack, if they must have a licence, could not you get it for them? Are such things to be procured in London? Do they, perhaps, cost a great deal of money?"

"Yes," said Mr Westruther, "they do, my dear Kitty! And if you are indulging your imagination with the notion that I mean to drive to London and back for no better purpose than to provide Dolphinton, in whose affairs I take not the smallest interest, with a marriage license, you very much mistake your man!"

She laid a hand on his sleeve. "No, no, Jack, you cannot be so disobliging!" she said pleadingly. "It is vital to Dolph's happiness!"

He looked down at her, a mocking smile in his eyes. "I am quite unmoved, Kitty. Show me that it is vital to *my* happiness, and I might oblige you!"

She stared up into his face with puckered brows. "To yours? What can you mean?"

He lifted her hand from his arm, and held it. "My dear Kitty, let us have done! Between us, we might, I fancy, induce my uncle to change his mind."

An indignant flush rose to her cheeks; she pulled her hand away, saying hotly: "I don't wish him to change his mind! I hope very much that he will marry Fish!"

His brows snapped together. "A sentiment that no doubt does credit to your heart, but very little to your head, believe me!" He broke off, as Lord Dolphinton, uttering a strangled sound, almost leaped from his chair. "What the devil ails that lunatic?" he demanded irritably.

"*Listen!*" gasped his lordship, fixing dilating eyes upon the window.

The rest of the company now became aware that some vehicle had drawn up outside the Rectory. Kitty ran to the window, and peered out. It was by this time too dark for her to be able to distinguish any object, but she could perceive the glow of carriage-lamps beyond the hedge, and could distinctly hear the fidgeting and blowing of horses. She said uneasily: "It sounds as though there are more than two horses. But it *could* not be your Mama, Dolph!"

Lord Dolphinton, feeling no such certainty, made a bolt for the cupboard, but was intercepted by the Rector, who took his arm in a firm grip, and said in a voice of authority: "Foster, I will not suffer you to behave in this nonsensical fashion! Now, calm yourself! In this house, you are perfectly safe, whoever may have come to visit me. For shame! Do you mean to leave Miss – er – Plymstock to face what you imagine to be a danger?"

"Both go into the cupboard!" suggested his lordship imploringly.

"Certainly not! You will protect Miss Plymstock," said Hugh.

Rather to Kitty's surprise, these stern words appeared to inspire Dolphinton with courage. He gulped, but he made no further attempt to reach his refuge. The sound of the knocker on the front door did indeed make him jump and shudder, but he said resolutely: "Protect Hannah!" and stood his ground.

Mr Westruther drew his snuff-box from his pocket, and flicked it open. "If someone would have the goodness to inform me whether I am assisting at a tragedy or a farce I should be grateful," he said sardonically.

The housekeeper's unmistakable tread was heard, followed by the sound of a lifting latch. Lord Dolphinton acquired a firm hold on Miss Plymstock's hand, and swallowed convulsively.

"Affording protection, or seeking it?" drawled Mr Westruther, taking a pinch of snuff from his box, and expertly shaking all but a grain or two from between his finger and thumb.

The door into the parlor was opened. "Mr Standen, sir," announced Mrs Armathwaite placidly.

Surprise held the company silent for perhaps thirty seconds. Mr Standen, not a hair out of place, walked into the room, found that five pairs of eyes were staring at him in astonishment, and said apologetically: "Thought you might be needing me! No wish to intrude!"

Kitty found her voice. *"Freddy!"* she cried thankfully, hurrying towards him. "Oh, how glad I am to see you! We are in such a dreadful fix, and I don't know what to do!"

"Thought very likely you would be," said Freddy. "Not sure, mind you, but I'd a strong notion you'd forgot to buy the special license."

Kitty caught his hand. "Freddy, you have not *brought* one?" she demanded incredulously.

"Yes, I have," he replied. "That's why I came."

For the second time in her life, Miss Charing lifted his hand to her cheek. "Oh, Freddy, I might have *known* you would come to our rescue!" she said, in a choked voice.

Mr Westruther, who had been watching them with an odd expression on his face, shut his snuff-box with a snap. As though this sharp little sound released him from a spell which kept him standing with his eyes starting from their sockets and his mouth falling open, Lord Dolphinton suddenly released Miss Plymstock, and surged forward, saying, with gratifying delight, if somewhat unnecessarily: "It's Freddy! Hannah, it's Freddy! My cousin Freddy!" He then seized Freddy's hand, and shook it up and down, beaming upon him, and pawing his shoulder with his free hand. "I'm glad you've come, Freddy!" he said earnestly, in a burst of confidence: "I *like* you. Like you better than Hugh. Better—"

"That's the dandy, old fellow!" said Freddy, stemming the flow. "No need to stroke me, though. Now, stop it, Dolph, for the lord's sake!"

He managed to disengage himself, but Lord Dolphinton had not reached the end of his disclosures. "When Jack came, I wasn't glad," he said. "Sorry. Because I don't like him. I'll tell you something, Freddy: Hugh wouldn't let me get in the cupboard, and I'm glad of that too."

Mr Standen, who had long since ceased to feel surprise at anything his eccentric relative might say or do, thrust him gently into a chair, and said amiably: "Of course you are. No need to sit in the cupboard on my account. If it's your mother you're worrying about, no need to do that either: she ain't coming here."

"You *know* that, Freddy?" said his lordship.

"Lord, yes! Gone to a party – thinks you're at Arnside!" said Freddy, improvising cleverly.

Lord Dolphinton, on whom the repeated assurances of Miss Charing and Miss Plymstock had made no impression at all, appeared to accept this. He turned to relay the information to Miss Plymstock; and Freddy was at liberty to turn his attention to his betrothed, who was tugging at his coat in a way which drew a protest from him.

"Oh, I beg your pardon!" Kitty said. "But how in the world did you guess that I had forgot the license?"

Mr Standen rubbed his nose reflectively. "Struck me when Meg gave me your letter. What I mean is, told me everything else, but didn't say a word about the license. What's more, knew dashed well you hadn't enough money to purchase it, and had a strong notion

Dolph hadn't either. Meant to have been here with it
sooner, but the thing was I got detained. Had to buy
the Broughty girl a toothbrush."

"Had to do *what?*" exclaimed Kitty.

"Dash it, Kit, couldn't let her go to France without
one! Must see that!" expostulated Freddy. "Not the
thing at all! Bought her a hairbrush and comb as well.
Meg saw to the rest, but if ever there was a hen-witted
female it's Meg!"

"Freddy, are you telling me Olivia has gone to
France?" demanded Kitty, dazed.

"Gone to Dover," corrected Freddy. "Boarding the
packet tomorrow."

Mr Westruther, regarding him out of narrowed
eyes, said silkily: "You have been busy, coz, have you
not?"

"I should dashed well think I have!" said Freddy,
stirred by the memory of his activities.

"You have – you will agree! – a trifle of explaining
to do!"

"Not to you, Jack!" said Freddy, meeting his eyes
fair and square.

The Rector, a silent and puzzled auditor, at this
point moved a pace forward, but it was Kitty who intervened. "Good God! Freddy, she has not eloped with
Camille?"

"That's it," said Mr Standen, pleased to find her of
such a ready understanding. "Best thing she could do.
Saw it in a flash. Thing was, Gosford offered for her
– poor girl cast into despair – came to find you – found
me instead! Left her with Meg, and went off to your
cousin's lodgings. Silly fellow flew into his high ropes:
never met such a gabster in my life! Give you my word,
Kit, he enacted me a whole Cheltenham tragedy!

However, contrived to settle it all right and tight in the end. Saw 'em off from the Golden Cross, told the hack to take me to Doctors' Commons, got the license, and posted down here as soon as I could. Here, Hugh! You'd better take the thing!"

With these words, he handed over a folded document to his cousin. Hugh took it, but before he could say anything, Kitty exclaimed: "But, Freddy, an elopement! Have you considered – I own, the thought did not occur to me until quite recently! – that Camille must be a Catholic?"

It was plain that Mr Standen had not considered this possibility. He once more rubbed the tip of his nose, but said philosophically, after a moment's reflection: "Oh, well, no sense in teasing ourselves over a trifle! If he is, she'll have to change! Shouldn't think she'd object: seems a very biddable girl!"

Kitty drew a breath. "Then – then everything is settled! At least, it will be, when Dolph and Hannah are married, and there can be no difficulty about that, now that you have brought them that stupid license! Oh, Freddy, it is *all* your doing!"

"No, no!" said Freddy, embarrassed.

"Yes, indeed it is! For although it was I who wanted Olivia to marry Camille, I should never have thought of telling him to carry her off to France; and you see what sad work I made of poor Dolph's elopement! I am so very grateful to you! Oh, and Jack says that Uncle Matthew is going to marry Fish, and that is a very good thing too, though, to be sure, it was none of our doing!"

"Is he, though?" said Freddy, mildly interested. "Well, I daresay it don't matter, because he's a deuced rum 'un himself, but that Fish of yours is queer in her attic."

"Freddy, she is not!"

"Must be. Dash it, wouldn't write to you about Henry VIII if she wasn't! Stands to reason."

"You are mistaken, coz," interrupted Mr Westruther, in a brittle voice. "The Fish is cleverer than we knew. I have not the slightest desire to dwell upon all she saw fit to pour into my ears not an hour since, for I found it nauseating, but if the matter teases you, you may as well know that she believes herself to be comparable to Katherine Parr – tending the aged and irascible monarch!" he added sarcastically.

"So *that* was it!" exclaimed Kitty. "Of course! *He* had a bad leg too! Though I fancy it was not precisely gout that afflicted him, was it? Now I see it all! How very like Fish to be so absurd! If only Uncle Matthew has not bullied her into saying she will marry him, I must say I think it an excellent thing for them both, don't you, Freddy?"

"Well, Freddy?" said Mr Westruther. *"Do* you think it excellent, or does some grain of common sense exist in your mind?"

"Not my affair," said Freddy. "At least – come to think of it, not sure it isn't, in which case I do think it's an excellent thing. What I mean is, I don't want that woman living with us, and if she marries my great-uncle she dashed well can't."

Miss Charing's cheeks became flooded with color. "But, F-Freddy—!" she faltered.

Mr Westruther laughed. "Just so, my love! You have been so busily employed in making what I can only call infelicitous matches that you have left your own future out of account, have you not? Oh, don't look so conscious! I imagine Hugh cannot be so wood-headed that he does not know very well what game you have been playing! Dolphinton, I am sure, we need not regard; and as for Miss Plymstock, I look upon her as quite one of the family! It has been an amusing game, my little one, and you must not think that I blame you for having played it. It was very unhandsome of me not to have come to Arnside that day, was it not?"

He moved towards her as he spoke; his eyes were laughing again; and he held out his hands. The Rector cast a glance at Mr Standen, but Mr Standen had discovered an infinitesimal speck of fluff adhering to his coat sleeve, and was engaged in removing it. It was a task that appeared to absorb his whole attention.

Miss Charing took a step backward. "If you please, Jack," she said, rather breathlessly, "no more!"

"Oh, nonsense, Kitty, nonsense!" Mr Westruther said impatiently. "This folly has gone far enough!"

Miss Charing swallowed, and managed to say: "I collect that you mean to ask me to marry you, but – but I beg you will not! If you had come – *that* day – I should have accepted your offer, which would have been a very great mistake, and makes me so *deeply* thankful now that you did not come! Pray, Jack, say no more!"

He paid no heed to this, but said: "The fair Olivia admitted you a little too deeply into her confidence, did she? I was afraid she would. Don't trouble your pretty head for such a trifle as that, Kitty! You will own that I have borne with tolerable equanimity the news that she has fled to France with your enterprising cousin."

"No, no, it is not that! I can't tell what it is, only that perhaps I have changed, or – or something of that nature!" said Kitty. "And, indeed, Jack, I am excessively fond of you, and I daresay I shall always be, in spite of knowing that you are quite odiously selfish, but, if you will not be *very* much offended, I would much prefer not to be married to you!"

He stood staring down into her perturbed face. The laugh had quite vanished from his eyes, and there was a white look round his mouth. Miss Charing had never before had experience of the temper Mr Westruther's cousins knew well, and she was a little frightened.

"So that's it, is it?" he said, quite softly. "George was right after all! Dolphinton was a little too much for you to swallow, but you had indeed set your heart on a title and a great position, and so you laid the cleverest trap for Freddy that I have ever been privileged to see! You cunning little jade!"

It was at this point that Mr Standen, the most exquisite of Pinks, astounded the assembled company, himself included, by knocking him down.

For this, two circumstances were largely responsible. He took Mr Westruther entirely unawares; and Mr Westruther, recoiling from the blow, tripped over a small footstool, lost his balance, and fell heavily.

"Good God!" said the Rector, forgetting his cloth. "Well done, Freddy! A nice, flush hit!"

Lord Dolphinton, who had found the interchange between Kitty and his cousin rather beyond his power of comprehension and had allowed his attention to wander, now realized that a mill was in progress, which he was perfectly well able to understand. In high glee he called upon Miss Plymstock to observe that Freddy had floored Jack, and begged Freddy to do it again.

Freddy himself, rather pale, stood waiting with his

fists clenched while his cousin picked himself up. There was a very ugly look in Mr Westruther's eyes, which caused Hugh, who had helped him to his feet, to maintain a grip upon his arm, and Kitty to say hurriedly: "Oh, Freddy, it was splendid of you, and I am so very much obliged to you, but *pray* do not do it again!"

"No, no!" said Freddy, conscience-stricken.

The ugly look faded. "At least admit you could not!" said Mr Westruther.

"No, I know I could not," replied Freddy, "but I dashed well don't mind trying to!"

Mr Westruther began to laugh. "Freddy, you dog, you took me off guard and off balance, and I have a good mind to knock you through that window! Oh, take your hand off my arm, Hugh! You can't be fool enough to suppose I mean to have a turn-up with Freddy!" He shook the Rector off as he spoke, and straightened his neckcloth. That done, he held out his hand imperatively to Kitty. "Come, cry friends with me!" he said. "I will apologize for the whole, confess that I entirely misread a situation that is now perfectly plain to me, and remove myself immediately from your presence." He held her hand for a moment, grinning rather ruefully at her; then he lightly kissed her cheek, and said: "Accept my best wishes for your happiness, my dear, and believe that I shall do my utmost to cut you out with Uncle Matthew! My felicitations, Freddy. I'll serve you trick-and-tie for that leveller one of these days. Oh, no, pray don't accompany me, Hugh! Really, I have had more than enough of my family for one day!"

A bow to Miss Plymstock, a wave of the hand, and he was gone. The front door slammed behind him;

they heard his tread going down the garden path, the click of the gatelatch, and, in another moment or two, the sound of his horses' hooves.

Miss Plymstock rose and shook out her skirt. "I'm bound to say I ain't at all sorry to see the last of him," she remarked. "Nor I haven't told you yet, Mr Standen, how very much obliged to you I am for bringing that license."

But Mr Standen was not attending. He addressed himself to the Rector. "Oughtn't to have done it, Hugh. Not the thing! He wasn't expecting it."

"Very true," agreed the Rector. "It was, in a sense, improper, but since you could not, I fear, have landed him the smallest punch under any other circumstances, I cannot regret it. He came by his just deserts. The most deplorable feature of the business is that such a scene should have been enacted in this room, under the eyes of two ladies."

"Better have gone into the garden," nodded Lord Dolphinton. "Like watching a good mill."

"What you would have watched, my dear Foster, would not have been a mill, but a murder!" said the Rector tartly.

"Why, Hugh!" exclaimed Kitty. "I do believe you are quite cross because it was Freddy who knocked him down, and not you!"

"I would remind you, Kitty, that I am in Holy Orders," said the Rector austerely. "And let me tell you that if *I* had chosen to come to fisticuffs with Jack— However, we have said enough on this subject! The license which Freddy has handed to me does indeed enable me to marry you to Miss Plymstock, Foster, but it in no way alters my reluctance to do so. Pray do not misunderstand me, ma'am! I do not wish to oppose the marriage. From what I have observed I am inclined to think that Foster would derive considerable benefit from it."

"Well, for the lord's sake, Hugh, stop prosing!" recommended Freddy. "Dashed if you aren't as bad as Kit's French cousin!"

The Rector cast him a withering look. "Have the goodness not to interrupt me, Freddy! While I am prepared to support Foster in his determination to marry Miss Plymstock, I cannot approve of his clandestine way of going about the business."

"What you mean, old fellow," said the irrepressible Mr Standen, "is that you don't want to be mixed up in it. Scared of Aunt Dolphinton."

"I am not in the least scared of Aunt Dolphinton!"

"Well, if you ain't scared of her, you're scared of what the rest of 'em will say. Don't blame you: told Kit I'd as lief have nothing to do with it myself. However, shouldn't be surprised if the family thought you'd done the right thing. I can tell you one who will, and that's m'mother. What's more, there's two of us in it. I won't hedge off."

The Rector hesitated. "That is all very well, but—"

"I'll tell you what it is, Hugh: no sense in refusing! Paltry thing to do, because if you won't come up to scratch there'll be nothing for it but for me to take 'em to the next parish first thing tomorrow morning, and hand 'em over to the parson there."

Miss Plymstock was moved to grasp him by the hand, saying warmly: "You've got a great deal of common sense, Mr Standen, and I like you for it!"

"You like Freddy too?" said Lord Dolphinton, pleased. "*I* like Freddy! I like him—"

"Now you've set him off again!" said Freddy reproachfully.

"That will do, Foster!" said the Rector. "If you are determined on this course, I will perform the ceremony."

"Then that's settled all right and tight," said Freddy. "They'll have to stay here till the knot's tied, but you won't mind that. Going to drive Kit to Arnside now, but we'll come over in the morning and take 'em to Church."

Miss Charing, blinking at these competent plans, said: "Yes, but, Freddy, where are they to go when they are married? The thing is, you see, that it will take a little time for Hannah's lawyer to settle everything with Dolph's Mama, and until it is all quite safe she does not wish Lady Dolphinton to see Dolph, and also they will not have any money, which makes it particularly awkward for them."

"I shall be happy to offer you the hospitality of my house for as long as you wish to remain here, Miss Plymstock," said the Rector, untruthfully, but in a very Christian spirit.

"No, that won't do," said Freddy, considering the matter. "Aunt Dolphinton's bound to come after them. Don't see how you could keep her out. They'll have to go to Arnside."

"Arnside?" repeated Kitty blankly. "Freddy, they could not!"

"Yes, they could. I don't say it's where I'd choose to spend *my* honeymoon, but there's nothing else for it. Thing is, it's the one place my aunt dashed well can't get into. Told me yourself the old gentleman had all the doors barred against her!"

"Yes, he did, but you know how much he dislikes

to have guests staying with him! He would never permit them to do so!"

"Got a strong notion he will," said Freddy darkly. "Going to tell him it'll make Aunt Dolphinton as mad as fire if he does. Lay you odds that card will take the trick! Shouldn't wonder at it if it put him in high croak, what's more."

"Freddy, you are perfectly right!" said Miss Charing, awed. "Nothing ever puts him in such spirits as being disagreeable to Dolph's Mama! I daresay he will be very much obliged to us for putting him in the way of serving her such a turn!"

"Just what I was thinking," nodded Freddy. "Going to tell 'em to put the horses to now. No sense in dawdling here any longer: might put the old gentleman in a bad temper if we were late."

The Rector begged them to dine with him, but they were resolute in declining his invitation. Kitty put on her bonnet and pelisse, the chaise was brought to the front gate, and after faithfully promising to return in time to support the bride and groom through the wedding ceremony on the morrow, Mr Standen and his betrothed left the Rectory.

"Oh, Freddy, what a day this has been!" sighed Miss Charing, sinking back against the squabs of the chaise.

"Devilish!" he agreed. "Brushed through it pretty well, though. All we have to do now is to see 'em safely married, and then we can be comfortable. Mind, there may be a kick-up over the business, but we can't help that."

"I know it, and I wanted so much *not* to drag you into it!" said Kitty remorsefully. "I thought, if only you knew nothing about it, it would serve as a reason for you to put an end to our engagement!"

"Yes, I know you did. Told me so, in that letter you wrote me. Dashed cork-brained notion! Stands to reason if you're in it I must be too."

"No, Freddy, it does not," said Kitty, in a constricted tone. "You know it is all a hoax, our engagement. I am determined to end it. I ought never, never to have thought of such a thing!"

"Now, Kit, don't say we must quarrel, because I won't do it!" begged Freddy.

"Oh, no, how could I quarrel with you? I think we should tell everyone that we – we find we are not suited."

"No, we shouldn't," said Freddy. "Silly thing to say, because everyone must know it ain't true. Got a better notion. Dare say you won't like it, but it's what I should like."

"What is it?" asked Miss Charing rather huskily.

"Send that dashed notice to the *Gazette*, and get married," replied Freddy.

Something that sounded suspiciously like a sob broke from Miss Charing. "Oh, no, no! Freddy, pray do not! You know it was all my doing! You never wanted to be engaged to me!"

"No, I didn't," he acknowledged. "Thing is, changed my mind! Haven't said anything, because, to tell you the truth, I thought Jack was right: got engaged to me to make him jealous."

Miss Charing blew her nose. "I did. I was utterly wicked and shameless, and *stupid!*"

"No, no! Very understandable thing to do. Devil of a fellow, Jack! Trouble is – wouldn't make you a good husband, Kit. Been worrying me for a long time. Thought you was in love with him. Don't mind telling you it was as much as I could do to keep a still tongue in my head when he asked you to marry him tonight. What I mean is, like you to have everything you want. Wished it was me, and not Jack, that's all."

Miss Charing raised her face from her handkerchief. "I was never in love with Jack in my life!" she said. "I thought I was, but I know now it was no such thing. He seemed just like all the heroes in books, but I soon found that he is not like them at all."

"No," agreed Freddy. "I'm afraid I ain't either, Kit."

"Of course you are not! No one is! And if somebody was, I should think him quite odious!"

"You would?" said Freddy hopefully. "I must say, Kit, I think you would too. Well, what I mean is, if you ever met anyone like that fellow the Fish talked of – fellow who snatched up some female in the middle of a party, and threw her on his horse – dashed embarrassing, you know! Wouldn't like it at all!"

"No, indeed I shouldn't!"

"You don't feel you could marry me instead? Got no brains, of course, and I ain't a handsome fellow, like Jack, but I love you. Don't think I could ever love anyone else. Daresay it ain't any use telling you, but – well, there it is!"

"Oh, Freddy, *Freddy!*" sobbed Miss Charing.

"No, no, Kit, don't cry!" begged Freddy, putting his arm round her. "Can't bear you not to be happy! I won't say another word. Never thought there was any hope for me. Just wanted to tell you."

"Freddy, I love you with all my heart!" Kitty said, turning within his arm, and casting both her own round his neck. "Much, much more than you could possibly love me!"

"You do?" exclaimed Freddy, tightening his hold.

"Well, by Jove! Here, take this dashed bonnet off! How the deuce am I to kiss you with a lot of curst feathers in my face?" He found the strings, tugged ruthlessly at them, and cast the offending bonnet aside. "That's better! Been wanting to kiss you for weeks!"

Miss Charing, assisting him to achieve this ambition, was for some moments unable to make any remark. But the rude handling of her headgear seemed to her to call for reproof, and she presently murmured, with her head on his shoulder: "I daresay my bonnet is quite ruined."

"If it comes to that, I'm dashed sure my neckcloth is," said Mr Standen. "It don't signify about the bonnet. I don't like it above half. Buy you a new one."

"No. Just a set of garnets!" said Kitty, with a tiny gurgle.

"Garnets?" said Freddy scornfully. "You don't suppose I'm going to buy you trumpery things like that, do you? Got my eye on some good rubies. Just the thing!"

"Oh, *no*, Freddy!"

"And don't you say "Oh, no!" because now that we really are engaged, I can dashed well give you anything I like!"

"Yes, Freddy," said Miss Charing meekly.

GEORGETTE HEYER, author of over 50 novels, was seventeen when she started writing her first book. Although she is primarily known for her historical romances set in Regency London, she also wrote eleven detective stories. Ms. Heyer died in July, 1974, at the age of 71.